1

A Novel of an Epic Friendship

"*Blood Sisters* is an epic novel of the very best kind. Its characters are fascinating, their adventures profoundly human, and the suspenseful plot kept me turning pages addictively until the very end. Deeply philosophical, political, and sensuous, the book explores love of all types, relationships of all varieties, and most importantly, the irresistible pull of passion in our lives. Like the best of May Sarton's work, *Blood Sisters* honors the important things: our deep connection to ourselves, each other, and our past.

This is a book about the different ways we humans love each other and the inevitable difficulties that come from this need to connect. A beautifully written love story, *Blood Sisters* is so much more than that, revealing the limits of erotic love while honoring its power at the same time."

—Carla Tomaso,
Author of *Maryfield Academy*

"Mary Jacobsen's epistolary novel *Blood Sisters: A Novel of an Epic Friendship* delivers its title promise, tracing in epic fashion the evolving and enduring love between two women whose thirty-year relationship is forged when they first meet in college in the late 1960s. Out lesbian Val is vocal and unapologetic about her love for Ashmont, whose heterosexuality does not diminish her equally powerful love for Val. The relationship itself is the real protagonist here, changing and examined from every angle over time as the women struggle with the fundamental lesbian conundrum of an all-consuming but sexless love between a straight woman and a lesbian. Through their letters we witness the power that each woman holds for the other as they each mature and strive to define exactly what they are to one another.

Haunting, lyrical, and deeply moving, *Blood Sisters* pulls all the right heartstrings in its evocative portrayal of the profound and immutable bond between these two women. An immensely satisfying read."

—Cameron Abbott,
Author of *To the Edge* and *An Inexpressible State of Grace*

"The friendships that begin in college and continue for the rest of one's life can be richer and more meaningful than most marriages. Mary Jacobsen has written a wonderful novel that follows twenty-five years of such a friendship. Val and Ashmont are two very different women who grow and change, repeatedly surprising us and themselves with who they are. That one of the women is gay and the other straight only gives a wider scope to their tale. Jacobsen captures so many truths here, but she is especially good at the roles that people take in any friendship, for good or ill, and how those roles can suddenly shift: The strong reveal their weakness, the foolish their wisdom.

Jacobsen tells her story in letters, which enables her to concentrate an enormous amount of experience in a relatively short space. We get the extended conversation of two people talking to and through each other over the years about all the important things: work, love, family, sex, religion, pain, and joy. This is a lovely book that stays with the reader long after one has finished it."

—Christopher Bram,
Author of *Gods and Monsters* and *Lives of the Circus Animals*

Blood Sisters
A Novel of an Epic Friendship

Blood Sisters
A Novel of an Epic Friendship

Mary Jacobsen

Alice Street Editions™
Harrington Park Press®
An Imprint of The Haworth Press, Inc.
New York • London • Oxford

For more information on this book or to order, visit
http://www.haworthpress.com/store/product.asp?sku=5427

or call 1-800-HAWORTH (800-429-6784) in the United States and Canada
or (607) 722-5857 outside the United States and Canada

or contact orders@HaworthPress.com

Published by

Alice Street Editions™, Harrington Park Press®, an imprint of The Haworth Press, Inc., 10 Alice Street, Binghamton, NY 13904-1580.

PUBLISHER'S NOTE
The development, preparation, and publication of this work has been undertaken with great care. However, the Publisher, employees, editors, and agents of The Haworth Press are not responsible for any errors contained herein or for consequences that may ensue from use of materials or information contained in this work. The Haworth Press is committed to the dissemination of ideas and information according to the highest standards of intellectual freedom and the free exchange of ideas. Statements made and opinions expressed in this publication do not necessarily reflect the views of the Publisher, Directors, management, or staff of The Haworth Press, Inc., or an endorsement by them.

This is a work of fiction. Names, characters, places, and incidents either are the products of the author's imagination or are used fictitiously, and any resemblance to actual persons, living or dead, business establishments, events, or locales is entirely coincidental.

Excerpt from GILGAMESH: A Verse Narrative by Herbert Mason. Copyright © 1970 by Herbert Mason. Reprinted by permission of Houghton Mifflin Company. All rights reserved.

Cover design by Marylouise E. Doyle.

Library of Congress Cataloging-in-Publication Data

Jacobsen, Mary H.
    Blood sisters : a novel of an epic friendship / Mary Jacobsen.
        p. cm.
    ISBN-13: 978-1-56023-322-0 (pbk. : alk. paper)
    ISBN-10: 1-56023-322-2 (pbk. : alk. paper)
    1. Lesbians—Fiction. 2. Female friendship—Fiction. I. Title.
PS3610.A3567B58 2005
813'.6—dc22
                                                                        2005007716

For Mary Gentile
and

In memory of
Karen Mary From
and
Robert Bray

*"All that lay behind them
passed from view . . ."*

❧ CONTENTS ❧

Editor's Foreword

Alice Street Editions provides a voice for established as well as up-coming lesbian writers, reflecting the diversity of lesbian interests, ethnicities, ages, and class. This cutting-edge series of novels, memoirs, and nonfiction writing welcomes the opportunity to present controversial views, explore multicultural ideas, encourage debate, and inspire creativity from a variety of lesbian perspectives. Through enlightening, illuminating, and provocative writing, Alice Street Editions can make a significant contribution to the visibility and accessibility of lesbian writing and bring lesbian-focused writing to a wider audience. Recognizing our own desires and ideas in print is life sustaining, acknowledging the reality of who we are, as well as our place in the world, individually and collectively.

Judith P. Stelboum
Editor in Chief
Alice Street Editions

Acknowledgments

I am indebted to the following authors and books for information used in writing *Blood Sisters:*

Herbert Mason's translation of *Gilgamesh: A Verse Narrative* (New York: NAL, 1989) was the source for all direct quotations from the epic.

Carol Lee Flinders' *Enduring Grace: Living Portraits of Seven Women Mystics* (Harper San Francisco, 1993) provided information about the women mystics mentioned in Val's letters and inspiration for the character of Mary Patrick.

Christine Downing's *Myths and Mysteries of Same-Sex Love* (New York: Continuum, 1989) provided interpretations of the "myth of the round people" from Plato's *Symposium* and of the creation myth in *Phaedrus.*

Karen Armstrong includes the story of the rabbis at Auschwitz putting God on trial in her *History of God* (New York: Knopf, 1993).

The topic for Emily's dissertation and some of the specific examples of child abuse cited were influenced by *The History of Childhood,* edited by Lloyd DeMause (New York: Jason Aronson, 1995).

Emily's description of her sexual encounter with Val pays homage to the "Song of Songs."

I also wish to acknowledge the work of Healthy Families America. Their volunteer home visitor program, sponsored by the National Committee to Prevent Child Abuse, provided inspiration for Emily's "All for All" program.

Finally, I thank my mother, Kathryn C. Jacobsen, who taught me to read, and shared with me the joy and wonder of stories.

1993
Prologue

June 1993
Dear Val,

Here it is at last. The book of our friendship—our female *Gilgamesh*—which you thought we would never finish. I gathered the letters you wrote me faithfully for twenty years. From these, I selected eight years which tell our story best. And I added the letters I wrote but never sent. Together, they do the job.

An epic should begin with an epigram. Here is ours.

> Gilgamesh was called god and man;
> Enkidu was an animal and man.
> It is the story
> Of their becoming human together.

Gilgamesh

I call our book: *Blood Sisters,* for there is no truer name for what we are. Here it is. I hope you like it.

Love,
Your friend eternally,

Ashmont, Emily

P.S. I found our sophomore papers for Dr. Woolrich's Humanities class summarizing *Gilgamesh* as I was packing last month. They're in the appendix to our epic.

1973

June 1973
Dearest Ashmont,

I am desperate to talk with you!

You should have warned me how lonely life after graduation would be. Why didn't you insist that I move to Ann Arbor with you? You should have made me realize that I needed *you* more than a masters degree in fine arts. You are my patron saint. And saints must guide their mortal chicks.

You will say that you have other chicks to care for, younger and more vulnerable. And getting your PhD in psychology will enable you to be a better saint. But Ashmont, I knew you first! You must leave the largest cubicle in your heart for me. How I wish you had agreed to visit Provincetown for a few days before you left for Michigan.

"Life must move forward," you are fond of saying. You said it yesterday when I accused you of escaping me, and even though you protested that you were escaping *yourself,* I am not convinced.

The way to prove yourself is to visit me here this summer.

Good cousin Desmond has given my summer job the distinguished title of Assistant Manager of Domestic Maintenance. In other words, I am a maid. His inn has grown baroque since I visited two years ago. There is barely an inch of table top or wall that isn't covered with art deco bric-a-brac. Desmond's paramour, Raymond, calls it deco-mania and claims it is both incurable and degenerative. Still, the inn is lovely, set on a hill in the quiet West End, surrounded by lush flower gardens and a tiny pond with a small footbridge and the largest, orangest goldfish you could ever hope to see. From the deck, you can look out over the whole inner Cape.

Desmond and Raymond live in a suite of rooms under the steeply pitched pagodalike roof of the octagonal "tower," which sits anomalously atop the ramshackle gray clapboard of the rest of the inn as though a storm blowing in from the orient had dropped it *kerplunck* from the sky. Windows face north, south, east, and west, so if you spin around you can take in the whole world. If heaven is what we imagine it to be, then when I die I shall find myself ensconced with you in the prow of this heavenly pagoda, navigating earth, sea, and sky.

Since I last saw Desmond, he has lost much of his fine brown thatch. He has grown a bristly mustache, frosted with gray, to balance his bald pate. His eyes are kind and brown as ever behind his wire-rimmed hippie glasses, and his body is short, solid, and square as Raymond's is lithe and angular. Their clothing highlights this beagle/greyhound contrast. Desmond wears canvas pants and denim shirts—a proletarian look. Raymond wears tight-fitting polo shirts and slim, pleated pants. His hair is prematurely white and cut as close as an army private's—but on Raymond it looks aristocratic, accentuating his fine-boned, handsome face. They've been together for twelve years, Ashmont. Can you imagine? Desmond was only twenty-eight and Raymond thirty-four when they first met. They have lasted fourty-eight times longer than my longest relationship to date!

As befits my humble station, I live in a small room in the back of the inn. I have a bow-shaped picture window overlooking the hummingbird feeder and a bed of tiger lilies. Desmond gave me permission to undeco my room in favor of my Spartan tastes. I have a bed, a chair, a cabinet for paintbrushes and paints, and a small oak rolltop desk, from which I write you about the trivia of my life. You have already warned me in your prim way that you'll be *ever* too busy to write and I mustn't interpret silence as indifference. I don't care. I plan to write you even if you never write back.

Writing you is like talking to the stars. Seeing my tiny life refracted through your light pulls all my fragments together—broken thoughts, scabby knees, scuffed shoes, messy emotions—and makes me feel that I am whole. I am Val. I am brave enough to live. If I did not write you, I wouldn't know how to be me.

At dawn today, I walked to the little spit of deserted beach across from the lighthouse. As I faced east and watched the sunrise, the sky rose all around me like a vast blue bowl. There was no escape from the piercing, X-ray brilliance of its light, laying bare my smallness and insignificance. Suddenly the sky seemed like a cosmic taunt. There is nowhere to go but earth. Nowhere to be but inside my own body.

I *panicked* and ran back to the inn, feeling mocked by the cruel blue bowl. I am not sure I am up to the task of leading my life. I fear I shall stumble in circles, making no progress, forever.

I know you will be a great psychologist, but I am not sure that I can paint. *You* like my paintings. *You* believe that a passionate desire to do anything is a kind of talent all by itself. But I don't know if I will ever paint anything truly good, anything that will make a difference. Not the kind of difference you will make saving souls as a psychologist. I will probably live the rest of my life wielding a dust cloth and broom instead of a paintbrush.

I feel like Gilgamesh without his Enkidu, his grief deepening as he wanders into new places without the guiding light of his beloved friend. Anyway, I have started the first chapter of the adventure of our friendship, *Val and Ashmont: The Story of an Epic Friendship*—our very own *Gilgamesh*. Since no one else but you will ever read this, I have written it to you.

⟨❧⟩

Chapter 1

Our Two Heroes Meet

We met on our first day as freshman at "small, prestigious Barclay College" a few miles west of Boston. We always called it that as an example of redundancy in speech, rather like "the brilliant, capable Ashmont," or "the impulsive idealist Val." I arrived at our dorm in a cab, since my parents, "the erratic and alcoholic Russ and Shiela," had recently demolished the family Buick while driving under the influence. I cadged cab fare out of them saying it would be easier on me to arrive alone at my first day of college.

Laden with suitcases, arms and calves sore from five flights of stairs, I arrived at my dorm room door, a single which I had fought long and not entirely honorable battles with the Housing Office to be assigned to. The door was ajar, so I nudged it open with my knee.

There you were, calmly putting your clothes away into *my* bureau drawers. I took in your straight, brown, shoulder-length hair, pale and perfect complexion, your navy blue jumper and white cotton blouse with a Peter Pan collar, and a small strand of *pearls!* You looked like a refugee from Catholic high school. It flashed through my mind that I had overshot "small prestigious Barclay College" and landed on the campus of Our Lady of Perpetual Sorrow.

My next thought I am ashamed to admit—but since we swore always to tell each other the truth, I must—was a contemptuous critique of your appearance. I stood there sweating in my high school basketball jersey and torn denim cutoffs, my never tidy henna tresses plastered against my forehead, feeling ungainly and smelling foul. You looked like every cool, perfect, snobby, cliquish high school girl who had ever made me feel inadequate, untidy, and short. The kind of girl I had dreamed of escaping in college. And here you were, encroaching on my precious college turf: *my single.*

"What do you think you're doing?" I asked in a hostile tone.

"I don't *think* I am putting my clothes in my bureau," you said, barely glancing up, "I *am* putting them away." You were completely unruffled by the apparition-like suddenness of my appearance or the rudeness of my tone. Such composure enraged me. But since I freeze when I am angry, I stood silently, sputtering and sweating.

"Why do you ask?" you said.

"It isn't your room, it's *mine,*" I exploded. I dropped my suitcases, reached into my pocket and tugged out a torn slip of paper with my room assignment on it and shoved it in your face. "See! See!"

You glanced at it and continued unpacking. "Look at it," you said.

I was confused. I looked at the paper, with ROOM 517 clearly written on it.

"Look at the door," you prompted.

The three-inch brass numbers read 511.

"Oops! Sorry," I said, feeling like an idiot. "I'll hit the road now." I picked up my bags and what remained of my dignity, and skulked down the hall to find my own room, but not before I detected both a tiny grin creeping around the edges of your lips, as well as your efforts to suppress it.

"At least we're neighbors," you called out. I grunted, feeling a high, fine hatred for your clothes, your jewelry, your imperturbable manner, and your accuracy in reading numbers. I was sure *your* room assignment letter was already filed away in your desk drawer, tidy as the day you had received it, probably in white-gloved hands.

Then I forgot about the incident. Except for the little amused smile that crossed your face, and the effort you made to hide it. This suggested a kindness that I did not associate with perfect, proper girls like you.

At the end of the first day of classes, I rushed to "the overcrowded, understocked college bookstore" and began frantically tracking down the textbooks I needed. The huge responsibility of college had begun to dawn on me. I had to find the books, make sure I had enough money in my checking account to pay for them, lug them home, and then study hundreds of pages in a single night.

There were only twenty minutes left until closing, and my panic mounted as I discovered few books left on the shelves. I rushed to the biology aisle while juggling a huge stack of books in both arms. There was one copy of *Biology 101* left on a high shelf. As I clumsily reached up, a long arm reached up beside me and stole my book.

"Hey! I was just about to . . ." Turning, I saw the arm was yours. I shut up, but seethed inside. I damned you for your height, your speed, and your perverse insinuation into humiliating moments of my life. I was sweating in front of you again.

"About to what?" You smiled politely.

"Nothing," I said, disheartened. How in hell was I going to become an expert on photosynthesis before tomorrow *now*?

I walked away. But you followed.

"Were you going to take this book? Do you need it for tomorrow's assignment?"

"No. Forget it! Leave me alone!" I wanted to get away from you and the embarrassment I experienced in your presence. I was worried, frustrated, and close to tears which I did not intend to let you see.

"Oh," you said. You sounded hurt, which surprised me. "I was just going to say that we could share the book. If you want."

I looked at you, wondering why you had made the offer. I felt alone and afraid. For an instant, it occurred to me that perhaps you did, too. That your following me might be the beginning of an offer of friendship. But the idea was absurd. Girls who looked like you were never interested in friendship with a galumphing hoyden like me.

"No thanks," I said. I was starting to recover myself. Starting to feel tough and rebellious. "Screw the biology assignment. I'll take my geranium to class and let *her* answer questions."

"Yes," you said, smiling. "That's a marvelous idea. Bye." And you walked—your books stashed manageably in a canvas bag—to the checkout counter. Marvelous. You must be culturally deprived, I smugly decided. Still, something about our encounter left me feeling miserable and more alone and lonely than ever. And I had been lonely all my life.

Except for passing awkwardly in the hall, I didn't see you again until a month later, at Lettie Gorman's memorial service. I had known Lettie better than anyone else at Barclay except you. We had been team-mates on my high school basketball team. We weren't best friends, but I liked and respected her. She laughed at my jokes. She wanted to be a veterinarian. Animals thought she was one of them. Lettie did, too—felt more animal than human, that is. She said that animals were her soul mates.

There were a few girls at my high school who, like me, preferred girls to boys. But Lettie was the only one who wasn't completely paranoid and depressed about it. We threw a blanket over our heads and made out once in the back of the team bus. The coach and assistant principal were sitting two rows in front of us. That was another thing Lettie and I had in common: we liked a good challenge, even not particularly mean-ingful ones. She was an important person in my imitation of high school life, and I'd been happy to know she would be at the same college.

Little did I know Lettie had a secret life as a Latin scholar. She must have been afraid I'd think she was weird. She was probably right, al-though it wouldn't have lessened my affection. I would have admired her for being a state champion Latin wrangler. That was how Lettie knew you, from halfway across Massachusetts. You were both Latin gold medalists, and would compete at statewide meets or orgies or whatever you called them. Now there's something I will go to my grave sorry to have missed—seeing you and Lettie in your Latin team togas declining your way to victory over lesser, perhaps more contemporary intellects. When I learned about your Latin feats, I understood why you used words like *marvelous.* You couldn't help yourself.

The day Lettie died she was walking dogs. A St. Bernard, a grey-hound, and a mutt she exercised for a couple professors. No one knows what got the St. Bernard excited, but it bolted into traffic, dragging Lettie behind. She and the St. Bernard met the Grim Reaper in the form of an oil truck. Somehow, Lettie managed to release the other two dogs. I hope she knows they survived. It would have meant the world to her. Lettie would have given her life for any stray. She was a kinder, better person than I was by far. But death uses other criteria.

I liked to think of Lettie's soul mingling with the St. Bernard's as they rose into heaven. Lettie would have been thrilled. Maybe it would mean she could come back to life as a canine. Even today, I'll sometimes see a large, rambunctious dog, and I'll say, "Lettie" just to see if she re-sponds.

It was shocking for someone our age, eighteen, to die. And in such a random, fickle way. It seemed impossible. Like the sky turning green, or snow in August, or "the brilliant capable Ashmont" getting an F in psy-chology. Even now, though we are twenty-one, it is still hard to fathom.

It hit me hard. They sent Lettie's body home, but they held a memorial service in "the solemn, august Stillman Chapel."

I sat in the back row, sniffling, barely tolerating the service. We should be outside, I kept thinking. There should be animals. I felt sorry for myself, because my loss was real, and most people there hadn't even known Lettie. The chaplain didn't. He meandered on about Lettie being a "sweet, wholesome girl, an ornament in the lives of all who knew her." I blanched at the appalling, anonymous triteness of his words. And from across the chapel, I heard someone sniff in disgust.

I looked across the row of silent, bowed heads, and saw you, Ashmont, head raised high, looking as disgusted as I felt. We exchanged an understanding glance, then sought each other out after the service. I introduced myself, and you said your name was Ashmont mumbledy mumble. For the entire first semester of freshman year, I thought your first name was Ashmont, because who but you would introduce herself last name first? The habit of calling you Ashmont stuck. You never corrected me. And it suited you better than Emily.

We shared a slow, sad dinner together at the cafeteria. You told me about Lettie's secret life as a Latin scholar. And I told you about the fantasy I'd had while the chaplain read the Twenty-third Psalm. I couldn't imagine Lettie in the shadow of anything, and pictured her soul as a floodlight illuminating the valley of death. The Lord who accompanied Lettie was no shepherd, but a huge, slobbering sheep dog. There would be a party in the valley of the shadow of death when Lettie arrived, for sure.

I also told you about my beloved Gilgamesh and Enkidu, and how I hoped to find a devoted friend about whom I could some day write a female epic of friendship. Already that night, I was wondering if you could be my Enkidu, as unlikely a match for the job as you at first seemed. You seemed more approachable and vulnerable than your pearls had suggested.

You seemed genuinely interested in me, which amazed me. The more we talked, the more I discovered to admire about you. You were kind. You were unbelievably intelligent. You were private and reserved. You didn't care what anybody thought of you, which awed me. You seemed to carry some deep disappointment within you. It wasn't that you never laughed, but that before you did, first you had to forget your pain. It was that depth of pain that made you different from other girls. That made you like me. You are my soulmate, Ashmont. My Enkidu. And I was destined to be yours.

Before I knew it, I was sharing your biology book. And I was studying with you every night, when I wasn't trying to lure you into some outrageous prank. I soon realized that you had in abundance what always eluded me: clear goals and the discipline to achieve them.

Well, enough of Chapter 1 for now. Not bad, hey? It's easy to know where to begin an epic, but hard to know what should come next. Still, I regret that unlike Gilgamesh and Enkidu, we never wrestled when we first met. Perhaps in a female *Gilgamesh* the wrestling comes later. I hope so.

I am truly glad you are going to graduate school in psychology, even though I whine about it. It's just that I'm afraid to be without you. Promise me that you will never die. Or that we will die at the same moment. A century or two from now.

Tonight, after I finish my domestic maintenance, I am going to a bar with Desmond and Raymond. Perhaps I will meet the love of my life. The one who will let me love her completely and dedicate myself to her utter happiness. And that will become *my* happiness. If only that could have been *you.*

I know. I know. I know. It never can be. I have accepted that you are a self-avowed heterosexual, although my soul rebels against it. Sometimes I think the barrier isn't that you are heterosexual but that you are stubbornly, irretrievably determined to be single for all time. What I haven't been able to figure out yet is why.

Nevertheless, I must look for the great romance of my life elsewhere. That is the only clear goal I have ever had. No one will ever be able to say I don't work at it, albeit without much success in a life of many lusty frogs and, to date, no princesses. Remember, Love Rules. Love will triumph in the end. Of that I am sure. I am . . .

Your ever ever ever ever ever-loving,

Val

June 1973
Dear Val,

Your letter cheered me. I miss you too. In between classes and my job at the Youth Hotline, I think about you. I have a tiny studio apartment off campus. It's in an old house, with broad, uneven floorboards and large, leaky windows that let in equal amounts of drafts and sunlight.

You are so funny. You never remember things the way they happened. You prefer what you invent. Perhaps I shouldn't complain. After all, your stories show me in better light than the truth. But give me a harsh truth over a kind lie any day.

Your epic tale of our friendship is heartfelt, but riddled with distortions. You have pushed way past poetic license to outright fabrication. When you arrived at my dorm room door the first day of college, you knocked politely. You said, "Hello, I'm Val Summer." You were smiling, and I was, too. I liked you having a name that made people smile. A name like that would never work for me, but it fit you beautifully.

You said you thought there must be some mistake, and suggested we double check our room assignments. As soon as you looked at your letter, you acknowledged your mistake, apologized, and left. The conversation lasted one minute.

There were no pearls. I wore them to Lettie Gorman's memorial service, but even I do not wear pearls to unpack. I make no excuses for the jumper and the Peter Pan collar. It was a school uniform, and I liked the look. It keeps a certain element away. And while it attracts another element, they're easy to get rid of if one merely growls or spits.

And for heaven's sake, Val, let's clarify your obsession about height. You are 5'3" tall. I am 5'5". Scarcely a giant. And I'm sure I was sweating as much as you on that hot day in early September. Besides, sweat is healthy. It prevents overheating and death.

The truth is, I thought you were sweet. I liked your self-conscious, polite manner. I have always been stiff and formal. I envied you your jersey and shorts, although I would have looked phony and ridiculous in them. I am doomed to a lifetime of tailored clothing. While I am just as glad to be perceived as cold and off-putting by most people, I lose some of the few good ones that way. It's a price I pay. But I'm glad I never had to pay it with you.

As for that biology book, I believe we reached for it at the same time in "the overcrowded, understocked college bookstore." You said I could have it because you knew someone from high school with whom you could probably share.

Although it is true that I was appalled by the minister's eulogy for Lettie, I was sniffing not to express disgust but because I am allergic to dust and the chapel was thickly layered with it. It is, however, true that we had our first real conversation that night. I, too, date that evening as the beginning of our friendship. But, you dear, sweet idiot, not only did you reveal your passion for *Gilgamesh* to me that evening—after three beers at the pub—you also invited me back to your room and read the entire epic aloud. I was astonished enough by your innocent presumption that I stayed and listened.

I was puzzled that a college freshman in 1969 could be transfixed by an ancient epic, one that glorifies misogyny and violence. You know I don't care much for literature, especially the "classics," because of such reactionary polemics. As you're fond of pointing out—not uncritically—I'm an empirical woman.

A story of folly, ego, and the misuse of power, I thought at first as I listened to you read. But I watched your face. You were joyful when the two heroes found each other. Your eyes teared up when you described the friends recognizing their equals in one another's eyes. And when poor Enkidu died, the tears streamed in torrents down your face.

Watching the depth of your emotions, I was amazed at how openly and completely your feelings were churned up by a mere story. I asked you which of the two friends you identified with. You were surprised at the question, and said you'd never thought about it.

You said it wasn't either character you liked, it was the thing they had between them that you loved. You had invented a story beneath the facts of the story that expressed the yearning and grief in your heart. I was both suspicious and envious of your ability to do so. The story could have been rewritten about two Russian peasants in the nineteenth century or two suffragettes in the 1920s, and you would have made it exactly the same story, and would have been as deeply touched.

As I watched this yearning for a special friendship play across your face, I found myself touched not by *Gilgamesh,* but by you. You had known about your desire for friendship all your life. But it wasn't until I saw the yearning in your face that I recognized it as an echo of my own.

It never would have occurred to me to look for myself in an ancient Sumerian myth. It never would have occurred to me to seek a loyal, passionate friend. I had been liked and respected by people, but have rarely liked or respected in return. I expected to be a loner all my life. But there you stood. Sobbing. Drunk. Grieving along with a despotic, three-thousand-year-old king.

Who could not love you, Val? Who could not open her heart to your quest for a companion and an equal? You left me no choice. I believe you had been tracking me with some mental sonar from afar, and your arrival at my door was not an accident, but the final step in a grand plan.

You confided that someday you planned to write a female version of *Gilgamesh.* I knew that reading me the myth aloud had been your way of inviting me to be your Enkidu. I could say yes or no, but I couldn't pretend I had not been invited.

After you finished reading, you fell on your bed, nearly sliding off from exhaustion. I removed the book from your hands, took your shoes off, tucked you in, and turned out the light. I may even have patted you on the head. Then I left your room knowing that by the act of staying and listening, I had already made a commitment to be your friend for life. I knew you would be hard work. You would demand a lot from someone who loved you. You would not always be reasonable or kind. But you would be open and generous and warm. And loyal till death do us part.

No one could have been more surprised by my commitment than I. But I saw myself in you. Just as you saw yourself in your Sumerian pals. I saw the person in you I might have become—warm, vibrant, daring, a little reckless and impulsive—if I had not been spoiled. If a part of me had not long ago been frozen and shut down. I not only liked you, Val, I liked the me I saw in you. And that liking felt like stepping unexpectedly into a warm breeze in spring, a pleasure that the cold of winter had made me forget was possible.

The one thing you wanted that I could never offer you was sex. You used to ask repeatedly. Sometimes sweetly, sometimes annoyingly. I knew you were a lesbian the first time I saw you. And I didn't care. Rather, since it was part of you and since I loved you, I loved that about you, too.

Sometimes you would try to seduce me simply by stopping by my room on your way back from the shower. You would accidentally allow your belt to become untied and your robe to fall open revealing your breasts, pretending you hadn't noticed. Then I would pretend not to notice your hidden agenda. I was fond of your childlike faith that innocent display of your body would entice me with overpowering desire. I believe you always left my room genuinely surprised that it hadn't worked.

At other times, you would visit me after a date, beer in hand, and casually discuss how the "sex had been okay," but of course the "very best sex" was always with people you were closest to. And I would always agree with you. The problem, I would say, was that the people you were closest to might not remain as close to you after sex. You would argue that when people are truly close nothing could ever draw them apart. We both knew what we were debating.

Only once did you proposition me directly, just two weeks ago. Since this encounter provides a verbal substitute for an epic wrestling match, I'll recount it for Chapter 2 of your epic.

Chapter 2

Our Heroes Avoid Having Sex

The last Saturday night before graduation, you had gone to five or six keg parties. This was not an atypical Saturday for you at all. I, also typically, had stayed in my dorm room to finish packing. I was leaving for the University of Michigan as soon as graduation was over the next day. You stopped by my room around midnight—an early Saturday for Val Summer—pretending to be drunk.

I knew you weren't, though. You were feeling truly sad, and you never liked to drink when you were sad—a quality that reassured me that you would never become an alcoholic, in spite of your affinity for excess and your family history.

I knew you were upset about saying good-bye the next day. You looked at me with vulnerable, soft-focused brown eyes, and I knew exactly what you wanted from me. You looked just like all those pitiful sailors in World War II movies on their last night before shipping off to battle, making carpe diem appeals to their girlfriends for sex.

I would have made a terrible sailor's girlfriend, because I would never have sex out of pity with anyone. Including you. I knew that you knew I would not be swayed by mooning and moping. I was curious, though, to see what you would try next. So I kept packing, while you tracked my every movement with your eyes. After a few moments, to my surprise, you said good night and left.

I was certain I had not seen the last of you. I heard the shower down the hall, and chuckled, anticipating what was to come. But I underestimated you. I heard the slapping sound of your bare feet headed my way. I heard the creak of my door opening. When I looked up, you were stark naked. Naked and shivering. You grinned and said, "Last chance."

I looked straight at you, determined not to avoid your eyes or any other part of you. "Thanks for the offer. No thanks." It was the first time I feared you might be hurt or angry rather than baffled by my rejection.

But you were gracious. You were pleased with yourself for trying.

"Aren't you afraid you'll regret this decision in the morning?" you asked.

"I'll live with it," I said.

"Can't blame a girl for trying. You don't, do you?"

"I never have," I said. And I meant it.

"Just let me ask you once. I have to know. Answer honestly. Don't you find me attractive?"

I owed you an honest answer. So I looked you up and down. I wanted you to understand once and for all that I wasn't afraid of finding women attractive. I just didn't want to have sex with them. Including you.

"You are very attractive, Val Summer. You are Venus de Milo—with muscle tone and a head. If I were interested in having sex with a woman—which I am not—I would jump into bed with you in a flash."

"Oh well," you sighed. "Perhaps you can't have everything in life. But you should try. Maybe another year. Maybe you'll grow up." You grinned.

"Maybe another lifetime," I groaned. And I unpacked a towel and threw it at you. You wound it around your dripping hair.

"By the way," I asked, "what do you plan to wear back to your room?"

"I'm already wearing more than Venus de Milo," you protested, and walked naked down the hall to your room.

As I read this over, I am relieved you took rejection gracefully. I know you still do not understand why, loving you as I do, I could turn you down. You think being a heterosexual is like being a vegetarian—a moral choice which excludes life's most interesting flavors. You are eager to create a myth in which all close friends can also be lovers.

But that is not the truth. Your wanting it to be so will never make it so. I know that hurts you. But what you have never tried to understand is that it hurts me, as well. It is your blind spot.

I don't know how to convey to you that just as you need to believe that the love of friends ideally should embrace sexuality, I need even more strongly to believe that there are some kinds of love in the world, including ours—especially ours—that leave sex behind. Somehow, we always failed to meet minds on this. For example:

Chapter 3

Our Heroes Fail to Communicate

In a rare irritable mood one night, after one of your brief, tormented affairs with some sexual adventuress you picked up in a bar (really, Val, to watch the traffic in and out of your dorm room one would have thought half the women at Barclay College were lesbians), you found me studying in my room. You were carrying a nearly full quart bottle of malt liquor. You were in the habit of buffering yourself from difficult emotions not by actually consuming alcohol, but carrying it around with you like a talisman.

You sat down on my bed, squeezing the bottle between your thighs, and waved at me to continue reading. I did so, and you sat meditatively for a few moments.

"I've decided," you broke the silence, "that you are essentially a virgin."

I snorted, thinking you were joking. You knew I was having sex with one of what you called "those stiff-backed science majors." But as I met your eyes, I saw a rare hardness there. It was because I was having sex that you were upset. You had said it to be mean.

"That's interesting," I said, refusing to gulp your bait. "Do you really think so?"

"Yes, I do."

"Well, you know, Val, the original meaning of virgin was someone who is one by herself, who is owned by and obliged to no one. And that is how I plan to be all my life. Whether I have a lot of sex or not. And whether it pleases you or not."

Gracelessly, you sneered, "Why don't you just become a nun? You aren't interested in really loving anyone."

"I'm not religious, for one thing. For another, those women are escaping love. Rather, they're pretending there is some pure kind of love they can receive from Jesus as a substitute for real, debased human love. I'm not escaping or pretending. I'm simply choosing to live my life without it, and to be happy that way."

"But aren't you curious?"

"That's why I have you," I laughed.

"Harumph." You didn't like that. "But," you asked earnestly, "don't you need love?"

"Of course I do. Believe it or not, there are varieties of love in the world that are not contingent upon sex. Our friendship is one of them, but there are many others."

"I don't know." You frowned, offering me a sip of malt liquor. I took the bottle from you and poured it down the sink.

"You'll thank me tomorrow," I said.

But you hadn't even noticed. Your brow was furrowed. "Sometimes," you began hesitantly, "I feel you really are escaping something. Other times, I think you are just stronger and braver than anyone else."

"Maybe I just have my own forms of love. Why can't studying on Saturday night be just as much a search for love as barhopping and pressing flesh?"

"I don't know," you said, unconvinced. "I just don't think it's the same." You left, looking hurt. You thought I was saying I loved studying more than I loved you. I can read you like a headline.

I don't remember being annoyed with you when this happened. But I am now looking back on it. You can be so smug, Val.

You have always had more of my heart than anyone else, yet you always want more. And I don't mean just sex, but the deepest, most private parts of me that I will never share. You think if you know my secrets, you'll have my soul. And then you think I'll need you, because my soul won't be mine anymore. That is what you think lovers should do—possess each other's souls.

Forget it, Val. No one, not even you, will ever own my soul. That is why I will never get married. And there is nothing wrong with that. It isn't cowardice or pathology. It's just different. I love the things about you that make you different. Why can't you love the ways I'm different, too, instead of taking them as personal slights?

Love rules, you are fond of saying. But I tell you, as I have a million times, you are wrong. Power rules. Corruption rules.

Love is predatory. As your Enkidu says when he warns Gilgamesh of the perils of the forest, "It is a road you have never traveled." But I have. You believe that deep inside the heart of every tiger is a wounded lamb, longing to be taken care of. But the truth is that deep inside the heart of every lamb is a savage beast, waiting to pounce on the unwary.

What am I saying? I am too tired to write a letter. I can never mail this. I am ranting. I am lashing out, but you don't deserve it.

I had sex with a graduate student I met at orientation last night. Another "stiff-backed" boy. He was funny and charmingly red-headed, but when I sent him home this morning, I felt how alone I am. How massive the undertaking of getting a PhD is. I'll be here for years, Val. Living in tiny apartments. Studying constantly and working at part-time jobs. Competing with equally smart students for faculty attention and good grades. My little apartment feels right now just as your intimidating blue bowl of sky did to you at the beach that morning.

I will not yield to discouragement. I must get some sleep. I have three papers to write tomorrow, and a double shift at the hotline. I would write about the crazy calls I get, but there is no point. I will never send this letter. You would be too curious. If I give you a little, you always want more.

Stop. That's not fair. I'm protecting myself. The truth is that how you see me is more important than how I see myself. And the irony is that although I accuse you of hiding from the truth—and although we have sworn to always be honest with each other—I am a coward. I withhold the truth from you. I am ashamed.

I will send you a postcard tomorrow telling you all is well. I hope I remember to add that I miss you, and to sign it with

Love,

Ashmont

July 1973
Dearest Ashmont,

Eureka! The love of my life has appeared. I am not cursed, after all. As in the song from *The Sound of Music,* in spite of my wicked childhood, I must have done something good. God has lifted the curtain of loneliness, and given me Dolores.

Let me get the part you will disapprove of out of the way. She is older than I. To be exact, twenty-five years. But when hearts are true, age is equalized by passion. And oh, Ashmont, my Dolores's heart is ever so true. True, square, and plumb as the beams on the best built houses.

Not that Dolores looks like a house. Although, to my artist's eye, she resembles a lighthouse in that a beacon of wisdom seems to radiate from her forehead. I painted her portrait. She is posed in a blue evening gown, standing in moonlight next to the lighthouse. In profile, she gazes through a telescope out to sea. I am trying to combine the elegance of her personality with the depth of her wisdom-seeking soul.

I have been in love with her since I met her my first night at Lucky's, the bar Desmond took me to. Never has a bar been so aptly named. I spotted her from across the dance floor. Her silver-blonde mane of sparkling hair served as candle to my moth. I thought she was my age at first. She was holding court in the middle of a gaggle of adoring gay men, as if she were Auntie Mame. She wore a white pants suit with gold epaulets on the shoulders and a double row of gold buttons down the front. The military look was appropriate, since she commanded everyone's attention.

When I mentioned this to Desmond, he snorted and said it was her vast fortune that commanded everyone's attention. I told him that our grandmother Norma always said that envy was a bilious emotion that spoiled livers and complexions. Desmond opined that in our family alcohol alone did a fine job of that.

I begged him to introduce me to her. At first he refused, saying Raymond thought she was a *fag hag.* Can you believe such an ugly word could be used to describe such a beautiful woman? I pretended I knew what he meant and said she certainly was not, and kept begging. Later, I asked Raymond what it means. Do you know, Ashmont?

With all your Freudian theory, you probably do. But in case they don't include vulgarities in your text books, it means a woman who hangs around with gay men. Raymond said it was very pathological. But then Raymond, who thinks nothing of dressing up like Barbara—excuse me—*Barbra* Streisand for breakfast, thinks people who drink instant coffee are pathological. Besides, I hang around with Desmond and Raymond, so I guess that makes me a fag hag, too. And how pathological am I? Never mind.

Anyway, I pestered him until Desmond finally walked me over to Dolores's circle of admirers and introduced us. Dolores was immediately gracious, so I shot Desmond a look that said, *"See . . ."* and he left us alone.

Dolores was telling a story about an auction of Shaker antiques in upstate New York. She and her friends were comparing antique dealers, and I was feeling like a canine at a cocktail party. Then Dolores flashed me a smile said, "What about you, Val? What do you collect?"

I had a few minutes to make an impression or I might never see her again, so I had nothing to lose.

"I collect heads," I said.

"I thought they only did that in Borneo," one of the guys said.

"A primal woman," said another one. "Don't let her escape, Dolores. I've a list of heads I wish she'd gather."

They were laughing their miniature brains out, but I focused on Dolores. She shushed them regally, with a wave of her hand.

"Don't worry," I grinned, pretending only the two of us were present. "I leave them on the bodies. I paint portraits. I'm an artist. I'm always looking for great heads to paint. My friend Ashmont and I have a theory that great minds go with great heads. She thinks that since Einstein died, there aren't any truly great heads *or* great minds anymore. But I'm always on the lookout."

"Provincetown may not be the most promising territory," Dolores said.

"Don't be too sure," I said with my best flirty grin, "Actually, I like *your* head. I was hoping you'd let me paint your portrait."

The hyenas were amused and started whistling and clapping and calling out, "Portrait! Portrait! You must, Dolores! You must!"

I felt bad to have incited such rude behavior, but Dolores didn't seem to mind. In fact, she looked amused. I hoped I was starting to charm her.

"Your friend, Ashmont. Is he or she here with you this summer assisting you in your quest?" Dolores asked.

"Oh no," I said. "Ashmont and I are best friends. But she's in Ann Arbor earning a PhD in psychology. And we are forever chaste, anyway. I am available body, mind, and soul."

"First rate!" The chorus of fools began chanting. I wasn't used to flirting in front of an audience and found it distracting.

"Take her, Dolores! How can you resist?" they chimed.

"Maybe I will," Dolores murmured lightly, more to the guys than to me. "But not tonight. I need to keep my head until after my dinner party Saturday night. Which you, my dear—" she pointed her index finger at my heart and touched my shirt lightly *(I trembled with excitement)* "—must attend."

She walked away, trailing a wake of inebriated, tittering fools. As she stepped, she made charming little jingling noises with the bangles she wears on her slender, elegant wrists, and left a trace of perfume in the air, which I inhaled deeply. I felt buoyed. Maybe this summer wouldn't be so lonely after all. Maybe I could stand to live my life until fall. I hummed and skipped back to the inn, and even Desmond's and Raymond's grunts of disapproval couldn't dim my spirits.

After an eternal, infernal three days, Saturday night came. And since then, Ashmont, I am a goner. Her dinner party was unlike any I've ever been to. You will say that is not surprising, since cafeteria meat loaf and fast food burgers do not dinner parties make. But even *you* would have been impressed.

She lives in a house just a few doors down from the inn, but set back discreetly from the street by a tall fence. You follow a narrow driveway back to a gigantic white house with Tara-like columns and a widow's walk on the roof from which you can gaze at the monster sea.

In the middle of the backyard nestles a kidney-shaped swimming pool surrounded by two huge hammocks and white wicker sofas and armchairs.

Inside, the house is full of glass tables and shelves with Chinese vases and African masks and what Dolores explained to me were "museum quality artifacts." Her dining room table is the longest, glossiest one I've ever seen. She never bothers with tablecloths, just fine lacy placemats. The candlesticks are *real* silver, and you can actually see through the dishes if you hold them up to the light. One night the guys filled their crystal goblets with different levels of water and played "Some Enchanted Evening" with their spoons. Very juvenile. But Dee (which is what I now call her) is incredibly tolerant. She smiled and said, "Keep your day jobs, boys."

They howled, as they do at everything she says. Most of them are hardly boys, except for two or three bronzed young gladiators who are probably younger than *we* are. None of them seem to have night jobs or day jobs or even constructive hobbies. They spend their time tanning and fawning over Dee. I know this sounds harsh. I suppose I am a bit jealous. All right, I am *insanely* jealous. But when you're as much in love as I am, you shouldn't have to be objective. What I truly resent about Dee's friends is that they take up so much time that she could be spending with me.

Dee is filthy rich, to use her words, and sometimes I fear these people are using her. Sometimes, I get afraid that perhaps I am, too. At first I didn't like being around so many simply exquisite things. I was afraid I'd break a plate, use the wrong fork, or spill my wine. But Dee is very reassuring. She says it's only stuff, and can be replaced, whereas friends are irreplaceable. Her stuff is consoling for her. I think she's suffered a lot.

Dee is always trying to make people feel comfortable. She says that Oscar Wilde said you had to feed people, amuse them, or shock them. She leaves shocking to younger people, and focuses on feeding and amusing. Except that she is so very beautiful, she reminds me of Gertrude Stein, having a salon and all. Sometimes I wish there were other women besides me at her parties, for balance, you know. And because of Raymond and the "fag hag" thing, which I can't entirely put out of my mind. But then I tell myself that I am glad to be the only other woman there, or I'd be so jealous I couldn't be responsible for my actions.

Sometimes, when she holds court in the evening, wearing mint green silk in her wingback chair, I feel like Lily Briscoe to Dee's Mrs. Ramsay from *To the Lighthouse*—suppressing the urge to fling myself at her feet, bury my head in her knees, and declare my love both for her and for the atmosphere of beauty and refinement she creates.

As you know, the environment I grew up in could be downright squalid. When my parents were drinking, which was always, I was responsible for keeping the house clean, and you're familiar with the "high pigsty" style in which my dorm room was maintained.

By the time I was ten, Russ and Sheila had given up even the pretense of behaving like parents. That was the year they decided it was too much trouble to buy a Christmas tree. When Jamie and Ralph looked disappointed, Mom and Dad just took a stiffer drink. I was the one who saved money for a Christmas tree and bargained chores with Uncle Rusty to get him to drive it home for us. One year, Rusty refused to drive the damn tree home, and I had to move two potted plants together and drape them with lights. That was the same year I took money from my college savings to buy Christmas presents for my brothers. My parents were so busy drinking they didn't have time to shop. They handed a twenty dollar bill to a five-year-old and a seven-year-old and said Santa wanted them to go out and buy something they really wanted. Pathetic.

On Christmas Eve, I used to love walking down Jefferson Avenue, where the rich people lived. Looking inside the frosted windows at brightly lit trees, I'd watch long, wide cars pull up and deposit expensively dressed partygoers at festive doorways. I yearned to be transported inside. Everything would be warm and bright. No one would be rude or loud. Or comatose in front of a TV.

Food would be hot, homemade, and plentiful. There would be bowls and bowls of candy. Peanut clusters. Malted milk balls. Gumdrops. Chuckles. Licorice bits. Necco wafers. And M&M's, of course. Sometimes I would fantasize that a woman in a red and white striped apron would throw open the door of a house on Jefferson Avenue as I walked by. She'd be carrying a huge mixing bowl filled with chocolate chip cookie dough. She would recognize me as her lost child, throw her arms around me, and give me the whole bowl of dough to express her joy at being reunited.

I would walk through the magic doorway on Jefferson Avenue, and my life would change forever. I would ask if Jamie and Ralph could come live with us. She'd say yes, of course. I'd call my parents and they would agree to relinquish their children, glad to be rid of the pests. I used to wonder what the children born to people on Jefferson Avenue had done to deserve it, and what defect in our souls forced the rest of us to wander in the cold staring in at such abundance.

Ashmont, when I am in Dee's house, I feel as though I have walked through the magic doorway into Jefferson Avenue, where life is expensive and sweet instead of cheap and begrudging. I feel that I've been rewarded at last for trying so hard to be good. Dee seems like the fairy godmother in Pinocchio to me, and I feel deeply grateful to her.

I call her the golden one. Do you remember my dragging you off to see *Maedchen in Uniform* at the Fine Art Cinema? That is what the children in that oppressive boarding school called the beautiful, kind teacher who helped them transcend their surroundings. That is what Dee has done for me. She has helped me transcend my upbringing. She says I am too self-critical, and she encourages my painting. She even has the portrait I painted of her on display in her bedroom. She said she was saving it for her own gaze. I thought that was very romantic.

Sometimes, Dee flies down to New York for a day or two, and I feel forlorn without her. But she always brings me back some exquisite little treat that tells me she's been thinking about me—last week it was a white sugar mouse, perfectly in scale, with a green frosting collar and a red licorice tail. I couldn't bear to eat it, so I painted it with shellac and perched it on my bedstead. Now its sugary rodent smile is the first face I see every morning.

Last Sunday morning, we were laying together in Dee's huge four-poster bed. Yes, Ashmont, I can see your eyes narrowing, we *are* having sex and it was entirely my idea. Unlike some people we both know, Dee is unable to resist my entreaties. Anyway, her bed is covered with beige satin sheets and surrounded with piles of feather pillows. I felt like a baby bird in a giant nest. Dee's maid even brought us a tray of worms—I mean coffee and croissants. I felt peaceful. And I realized it was because I felt completely safe. Truly safe, for the first time in my life. The harsh edges of the big, bad world soften when I'm with Dee.

Dee says I am a gifted lover. She comes more slowly and often than anyone I've ever made love to. Of course, my other lovers have been no older than twenty-one or twenty-two, max. Maybe slow, multitudinous orgasms are something we can all look forward to. I hope so. Unlike my other lovers, Dee isn't the least bit shy about telling me what she wants. "Val, sweetie, what's the rush? Take the scenic route. Aw, there, now, off to the left, now around the sides. Perfection, dear. Steady, just like that."

My coaches on the basketball team always said that I might not be the most graceful athlete on the team, but that I took direction well. Dee, however, insists that I am a skillful partner. Whether it's true or not, I feel proud that I give her so much pleasure. Regardless of my failures in other arenas of life, in Dee's bed, I don't just succeed, I triumph.

She asks me why I want to make love to an old wretch like her. She is very ruthless and crabby about her age and her body. When I insist that she is beautiful, she will shush me. But she lets me whisper "I love you," as I kiss her neck and stroke her fine spun hair. What happiness, Ashmont, to lay my head across her bosom and hear her heartbeat, steady and reassuring, keeping me sweet company all the night.

Do you remember the myth of the round people we read in Plato's *Symposium* for Dr. Durvin's philosophy class? It said that the original people were round, but they angered the gods, who split them in two for punishment. One became a male and female. One became two males, and one two females. These broken creatures were so miserable and despondent that even the gods pitied them, and moved their sex organs to the front so they could at least, through lovemaking, feel round and whole again.

You thought the myth demonstrated how moronic and dependent romantic love makes people. But I thought it explained everything I ever thought about love. I remember thinking that the loneliness I had felt all my life was simply yearning for my other half. That's why I have trouble concentrating on goals and plans and practical things. I need to find my other half. And our love will make everything right.

Well, that is what Dee is for me. I told her that in bed one morning. "Dee," I said, "you're the other half of my round being, and I have found myself in us." She thought the myth was a charming story, and said that she was flattered by my analogy.

Although Dee has not yet told me she loves me, I take her being flattered favorably. If she didn't feel something for me, she wouldn't like the idea of being the other half of my round being. Don't you think? I need your advice. I know I get carried away. As you say, I put not just the cart before the horse but before the invention of the wheel!

Sometimes Dee will send me away because she needs time alone. She has photos in the living room of a bald, gnomelike man named Duncan—a zillionaire financial wizard who works on Wall Street— to whom she used to be married. I know because I asked about the picture one day and she said they rarely see each other, only when the children bring them together for holidays or graduations. They have two kids, both of them older than I am: a girl in Long Island and a boy in San Francisco.

I said I was sorry about her marriage, but she waved me off, saying it was better now than ever before. I guess they must have been pretty unhappy. She never brings up the gnome herself, so I didn't ask any more about him. Dee says she has always had "special friends" who are women. She won't use the word "lesbian," and we came close to an argument over this. She said "lesbian" connotes "mannish hoydens," and she didn't see either herself or me that way. I said that she was prejudiced, and that I loved the company of "mannish hoydens." I also told her I liked being associated with Sappho, the greatest poet in history. We compromised on the term "Sapphic friends." See, Ashmont, she is open minded.

I see your face in front of me, your eyes glaring, telling me I'm a fool. Or am I projecting my own doubts and fears about Dee? Such as, what happens in September when Dee returns to her Park Avenue penthouse and I go to Boston for art school? I try not to think about it, but I'm terrified. What if she finds some other "Sapphic friend"? Maybe I should get a job in New York in the fall, and apply to Pratt for the following year?

Still, for now, I am happy. And if you could see how happy I am you would unnarrow your eyes and be happy for me. My only moment of unhappiness came at Dee's last dinner party. And then I was unhappy for her, not myself. She's so generous to those bums. They all flatter her, but they never sound sincere. Dee doesn't seem to notice, or she's so kindhearted that she doesn't care. Anyway, I usually ignore the buffoons, but that night one of these parasites had the audacity to accuse Dee of exploiting me. I was so angry, I nearly socked the fool.

Halfway through dinner, Clive, a middle-aged bearded guy that before that night seemed perceptibly smarter than the others, stuck his thumbs in the sides of his suspenders and leaned back in his chair. He had been staring at me all night, but now he stared at Dee.

"Hail, Lady Bountiful!" he says in his bass voice, so it's impossible to ignore him.

"Hail, Clive," Dee says good naturedly.

"Have you no shame?" He's talking in this stupid, exaggerated way, but he looks serious. He's not drunk. I can tell. His eyes are focused. He is actually seeing what he is looking at. So there was no excuse for what he said next.

Dee raises her wine glass in a mock toast. "Shame is boring. I banish it from the dinner table."

Well, the guys are making their usual syrupy sounds. "Right, Dee!" "Well said, Dee!" And all that slop. But Clive is undeterred.

"No, listen to me. I've been watching you set your snare." And he looks at me. "Is there no tender veal you won't buy for your table? No unripe grapes you will not squash to see what flavor wine they make? Does your Epicurean appetite have no conscience?"

Well, the guys were quiet now. This high drama was just their style. I was angry, but I wasn't ready to pounce.

"She doesn't know about the aged, expensive brandy you imbibe while in New York, does she? You are a shameless voluptuary, Dee, and if I weren't one myself, I'd be embarrassed to sit at your table."

That cut it. I jumped up from my chair and shouted, "Get out of here! What do you know about anything! I know everything about Dee's old, bald brandy, not that it's any of your business. And unlike you and your pals, Dee would never take advantage of anyone. You're just jealous of the time she spends with me. Don't pretend you care about anyone but yourself. I was raised by people like you, and trust me, I recognize selfishness when I see it! You're nothing but an old . . ." Oh, Ashmont, you know how inarticulate I become when enraged. I scanned my mental files for invective, and all I came up with was ". . . *codger!*"

All the guys laughed. I could see Dee was amused, too. I thought she would toss Clive out of her house. But she said, "Val, sit down." Her tone was concerned, but there was a sharpness to it. "You're on the verge of shocking. Tone it down."

I sat down, but I glared at Clive. My fists were clenched on the table. It confused me that Dee seemed more concerned about my behavior than Clive's. Maybe she was afraid that I would punch him. I wouldn't really.

We sat silently for a few minutes, except for the guys' clearing their throats over and over. They were dying to titter, but they didn't dare until they got a signal from Dee.

Finally, Clive said, "Val, I apologize. Your earnestness puts me to shame. I'm as bad as Dee." He must have seen my face redden at that, because he added, "Now calm down. But if this protective outburst doesn't prove my point, I don't know what would. But to avoid inciting a riot, I won't say anything more about your precious Dee." Then he drained his wine glass, and looked at Dee as if to say, "I rest my case."

"Clive's an old friend, Val," Dee said soothingly, as if that explained everything. But I was angry at all of them now. Clive for his attack. Dee for sympathizing with him instead of tossing him out. The others for being alive.

"Clive's an old fart!" I exclaimed. And everybody burst into laughter, including Clive and Dee. The worst thing about these people is they're beyond insult.

Then it was as if everybody thought things were back to normal. Dee started talking about the burden of real estate taxes in Province-town. Not a topic I had much to contribute to. I sat there feeling completely alone. Maybe in addition to sleeping in beds like nests and "imbibing brandy" with your ex-husband, there are other rules of speech, courtesy, and amusement on Jefferson Avenue that I will never understand. Do you think Clive really meant that Dee and the gnome still have sex together? I shudder to think of Dee in the arms of such an wizened old goat, whether she was ever married to him or not; it makes me realize that there are many, many things I still do not know about Dee. I loathe the idea of sharing Dee's body, mind, or soul with anyone. But I love Dee so much that I will simply have to learn.

So Ashmont, please write. I hate it when you don't, which is always. Tell me more about the hotline, the soup you cook for dinner on your hot plate, the landlord who beats on the ceiling with a broomstick when you play your Brandenburg Concertos. All the luscious details of your life. I know you don't have time. I know I'm not supposed to complain, but I have to whine a little bit. I am so in love. I want to share my happiness with you. And to say in triumph so you will remember for all time: Love Rules!

Your ever-loving, happy at last in love,

Val

July 1973
Dear Val,

When I see you at the end of the summer, I am going to wring your neck. If you survive the summer, that is. By then, precious Dee will have broken your heart. It will be all I can do to refrain from saying "I told you so" as I pick up the pieces.

I've a mind to fly out there right now and yank you back to Ann Arbor with me. Can't I let you out of my sight for a month? Haven't you learned anything? Clive is right. You are a tasty morsel of youthful flesh for this carnivorous woman. She will spit you out the moment she is bored. Trust me, she's not going to let you follow her to Manhattan, you besotted moron. I can't believe you are entertaining the thought of abandoning art school. You owe it to yourself to go. You owe this craven opportunist nothing.

If she hurts you badly, I'll kill her. I may, however, kill you first. There's a certain point at which your brand of romanticism stops being merely harmless naivite and becomes imbecility. You have crossed the line.

She's using her wealth to trap you, which is unforgivable. Worse, if she cared a whit about you, she would have thrown you out of her bed the first time you waxed all starry-eyed and moonstruck about "finding yourself" in this relationship. A sock on the side of the head is what any true friend would have delivered.

I remember that myth about the round people. You babbled about it incessantly. You find it touching and romantic. I find it chilling. What a repulsive thought, being bound to someone, losing your identity in an amorphous blob. No thank you. I'd rather be alone. It may not always be fun to be alone, but at least I know who I am. At least I run my own life. Really, Val, you could romanticize slavery. I worry about you.

Shall I tell you the truth about Professor Durvin, the purveyor of this putrid myth? Would that shock you out of your trance? So funny that you mention him in the same letter as your hagiography of Dee. Many students thought he was a saint, as well.

Dignified, bearded Professor Durvin. Winner of the Fielding Teaching Award three years running. Tenured at the age of thirty-five. Expert at using the Socratic method to wrench from tongue-tied students little nuggets of wisdom they didn't know they had until Professor Durvin interrogated them. Sadism masking as pedagogy. Not unusual. Not original. But practiced and refined.

That much you know. What you don't know is that Professor Durvin invited me to his apartment second semester junior year to "help" me with my philosophy paper. Only his brightest, most gifted students, he told me in his office, were honored with invitations to work at his home.

"Really," I said innocently, "male and female students?" He flinched a little. I knew no male student had ever been gifted enough to garner an invitation to the professor's house. He knew, too. But he didn't miss a beat.

"Of course," he said impatiently. "But if you're too timid to come, we'll just meet here in my office instead." He was insinuating that any hesitation on my part reflected my own paranoia. My fevered imagination. He looked down at his date book to check his next appointment. I had become just another boring philosophy student instead of a potential "lay." It was his lack of respect for the sacred trust of teaching as much or more than his sexual corruption that made me decide at that moment to take him down.

"Oh, yes, Professor Durvin, I'd be very happy to meet with you at your house. I'm sure my paper will be better for it."

He indulged in a pleased, predatory grin. "I'm sure it will be brilliant. The best in the class. An A for sure, Miss Ashmont."

I did a background check on Durvin. It's amazing what you can find out if you act as if you had a reason to know. Durvin was divorced from a woman who had been an undergraduate student of his ten years ago. Two years ago, a junior philosophy major had gotten pregnant by him and left college. He had denied paternity and insinuated that this girl was a dangerous seductress out to destroy the careers of innocent professors. Durvin's profile came into focus. He was a slithering reptile whose bloated ego required the constant conquest of vulnerable coeds.

You know, Val, that I am not sentimental. I hold people accountable for their actions, even impressionable eighteen-year-old girls. My general view of life is that if people are dumb or irresponsible enough to make messes of their lives, they are responsible for cleaning them up.

Still, there are times when the predators must be stopped. Times when I am willing to disguise myself as an innocent long enough to win the predator's trust, and then slit the beast's throat. Someone has to stop them. When men take action to stop injustice, they are called avengers. When women do it, we are called harpies. I don't care. I'd rather be a harpy than a doormat.

So I appeared at Durvin's house in costume, with my Peter Pan collar and my book bag declaiming: "Victim!" And my cassette tape recorder silently recording all the evidence I would need to hang the bastard.

As I expected, Durvin encouraged me to have a drink. A gin and tonic with double gin and a drop of tonic. I pretended to sip it, and pretended to get tipsy.

"Professor Durvin," I said coyly, "now tell me why you invited me here."

"I think you know why I invited you here, Miss Ashmont," he said in a flirty tone.

"You wanted to help me with my philosophy paper?"

"That's right," he grinned. "I'm going to give you some very special help. The kind only the brightest, most attractive students deserve. Don't you think intelligence makes a woman sexy, Miss Ashmont—but perhaps you wouldn't mind if I called you Emily?"

"I prefer Miss Ashmont. But tell me, do your male students ever receive this 'special' help?"

"Of course not!" He was annoyed. Offended, even. He might be a pedophile, but he was no bugger.

"Professor Durvin—"

"Really," he interrupted, "you might as well call me Dick. But only here, not at school."

"Okay, Dickie," I giggled.

"Not Dickie, Dick," he said.

"What happens, Dickie, if a student turns down the special help once she's here and has drunk your gin?"

He was irritated. This was taking too long. "They might find," he said darkly, "that if they can't benefit from the special help, that their grade suffers."

I had him. He was blackmailing me for sex, and I recorded it on tape. I went on for a while, asking him how low my grade might fall, until he threatened failure. Then, at 9 p.m., right on schedule, his doorbell rang.

"Who the hell can that be?"

"Oh, Dickie, do you mind? I told a friend he could pick up notes from today's class here."

He minded a great deal. "Well, that was poor judgment. You know, other students might get jealous of the help you're getting."

"Oh, not this one. He won't be jealous." I picked up my bag and opened the door for Mike, my psychology lab partner, whom I had asked to meet me at Durvin's house without explaining why. I moved outside the front door with Mike, and lifted the tape recorder out of my bag, so Durvin could see it clearly.

Very soberly, I said, "I got it all on tape, Dick. Every bit of your disgusting 'come on.'"

"Yeah, right," he said, covering his surprise with nonchalance. "No one will believe you. I'll say it isn't my voice."

"Oh, everyone will believe me. Your department chair will recognize your voice. The newspaper will love this story. Maybe the American Philosophy Association newsletter would like to print the transcripts. You may never teach ethics again, Dick."

"Bitch," he said. "You wouldn't. I'll flunk you."

"Try me," I said. "I haven't turned off the tape recorder, did you know that? Mike, did you hear Professor Durvin just threaten me? Now I have a witness as well as a tape recording."

Durvin had forgotten about Mike, who stood, mouth agape, staring back and forth between us.

"What do you want?" Durvin was ready to bargain.

"I want you to pick on women your own age. No younger than thirty seems reasonable, considering you're at least fifty. Anyone over thirty who has sex with you has only herself to blame."

"Why are you doing this to me? You knew what was happening. You came here of your own free will." He sounded weary and harried. In his own twisted logic, he was the victim.

"Because you deserve it. And no one else was available to stop you. Because of Deb Harry. Claudette Corbin. And Paula Humphreys."

"Get out!" He was shouting now.

"But you haven't promised to be good yet."

"All right. All right. Just leave."

"You better keep your promise. I have a network of spies. We'll be watching who comes to your house."

"Okay, okay. I promise. Now get out of here before I call the—" He had the good grace to stop himself from threatening to call the police, which I would have loved.

Mike and I walked down the front steps. But I paused at the bottom and yelled up, "Dick! Dick!"

"Now what?" he asked.

"I want an A. Don't even think about anything less."

"Get out of here, bitch." He slammed the door.

"Well, no need to be rude."

I don't kid myself that my actions triggered a redemptive transformation of Professor Durvin. I never used the tape. I had no delusions that other faculty or the American Philosophy Association would have given a damn about Durvin preying on students. His colleagues would have covered for him—too many of them are corrupt in the same way. Durvin gave me an A. I deserved it. I won the philosophy department's yearly award for the paper I wrote for his class. I'm fairly certain that he stopped offering "special help" to female students until I graduated. He thought I was crazy and dangerous. He probably believed I actually did have a cabal of girl spies staking out his house.

Did he learn anything? No. But he was forced to restrain himself. And he was beaten by a girl. Given his contempt for women, I'm sure that was the greatest punishment of all. And that was my reward. Piercing that arrogance, that colossal presumption. Finding the vulnerable spot that at least for a moment equalizes predator and prey.

Mike was shocked at what I had done. "Geez, are you really sending that tape to the *Boston Globe?*"

"That's largely up to Professor Durvin and how he behaves."

"Geez," Mike kept saying. "Geez, you really squeezed his balls."

"Did I?" Mike was having a little crisis of identification.

"You must really hate Durvin," he said. He was trying to make sense of my behavior. For Mike, stopping Durvin from preying on his female students was not sufficient motivation for such dangerously aggressive behavior in a woman.

"Why do you say that, Mike? Do you think Professor Durvin hates the students he seduces and blackmails into having sex?"

This confused Mike. "No," he said. "He's just a dirty old man."

"Oh," I replied. "'Just' an exploiter of females, not a hater of females. Well, if you don't think he hates the women he exploits, why do you assume that I hate him because I stopped him?"

This confused Mike even more. "Geez, I don't know." He looked at me as if the strands of my hair were turning to snakes. "It's just different. I can't explain. You're weird, you know. I mean, you're brilliant. I'm glad you're my lab partner. But you're really strange."

"Yes I am. But here's a way to think about it. If Professor Durvin is 'just' a dirty old man, think of me as 'just' a dirty old man's nemesis. The fates drew us together."

"I have no idea what you're talking about," Mike said.

"Mike, I believe you. Let's go study."

Val, your precious Dee is a variation on Durvin. Love does not rule. Lust does. Before the end of the summer, you will see that your "love nest" is really a snare. You can't retreat from life. You have to be faster and stronger so it doesn't pounce on you. I'm afraid you've already been pounced upon. The fact that you went willingly, belly up, won't diminish your pain.

Well, Val, look what I've done. I've written you another letter I can't mail. I've revealed too much. You would never forgive me for not telling you about Durvin long ago. You would be angry and hurt that I asked Mike to be my accomplice instead of you. You would quiz me about my motives, and like a dog worrying a bone, you wouldn't stop until I was all chewed up.

I couldn't take that. That's why I asked Mike instead of you. You would have probed too much. I knew Mike wouldn't care. I know this is unfair to you, but it is the truth. I am overwhelmed with work. I am exhausted all the time. I hope that someday, I can talk to you about all this, but not now.

There's another reason why I asked Mike rather than you. When we took mythology together, I remember discussing the story of Artemis with you. She was always your favorite goddess. You liked it that she rode and hunted. And you liked her band of nymphs. You envisioned them as a kind of lesbian harem, always available for easy sex.

We read the story of Actaeon, the huntsman who lingered behind a rock to watch Artemis bathing. She punished him by changing him into a stag. He was then torn apart by his own hounds. Artemis wanted to ensure that he would never boast of seeing a goddess naked. You kidded about it. You said you were glad none of the women you stole glances at in the locker room in high school had Artemis's powers. You thought the huntsman had been punished too severely for the crime.

I said the punishment fit the crime. If a goddess is not protected from voyeurs, what hope do mortal women have for respect? You became cranky. We nearly had a fight. You felt I was judging you. You refused to understand that it wasn't Actaeon's looking—it's only human to look—that I was judging. It was the bragging that had to be stopped. The bragging made looking about power, rather than admiration or desire.

Actaeon and Durvin are different. But I like to think that if Artemis were alive today, she would have taken the steps I did. I couldn't, however, risk your responding to me the way Mike had, as though I were strange, weird, extreme, or dangerous. A bitch. I couldn't stand it. I would have lost you over something stupid. And I needed you. I need you now.

I can't send you this letter. Instead, I will send you a postcard tomorrow that says, "Val: watch your back!"

Love,

Ashmont

August 1973

Dear, discerning Ashmont,

My heart is heavy with grief and remorse. It barely pumps enough blood through my arms to pick up my pen and write. How I wish I had listened to the warning phone call you made last week. Remember, my skull is stuffed with cotton instead of neurons, and forgive me for disparaging what turn out to have been *accurate* warnings about Dolores as the products of a mistrustful and cynical mind.

I feel so betrayed, Ashmont. So terribly hurt. She might as well have kicked me in the stomach. I keep finding my hands crossed over my middle, as if to keep my guts from spilling out. But it didn't happen the way you predicted. It happened sooner. And it was *worse.*

I might as well tell you from the beginning. I was supposed to be working at the inn on Sunday night, so I wasn't expected at Dee's until Monday afternoon. But I helped Desmond wallpaper his kitchen that afternoon, and he gave me the night off. I decided to surprise Dee, and skipped to her house.

When I arrived, the French doors to her living room were open. I paused, hearing an unfamiliar voice, a high falsetto. Curious, I walked close enough to see and hear, but not be seen. Clive knelt at Dee's feet as she sat in her wingback chair, burying his head between her knees in exactly the position I had fantasized for myself. I felt a stab of jealousy. He was paying homage to *my* queen in *my* way *before* I had gotten around to it.

Then I heard what he was saying.

"Oh, my golden one . . ." She had told Clive my private name for her. I was stunned.

"You are my queen. Let me be but the chewing gum beneath your shoe! The sludge in the drain of your tub!"

He was mocking me. Making fun of my love for Dee. I couldn't believe it. I thought Dee would tell him to shut up and get lost. But the sound she made next was horrible.

She chuckled. She could have called me names, hurled insults, criticized my hair or my clothes—*nothing* could have hurt me more than that chuckle. It told me everything I needed to know about what I really mean to Dee. Which is exactly *nothing.* Just some hayseed the Jefferson Avenue regulars kicked around for their amusement.

"Please, please, please let me paint you on black velvet," Clive whined, "with sad, round eyes. Let me paint a portrait of your little toe. Please, any body part will do."

Dee chuckled stupidly again. "Her painting *is* a bit naive, isn't it?"

I couldn't believe what I was hearing. The same woman who encouraged me to "believe in my talent," who urged me to give art school "a serious try," was savaging my work. I felt humiliated for pretending I could be an artist. I wanted to steal my painting off her wall. I wanted to disappear and never be seen again. And I wanted to choke Dee. To feel her gasp for breath beneath my hands.

"*Trite* is the right word," Clive snickered. "She should be painting furniture, not canvas. Still," Clive spoke normally, standing up. "She's just a kid. She's going to get hurt. She thinks you love her."

Dee snorted. "Val is very sweet, but she's a grown woman. And she thinks nothing of the kind."

"She's twenty-one years old. And when you're twenty-one, you assume other people take your feelings just as seriously as you take them. At that age, you can't begin to imagine the cynical self-absorption of people like us." Dolores frowned and drained the rest of her wine.

"Drop it, Clive. You're becoming moralistic in middle age. Besides, I knew better when I was twenty-one. I was twenty-one when I married Duncan. And he'd already cheated on me three times—once with my best friend. I had no illusions about love when I was twenty-one."

"Dearest, you were never twenty-one. Neither was I. You have to calculate age in upper-class years rather like dog years. You were way past twenty-one before you were out of diapers."

They laughed nastily, as if their cynicism gave them special claim to self-pity and superiority.

"Nonetheless," Clive continued, "Val is twenty-one for real. She has no idea she's a summer diversion to keep score with Duncan's summer diversions. She's earnestly in love with you, and I'm telling you she thinks you're in love with her. She's probably wondering right now when you'll invite her to live with you in New York. You're leading her down the primrose path."

"Clive, this is boring," Dolores said. Amusement was failing fast. "Let's change the subject. But for the record, I am not leading Val down any kind of path—"

"No, she's not!" I shouted. I don't remember deciding to do so. I don't remember deciding to do any of the things I did next.

I knocked the French doors wide open with my fists, and strode into the room with my hands on my hips.

"If anyone's leading anyone here, it's me. I'm laughing. Hear me! *Ha!* As if I could be interested in Dolores . . . in anyone *so* . . . *so* . . ." Ashmont, I wanted to say something insulting and hurtful, but the turnabout in my emotions, from adoring Dee to excoriating Dolores, was too fast. I couldn't say something hurtful to Dee without my voice catching. I sounded like an idiot, but I just said, "Ha!" again.

"Val! How much did you—" Dolores started to rise, but I raised my hand and spoke sternly, not looking at her because she had just broken my heart and I couldn't bear to meet her gaze.

"I'm laughing at you and all your sycophants and parasites." Clive stood by silently, staring at Dolores as if to say *I told you so.*

"Val, honey. You don't understand the way Clive and I—"

"Oh, but I *do!*" I said. "That's why I've been coming to your simply *fabulous* dinner parties. I wanted to find out firsthand how a fag hag and her minions act. I think I'll write a book. You'll see—my writing is much less *naive* than my painting."

Dolores' face went cold. I had hurt her. I called her fag hag to save my pride, but it was going to cost me more than it did her.

"All right, Val," she said coldly, "you will leave. Now."

I couldn't believe it. I was the one who had been treated badly. And she was throwing *me* out. I felt like a grounded fish in an airless room, gasping for some understanding of what was happening. I looked in her eyes, but all I saw was detachment. I understood then how easy it was going to be for her to cut me off. And how hard it was going to be on me. I didn't want to, but I started crying. Then I turned and ran away.

At the end of her driveway, I stopped running, wiped my tears, and looked back. I half expected Dee to be standing at the open doors, waving frantically for me to return. But all I could see was the golden light radiating from the inside of Dee's house, brightening up the night sky for a kid who was never going to break the barrier to a house on Jefferson Avenue.

"Good-bye," I whispered. Not entirely to Dee.

Back at the inn, Desmond and Raymond found me on the back porch, drinking beer—well, not actually drinking but holding the bottles as if I were planning to—and shredding the paper labels. They could tell that I'd been crying, and they knew it had to do with Dolores, because, like you, they'd been warning me to watch out for her all summer.

They had the decency not to say, "I told you so." Instead, Raymond invited me to accompany them on a night time walk down the beach.

"I can't," I said, feeling miserable. "I'm afraid of getting stained by the ink, and falling into the blowhole."

Raymond looked at me as if I'd lost my mind, so Desmond explained my long-standing fear of the ocean at night. The water turns to ink at night, and will stain your skin. And the black liquid harbors a monster with a huge blowhole like a whale's that can pop up anywhere and suck you in.

"Is she serious?" Raymond asked.

"She's serious," Desmond said. So they sat down on either side of me. Desmond took my beer bottle and poured it off the porch. *(Who does that remind you of?)*

"Sweetie," Desmond said, "is it over?"

I nodded. I could feel them making eye contact over my head.

"Some people are just bitches. And nobody goes through life without loving at least one bitch. Right, Raymond?"

"One if you're lucky," Raymond groaned. "Some of us get stuck with dozens."

"Oh, Raymond," I moaned, "you told me she was a pathological fag hag to begin with. You guys are being so nice you're just making me cry harder. Why don't you just say *you told me so*. There, *you told me so*. Now it's out in the open. I was a fool to trust her."

"No!" Raymond said sharply, to my surprise. "Never think *you* did something wrong. Trusting people is always a risk, and it's always noble. Because it's the only way connections happen. 'Only connect,'

right Dez? That's Forster himself, you know. And every time you connect, you're a hero."

He told me I was a brave soul, and that I deserved better. Desmond
told me I'd forget about her in a year. Raymond said two.

They were kind and gentle in such unexpected ways that I couldn't
help but feel better. But they're wrong about forgetting Dolores. I'll
carry her scar forever. It feels jagged and deep.

If Dolores cared so little, how could she have sex with me? Didn't it
mean anything to her? How could she let me fall so hard in love with
her if she didn't care? Why did she bother encouraging and flattering
me about my painting? I thought because she fussed over me that she
was different from my parents, different from anyone else I ever met.
And now, I find out that someone can fuss about you on the surface,
but beneath the surface it doesn't mean a thing. Rather, it's just to get
what she wants. Which means that, beneath the surface, she is exactly
like my parents, except they never bothered with the fussing.

Or is it me, Ashmont? I can't stop wondering if she would have
treated anyone else this way. Am I *nothing*? Someone whose feelings
aren't worth bothering about? I certainly feel like nothing right now.

Desmond and Raymond finally cajoled me into walking with them.
They promised to wash my feet if the ink stained them, and to snatch
me back from the belly of the beast if I got swept into the monster's
blowhole.

They walked on either side of me and lifted me off the ground when
the waves got close. I came back to the inn chilled but cleansed.

The next morning, Dolores had the gall to send her maid over with
the following reprehensible missive (it's taped together because
when I received an envelope made of Dolores's "simply exquisite
handmade Florentine paper," I ripped it up; about two seconds
later, I taped the damn thing together so I could read and be out-
raged by her feeble comments).

Valerie, mon cheri—

Because you fled my house like a burglar *the other night without bothering
to say good-bye, I must write, not speak, this brief farewell.*

*I want you to know that despite your having eavesdropped on a private conver-
sation and then having called me—whom you professed to love—the* foulest

name imaginable, I harbor no ill will toward you. I long ago passed the point of being shocked or disappointed by anyone or anything. As for my own behavior, I will not explain or justify it to anyone. Including you. Clive seems to think you are a naive waif. Pity me for thinking you a grown up, capable of a grownup's discernment, maturity, and resilience.

In spite of our unfortunate last meeting, I want you to know that I will always remember our interludes fondly, my Sugar Mouse. *You have qualities in abundance,* Valerie dearest, *that I was born without a single gene for, sweetness and—trust me, I never use this world lightly—an innate goodness deep inside. So if I am wrong and you are not tough already, learn to be so now so you can preserve and protect these rare qualities at all cost.*

There will be times, whether you think so now or not, when you will wonder whether you mattered to me. Whether I cared. The answer is, yes. Just not in the way you wanted—but darling, such wants are merely luxurious fictions. They are not the stuff of this world.

So you know, I received each of the six phone messages you left last night and this morning demanding the return of your portrait of me "forthwith." You, however, gave me that painting as a present. I shall not return it to you "forthwith" nor in any other manner. Remember, Valerie, not only is there no sin in one's talent's being naive, but if you want to be an artist, you cannot afford to give a good goddamn what Clive or I or anyone else thinks of your work.

By the time you receive this note, I will have flown back to New York. From there, I depart for a fall vacation in Barcelona. For reasons completely unrelated to you, I have directed Duncan to put the Provincetown house on the market and to look for a new vacation home in Palm Springs. My children feel more comfortable visiting me there than in Provincetown.

Years from now, Valerie, when you're a famous artist and can look back bittersweetly on our summer rendezvous, perhaps you will pay me a call. I shall be happy to hear from you. Until then, my little maid of Lesbos, I shall remain your "Sapphic friend."

Warm regards,

"D"

What a load of pretentious crap. Right, Ashmont? When I read it the first time, I picked up the Sugar Mouse from my bedstead and bit its repulsive little head off (later I flung the rest of it in the *literal* shit heap Raymond uses to compost his rose garden). Then after the next six or seven times I read her letter, I ranted and raved about my room, furious at the way she twists everything around so it sounds like I was the one who screwed up and she's ready to be canonized.

And yet, Ashmont, furious with her as I am, when I walked home from Lucky's Saturday night and saw a "For Sale" sign hanging from the closed gate to Dolores's driveway, I felt such heaviness in my heart I could barely stand. I touched the cold metal sign with my fingertips and traced the letters, one by one—F-O-R S-A-L-E—as if each of them held some precious memory of beauty and refinement, and of Dee herself: her satin sheets; the gloss of her dining room table; her mint green silk evening gown; the gold epaulets and buttons of her nautical pants suit; and her regal wingbacked chair. I believe that Dee is right about one thing: such wants are luxurious fictions. They are not the stuff of this world. Not mine, anyway.

And now the part that's harder to explain, because you will think it's because of Dee and Clive and what they said about my painting, and it's not. Well, maybe a tiny bit but not the most important part.

I'm *not* going to graduate school in the fall. I'm not ready to paint. I don't know why I'm painting or what I'm trying to say by painting. I feel strongly that—strangely enough—the next thing I need to learn in life is right here in Provincetown.

I feel as though the things I started learning this summer aren't through with me yet. No one could be more surprised at this than me, although Desmond isn't. He says the best education an artist can have is to get to know herself really well. And he says you can do that anywhere, as long it's in a place you feel called to be. He says it's like Georgia O'Keefe and the desert. The desert called her, and showed her who she was and what she needed to paint.

Desmond has decided to keep the inn open all year, and he's offered to let me keep my room and my job. I think he and Raymond like having me around. And they're the closest thing I have to a family now that my parents have moved to Florida and Jamie and Ralph have both moved to California.

Ashmont, I so wish you were here to talk to. You're leaping ahead of me in graduate school, while I refine my housekeeping skills. At least I'm young, so if I'm making a bad decision, there'll be plenty of time to reverse it. I hope I'm not being a coward. I hope I'm being brave. Isn't it funny, how hard it can be to tell the difference?

Anyway, you'll think I'm an incurable romantic—or a dunce—but I still believe that Love Rules. The fact that I'm a fool for love doesn't diminish its power. I simply haven't found the real thing. But I *will*. Dolores never loved me. I only *thought* I loved Dolores—that like a great Mother Bird, she would shelter me in her satin nest. Well, Dolores had a seductively beautiful nest, but she was a lousy mama. I know! I know, Ashmont! You will say I've no business looking for mamas at my age! I can't argue with you.

But Ashmont, please understand why nonetheless I feel so wounded. I thought that in Dolores and her world I had found my vision—like Lily Briscoe at the end of *To the Lighthouse* when she paints a final stroke in the center of her canvas and lays her brush down, knowing her painting is finished. But when I walked up and touched *my vision,* it shimmered like a mirage and disappeared. Discovering how profoundly mistaken I can be has humbled and frightened me. Now that I realize how infinitely far away I am from putting down my final stroke, I don't think I can even pick up my brush. Not for awhile.

I'm sorry to hear how tired you are. I wish I could be there to ease your burdens. I don't know much about developmental psychology or reassuring panicky adolescents on the telephone, but you'd be amazed at how effective I've become at making beds and mopping floors. I'd make your apartment sparkle.

I miss you. I promise to listen to you always completely carefully in the future.

Your ever-loving fool for love,

Val

August 1973
Dear Val,

Poor heartbroken Val. There's a special circle in hell for Dolores and her kind. If only behavior like hers could be criminalized, we could toss her in jail. Her letter oozes self-pity. Even her apprehension of your fundamental goodness, which might redeem her slightly, is canceled out by her posturing as some kind of hard-edged but benevolent patroness.

I might as well abandon the fiction that I am actually writing you letters. I suppose I'm writing a journal, addressed to you. Maybe some day, if I'm brave enough, I'll give them to you as source material for your *Gilgamesh*. Earlier this summer, you wrote that your letters to me were like bouncing your life off a star.

For me, writing you is like sitting by the ocean, thinking aloud while I listen to the waves—the heartbeat of earth, pounding and thrashing, distressed and appalled at what she's witnessed. Writing you helps me to conjure up a conscience for this pitiful planet. There's a cleansing and catharsis. You said you couldn't stop writing me or you wouldn't know how to live. I can't stop writing you letters—even though I'll never send them—or I couldn't bear to live.

What different assumptions we bring to love. You expect lovers to be trustworthy above all. I expect the opposite. A stranger is more likely to be trustworthy than a lover. Strangers have no hidden needs that warp integrity and truth.

What you expect from lovers I expect from friends. And since I never had a real friend until I met you, Val, I guess you're the only one I trust. That's why it's important to me that we never became lovers. How ironic that the very thing that I believe cements our trust—lack of sex—is the very thing you believe impedes it from reaching its full potential.

You assume that sex should open mind and heart, as well as body. Sex should melt flesh into pure spirit. The oceanic feeling of mystics and infants. I don't mean to condescend. It just comes out that way. I don't want to melt and merge. I don't want to transcend reality. I merely want to survive it. To do that, I need my wits about me.

For me, sex is cold comfort. I like it that way. That's what makes it erotic. Bumping up against a body whose mind is closed. The contrast between heat and detachment. The excitement of sinking deep inside and releasing a moment of pleasure and need, fragments of memory and desire, but with someone who isn't the least bit interested in snatching up these glimpses of my inner self, patching them together, and trying to get to know me. Men let these glimpses float away. If you want the secret to my heterosexuality, Val, here it is.

Of course, men don't like women allowing *them* to float away, but they won't admit it. Men pretend that being snatched after is a burden they indulge in order to placate women. But when women don't pursue, men feel empty and sad. In *themselves,* they view self-sufficiency as strong. In a woman, they call it cold. If they've grown to care about you and want you, they call you a bitch. I've heard it so often; it no longer surprises or wounds me.

I confess to feeling hurt when you claim no one ever fussed over you before Dolores. I fussed over you constantly. I drained your beer bottles. I attended your basketball games. I encouraged you to write and paint. And I showered you with affection. Yet it never occurs to you that I might be hurt by your oversight. Nor that I might not be brave enough to confide that I was hurt. It's my own fault in a way. I like having you see me as a Superwoman, but I don't want you to need me to actually be one. I want you to search for my vulnerability as diligently as I do your strength.

I'm in trouble, Val, big trouble. Not academically. I'm getting A's in my courses. They aren't that hard. Critical thinking, it turns out, is irrelevant to the professional indoctrination that passes for advanced study in psychology. What graduate students must do is regularly genuflect to the Great Beards of Psychology. And they are all *beards.* The one or two female theorists who find their way into textbooks were only overcompensating for their lack of ding-a-lings, or so psychoanalytic theory would have us believe. As a female graduate student, if you take exception to this belittling of women, you're not only overcompensating, you're man-hating, humorless, and probably a lesbian. Oddly, this flagrant misogyny never leaves its purveyors themselves open to much more justified accusations of woman-hating, humorlessness, or sexual "inversion" (as the classic texts would have it).

This strategy to control dissent is pathetically effective. Like your Dolores, the threat of being thought "mannish hoydens" by a pack of intellectually timid yet pompous psychology professors terrifies and silences the other women graduate students. It saddens and befuddles me that they find greater danger in being *thought* humorless and lesbian than in actually *living* without voice, equality, or integrity. I know this sounds harsh. This is harsh. But when I open my eyes, the truth is what I see, whether or not it's harsh. Whether or not it would be easier to see something different.

If others see my self-respect as "mannish," so be it. I know better, and I hold my ground in class. But when it comes to clinical work, my values have clashed with those of the powers that be. You know that I'm not any good at deferring to someone else's judgment. I can't even pretend to do so. Therefore, I'm in hot water at the Youth Hotline. It boiled over a single case.

A thirteen-year-old boy called on my shift. His seventh grade gang have become bad seeds. They're extorting lunch money from less ruthless children by beating and harassing them. All the kids are afraid to "snitch." If one of them risked a beating by reporting the violence, the bullies would deny their transgressions. It would be one child's word against another's. Since the gang's leader is the nephew of the school's principal, the children are sensibly afraid that the little thug would be believed, not them.

Some of the children have begun making regular payoffs of lunch money to the gang. In Mafia parlance, they're buying protection. A practical plan. But then, seventh graders understand power. Bullies have more of it than teachers or parents, and bullies are everywhere. Unless they're stupid enough to get caught in the act, your only recourse is to avoid or placate them.

The problem for my caller was that he didn't yet have a bully's stone cold heart. He was a follower who got in over his head when his gang escalated from vandalism to extortion. He was having stomachaches and bad dreams. He wanted out, but couldn't find a way. He couldn't quit or he'd be assaulted. He couldn't snitch, or he'd be battered.

In his family and his school, the only thing worse than being a fag is being a snitch. I'm quoting, Val. It hurts me to write words that would hurt you. It hurt me to hear this child's life being contorted by ignorance and hatred. Anyway, if the boy told his parents, they would call the other boys' parents, and everyone would know he'd snitched. If he told his teachers, they'd call his parents. If he told the police, they'd call his parents. One way or the other, the whole school would eventually know who had "snitched."

I sympathized with the boy's plight. He had considered every authority he could turn to, and had rejected them for credible reasons. If I had simply urged him to reconsider these choices, he would have hung up the phone and been more alone than ever.

What he needed was a realistic strategy to survive the Hobbesian environment of middle high school. First of all, I told him that there truly was no such thing as a snitch. The concept "snitch" is something bullies invented to make people who care about justice feel bad about themselves. You know how strong my feelings about this are, Val. When I hear adults chide children for being tattletales, I grow livid. It teaches children to tolerate injustice, to silence themselves out of fear of being shunned. It turns so-called "normal" children into passive bystanders and conformists, and courageous children who stand up for themselves into isolated freaks, whose moral courage is rewarded with scorn.

I told the boy to think of himself as a whistle-blower. I said it was brave of him to want to stop his friends from hurting people. Whistle-blowers often stand alone. They have to be strong.

I told him we would figure out a way for his friends to hang themselves. He should think about when and where the gang's usual shakedowns take place. Then he should write a note to a teacher he thinks would care, telling him or her where to hide to witness the shake-down. He shouldn't use his own handwriting, but either use the type-writers at school, or cut words out of the newspaper. Then he should arrange to vomit in public the next morning and either go home or spend the day at the nurse's office. That way, he'd have a cover for not being present at the bust.

If the plan worked, the bullies got busted and were suspended for awhile. That gives my kid the time to find a new crowd. If the teacher didn't take the note seriously, nothing would happen. But at least my kid would know that he tried to intervene. If need be, I reassured him that I'd help him think of something else to try.

The boy was enormously relieved after our conversation. He was supposed to call me back and let me know what happened. That was before I told my supervisor about the call.

My supervisor was furious. He said I was only supposed to listen, not give advice. Second, I was giving the child the message that authorities were not to be trusted. Third, I was planting devious and paranoid ideas in a child's mind, and possibly promoting future antisocial behavior.

In spite of this scathing assessment of my work, I might have kept my position at the hotline if I hadn't argued back. After all, we're students. We're supposed to make mistakes and learn from them. Cody, the other graduate intern at the Hotline, advised me to let my supervisor think I was grateful for his feedback. Cody is fond of telling me to "cool it." He says I turn everything into Custer's last stand, and that I'll burn myself out if I keep up this pace. His philosophy is that you have to accommodate the hierarchy while in graduate school in order to get job recommendations. Then, once you're an established professional, you can do whatever you want. Become a force for good.

This strategy seems to work for Cody. He believes you can act in hypocritical, cowardly ways, but if you have good intentions on the inside, you don't have to feel ashamed or guilty. The inner person is the real you. You can therefore feel okay about yourself no matter what you do. I know I sound judgmental, but the truth is, I often wish I could follow Cody's advice. Life would be simpler.

I can't. It would destroy me. Your actions define who you are, not what you intend or feel about them. If I did as Cody suggests in order to succeed in graduate school, there would be nothing left of me to become a psychologist. Nothing good, anyway.

So I argued with my supervisor. He told me sarcastically that I showed so much interest in undercover operations that perhaps I should become a cop instead of a psychologist. I said I wasn't interested in undercover operations for their own sake but as a means to a just end. And that if therapy didn't concern itself with justice, then it was worse than irrelevant—it was corrupt. That as far as I could tell, the discipline of psychology was totally tangential to the knowledge and skills required to help human beings. And perhaps I should indeed become a cop. Or better yet, a judge.

He then told me that I was not only insubordinate, but dangerous, because I was resisting insight into the countertransference issues that led to my inappropriate advice. I was revealing serious issues with authority in my relationship with him that underscored the authority issues of my interaction with the caller. When I suggested that his sarcasm and loss of temper indicated he himself had transference issues that prevented him from evaluating my work objectively, his face turned blood red and he demanded an apology. When I replied that I didn't believe rational discussion of the observable truth warranted an apology, he crushed the paper cup he was holding into a small waxy ball and threw it at the trash can. He missed—which made him even more irate.

My biggest mistake was remaining logical and calm. I was supposed to panic over his disapproval. My self-confidence insulted him, led him to exaggerate the threat I posed to youngsters, and then to doggedly pursue my termination with the graduate department.

I felt like a prisoner who knows she's innocent. The only way I can get paroled is to say I'm guilty. As long as I maintain I'm innocent, it's proof that I'm guilty and I deserve to be in jail. The assumption, of course, is that the system could never have been wrong to send me to jail in the first place.

So, Val, Superwoman has been fired from her first psychology internship. I suppose I should feel ashamed. I don't. But I do feel discouraged and demoralized. I wonder if psychology is a field where I can do the work I want with children. My consolation is knowing that I gave that boy useful advice. He was listened to by someone who believed him, understood the complexity of his situation, and tried to help.

I'm disturbed that when the boy calls back and asks for Emily, he'll be told I'm no longer available. I failed him. The last thing that child needs is another unreliable adult. If there were anything that might motivate me to adopt Cody's policy of accommodation, it would be to remain accessible to kids like him.

My other consolation is in thinking about what you would say, Val, if I told you this story. You'd look troubled at first. Then you'd say it was true that kids can't always rely on their parents or teachers to protect them. You would back me up 100 percent. And if anyone else didn't like it, that was just too bad. Who needs them? It is this indiscriminate loyalty, this passionate belief in me that endears you to me. Being viewed as Superwoman is .perhaps a small penalty to pay for such extravagant friendship.

I believe in you passionately, too, Val. I know you expected me to be shocked at your news about graduate school. I was surprised at first, but the reasons you articulated are sensible. What's the point in going to art school if you aren't ready? Sometimes, I wonder—well, I was going to say I feel so out of place and alone here that I wonder whether I myself was ready for graduate school. But the truth is that graduate school wasn't ready for me.

From the day I met you, I knew with utter certainty that you will create something great someday. Whatever it is, I doubt any school can teach you how. You're silly to worry about "falling behind." I'm afraid mine is, as your muse Blake said, the "straight and narrow path" that leads to improvement. But yours is the "crooked path without improvement" innate to genius.

It's after midnight. I'd better go to sleep. I have an interview for a new internship tomorrow. Afterward, I'll take my tip money to the flower shop and send you a dozen roses. Sun-colored, fragrant yellow ones to remind you of better times, and that friendship endures, even when romance falters.

Love,

Ashmont

1976

May 1976
My darling Ashmont,

After the longest, most brutal winter ever the temperature is rising and days are getting blissfully longer. Tourists are returning to our quaint Cape Mecca. I have turned twenty-four and cannot believe how close I am to being a quarter of a century old without having discovered the meaning of life. And after a lengthy but not entirely unpleasant hiatus, my love life—if you can dignify it as such—has taken a *bizarre* turn. *Uh-oh,* I can hear you thinking, *what kind of pickle has Val gotten herself into this time?*

Three weeks ago, as I was hurrying back to the inn from my early morning bank deposit—I've been doing Desmond's bookkeeping, and am amazed to discover that I enjoy it—I was holding my head low to protect it from the frigid wind. As I passed the doorway to Schrod and Company, I stumbled and fell forward. As I picked myself up and turned around, prepared to curse whatever detritus had blocked my path, I saw a girl hunched up on the ground, with nothing to keep her warm but a torn flannel shirt and filthy blue jeans.

She lifted her head, squinted up at me and mumbled, "Sorry, greyhound. Better slow down. You might trip."

I was mad. But I couldn't help but laugh. Then I saw she wasn't a girl at all, but a very thin woman, with pale skin stretched taut across high cheekbones, catlike yellow-green eyes, and flyaway honey-blonde hair whipping across her face. Up close, you could see microscopic wrinkles branching around her eyes and mouth. I guessed she must be about thirty-five. Then I noticed a small stream of dried blood trailing from one side of her mouth, and a mean-looking bruise under one eye. She was holding her ribs, and I could tell she was hurting there, too.

"Hey," I said, "you need a doctor."

"Hey yourself, Einstein," she said. "Don't it just prove there's a God. That on the morning after I get thrashed, I am found by such an observant Samaritan." She smiled and winced.

I realized she was teasing me. She was freezing and in pain, yet she was making wisecracks. In a different setting, I'd have called her behavior flirtatious. All the feelings I have for Pamela—or *Lupe* as she and a tattoo on her right arm would have it—began in that moment. I was charmed. I was aghast. I was worried. I was intrigued.

"Let me help you up," I said, offering her my hand.

She grasped it with one thin, papery dry hand, pulled herself up half an inch, grimaced in pain, released my hand and moaned. "Oh shit, forget it. Go away. Shoo. I'll die here."

"Death is not an option," I said, feeling oddly powerful and energized as I did so—as if it truly were up to me. I felt keenly aware not only of my greater physical strength compared to her, but of the greater clarity and forcefulness of my will. It was a new feeling for me, and as concerned as I felt for her, I enjoyed a flush of pride in the competence this frail creature drew from me.

"I never asked you to help me," she said. "Remember that."

"I will," I said. "But I'm going to, anyway. Right now, you don't have a choice, and neither do I. I won't have your ghost haunting my dreams."

I called Desmond, who brought the van. When "Lupe" stood up, she was taller than I by about six inches, but so scrawny, I'm sure she weighed about fifteen pounds less. She kept calling me "Shorty" as Desmond and I lifted her into the backseat. Then I drove her to the hospital in Hyannis. She was quiet, moaning lightly during the drive down. They admitted her from the emergency room, and I waited, afraid the doctor would return and tell me she'd died. Instead, they said she'd be okay, and to come back the next day.

I drove down the next afternoon, and found her sitting alone in a lounge, slumped in a wheelchair, staring out the window, smoking filterless cigarettes. She had some bags and tubes hooked around her waist, attached to a metal apparatus she wheeled around with her.

Without turning around to see who had entered the room, she started talking as though we were in the middle of a conversation. "The thing is, Shorty, I'm straight. I wish I could be a lesbian, because the nicest women are. And I'd probably live longer if I were, but I'm not. In fact, it was my fucking shitface of a boyfriend did this to me. Well, not all of it. My ex-husband pushed me off a roof one particularly grouchy day, that's how I got the kidney condition and the rod in my spine." She wheeled around to squint at me.

"Oh, and I saved the best for last. I'm a junkie, too. Ex-junkie. I quit two months ago." And she stared at me, waiting to see if I'd run. In fact, I did consider fleeing.

But I had saved her, and felt a strangely intimate bond with her because of it. I felt the weariness and mistrust in her voice. I felt a kinship with the beaten-down, used-up hunch of her shoulders. I wanted to save her some more. She may have been pushing me away with her words, but her eyes and tone were pleading for help.

More than anyone I've ever known, Pamela lives in her eyes—the eyes of someone who has been knocked around a lot, and whose only defense has been to watch and study and learn to predict the intentions of others. Her eyes knew everything about me, including the effect she'd had on me yesterday, the effect she was having on me right now. This was how she had survived. She *knew* I wanted to save her some more.

"The thing is," I said, "I know you're straight. Don't flatter yourself by thinking I care. The other thing is, you're *still* a junkie. You didn't quit two months ago, you quit two minutes ago, when you heard me come in the room." I instinctively knew Pamela's code: talk tough, laugh through pain, never show vulnerability.

She stared at me. Then she grinned, "You're all right, Shorty." And for some reason, I flushed with pleasure, which I tried to disguise. I had passed her first test.

Over the course of several hospital visits during the next few days, Pamela told me her life story. Her father had murdered her mother when Pamela was just thirteen. He'd been sent to jail and she'd had to stay with an abusive aunt and uncle who had made her work and pay rent so she could never save for college.

She'd married the famously irritable and violent John Barton when she was seventeen, and it was from him she'd learned about alcohol and drugs. He used to hit her, and one night he'd been so furious to find out she'd gotten pregnant, that he'd chased her up to the roof and come at her with a baseball bat. She'd jumped to save her life, and had lost the baby. She also developed chronic kidney and bladder problems, and had a steel rod surgically implanted in her spine. She'd been on disability and never been able to work after that, although she'd dreamed of becoming an elementary school teacher, like her mother. She became so depressed she took to drink and drugs, figuring if she was lucky, she'd die young.

I was agog at the tragedy she'd been through, and came close to tears several times. But she talked about it all quite coolly. I concluded she was either a pathological liar, or the toughest, most resilient person I'd ever met. The funny thing was, that the latter seemed true even though the former did, too. Whether the events were real in details, the imprint life had left on her fit the story she told. I know you believe there is only one truth, Ashmont—that constituted by the facts—but I believe in another equally important truth constituted by the lies one tells to distort the truly unbearable facts.

Pamela asked me if I'd lend her money for soda and cigarettes. I did. She asked me if I'd bring her some magazines. I did. And chocolate cake. And lipstick. And nail polish. She also asked, as I hoped she would—because I knew it would violate the code for *me* to bring it up—if I knew of a shelter for battered women.

I offered to call some for her. Actually, first I called Desmond to see if she could stay in a vacant room in the inn. When he heard she was a junkie—*ex-junkie* I assured him, having been told by Pamela's nurse that she had indeed been through a detox program at the hospital two months ago—he emphatically and rudely said *no,* that she would rob him blind, and to watch my wallet. About twenty phone calls and three hours later, though, I'd found a shelter in Plymouth where Pamela could take refuge in a few days, as soon as she was well enough to be discharged from the hospital.

It took some fancy logistics to plan Pamela's arrival at the shelter, since the location was secret and her infamous boyfriend, Buck— whom Pamela claimed was twice her age at sixty and a hunchback with a wart on his nose—had tried visiting her twice at the hospital. Several of the nurses and one of the doctors took me aside to say I shouldn't get my hopes up, that Pamela had asked hospital social workers to find shelters for her before, but she never followed through. She always went back to Buck. I told them I knew she might go back to Buck instead of to the shelter, but I had to try. And in part, I do know. But in part, foolhardy or naive as it may be, I hope I can succeed in helping her where others have failed, because Pamela likes me and trusts me, and has opened up to me.

Desmond disapproves of my friendship with Pamela. Although he is a small man, evolution has compensated him with a withering gaze that can slay small mammals at twenty paces. Whenever I ask to borrow the van, he knows I want to drive to Hyannis to visit Pamela at the hospital. He grunts in disgust, casts the evil eye in my direction, and throws me the keys. I believe our family's resplendent alcoholic past has left Desmond with a fear that addiction is contagious, that it can spread—germlike—from carriers to innocent bystanders.

"I don't like the idea," he said one day, "of someone"—meaning me—"who has been spending time with her"—he refuses to say Pamela's name—"sleeping in my inn."

"But you rent rooms to people all the time without knowing anything about them, much less who they've been spending time with," I protested.

"Yes," he agreed, "that's exactly right. I don't know about it. That's what makes it tolerable. Besides, they aren't family, and you are."

Apparently, in Desmond's mind, the addiction germ is only dangerous if you're aware of its presence. It's like saying that if you don't *know* someone has a cold, you can't catch it from them. I know I'm being sarcastic. It troubles me to go against Desmond's wishes. But I feel compelled to play out my fascination with Pamela to the potentially bitter end. Anyway, it can't last much longer since I'll never see her again once she leaves the hospital for the shelter. In the meantime, I'm afraid my response to our family's resplendent alcoholic past appears to be curiosity about the germ rather than disgust and avoidance. Who gets it? Why? How am I like or unlike the carriers?

I thought Raymond shared Desmond's attitude, but the morning I was preparing to drive to the hospital to say good-bye to Pamela— the day she was being discharged to the shelter—Raymond appeared in the kitchen with a small pile of clothing. He held up a pair of gold knit pants and a floral print jersey top.

"Let's see, she's tall, right? Well, these are stretchy. They'll probably fit."

"I thought you agreed with Desmond about Pamela—that she belongs in a leper colony," I said, taking the clothes from him.

"Of course I agree with Dez," he said. "She'll rob you blind with no remorse. But she still needs clothes. Everybody needs clothes. Preferably comfortable ones. The more people in the world who wear comfortable clothes, the calmer our little planet will be."

"Yes, you're right," I said, my voice catching a bit. I felt touched by Raymond's thoughtfulness. Not just for Pamela, but for me—for my concern about her.

To break the mood, so I wouldn't cry, I held the clothes up and grinned teasingly at him.

"Not your usual style, Ray. These look like something a middle-aged matron would wear to a church social."

"Of course," he said dramatically, "they belonged to a middle-aged matron. Although my sister Gracie would never have darkened a church social with her presence. Happy hours were more her style. She shared your family's penchant for the devil's brew. But Gracie claimed it wasn't *she* who thirsted for spirits, but the wicked little demons who gnawed on her spine—it was only when they got drunk that they gave her any respite from a bad back. I can't believe you thought for a second these clothes belonged to me. Really, you wound my pride."

"I didn't know you had a sister," I responded. Much less an alcoholic one. Ashmont, it seems that once you shake the branches of anyone's family tree, the drunks fall like overripe fruit.

"Indeed, I did," Raymond said, looking somber, "In fact, Gracie died here in the inn. She had metastasized cancer throughout her body. She'd burned her bridges with everyone else in the family. She'd been hellish to me fifteen years ago when I told her that I was gay. But Gracie wanted to die by the ocean. She wanted her ashes cast at sea— she said it was the only dignified ending she could imagine. 'Before there were ashes, before there was dust, there was water,' Gracie said. She expected to feel more at home in water than she ever did on solid ground. Frankly, I feel the same way.

"Des didn't want her to come, and the truth was, neither did I. But I was too chicken to say no. As it turned out, she didn't linger long. Which was good, because she was in a lot of pain. God, she was a tough nut. She yelled for morphine constantly, and she swore like a truck driver. She wouldn't let me flinch for an instant. 'Goddamn you, Ray, if I can stand *feeling* the pain, you sure as hell ought to be able to *watch* it.' In the end, I was glad she came. I learned a lot from watching her die."

"What?" I asked.

"That people can endure anything," Raymond said emphatically. "And that people are astonishingly consistent. They check out the same way they lived. Do you know what Gracie's last words were?"

"What?"

"She squeezed my hand and whispered so I had to lean over and put my ear right next to her mouth. 'Raymie,' she said—it's what she called me when I was a kid, but she hadn't done so in thirty years—'Raymie, there'd goddamn well better be booze in heaven.' Then she closed her eyes and five minutes later she was cold. She died hoping that St. Peter would meet her at the pearly gates with a double vodka."

Raymond stared intently at me for a moment, as if waiting for the lesson of his tale to sink in. I was confused.

"I don't get it," I said finally.

"Oh, there's nothing to get. In fact, that's exactly how I felt when Gracie died. That there was nothing in particular to 'get' from her death. Well, enough babbling. Take the clothes and go say farewell to your Pamela."

As I turned to leave, though, Raymond put his hand on my shoulder to stop me. I turned.

"What, Raymond?" I was starting to get annoyed. He was being so cryptic.

"Don't expect too much," he said.

"I expect nothing," I said.

"I know," he said, pressing his lips together. "But that may be too much."

I shrugged his hand off my shoulder and left, feeling suddenly alone, as though I had a mission to perform that no one but me understood, but which I had no choice but to finish. I drove to the hospital, and found out that Pamela was waiting to say good-bye to me before leaving for the shelter.

I found her standing in the lounge, leaning on an aluminum rubber-tipped cane. She wore a clean, black cotton turtleneck and black jeans, donated by the hospital. They suited her much better than Gracie's polyester pants. Her hair was clean, and brushed up and held in place with a black velvet barrette. For a moment, as though glimpsing an alternate reality, I saw how beautiful Pamela must have been, before illness and ill use had left her body gaunt, her face prematurely wrinkled and preternaturally pale. The pathos stuck in my throat with a stifled sob. And it was then that I became aware of the other feeling I had for Pamela, because it swept over me like a rash. I felt completely, profoundly aroused by her.

The bizarre thing is, Ashmont, that I didn't want to touch her. In fact, the idea of touching her repelled me. Nor did I want her to touch me. I don't even always like looking at her, to be honest, because she's sickly and bony, and she has yellow teeth. But I felt an incredible sexual rush in her presence, as though I were in heat, or had drunk some deadly aphrodisiac. In a paranoid moment, I thought Pamela had hypnotized me, slipped a mickey in my Coke, and tossed a psychic lariat around my loins which she could rein in or release at will.

You know how when you're having sex and you're close to orgasm but you haven't come yet but you want and need to so much, it's not pleasure anymore but downright uncomfortable, like needing to sneeze and not being able to? That's what it feels like being around Pamela, all this arousal without any possible climax. No sneeze.

I am confused by these feelings. I know you have always told me sex could be separated from love, but I thought you were just being cynical. That sex could be mixed with repulsion, that my body could generate powerful sexual feelings separate from my will, from my heart's desire or my mind's approval—Ashmont, you are right (as always, when will I learn to stop questioning you?)—sex has its heart of darkness. I had encountered it briefly once before, but had diligently put it out of mind.

I tried to mask my arousal from Pamela, but I feared she sensed it. I was afraid she would say something embarrassing, and I would have to flee in shame. But she didn't. She was uncharacteristically somber. She thanked me graciously for giving her a fresh chance at life. She said others had stopped believing in her, but that my faith gave her the courage to try again. I blushed and my heart swelled up to the next largest size. We walked down to the cab together, and I told her to call me if she needed help. She said she'd call, but she hoped it wouldn't be to ask for help. And as I watched her drive away, she turned back once and looked at me with serious, scared eyes. Meeting her gaze, I started to cry. And I wept deep, heaving sobs all the way back to Provincetown.

I knew I wasn't crying for Pamela alone, but for both of us. I felt as though I had fallen through the rabbit hole into a parallel universe and met my other half. And it wasn't Dolores or anyone else from Jefferson Avenue, it was a frail ex-junkie with a passion for self-destruction and eyes that reflected only the dim light of broken dreams. I could have been Pamela so easily. The distance separating us was no thicker than an abstraction: luck.

You know what I'm talking about, Ashmont. In fact, I wrote another chapter for *The Story of an Epic Friendship* about the time you saved me from becoming a junkie.

Chapter Two

Ashmont Saves Val from Becoming a Junkie

You wanted to study on a Saturday night in October of our senior year. I was sulking because I wanted you to go to the college rathskellar with me. In an effort to make you feel guilty, I declared I would go to the Panther Club all by myself. The Panther was notorious among Barclay students. A smoky, sleazy biker bar on the outskirts of campus, it was known for serving hard liquor to underage patrons, for drug deals—and not just benign, baby drugs like marijuana and speed, but malignant, grown-up drugs like heroin and cocaine—for danger, and for enough black leather jackets to upholster a warehouse of sofas. It was unimaginable for a female student to go there alone.

Your refusal of my invitation to the rathskellar was only the surface reason for my sulking. I was longing to touch you, Ashmont, and I couldn't. Sometimes, it was pleasant to be near you, to allow my impossible yearning to spread like a warm flush all over my body, and to hover as close as possible, inhaling the air you had recently breathed. But at other times, it was sheer torment. A hormonal storm of pent-up urges would spread like a painful itch all over my body until I was sure I would go mad.

Nothing I tried soothed me: not picking a fight with you, not alcohol, not cruising bars for lonely undergraduates, curious about their Sapphic potential, with whom I could share an evening of clumsy, self-conscious sex. But I imagined that within the Panther's smoke-filled, infernal rungs I might find a more potent and distracting brew of vice and drugs. If your back is driving you crazy with an itch beyond your grasp, chances are that if you bang your head hard enough against a wall, the pain of the itch will fade. It was in that spirit that I set out for the Panther.

You said I was free to go, but not to look to you for sympathy if I came back missing an eye, arm, or lung, not to mention innocence and sobriety. I said I had heard that some biker dykes hung out there, and I announced that I was going to find some action. You, of course, were supposed to feel stodgy and guilty, and volunteer to accompany me to the relative safety of the rathskellar. But you refused to play. You ignored me. Enraged, rejected, and dejected, I set out for the Panther determined to prove something—what it was other than my idiocy and immaturity escapes me in hindsight.

Lucky for me, there was a biker convention in Portsmouth that weekend, and the Panther was sparsely populated. I ordered a Wild Turkey and sat at the bar, twirling a toothpick in my drink and feeling morose and lonely, staring deep into the golden liquor as if there were wisdom to be found at the bottom of the thick-bottomed glass. I overheard some whispers to one side, and the next thing I knew the bartender, a burly guy named Rusty, was pushing a shot glass of Wild Turkey under my face. I looked up quizzically, having forgotten where I was.

"Ronnie likes you," he winked. "But be careful, the last girl Ronnie liked was found belly up in the Charles with a bullet in her head"—he put an index finger to his temple—"right *here*."

"Yeah, right," I said sarcastically. I was pretty sure he was teasing me, but I felt a little scared, too. After all, this was the notorious Panther, and I was here all alone.

I turned around, following Rusty's nod, expecting to see a greasy biker boy with a fat belly encased in chains. Instead I saw Veronica, a compact, muscular woman. She dressed like James Dean, in a white T-shirt and black leather jacket. She had a pouty lower lip worthy of young Marlon Brando, but her definite eyebrows and intense, sensual stare reminded me of Ava Gardner. She was the most androgynous person I'd ever seen. And the most attractive.

She stared at me, and I felt myself flush with embarrassment. I stared back, although it was hard to sustain the skeptical leer I was striving for. My feelings were mixed. I was curious, flattered in spite of myself, but I was also afraid. Not only did Ronnie look tough in her leather jacket decked with biker chains, she was surrounded by a group of similarly garbed women dressed like Jets—eyeing me as if I were a Shark. Suddenly, I wished I'd left my leather jacket at home and worn my innocuous blue nylon Barclay Windbreaker instead.

So when Ronnie curled her finger and grinned, inviting me to join them, I looked behind me at first, as if checking to see if she was motioning to someone else. I pointed at my chest as if to say, "Who? *Moi?*" and when she nodded, smiling, revealing a stem-sized gap between her front teeth, I walked to Ronnie's table, drink in hand.

"I'm inn-arrested in you. You a college kid?" Ronnie asked in a thick Boston accent. I was surprised. The accent humanized her. I'd expected her to sound like Ava Gardner, too.

"I'm in college, but I'm no kid," I protested. They laughed.

"Sure you are, baby," Ronnie said gently, as if she were breaking bad news. "Every now and then one of you slumbangers wanders in here to chew up the scenery. None of you got the common sense of a chiclet. Don't matter how many books you've festered your way through, you don't know squat." Ronnie's improbable diction humanized her further. I was both relieved and disappointed. Beneath the black leather and the ominous aura of her girl gang was a human being, and a not particularly well-educated one, I noted, feeling a tad smug.

"Oh, we don't, do we?" I retorted, deciding to play along.

"No, you don't know a sesame biscuit about the true erudition of life."

"Such as?" I tried to sound challenging.

"Such as, none of you kids knows how to swill your liquor with propriety." And she chugged a shot of whiskey.

"The hell we *don't!*" I said. And I chugged my Wild Turkey to applause from Ronnie's gang. I knew I was acting like a moron. I didn't care. Nor did I care what Ronnie's motives were. I was absorbed by her attention, which at the moment was focused intensely and entirely on me. I felt flattered by her boozy biker glamour.

As I drank, my mind became soft and loose, and my sense of time altered. One part of me could wander off—for what felt like hours but passed on the clock as seconds—into contemplation of small details. A single white hair in the middle of one of Ronnie's coal black eyebrows, a curl of sweat-dampened hair that fell across her temple, the oversized gold watch she wore on her left wrist, a few flakes of dry skin across her nose. The rest of me sat still, drinking and sweating, allowing my judgment to fly. And throughout, a part of my mind wondered what *you* would think if you could see me now—and felt wistful and sad.

Each time I chugged one, Ronnie claimed that I'd *overutilized my wad.* I'd claim I hadn't, and a new glass would appear. That was how I progressively lost my sobriety. The drunker I became, the more intense and palpably sexual Ronnie's gaze became. It was more a carnivorous than a lusty or friendly gaze. It wasn't aimed at me, just at my body and whatever it was that college girls symbolized for Ronnie. But I liked that. At that moment, all I wanted to be was an object to be flirted with and seduced. That last thing I wanted to be was human, individual, Val.

The longer I looked at Ronnie, however, the less attractive she became. Her chiseled features became haggard rather than refined. Her full lips became gross rather than sensual. Her coloring began to look yellow rather than bronze. Alcohol seemed to release a deeper, sharper perception in me—a kind of "night vision"—through which I saw a coarseness at Ronnie's core, something raw and vulgar which both repelled and, quite frankly, excited me. A coarseness which magnetically attracted something similarly coarse in me that I always tried to keep at bay.

Sex, I always argued—to your cynical disagreement—should be refined and sublime. And sex between two women should be downright transcendental. Yet here was Ronnie personifying everything the church, the nuns, my parents, teachers, and society ever told me or implied about sex—that it was defiling, low, and dirty. And that sex between two women was the most depraved of all. But what they had left out—what I was discovering—was that it was also exciting and intense and overpowering. The current of sexual feeling running between Ronnie and me wasn't pretty or ethereal or romantic. It was visceral and crude and primal.

After a while, Ronnie sent her friends away. She would stroke her hands over mine, which were laid flat on the damp, sticky table. Every now and then she would isolate one of my fingers and squeeze it—hard. A quick squeeze and a quicker retreat. Harder than was polite. Harder than simple flirtation. She was watching my face to see if I'd flinch. I didn't. There was something new and electric in Ronnie's harsh, unpredictable touch. I had finally found a game that completely distracted me.

Ronnie wanted to talk about drugs. In a probing, relentless way, she insisted on finding out what I'd tried, what I liked, where I got them. I lied. I told her I'd tried everything. Ronnie scoffed. She knew I was lying, but instead of being offended by my lies, she seemed pleased that I was trying to impress her. She said I couldn't claim I'd even done drugs if I hadn't tried heroin—Ronnie called it *smack*. Ronnie's tone telegraphed genuine awe when she referred to the "Queen of Sheba of drugs." I was intrigued, and I asked her what getting high on smack was like.

"Orbit, baby," Ronnie said, "it's like being in orbit. Far, far away from whatever or whoever you want to get away from. I'll take you there if you want. That is, if a yellow-belly college girl like you has the guts to feel that good," she dared. Her eyes rose upward, as if star-gazing, and mine followed her, imagining being lifted above and beyond the smoke-smudged Styrofoam panels of the Panther's low-slung ceilings and into the brilliant, remote ether beyond.

Ronnie had read me perfectly. She understood the release I was craving. She squeezed my whole hand, hard, clearly excited at the prospect of deflowering a heroin virgin. If coarseness was what attracted me to Ronnie, innocence attracted her to me. Some potent mixture of youth, inexperience, education, and a middle-class future. She was drawn to these differences, and she wanted to destroy them. Drunk as I was, I understood this. But I didn't care. Because she desired me. She wanted something that I had. And being desired was what I craved. Whether I liked it or not. Whether I approved or not. Whether or not *you* would approve or not.

Innocence was useless to me. I coveted experience. I wanted to go into orbit. Damn the consequences. If Ronnie could guide me there, I'd let her. I made a date to try heroin with Ronnie the following Saturday night. At the Panther, of course.

All of this, you know. But what I never told you—because I was too ashamed, was what happened as I was leaving the bar. Ronnie walked me to the door and kissed me. At first, her lips were soft and inviting. So I softened my own lips and let her continue. Then she *bit* me—hard enough to draw blood. She caught me off guard. She hurt me, and I felt enraged. But I was also intensely and deeply turned on. Instinctively, from some predator synapse inside the murky depth of my brain, I wanted to bite back. But I didn't.

I pulled away and jerked my hand up to my mouth, and stared at the blood on my fingers. Ronnie, her eyes a mixture of contempt and lust, smiled at me in a crooked, suggestive way as if to say, "There's more where that came from," and swaggered back to her friends, saying, "See ya Saturday, collegicum."

As amusing as Ronnie could be with her biker Mrs. Malaprop schtick, she was also danger and degradation waiting to happen. However hard I might bite Ronnie, she would bite back harder and faster. She would draw more blood, and she would enjoy it. I knew this. But the truth was, I wanted her anyway. I wanted to sink very far down, as far as I could. I suspected that the only way I could get down as far as my ambition required was under the influence of drugs.

If, I rationalized, I could never have sex with you, the woman I loved more than anything, then why not abase myself by shooting heroin and having mean-spirited sex with Ronnie? Cold, hostile, physically cathartic, absolutely loveless sex. Seeing what your rejection had driven me to would teach you a lesson. Would render me an object of pity and remorse. Right, Ashmont? Love may rule . . . but no one has ever claimed it makes anyone smart. Certainly not me.

I wanted to go to hell. Even if I found despair and pain that I'd previously only imagined, perhaps in hell I would also discover who I am. If I were fated to become an addict, as I half believed all my life, then maybe I postponed a necessary baptism. Is the *real* me the person who is attracted to—who wants to *be*—Ronnie? Or am I really the person who holds back and runs away?

After staggering back to my dorm room with the help of a kind security guard who found me throwing up convulsively by Lawlor Pond, I spent all day Sunday hungover. And I spent all week trying to decide what to do. My mind was a wild, overheated jungle. I couldn't stop thinking about Ronnie's kiss, and the raw, powerful attraction I had felt to her and to dangerous drugs. I tried to scare myself out of my temptation by generating horrible fantasies in which Ronnie stabbed me with a knife and left me to bleed to death in the alley behind the Panther. Or I become so hooked on heroin after a single encounter that I dropped out of college, sold my belongings, and wound up working the streets to support my habit. I'd catch hepatitis and syphilis, then die.

If Ronnie had access to heroin, she must know drug dealers. What if I didn't show up and she thought I was a nark? What if she came after me to shut me up? It wouldn't be hard to find out where I lived. In my haze of memory from Saturday, I thought Ronnie had told me she'd been in jail, but I couldn't remember whether it had been for possession of drugs or for assault and battery. I didn't know if my fears were realistic or the products of a feverish, divided mind. I was terrified to go, and equally terrified not to.

By the time I finally confided in you why I'd spent the week looking pale and distracted, there was only an hour left before my midnight appointment with Ronnie. I didn't tell you about the kiss, and I didn't tell you how tempted I'd been by heroin. I told you only that I didn't want to go, but I was afraid not to show up.

I thought you would be judgmental, but you weren't. You were just very firm.

"You'll have to go and say you changed your mind."

"But she'll *kill* me," I protested. "Ashmont, Ronnie carries a switchblade in her pocket. I saw it."

"Then you'll want to be polite. Be sure to apologize for breaking a date at the last minute."

"I don't believe you," I cried. "I'm going to be killed or become a junkie tonight and you don't care."

"Oh, I care. That's why I'm telling you what you have to do. You have to face up to this, Val. Frankly, with so few facts emerging from your overactive imagination, it's hard to assess the real danger you're in from Ronnie. But you know that taking heroin is risky. You either go tell her the date is off—or you simply don't show and risk having her arrive looking for you here at the dorm. Then you could call security on her."

"I can't do that," I yelled. "Then she'd really be out to get me. What if she had the drugs on her and they found them? She might go to jail and put out a contract on me from there."

"Then you'll have to go tell her at the bar."

You can be extremely single-minded, Ashmont.

I left your room feeling sorry for myself and terrified of my task. The truth was, I was less afraid of saying no to Ronnie than I was that at the last minute, I would say yes. I got ready as slowly as possible, showering and washing my hair, pampering my poor body on what might be its last night on earth. Finally, at quarter to midnight, I left for the Panther.

I stood outside the Panther's windowless gray steel door for a few minutes, staring up at the red light bulb overhead. There were several glossy black, overfed motorcycles in the parking lot—no wonder they call them hogs, I thought—and I wondered vaguely which of them was Ronnie's. In a burst of nostalgia for the magical protections of childhood, I muttered the prayer I used to say every night before I would shut off my bedside lamp and allow darkness to descend:

> Angel of God, my guardian dear,
> To whom God's love commits me here,
> Ever this day be at my side,
> To light, to guard, to rule, and guide.

Oh minion of God, I thought wistfully, where the hell were you last Saturday night?

I pushed open the door, expecting to see Ronnie and the gang at her regular table. Instead, I saw you. I blinked. But it was really you, sitting alone at Ronnie's table, wearing a Barclay Windbreaker, sipping cranberry juice through a straw. You looked completely out of place in this fetid environment filled with smoke and booze and crude, obnoxious people. You sat still and erect and refined, a center of tranquillity in the eye of a raging storm. For a moment, I thought you were my guardian angel.

Dumbfounded, I approached you.

"I really don't know how to swill a drink properly, do I?" you smiled.

"Ashmont, is it really you? Or an elf or angel come to bewitch me? What are you doing here? Where's Ronnie?" I looked apprehensively around. Suddenly, it occurred to me you might have killed her.

"Don't worry. I disembarked her from this booze moat."

"Well, you obviously met Ronnie," I said, exhaling fully for the first time in a week. I sat weakly beside you.

"How . . ." I trailed off. "Why . . ."

"I decided I couldn't afford to have you in drug detox. I need you around too much. And frankly, Val, I've never seen you so afraid—or so irrational—in all the time I've known you. I decided to step in. I hope you don't mind?"

"Mind?" I said in a small voice, "Are you crazy? I owe you my life. You can have my firstborn. If I get around to children. But how did you make her disappear? Did you tell her I'm contagious? That I have hereditary madness? What? *What?"*

"Nothing so exotic. I used the cleverest strategy of all. But one you never would have imagined."

"What?"

"I told her the truth."

"And what's that?" I asked, without at this point having the foggiest notion myself what the truth really was.

"I told her you had been furious with me last Saturday, and you were trying to prove a point by foolishly endangering yourself. That you had never used drugs before. And that I came as a friend who was deeply worried about you."

"And why did you say you I was angry at you? Because you wouldn't barhop with me? Jeez, I sound shallow."

"No, Val. I told her the truth. I told her that you were—" You paused, looked down as if deciding something, then looked me straight in the eyes and finished—"that you are in love with me. But that I love you as a friend. And that causes you a lot of pain."

I deflated, feeling all the air suck out of me. Why, I wondered, does it hurt so much more to hear the truth spoken aloud than to simply think it in your own mind?

I waited a minute until the stabbing pain in my heart subsided. I couldn't bear to talk about it. If I'd wanted to talk about it, I wouldn't have gone to the Panther in the first place. I hoped you weren't going to make me.

"And what did Ronnie do?"

"She said, 'How in tarnation do you like that? Well, Em, how do you think I got started on the path to perdition myself? If my friend had been as nice as you, maybe I wouldn't be here now. Tell Van—do you know, she thinks your name is *Van?*—she's lucky to have a friend like you. Take her home and dry her out, give her a hot bath, and tell her to get rid of that awful henna dye job.'"

I laughed. We weren't going to have to talk about it. We were going to laugh about it. You were kind and gentle. I felt immensely relieved.

"She did not," I protested. "Ronnie would never use the word perdition in such an unimaginative way. Tell me what she really said."

"Okay," you said, laughing. "She said, 'Fuck it. Keep her.' She summoned her gang, and they left."

"That sounds more like it."

As my nerves settled, I began to feel heavy and tired. "Ashmont," I groaned, "how can I ever repay you?"

"Promise me that in the future, you'll think for a least a microsecond before you act."

"I promise," I said. As we waited for a cab to drive us back to the dorm—*your* idea—I fully intended to think very, very hard about what had drawn me to the bar, to getting drunk, to saying yes to a date with Ronnie and with heroin. To low places and to danger.

But I never did. I wanted to forget all about it. And I pretty much did. Until now.

⌒∽

So, the thinking I didn't do then, I am doing now. I brood about Pamela. Hers is the life I was meant to have and truly deserve to have. I wonder what it would be like to go ahead and do every reckless, dangerous thing that enters my mind. Instead of spending my life feeling that I deserve to be punished, I could just go ahead and punish myself and get it over with. I know how stupid this is, Ashmont, but just because it's stupid doesn't mean it isn't true.

Whether I want her to or not, Pamela haunts my waking and sleeping dreams. I see a swirling gray tornado circling a single point deep inside her, and inside the vortex is a desperate child, acting crazy and laughing insanely. She shouts so there will be no silence. She stomps her feet and pulls her hair until it hurts so there will be something to feel. No one hears her. No one holds her. No one stops her from hurting herself.

I try to fathom what, if anything, makes Pamela different from me. What made her become an addict? How did I escape? Is she my future? Maybe I have too much time to think. It's one of the curses of living on the Cape off-season. Ironically, after spending all this time thinking about her, I will never see Pamela again. Sometimes that makes me sad, but I know it's probably a blessing.

Did I tell you I'm going to teach an art class at the high school? It's a noncredit summer course, but if it goes well, I might teach a regular high school course in the fall. If I like it well enough, maybe I'll get a degree in art education. Although I'm very happy at the inn, I feel I should be doing more to develop my mind. What if I never go to graduate school in anything? What if I wind up, as the notorious Clive of three summer's ago prophesied, painting furniture instead of art?

I fear I'm drifting, Ashmont. I don't know what else to do.

I'm thrilled your course work is over. I know how much you've hated it. I can't wait to hear your ideas for a dissertation. I know it will be stunningly brilliant. Call me. Telegraph. Send a smoke signal. I know better than to ask you to write.

Thank you again, Ashmont, from the bottom of my heart, for saving me from Ronnie. From myself. If you hadn't, I would *be* Pamela today.

In perpetual love and gratitude,

Your ever-loving Val

May 1976
Dear Val,

I am uneasy about this bond you feel with Pamela/aka Lupe. Unless she's been killed by liver damage or Buck by now, I doubt you've seen the last of her. She'll be back, asking for loans, pity, and your belief that she's an innocent victim of forces she can't control. Such people make weakness a virtue, dependence a way of life.

Pamela has no mystique for me. The difference between the two of you couldn't be plainer. She's chosen her path because she wants to die, slowly and painfully. She wants it to appear that it is some outer force that is killing her—her father, Buck, drugs, the cruelty of life itself. But it's not true. She has simply chosen death, not life. I find such people less interesting than those who choose life, as you did, Val. It doesn't matter that you felt the temptation of death—that only means you are human. The fact is, you chose life.

You chose it that night you turned Ronnie down. I knew you were petrified to go to the Panther, not because you thought Ronnie would kill you, but because part of you really wanted to try heroin. You weren't sure you'd have to strength to say no. But you did.

You are far too generous to people like Pamela and Ronnie. For every bad person, for every unkind act, you struggle to find an explanation. I think it is because you exaggerate your own defects. You identify with thugs and lowlifes, and if you can find a "reason" for their behavior, then you can forgive yourself as well. This habit of yours drives me insane. Taken to extremes, no one would be accountable for any behavior, no matter how heinous. If I shoot you, you must have stepped on my toe. My mother stepped on my toes when I was little. Therefore, it's okay for me to shoot you.

I remember arguing with you about Hitler. You insisted there must have been an extraordinary reason for his obsessive hatred of Jews. His abusive father. Pathological ethnic and sexual insecurities Larger forces of German history and economics. It isn't that you wanted to forgive evil behavior. But you needed to believe in a world in which, were it not for that extraordinary circumstance, six million people would not have been slaughtered. A lovely fantasy—as lovely as imagining what Pamela would have looked like without years of self-abasement to taint her beauty—but only a fantasy. The fact is, the Holocaust happened. And that's the most compelling argument for my own position.

I said that Hitler murdered the Jews because he wanted to. And no one cared enough about the deaths of millions of Jews to stop him. People are attracted to power. People are fascinated by death and destruction. They always have been. They always will be. There's nothing novel about it. It couldn't be more ordinary. It's those who oppose the misuse of power, at great risk to themselves, who interest me. It's the snitches and whistle-blowers in history whom I admire.

I don't know whether to mourn or celebrate your discovery that sex and love are not always entwined. I would grieve if you lost your innocence, but if you lost your idealism, I'd sleep better. People like Pamela exude a sexual charisma. It's probably regulated by the most ancient, reptilian parts of the brain, a holdover from the days when our ancestors chose partners based on pheromones rather than visual or emotional cues. Your Pamela sounds like such a creature. Your registering her magnetism simply reflects an acute sense of smell. There's nothing to worry about unless you allow your olfactory sense to overrule your cerebral cortex. Don't do it, Val.

I finally decided on a dissertation topic, although I have to apply for special approval since it's not the usual analysis of rats pushing levers in a maze. I call it The Failure of Empathy: A Comparative Study of Projection and Brutality in Childrearing Over the Ages. I'm going to compare the attitudes and behaviors of parents who exploit and abuse their children from the past through the present. I wanted to call it Sociopathic Nurture: A Study of Parents' Crimes Against Children. My advisor, however, insisted that since many of the childrearing practices I'm describing were normative for the times, the word sociopath was inaccurate.

I disagree. Many forms of brutality toward children are considered normative in numerous cultures and regions of the world today, but that doesn't make them any less sociopathic.

Consider the use of children as slaves in the textile industry in India; the genital mutilation of female children in Africa; the exploitation of child prostitutes in Thailand by wealthy Western businessmen; and the current failure to educate children and teenagers about sexuality and birth control in the United States. If these are not sociopathic, tell me, what is?

My advisor says that by my definition, half the people in the world are sociopaths. I said more than half are, if you take the safety and well-being of children and women of all classes and races seriously. We agreed to disagree. And we compromised on a different title. Although I loathe compromise, Cody has convinced me that getting a PhD is, like politics, the art of the possible.

Cody advised me to pick a lighter, easier topic. But these stories must be told. It's the truths that make others cringe that I feel it my duty to tell. I admit that sometimes my scholarly detachment fails. Several times, I've become so nauseated at the cruelty I'm reading about that I've vomited.

A mother in Ohio just last year dipped her eight-year-old son's hands in scalding water as punishment for touching his penis. Then she let his burns fester and become infected, because she was afraid she would get into trouble if she took him to the hospital. She told the hospital social worker, "The child had to be taught. If he hadn't been bad, I wouldn't have had to punish him. I didn't have any other choice."

Ten years ago, a father in New Jersey hit his son so hard with a board that he killed him. He told police he was "just showing the boy who's boss. That kid was always walking around here cocky and almighty as though he were king of the roost. I was just showing him he was too big for his britches. I never meant to hurt him."

In India, there's a proverb, "For a girl to be a virgin at ten years old, she must have neither brother, nor cousin, nor father." When laws were passed in 1929 to outlaw child marriage, they were protested by men claiming that early marriage was the only way to restrain girls from seducing adults. They said, "Cupid overtakes the hearts of girls . . . at an early age. A girl's desire for sexual intercourse is eight times greater than that of males."

As recently as the end of the nineteenth century in England, men who were jailed for raping a virgin were released because the practice was prescribed by medical texts as a cure for venereal disease. British doctors treating males with venereal disease regularly discovered the same disease in their patients' children.

During the Inquisition, the *Malleus Maleficarum* gave instructions on how to recognize changelings. Possessed infants tended to "howl most piteously." Martin Luther said they "are more obnoxious than ten children with their crapping, eating, and screaming." And of course, the demons had to be beaten out of the child, with whips, shovels, bundles of sticks, chains, and other instruments of torture.

And child sacrifice was common throughout the world. In Carthage, a cemetery was found filled with 20,000 urns from between 400-200 BC, containing the bones of children murdered by their parents so the gods would grant them favors.

The horror is endless. The violence breathtaking and unstoppable. And most horrible of all are the attitudes that link all these parents together, across time and space and culture—they all say they love their children, Val. They exploit them, beat them, punish them to the point of death. They endanger and hurt them in order to enrich, heal, and soothe themselves. *But they always say they love their children.* And this is the cruelest—is that why I begin to cry as I write this?—the cruelest hoax of all. To declare to children you love them, while you perpetrate horrors against them.

Maybe I am wrong and you are right, Val. Perhaps Love does Rule. But if so, it is an abomination and a crime. An excuse to torture and torment and do so in the name of love.

There are nights when I sit down to study, and I dread reading yet another account of the everyday savagery that passes for childrearing. But I feel that if I turn away, I become just another passive bystander to centuries of wounded children. As guilty, in my own way, as—if one existed—God. Sometimes, with my eyes closed just before sleep, I sense them hovering near my bed—wingless cherubs, broken, bruised, and bloodied, studying me with pleading and wary eyes to see if I, too, will ignore and bless their pain. If I stop watching and caring, these children will know it—and as alone as they already feel, they'll feel even more abandoned. Believe me, I envy your life on the Cape, Val. You at least are free to live your own life. My fate is merged with these tortured children. I can't be free until they are.

So that is what I've been trying to do at Protective Services, my placement for this semester. I try to free the suffering children from the battering parents. My supervisor thinks I'm "overzealous." She noted that my assessments always recommend foster care and adoption. She listened to a tape of an interview I conducted with a mother whose infant had been admitted to the hospital because it had been violently shaken. The mother kept insisting that she loved her baby and never intended to hurt it. She thought that her intentions rendered her innocent, and she should get her baby back. I told her that whether she intended to or not, she had endangered her child. I asked her: "Why don't you admit that you sometimes feel hatred and rage for your child? That you are unable to control these feelings? That makes you an unsafe parent for your baby. If you really care about your baby's safety and well-being, why don't you give it to someone who can keep it safe?" The mother nearly hit me.

Ever so tactfully, my supervisor pointed out that my question had been provocative. I knew it was provocative. But I owed it to that infant to confront the mother on her behavior. Who else was going to? It isn't my job to help that mother feel good about herself, but to make her see the pain she caused. To make her feel that baby's pain as if it were her own. To prod her to take responsibility for her behavior instead of making excuses for it.

I must have spoken with passion, because my supervisor started asking me how responsible my own parents had been. I've discovered that in the field of psychology, to express passionate, principled convictions about a case quickly leads to patronizing efforts by supervisors and colleagues to analyze the familial psychopathology from which they stem. Cody says that passionate outpourings from a colleague threaten the control psychologists keep over their own emotions—a control that enables them to surround themselves with clients whose emotions are out of control. Like a virus, they're afraid the passion will spread.

I disagree. I believe it's because most psychologists are simply interested in soothing their clients—who will then adore and admire them. They aren't brave enough to confront adults with their irresponsible and inhuman behavior, which will make their clients furious with them but will also ensure justice and protection for defenseless children. Cody says that the passions that drive me to psychology are those that drive others toward religion. He fears that I will never be satisfied with the limited tools available to psychologists to improve the human species, and that I'd be happier as an avenging angel. He's probably right. But since celestial ranks are closed to mortals, I'll have to settle for the earthly advocacy of psychology.

My supervisor recommended that the mother who had shaken her child attend classes on effective parenting, and that she work with a therapist to improve her self-esteem. Can you imagine, Val? The woman shakes her child to within an inch of its tiny, defenseless life, and Protective Services wants to improve her self-esteem. No doubt it bears work, but perhaps jail rather than a clinic would be the appropriate place to pursue it. The child was returned to her mother's care, under the supervision of a caseworker who will make weekly visits to monitor the child's safety.

Saving families is the proper goal of Protective Services, my supervisor insisted. I, in turn, pointed out that families pose more harm to children than any multitude of strangers. To her credit, my supervisor—a more honest and sensible person than most psychologists I've met—admitted that truth. But she described the evidence that foster care is fraught with hazards, too. Children taken from abusive homes are abused by foster families with appalling frequency. And competing social, political, and legal interests make adoption difficult and delayed. In addition, there just aren't enough money and resources to create substitutes for families. In short, she said, "We're stuck with them."

I saw her point.

But I still maintained that the inadequacies of society seemed a poor basis for determining mental health policies and treatment. Besides, I couldn't bear to think of that infant being violently shaken again. Then my supervisor muttered under her breath that if I were to survive as a psychologist I might have to learn to bear it, but when I asked her to repeat herself, she refused. Although it's rare to transfer midsemester, we agreed that perhaps I would find the pragmatism she recommended easier to practice with older children, and I was assigned to a different treatment team, which works with children over the age of twelve.

That makes the third placement in my graduate career that I've been fired from or invited to transfer out of. Although my transcript is full of As', with my checkered placement record, it will take, as Cody says, a very special clinic to hire me, indeed.

There is so much suffering in the world, Val. And so much indifference. It's a wonder any of us survive childhood. I know that you would say that what's remarkable is not the horror humanity perpetrates endlessly upon itself, but our ability to survive it. You say our diabolic natures are tinctured with angelic possibilities—that over a long enough span of time, even if it takes billions of years—humanity improves. I say that all that has improved is our ability to ignore and distract ourselves from the brutality we live among everyday. The facts support me. What's tolerable to believe supports you.

Because I am swayed more by facts than desire, I have decided that I shall never have a child, Val. Not only could I not in good conscience bring a child into this world, I have no reason to believe I would be any better a parent than the shakers, beaters, and exploiters I'm writing about. I can feel in my heart how deeply I would love a child, but I've seen too much to assume that loving a child guarantees that I would treat it well. I know that the need to take care of a small, helpless being can quickly descend—despite "good intentions"—into the need for the child to care for you.

Sadly, though perhaps it is for the best, this decision has cost me my relationship with Cody. Poor, sweet Cody is determined to be a father some day, and he was sensible enough not to become more deeply involved than he already was with a woman who doesn't want children. I miss him. Without him, life feels grim. Cody always reminded me of you, both in his open affection and his loyalty and devotion toward me. Neither of you has ever understood how exceptional that makes you, because neither of you can fathom why I evoke hostility and avoidance in everyone else.

The fact is that Cody and I were already experiencing strain in our relationship. My decision not to have a child simply stretched it to the breaking point. And despite your assessment of Cody as "suspiciously nice—too nice to be completely straight," our problems didn't stem from sex. Cody is nearly as romantic as you, Val. He envisions love as the union of souls. He came closer to me than anyone but you, but he sensed a private center that no one has access to. And he wanted to know that center. He could not feel as though he were loving me adequately if he did not know and love all of me. It's Cody's nature to love completely—it would destroy him to be asked for less. But asking for less is what I did. I only wanted 90 percent of his love, not the 150 percent that he needs to give.

I miss you, Val. For god's sake and mine, please take care of yourself. Some days, I feel you are all I have.

Love,

Ashmont

July 1976
Dearest Ashmont,

How sorry I was to hear from you on the phone about your breakup with Cody. As insanely jealous of him as I was, I liked him because he made you happy. I accepted the idea that you would marry him. So I'm deeply sorry, Ashmont, that it didn't work out.

Cody should have had more faith. I've always believed that private part of you will emerge when you are ready. If it takes you a decade—or two decades or three or four—to trust me enough, I'll wait. Because you're worth waiting centuries for.

I don't know what to say to you about your decision not to have children. I feel like such a child myself, it's hard for me to imagine wanting one of my own. The *older* I get, the *longer* it seems to take to finish growing up. Also, there's that *pesky* complication of my not having sex with sperm-bearers. But I know you feel sad about not being a mother, so I'm sad for you. And I'm sad in general, because it's people like you who should reproduce. I think you'd be inspirational as a mother. Not perfect, Ashmont—this is the part you can't accept—but wonderful nonetheless.

Meanwhile, back in my sordid life, your worries about Pamela exploiting me are unwarranted. I told you on the phone she was in the hospital again, but I didn't know then how ill she was.

Pamela—aka Lupe—is dead. I write it and say it aloud to make it seem real. To churn up some feeling about it instead of this numb stupor I've settled into. Now that she's dead, morte, muerte, pushing up daisies, and there's nothing for you to worry about, I can tell you the rest of the story.

I thought I would never see Pamela again after we'd said good-bye at the hospital, but I was wrong. Over the past few weeks, Pamela ridiculed, embarrassed, humiliated, and ultimately stole from me. And yet. *And yet.* And YET, Ashmont, as angry and insulted as I felt, something about her touched me deeply. And touches me still from beyond the grave.

Pamela never checked into the women's shelter in Plymouth. When she left the hospital, she told the cabdriver to take her to the nearest bar. I was sure that she'd gone back to Buck and they'd sunk into some den of iniquity together. Then one afternoon in June, I noticed a small crowd gathered in front of Town Hall, where jugglers, magicians, and musicians often perform.

Curious, I nudged my way to the front of the crowd, where I saw Pamela, dressed in the same black pants and turtleneck I'd last seen her in—only now torn and dirty—twirling and tossing a baton up in the air and catching it with surprising expertise. She also had a first-degree purple and yellow shiner under her right eye. Behind her, beating a tambourine, stood a small, wiry man with skin so tanned it looked like hide and eyes so cold and black they looked reptilian. He was probably forty or so, with greased back, dark brown hair. If it weren't for the contemptuous smirk that permanently creased his face or the small potbelly that pressed against the waistband of his jeans, he might have been considered handsome. Who could it be but the infamous *Buck?* Near the man's foot, a baseball cap was littered with a few coins.

Pamela dropped the baton and bent over to pick it up. Buck slapped her on the butt, sneering, "Pick it up, bitch. You can't even twirl a stupid baton."

"Stop it!" "What a jerk!" "What a pathetic creature," people muttered. And a few took bills from pockets and purses and dropped them not in Buck's hat but at Pamela's feet.

"Don't share it with him, sweetie, run away," said one woman who passed Pamela $20.

Pamela looked grateful. "I will," she said. "I've been trying. This will help." But as the woman walked away, she tucked the money in her pocket and gave a sidelong glance at Buck. If you didn't know Pamela, you'd have thought she was grimacing. She wasn't. She was suppressing a thin-lipped grin.

This was their *act,* I realized, or should I say, their shill. I was appalled.

"You don't have to do this!" I said to Pamela. "How *dare* you!" I yelled at Buck.

Pamela met my gaze, narrowed her eyes, walked over and spat on my face. At least she tried to. The spit landed mostly on my chin.

"Who the fuck do you think you are?" she asked in a tone of pure contempt.

"Hey!" was all I could think of to yell, while I wiped her spit off
with my hand.

"She's crazy," I heard someone mutter. "They're psycho . . ."

Pamela turned her back to me, tucked her baton under her arm,
and walked away from me, the crowd, and Town Hall. I looked at
Buck, who met my gaze briefly with smug, drug-dilated eyes, before
he picked up his hat, pocketed the coins, and followed her.

The strangest thing was, that I didn't feel angry at Pamela. I knew
instinctively that she had spat on me not because I had witnessed her
humiliation by Buck. She felt humiliated by *me*.

On her own with Buck, Pamela was beyond humiliation. What
happened between them was her lot in life. Cruel, perhaps, but inescapable. Who was I to suggest she could choose a different life?

The greatest kindness I could offer Pamela wasn't to help her but to
stop looking at her. But as I walked away from the dispersing
crowd—I hope I can explain this to you, Ashmont, because it mysti-
fies me still—I felt my heart break. It tore in two, a healthy, surviving
chamber pounding in my chest, and a dying, strangled, wounded
chamber, bound to Pamela. I felt hopeless and helpless and small all
the way back to the inn.

I remembered how I felt as a child when my parents would come
home from work, open up the liquor cabinet, and pour themselves a
drink. I felt as though I were standing on a dock watching my mother
and father climb aboard an ocean liner to embark on a lengthy voyage. There was nothing I could do to stop them. All I could do was
wave from shore, hoping they would remember to come home.

I thought of alcohol not as a liquid, but as a destination. Whiskey
sang to my parents like a siren. But I lacked the wiles to stop their ears
with wax, or the strength to lash them to the mast. Once they arrived
in *Alcohol,* only their bodies remained in this world. Their souls and
minds, their wills and hearts, were trapped in the fluid amber sphere
that overlapped our house. They would be zombies until morning,
and I could rely on them for nothing. Could receive nothing. Could
offer nothing. Could neither find them nor be found. Jamie and Ralph

and I would be mother, father, friend, family—in our child's way, we would be all in all to each other until morning.

Ashmont, I was so lonely as a child I ache at the memory. That loneliness is why I have never had many friends, with you as my notable exception. I don't know how to make them, and I'm terrified they'll leave me. But the loneliness wasn't the worst part. The worst part was watching my parents take the first sip, knowing they knew where they were headed, and that they wanted to go. They couldn't wait to get there. Even though it meant leaving Jamie and Ralph and me behind. The lure of the amber sphere was not only greater than me, but than the world itself, greater than life. Even as a child, I knew it was not some better life they were entering, but a limbo poised between life and death.

As I watched them take their first drink of the night, I yearned for some gear to shift, some spotlight to shine, so they might look at the world and see something, anything—a dash of color, a smile from me, a clean kitchen sink—that would make them think, "Maybe it's not so bad. Perhaps I'll stay." And they would put the drink down. It never happened. But the hope that they *would,* and the knowledge that they never *did,* hurt more than anything.

That gut-wrenching remorse over my parents' choice—or should I say, their inability to perceive they even had one—that is the same feeling I had walking away from Pamela. I couldn't hate her. I couldn't even feel angry at her. I felt profoundly pained.

You know, Ashmont, that I remain deeply curious about the amber sphere. I have been tempted to stroll those hazy pathways, to understand its lure, and thereby my parents' choice. But something stops me at the gateway. Perhaps I'm too fainthearted. I hate hangovers. I don't like feeling drunk. I don't deserve any credit for this anomaly—it's probably a slip of DNA, a tiny chemical guardian angel that looks out for Jamie and me but neglects Mom and Dad and Ralph. Did I tell you that Jamie is in the Army now in Japan? Ralph, of course, is living with Mom and Dad in Florida. The last I heard—a Christmas card two years ago—he was in and out of alcohol rehab every few months.

I didn't see Pamela for a couple of weeks. Then, as seems to be our pattern, just when I started to forget about her, she reappeared. I was walking down the steps from the inn to the street on my way to meet Desmond for dinner at the Trawler. I heard a rustling in the bushes behind me, and as I turned, I saw Pamela stand up and brush herself off. She'd been waiting for me.

She was disheveled and dirty, with smudges on her arms and face. There was a rosy flush on her cheeks that I attributed to alcohol. I felt wary, but curious. She wobbled as she bent over to pick up her cane.

"Are you okay?" I asked before I remembered what had happened to me the last time I tried to help her.

"I'm as good as a crippled drunk can be," she smiled as she drew herself erect. Her tone held the defiant irony of our first encounter, and I couldn't help but smile.

Pamela then tossed her cane high in the air so that it twirled several times before she expertly snatched it one-handed on its way down.

"I was Captain of the Morningstar Majorettes in high school. You didn't think I had any talent, did you?" She half smiled, playing to charm me. I couldn't fathom why.

"Being a majorette isn't half as amazing as the fact that you were ever in high school."

"Yeah," she laughed easily. "Either one is amazing, isn't it? You know the most amazing thing about me, Valerie?"

"What? Please don't call me Valerie. It's Val."

But she was wasn't listening. She was lost inside herself.

"I led a pretty normal life. An ordinary life." She looked perplexed.

"What are you talking about?" I asked.

"Nothing," she said remotely. Something shifted inside her. She became suddenly, self-consciously calculating.

Glancing furtively behind her, she turned back and smiled at me provocatively and stroked herself suggestively with one hand from her thigh up to her breast. It was as though she had thrown her lariat around my hips and was reeling me sexually toward her.

I turned abruptly and walked away.

"No, wait," I heard her say, with a note of genuine fear in her voice. Curious, I turned. Pamela looked toward the bushes behind her, where a man stood, not very cleverly hidden.

"Come out, Buck," I said. "The show is over." Buck stepped forward, looking as contemptuous as ever.

"Are you out of your mind?" I screeched at Pamela. "Did you plan to seduce me so Buck could watch? Was this the depravity du jour?"

"You know you want a piece," Buck said nastily.

Pamela wasn't looking at me. But she held up one hand, rubbing her thumb back and forth across her first three fingers.

"Money!" I shouted. "You thought I was going to pay you . . ." I couldn't even finish my sentence.

"He did," Pamela said unapologetically, waving toward Buck. "You can be sure it wasn't my idea, Lezbo."

I wanted to hit her, Ashmont. My fingers itched to slap her. But Pamela turned her cheek and stood submissively in front of me, arms at her sides, her mouth twisted downward in a defiant pout, like a child waiting for punishment.

In a burst of clarity, I realized that hitting her was exactly what Pamela wanted. It would make me no better than Buck. This understanding cleared me of everything—my indignation, my anger. I felt calm, centered, focused, and indifferent. Pamela could read the change immediately. I could see the hatred building in her eyes.

"Good night, then," I said casually, with no emotion at all, and turned away.

I heard shuffling behind me. Then *wham!* I felt a hard push in the center of my back, and stumbled forward. Pamela had butted me with her head. I kept walking straight ahead, while I heard mocking laughter and two pairs of feet scuttling away.

When I returned to the inn several hours later, the door to my room stood open. The lock had been jimmied. I knew who had been there, and what I'd find inside. The sheets were on the floor. The bureau drawers had been turned upside down. My stereo and radio were missing, as well as a few books and records. And on a pad of paper on top of the desk, the name *Valerie* had been scrawled numerous times in large, lunatic script burrowing angrily deep in the paper.

I sat on the bed, cupped my head in my hands, and tried to feel as angry as I knew I should. But all I could think of was pity and fear. You remember, Ashmont, Aristotle's definition of tragedy. It evokes pity and fear in the viewer, leading to catharsis. The rumpled sheets, the strewn clothes, the scribbled name—these were the signs of Pamela's pain, which she had tried to leave behind. I felt the pity. But there was no catharsis.

I had to tell Desmond what had happened. I knew that Pamela's pain was bottomless, and she might return to strew more of it around the inn. I had made myself a target the first day I met her, by trying to help. She told me then to remember that she never *asked* for help. I insisted on offering, anyway. It isn't something one should do lightly. Kindness is dangerous. A poison that has to be cleared.

Desmond convinced me that I should call the police, but I procrastinated. As it turned out, I didn't need to. Two days later, I received a phone call at 5 a.m. from a nurse at the emergency room in Hyannis. Pamela had been admitted. Buck had dumped her at the hospital at 4 a.m. Then he disappeared. Pamela's liver was failing, and she asked that I be notified.

Driving to the hospital—I never thought of not going—I wondered what to expect. Had Pamela summoned me to spit on me, or to have someone around with whom she could act vaguely human? Both scenarios seemed equally likely.

I never found out what Pamela's intentions had been. By the time I arrived, she was unconscious. All her systems were failing at once. Trust Pamela to die as hard as she lived.

The nurses told me she was jaundiced, but nothing prepared me for how she looked. Her skin was dark yellow. Even the whites of her eyes, which you could see when her eyelids reflexively fluttered, were yellow. She looked like an alien. Her body had curled up, her arms and hands distended in unnatural, stiff positions. I wondered for a moment if these otherworldly hues were the natural coloring of the inhabitants of the amber world. If you had seen her, even you—who would say Pamela chose her fate—would have pitied her and wished her an easier death than the one she chose.

I decided to speak, because I knew that Pamela always hears. And since she was halfway in some other world already, I didn't think kindness could hurt her now.

I didn't know what to say until I said it. What came out was, "Thank you. The truth is I'm not sure for what." That was all I had to say, except "Good-bye."

Later that day, I met her father. Instead of the monstrous ex-con I expected, he was an ordinary gray-haired fifty-five-year-old guy wearing a polo shirt and corduroys. He works as an electrician in Duxbury. He told me that Pamela was only twenty-eight years old! Just four years older than I! She *had* been a majorette. She'd been in the honor society. She'd sung in a Baptist choir. Her mother died of cancer—not been murdered by her husband—when Pamela was sixteen. There'd been no vindictive aunt and uncle preventing her from going to college. She had always been a happy and normal child until her mother died of cancer. Pamela "turned wild" after that, her father said. She began to drink and smoke pot, and eventually turned to harder drugs. When her father told her she couldn't use drugs, Pamela left home, married her high school sweetheart and dropped out of her senior year in high school. He divorced her when she wouldn't stop drinking. It turns out that she had actually fallen—or more likely jumped—from a roof when she was out of her mind with drugs one night. But Pamela had never been pregnant. She never lost a baby.

For the past ten years, Pamela would disappear for months at a time, then show up at her father's house when she needed money or a doctor and a place to heal. She'd been in and out of drug detox five times in as many years.

Pamela's greatest secret, her source of shame, was the one she confided the last night I'd seen her. She believed she had led an ordinary life. There was no external trigger she could point to and say, "It was because of this unbearable thing, this horror that was done to me, that I had to numb my pain."

Ah, but what this tells me, what I wish I'd had the chance to say to Pamela, is that the ordinary world, in which parents die before you're done with them, whether it's due to cancer or to booze, such ordinary lives of ordinary pain, may be the harshest sphere of all. Its dangers rarely spoken of. Its horrors little understood. Nonetheless, some people, like Pamela, are allergic to its dust. Their fates—if we don't look away in disgust and easy judgment—challenge us to understand how perilous life can be.

Pamela reminded me of the wretched buffoon in the *Brothers Karamazov*. You know, Papa Karamazov—who never encountered a sensibility he didn't offend, a sacred code he didn't violate. Watching Pamela die, finally still and at peace, she seemed just like anyone. I thought of what Dostoyevsky says of Karamazov: "As a general rule, people, even the wicked, are much more naive and simple-hearted than we suppose. And we ourselves are, too."

I believe this to be true of Pamela. And my parents. And me. And even you at some level, Ashmont. Maybe it is even true of the depraved parents who have maimed and slaughtered their own children—the brutal souls with whom you spend so much of your time these days. I wonder if their evil acts would prey less savagely on your mind if you could think of them as Dostoyevsky says. I know it hurts me less to think so. I know you will be angered at the hint of compassion these words suggest. In your mind, compassion for the guilty equates with indifference toward the innocent. But I do not believe it must.

I have discovered, to my surprise, that I still believe that Love Rules. But by that I no longer believe, as I used to, that kindness or generosity or civility also rule. I used to think that love struggled against selfishness, violence, hatred, and rage. That when love won, such things would disappear. I thought that love and evil were opposites. Now I understand that they are not. They are the right and left, up and down, call and response of human nature. Perhaps they always will be.

Love rules not because it must. Not because it should. Not because it's good—it isn't always good, and sometimes it's downright bad. Love rules just because it does. Love rules because love *is* life. Love is trying again. Love is having to feel things. Love is being in so much pain you want to hurt someone. Or, for people like my parents, love means leaving your children behind while you visit an amber sphere where you feel more alive, more at home, than in the real world. They're all side effects of the struggle to live. It takes a desperate commitment to life to be as creatively cruel as the human race has been. These things do not deny or refute love, they exist like giant puddles in the midst, around, over, under, and through love.

But here's the thing, Ashmont. I believe that if you can hold love in your mind and in your heart while you look evil straight in the eye—without flinching—then a strange thing happens. Love stretches and strengthens. *Love eats evil.* And with it, fear of evil. And after it's eaten, evil becomes as still and peaceful as Pamela does in death. This is what I learned from Pamela. Or because of her.

I know what you are thinking, Ashmont. You are thinking that I am making love mean what I need it to mean, because it helps me forgive my parents. You do not think forgiveness is an unambiguous plus for humanity, but provides an excuse for inaction. You think evil never gets eaten, it simply takes a holiday before it lurches upright, leaps out of its deathbed, and runs amok again. All of which may be true, but it is not a fact. It may be true because you need it to be true, for reasons stemming from that private depth in you that I do not fathom. Still, my truth is just as valid as yours. But then, I believe that not only can there be, there *must* be many truths, some of which disagree.

I've thought of you—of us—often as I've mulled these things over. I fear that in the past, I may have used my love for you as an excuse for bad behavior. Because I loved you, it didn't matter that I was demanding, irritating, unreasonable, or insensitive. As though love were an excuse for bad behavior rather than a call to greater care. I am sorry. I shall try to do better.

Please, please, please live as long as you can, so I can learn to love you better. Perhaps by the time we are eighty, I'll finally know how not just to say I love you, but to show you I do, as well. In the meantime, please know how hard I try.

I love you as well as I am able.

In friendship and in, I hope,
constantly improving love,

Val

1980

October 1980

Dear Ashmont,

Desmond bought the *Boston Globe* last Sunday. I pulled out the "Help Wanted" section to line shelves in the potting shed, and read the ads for psychologists. Given the fifteen or twenty jobs I saw, there are as many despondent teenagers in Boston as there are in Buffalo.

Why you refuse to leave the land of fried bologna, bowling, and beer, I do not understand. I suspect a streak of missionary in you that seeks not only to save souls, but to do it in the most comfortless surroundings imaginable. You're lucky I visit you at all in a place where a fashion abomination such as long underwear must be worn from November to May. I *will* some day entice you back to Boston, even if I have to start a loony bin myself. The inn's clientele will fill a ward all by themselves.

Now that I'm in the esteemed position of Associate Manager, Desmond has given me a small apartment behind the kitchen, overlooking the moors. I watch the evening sun fade from orange to purple every night, and wonder how I left art so far behind. Or how art left me.

The high school principal offered me a permanent job teaching art this year, but I turned it down. Teaching feels as hollow as my own feeble efforts at painting. Without a passion for art of my own, how can I inspire the passions of others?

I wish I knew what my purpose was. I used to think it was being an artist. Now, I think I was only attracted to living a bohemian life. You know—wearing black, smoking pot, sleeping all day, and drinking dry martinis at night. Anyone can do those things, but none of them make you an artist.

While I wait for a visiting angel to proclaim my calling, being an Associate Manager is surprisingly tolerable. To my astonishment, I'm developing passable business skills. And I love the inn. It's ballast for my roaming mind. Sometimes I think I was meant to be a *professional daydreamer*. Such a *useless* calling. Yet it is in pondering, and in writing you, that I feel most myself.

I can't believe you are dating a cop. Really Ashmont, I'd prefer a stiff-backed science major. But I can hardly tease you about dating a cop when the truth is that I appear to be dating a nun.

I say "appear to" because of the ambiguous nature of our entanglement. Her name is Sister Mary Patrick, although everyone calls her "MP." I met her at St. Mary's a few weeks ago when I drove the van to the parish house loaded with used furniture for the annual flea market. When I opened the door to the parish garage, Mary Patrick was standing on a chair reaching up to pull some baskets from a shelf. She lost her balance and began to topple. I grabbed her around the waist to break her fall, and we fell in a heap on the garage floor. This was before I knew she was a nun. Godless heathen that I am, how was I to know they're letting nuns run around incognito in jeans and sweaters these days? So I think I should be forgiven for the flush of attraction I felt, and for assuming that as she lifted her breasts from my face, she felt some tickle of attraction, too.

I was smitten immediately. MP has dense gold, flyaway hair, apple cheeks, and an exuberant laugh that radiates goodwill for miles. She looks like a slighter older version of Hayley Mills in *The Parent Trap*—I know I need not say more. As we stood up, her smile felt like a heat lamp, warming me everywhere—even the coldest, darkest recesses of my mind. Then I spotted the crucifix dangling from her neck, an immense, industrial crucifix.

I spoke without thinking, an emphatic, "Oh no!" I was afraid I'd hurt her feelings, but she laughed.

"Are you . . .?" I trailed off.

"Sister Mary Patrick," she proffered a pink, small hand. "I'm afraid I am. But please don't hold it against me. It was Jesus' idea, not mine. I pray that in my next life I can be a nightclub singer or a masseuse. You know, they're not so remote from being a nun. We all lift people's spirits!"

Mary Patrick was clearly no ordinary nun. But then, I realized I didn't know anything about nuns, but suddenly I wanted to know everything about *this* nun.

I invited her to ride back to the inn with me to pick up the next batch of furniture. As we drove by the last stretch of beach before the inn, she pointed to the setting sun and pronounced, "Oh, it's lovely. Stop, please. We must stop." We parked and ran to the water's edge, where MP knelt for a moment, dangling her fingers in the breaking tide.

She stared up at me and said, "We must go in, Val. I dare us! God's magnificent sunset is daring us!"

"But we don't have bathing suits," I protested.

"We have the skin that we were born with, that's covering enough for God, the fish, and the sea." She tore her clothes off, tossed them on the sand and ran into the water. There was nothing I could do, of course, except join her.

The water was so cold, it quickly cooled the *skin that we were born with* to an unnatural blue, so we raced back, grabbed our clothes, and tossed them over our shoulders. As MP stood up to put her clothes on, I realized I'd been staring at her when she said, "What's wrong, Val? What did you think nuns had under their clothes? Dough?"

In fact, I *had* assumed that under their habits nuns' bodies must be shapeless and formless—like dough. I felt idiotic and tongue-tied.

"We have all your basic body parts. Arms and legs and toes. We even have pubic hair and —" she tugged her sweater on over her head—"breasts." I thought I was as red as I could get until she added, "Yours, by the way are very nice." And I felt my blush darken to crimson.

"Um, thanks," I mumbled, and then added instinctively, "Yours, too." Then, appalled at myself for complimenting a nun on her breasts, I immediately apologized, "Oh my God, I'm sorry. I mean, I'm sorry I said oh my God. I mean, I'm sorry for everything!"

She laughed, and threw my sweater in my face. "You're a sweet soul, Val."

Her comment touched me. I don't think of myself as sweet. And I haven't thought about my soul since grade school, when the nuns at Sacred Heart condemned mine to hell, because I insisted that un-baptized babies went to heaven instead of limbo. I liked Mary Patrick so much, I felt honor bound to come clean about the state of my soul.

"Oh, but I'm not. I'm a sinner and—by Catholic standards—a her-etic. I must break God's rules ten times a day. And you know, I think it only fair to tell you since you may want me to drive you back to St. Mary's right away, that I'm a lesbian. I mean, you know what that is, right?"

"Why yes, Val, in fact, I do," she said, looking deeply amused. I felt about ten years old. "I do indeed know what that means." Then she looked at me gravely. "But Val, you must understand, those are not God's rules you are breaking. They're the church's. That's an important distinction. Believe me, *everybody* breaks the rules! God loves you no matter what!"

And Ashmont, for a moment, I believed her. Whether I believed in God or not, I believed Mary Patrick thought God should and did love me, and I felt warm and peaceful and innocent and very, very young—not like a child, but like someone who has been relieved from carrying the weight of themselves around the world.

She pulled me to my feet, and put her arm around my shoulders, giving them a gentle squeeze as we walked back to the van. After that, I thought about her constantly. I was drawn to her warmth and faith, but I was suspicious, too. I kept remembering Hattie Wilson from high school.

Hattie was a cheerleader and president of Youths for Christ. Ordinarily, I wouldn't have given a Goody Two-shoes like her the time of day. But Hattie's cheery friendliness seemed sincere. She was cute, with a little button nose and a Dorothy Hamill haircut. Junior year she took a special interest in me, and I was deeply flattered. I knew Hattie had a boyfriend, but I thought perhaps my charms had won her over.

I was thrilled when Hattie asked me to go out for pizza after school one day. On our way to the sub shop, she asked if I would mind if we stopped somewhere first. I said okay, and we walked to the parish hall of Hattie's church. I thought it an odd way to start a date, but I followed Hattie into a roomful of the smilingest group of teenagers I'd ever seen. Everybody grinned as I came through the door. At first I felt pleased. This is what it's like to enter a room when you're popular and cute, I thought. This is what Hattie encounters everywhere she goes. We sat down in the back row and listened as one person after another stood up and addressed the group.

I wasn't even listening at first. I was staring at Hattie and imagining what it would be like to kiss her, and wondering what on earth these kids were so damned happy about—because it was getting on my nerves. Then I began to listen. Darned if these born-again Christians weren't telling *conversion* stories.

Jesus buckled their knees while they were taking a shower before they could abuse themselves. *Jesus* knocked the beer bottle from their hands. *Jesus* stopped them in the nick of time from fornicating in the back of their father's Buick. Jesus served as an omniscient hall monitor, on the lookout for every lapse in morals—ready to zap sinners with remorse and reform. I found something unseemly and smug in the way they chirped and bragged about their faith. But I also felt envious. Because they all had Jesus, they also had each other.

Hattie and the others glanced expectantly in my direction. I realized that Hattie had brought me here to *save* me. Her interest wasn't carnal, it was evangelical. Perhaps I should have been flattered that she cared about my soul. No one else did. But I wasn't. I was offended and resentful. How dare Hattie assume that I needed salvation! How dare she invite me here under false pretenses! How dare she *not* want to kiss me!

I raised my hand and asked if I could tell my story. They eagerly agreed, and listened raptly. I told them that I went on a date my freshman year with John Ray Manfred, known as the Dog Kiss Boy because he liked to lick faces. While sitting under the gazebo in Portal Park with John Ray's tongue halfway down my throat, *Jesus* spoke to me. I paused for effect, and they waited breathlessly for the expected moment of repentance.

"*Jesus* whispered loudly in my ear," I said. "He whispered so loudly that John Ray heard him, too.

"'Val,'" Jesus boomed, "'the reason you are not enjoying this boy's tongue sliding down your throat is that *you are a dyke!*'"

"'Thank you, Jesus!'" I said. "'That explains everything.' And I've been a happy dyke ever since. Right, Hattie?"

I smiled at Hattie and put my hand on her knee. She yanked it off, looking like she might spit up

"This is so much fun. Who's next?" I said cheerfully as I sat down.

The room was silent. I could feel the gears grinding in their brains as they tried to figure out how good Christian youths should respond. Ultimately, charity lost out to baser instincts.

"Yuck!" said several of the boys. The girls suddenly had to go the bathroom en masse. Hattie left. So I left, too, whistling "Onward Christian Soldiers."

After my first, oddly intimate encounter with Mary Patrick, I found myself thinking about Hattie, and the mistrust I felt for self-avowed Christians who manifest an interest in my soul. But I couldn't stop remembering Mary Patrick's reference to my sweet soul. She sounded like she believed I really had one—and that she had peered deeply into it and liked what she'd seen.

From Mary Patrick's point of view, I soon learned, God bestows love promiscuously on the faithful and profane alike. I was helping her paint the garage behind the parish house one sunny afternoon. She stood on a plank balanced between two ladders. I stood under the plank, shielding myself from the hot sun.

"Move aside, Val," she called out. "If I fell, I'd squash you like a bug."

"Then I'd be spared the pain of seeing you fall," I declared.

But I got an itch on the bottom of my foot, and sat down across from the plank to take my shoe off so I could scratch it.

Just then, Mary Patrick did indeed slip and fall. The plank fell straight down on top of where I'd been standing, and Mary Patrick fell, as she had when we first met, on top of me. If I hadn't gotten the itch at just that moment and moved aside, I'd have been squashed like a bug, indeed. And I wouldn't have softened MP's fall.

"That itch of yours was an angel's warning," MP insisted. "It proves that God isn't done with either one of us yet." She closed her eyes, and I knew she was thanking God.

The timing of the itch did seem providential. I wanted to believe in MP's benevolent deity, but if the universe offers evidence of anything, it's that God's attention wanders.

"I can understand angels looking out for *your* welfare. But isn't God too busy," I asked, "to bother saving the likes of me?"

"Now really, Val," MP scoffed, gesturing at the yard. "Look at that dandelion over there. Is the sun shining brightly on it?"

"Yes."

"Now look at the roses on the trellis. Is the sun shining more brightly there?"

"No," I acknowledged.

"So it is with the love of God, Val. It's the great equalizer. All souls deserve and receive God's love equally. Hierarchies are human inventions. The love of God snuffs them out." She was very firm and sincere. And I was won. If MP believed that an angel had made my foot itch, I would believe it, too.

Over the next couple of weeks, I gave away half of Desmond's furniture, just so I'd have an excuse to drive to St. Mary's. I brooded sleeplessly for hours every night trying to decide what it meant that MP would reach out and hold my hand when we were driving together. That she would hug me good-bye and press me close just before she released me. Was she attracted to me? Or was I projecting my own base motives onto an innocent nun? I feared that I'd go crazy if I couldn't ask her, but feared that if I *did,* she would refuse to ever see me again.

Finally, MP asked one night if she could see my room. She sat quietly at my desk, studying my possessions as though each one yielded a precious insight into my depths. Then she wrote something on a piece of paper, stood up, and came to sit beside me on my bed. Then, Ashmont, a miracle happened. Instead of the awkwardness of trying to guess whether she wanted to kiss me, or whether I dared to kiss her, we were drawn into our first kiss like two magnets in space.

That was all we did that first time. We kissed. After she left, I found her handwritten note on my desk. It said, "God loves you no matter what. Believe it, Val." I nearly cried. I thought my spiritual side had died long ago. My response to her note, my attraction to MP herself, made me realize it was numb, not dead.

Then there was another night, and another kiss. And another night, and a little bit more than kissing. Each night, we went a little farther. I worried that if MP's religion were right, I would burn in hell for corrupting a nun. But I enjoyed kissing her so much, I couldn't force myself to care. I felt like Huck Finn—ready to *go* to hell.

I assumed that we would gradually continue removing one more item of clothing until we were completely naked, and then we would make love. It was fun to move slowly, like playing strip poker in junior high. I'd almost forgotten Mary Patrick was even a nun until one night, after kissing each others' breasts and rubbing each others' backs, I spontaneously moved my hand up her thigh. She moved it back up to her breast. I tried again, and the same thing happened.

I was befuddled. MP seemed to be enjoying our trysts as much as I. But as she returned my straying hand to her breast, I began to wonder if I'd gone too far. If I had been seducing her, rather than responding to her overtures. I remembered with great clarity that these were a nun's sex organs I'd approached with my wayward hand.

So, being me, I began to apologize. Profusely. I started to put my shirt back on and handed MP her sweater. But she pulled my head toward her breast. "You aren't going to stop, are you?" she asked cheerfully.

Ashmont, I have never been so confused in my life. I must have looked it, because MP sat up, and sighed, "Poor Val, I should explain. You know, I've taken a vow of celibacy." She looked at me as though this statement clarified everything.

I felt even more befuddled. "But MP, what do you think we've been *doing?* I mean, if it's okay to kiss you and touch your breasts, why won't you let me give you an orgasm, too?"

"Oh, that," she laughed heartily, as if I'd just told her a delightful joke.

"Yes," I said, *"that."* I was starting to feel annoyed, because I felt embarrassed and stupid.

"No, no. Please don't be irritated. I'm sorry. I shouldn't have laughed. It's just that in my mind what we've been doing isn't really sex."

"It's not?"

"Oh, no. Why kissing and touching each others' breasts—well, not only does it give us pleasure, but you see, Val, it's sacred, too. It brings us closer to God." At that moment, it occurred to me that MP wasn't a nun at all, but an impostor who had been waiting to see how long it would take me to catch on to the joke. But as I studied her face searching for mockery, all I saw was earnest conviction.

I was astounded. Over the years, other people had tried to tell me that sex—especially sex between two women—was many things. Dangerous. Wonderful. Sinful. Depraved. Thrilling. But no one had ever suggested it would bring me closer to God.

"Poor Val. You look like someone put your head on backward. But it all makes perfect sense. After all, why do you think women were given breasts in the first place?"

"I have no idea," I confessed.

"The nurture we give through our breasts is a symbol of the nurture God gives humanity. Everything in nature is a mirror of God, Val. Everything!" She looked me intently in the eyes, as if, indeed God were there, too.

Then MP explained that breasts—femininity itself, for that matter—have been "out of favor" with the church for centuries. But they were powerful symbols for the medieval mystics whose extravagant visions fuel MP's faith. She says that these mystics regularly compared Christ's death to labor pangs, and spoke of Jesus as "our true Mother." In one mystic's vision, Mary bragged of "suckling the sages and prophets before Christ was born." Later she suckled Jesus, and after that, she suckled "God's bride." Which, MP informs me, is Christianity itself. If we are to believe MP, the early Catholic Church ran rampant with suckling. Metaphorically, of course.

Her favorite story about the sacredness of breasts is a vision of St. Clare's—who was, it seems, a great pal of St. Francis. Clare envisions herself taking a bowl of water and a towel to Francis in his room. When she arrives, he opens his shirt and offers her a breast, saying, "Come, take a drink." She said that what she tasted was so sweet it was impossible to describe. When she took some of what she had imbibed in her hands, it became gold and clear and so bright that it reflected everything in the world as if it were a mirror.

So what MP and I do in bed together follows saintly tradition and actually brings us closer to God! Ashmont, I find MP's views stunningly pagan! They blur God's gender and elevate women's bodies to divine status. To me, these ideas are the antithesis of Catholicism. But MP thinks they are completely Catholic. More truly Catholic than the modern day church. I understand now why she told me that first day that everyone breaks the rules. She has constructed her own Catholicism without regard for the Catholic Church. And she tells me this is what all nuns do. She says she doesn't see how anyone could *be* a nun—or for that matter, a Catholic—if they didn't.

"But Mary Patrick," I said after a break in her speech. "There is still one thing I need to ask you. Why would it be so wrong to let me touch you in other places? Isn't it frustrating for you? I mean, to get all worked up and then not be able to come?" It certainly was for me, although I didn't have the nerve to say so.

"Poor Val," she said, looking concerned. "Am I driving you crazy? I'm sorry. Maybe it's wrong of me to be with you. I enjoy being with you so much. But if it hurts you, tell me now, and I won't come back."

I panicked. I wanted more of MP, not less. So I quickly added, "No, no. Please. Never think of going away. It only drives me a *little* crazy. I'm fine. But I don't understand why it doesn't drive *you* crazy, too. Unless, that is, you don't find me that attractive . . ."

"No," she reassured me. "Never think that. You are very beautiful. It's just that . . . I don't know how to put this without it sounding strange—" she began. As if everything she'd been saying till now had been common sense.

"Try me," I encouraged her.

"I have to save something for God. Every time I'm frustrated, I focus my mind on God. I pray very deeply for God to help me keep my focus on him."

"But can't you get closer to God through sex? If everything is a mirror of God, why not orgasms, too?" It seemed logical to me.

MP's face scrunched up with thought. Apparently, she was still working on the answer to this one.

"I don't know for sure, Val. But I'm afraid that if I lost myself completely in sex, I might never find God again. Not in the same way. And that would be . . ." She searched for an adequately powerful word.

". . . the worst thing that could happen to you," I completed for her.

"Yes." She nodded.

MP's eyes looked sorrowful and perplexed. I had never seen her depressed. Never seen her look so lost, so small. Her usual radiant, joyful glow had faded to a dim haze. I hated seeing her upset. And then I had the most mature thought, Ashmont. You will be surprised. I realized that MP had to sort this conflict out inside herself. As saintly as MP is in some ways, she is deeply confused in others. I could not, would not, should not pressure her in any way. There is too much at stake.

I know religion is a sore point with you, but I need to confide in someone about this perplexing relationship. And Desmond and Raymond, for reasons that surprised me, are absolutely unavailable. MP has become a sore point for them, because of the terrible disagreement they had about her.

Desmond, it turns out, feels more scarred by his Catholic upbringing than I do. He took it more seriously when he was younger, so it's left him bitter. He was friendly to Mary Patrick when he thought she was just a new girlfriend. But once he found out she was a nun—he asked one day, "So, what's with the *Patrick?*"—he became cold and distant whenever he saw us together.

I overheard Dez and Raymond arguing on the deck one night. Something they do so seldom, I had to eavesdrop.

"I can't believe that nun. What a hypocrite," Desmond said. "But then, they're all hypocrites. Worse yet, I can't believe Val. Our own sweet little Val is having sex with the enemy."

Raymond, who had been "uh-huh-ing" indulgently in response to Desmond's fulminations, took umbrage at this last. I was glad, since I felt hurt by Desmond's scorn toward my own sweet Mary Patrick.

"Oh, really, Dez. You're being awfully self-righteous. Val's friend seems like a perfectly nice person. You know, when I lived in the Village, half the men I met in gay bars were monks and priests. I used to think they sent them in by busload from the monastery on Saturday nights. Even monks and nuns have to have a sex life."

"But that's exactly it," Desmond was nearly shouting. "They're having a sex life at the same time that they belong to a church that hates sex. Especially gay sex. It's not just hypocritical, it's cowardly and cruel."

"Desmond, everybody breaks the rules." Raymond sounded exasperated.

I felt like chiming in, "Yes, that's exactly what Mary Patrick says!" But I had the good sense to keep quiet. I was astonished at the tension between them. Desmond was usually so fair. Raymond was usually so solicitous. Mary Patrick says religious passions and the passions of those abused by religion provoke humanity's most heated emotions. Dez and Ray were proving her point.

"But why belong to the big, bad church if you're going to break the rules? Start your own goddamned church. Start a church where homosexuals can be treated like God's creatures, too!" There was such hurt beneath the anger in Desmond's voice. He was like a lion with a spear in his heart—roaring in pain, but effectively frightening off any efforts to help.

"Dez, be realistic." Raymond softened his tone a bit. "Why do you stay in America? You hate taxes. And Republicans. You don't even like rock and roll. Why don't you go off and start a new country?"

"Because I was *born* here! Because it's my goddamn *home!*" Desmond roared. Not mollified in the least.

"Yes, exactly. And I'm sure that's how gay priests and lesbian nuns feel about the Catholic Church. They don't know how not to be Catholic. And they don't know how *not* to be gay. But it's obviously harder to not be Catholic than it is to pretend not to be gay."

Desmond jumped to his feet, his face closed with fury, and said in a dismissive tone, "There's no point in arguing with you. You're deliberately missing the point. The truth is, it's not *right.*"

He stalked off, leaving Raymond to say wistfully to the air where Desmond had been sitting, "Oh, Dez. It's not about being right. It's about being human . . ."

I felt bad to have been the cause of their discord. And I felt protective of Mary Patrick, and my tender feelings toward her. So after that exchange, I avoided talking about MP, and I timed our arrivals and departures from the inn so that we could avoid running into either Dez or Ray.

So you must bear with me, Ashmont, and be audience for tales of my nun. I fear you will think she is crazy. At first, I did, too. But I am starting to understand her better. Maybe you have to know MP. Maybe you have to see the strength her faith gives her, to fathom why she wouldn't want to do anything sexually that would mess it up. I don't know if I believe in God, but I believe in the light that shines through Mary Patrick.

Ashmont, I am a libertine and MP is a saint, but in her I have met my match. She is even more of a romantic than I am, only her romance is with Jesus. I had a hard time getting used to being with someone who talks about Christ so much, and not when she is swearing. Nothing could interfere with MP's love for Jesus. Terrible things only make Jesus more special to her. Her friend Mechthild—one of her medieval mystics—said that all human suffering, even that which arises from our own stupidity, is analogous to Christ's, and therefore unites us with Jesus. We must learn, MP says, quoting another of her saints, "to regard sweet things as bitter and bitter things as sweet."

Did you ever read *The Story of a Soul,* the autobiography of St. Thèrése of Lisieux? No, of course you didn't. And you'll be astonished that I *did.* She died an agonizing, premature death, but she experienced every stabbing tubercular breath, every wracking pain, as a connection to God. Pain winnowed out all *distractions* except the purity of her focus on God. She died a horrible death, and felt beatified with every pain. There is something both psychotic and noble in such desperate and fanatically determined faith. MP has it, and I am in awe.

Sometimes, when I probe her beliefs too deeply, MP will chide me with a saying from her favorite saint of all time, Teresa of Avila. "The important thing is not to think much but to love much," she reminds me. But MP admits that at times even Teresa found God's ways hard to take. Once Teresa and some traveling companions were crossing a river after there'd been huge floods. As they were floating their wagons across, a cable broke, and all their supplies floated downstream.

As she began to lose patience—which I was pleased to learn could happen to a saint—Teresa paused to speak inwardly to God.

"This is how I treat my real friends," God reassured her.

"Then it's no wonder," Teresa replied, "that your Lordship has so few."

MP bellows with laughter when she tells this story. I find it sobering, but I'm sure that's because I have no faith, whereas MP has bundles. So much it is always radiating outward to inspire infidels like me. And ultimately, faith is what it all boils down to.

One day when I was pestering MP to explain to me how she could know for *certain* that God existed, she sighed and spoke dreamily. Once, she said, when Teresa's spiritual director asked her a similar question, she explained to him, "In the dark, when someone is close by, you just know he's there." For MP, God hovers protectively in the dark. For me, the only things that hover in the dark are the goblins and ghouls of my own fears and insecurities.

She believes that God answers every prayer, although human intelligence is not always adequate to fathom how. I am reminded of how stalwart and stubborn God's partisans can be. They want God to be all powerful and all knowing, but they won't let him take the blame for anything.

When I was young, I used to pray to God every night to stop my parents from drinking. Of course, he never did. At the time, I thought he was too busy answering the prayers of children who were prettier, better behaved, more important than I. Sometimes, I'd get angry at God, thinking it terribly unfair of him to play favorites—that his doing so made him as untrustworthy and mean-spirited as most of the nuns at Sacred Heart.

In third grade, I remember challenging Sister Sebastian on this point. She had been telling the class that no prayer goes unanswered by God. I knew for a fact this was untrue. So I raised my hand and stood next to my desk, as was protocol for addressing the nuns.

"Sister Sebastian," I said indignantly, "God does *not* answer all prayers. He *doesn't!* I've been praying since I was practically a baby for God to stop my parents from drinking, and he hasn't done a thing!"

She looked at me seriously. Sister Sebastian was a rarity. She would actually try to answer children's questions thoughtfully, not shush us or imply the questions themselves were sinful.

Softly, she asked, "Tell me, Valerie Marie, were your prayers sincere?"

Ah, I recognized the fudge factor, always brought in by the nuns to excuse God and make everything the human being's fault. You could go to heaven if you said an Act of Contrition before dying—but it had to be a perfect Act of Contrition or it didn't count.

"Oh yes, Sister. I would never pray for anything I didn't really want. Because then, if God answered my prayers, I'd have no one but myself to blame." I'd given this some thought. I knew why God might choose not to respond to *some* prayers. By the following morning, for example, I might regret invoking divine power the night before to transform my brother into a bug.

"Why then," said Sister Sebastian, "I believe that God is allowing your parents to exercise *free will*, Valerie Marie." She walked toward me, and I flinched a bit until it became clear her intentions were benign. She took my hands and held them pressed together in her own surprisingly warm and soft larger ones. I found this oddly comforting.

"Suppose God controlled your every movement. He told you when to press your hands together like this and when—" she pulled my hands apart—"to pull them away like this. You'd be little more than a puppet, wouldn't you? God wants us to be more than puppets, so we must make choices about our actions. And that's what we mean by free will."

She smiled. She thought she'd gotten God off the hook. But I'd heard this free will baloney before. It was a cop-out.

"But Sister, if God was going to give us free will, and allow us to make choices, why didn't he make us smart enough to make *good* choices?"

Sister Sebastian looked surprised. I had her. And I knew it. I felt triumphant. But I also felt sad—because the truth was that I really wanted God to have an acceptable reason for his failings. It would have made me feel that at least he, like me, was trying to deal with my parents. That I wasn't completely alone.

I expected Sister Sebastian to snarl, "It's not our place to question the will of the Lord." But instead, she sighed.

"That's an excellent question, Valerie Marie. Sometimes I ask that question myself. All I can tell you is that God's ways are mysterious. That's why faith is such a challenge. All we can do is pray for greater understanding."

Sister Sebastian might have found solace in praying for greater understanding. Not me. From that day forward, I realized I could keep trying to redeem God—like Sister Sebastian and Mary Patrick—or I could treat God as the great irrelevance his behavior indicted him of, and get on with my life.

When we studied comparative religion at Barclay, I was struck by a passage about the life of Buddha in one of our texts. It said that Buddha grew up believing in the gods, but eventually decided they were useless to mankind. They were just as caught up in folly, flux, and pain as humanity. They had not attained enlightenment, and couldn't really help human beings, because the ultimate reality was higher than the gods.

I liked other Buddhist beliefs—that we must find enlightenment in ourselves, not in some external deity, and the idea of God not as a being, but as the vastness of mind itself. But thinking of God as impersonal—as a kind of infinitely intricate molecule transcending time and space—rendered God remote and useless. Almost as useless as the old father God.

For awhile, I tried meditating. But the same thing happened then that happens to me now when—as you will be amazed to hear—I have taken MP's advice and tried to pray. All I find is an emptiness and loneliness so unbearable I cannot stay there for long. MP says the emptiness is God, too, and that my willingness to bear the loneliness, however briefly, proves that God is strong and alive inside me. She says that my quest for perfect human love is just as much a spiritual quest as is hers for perfect closeness to God.

So Ashmont, I love Mary Patrick, *no matter what.* Loving her means accepting her restrictions on our sexual relationship. It means being satisfied with seeing her when she can get away from her innumerable parish duties. It means not pouting and whining about what I cannot have.

Perhaps I am finally growing up. I wish now that I could take back all the petulant complaining I used to indulge in when you would turn down my pleas for sex. How ironic you must find my situation with MP. Maybe falling in love with a nun is my karmic payback for the discomfort I caused you in the past. I'm sorry. Of course, I still want you. Some things will never change. But I promise never to plead with you again.

Even though I love MP, I don't yet fully trust her. I fear she'll confess to some priest that she's been cavorting with another woman, and they'll send her to a cloistered convent in Brazil. Then they'll send over a contingent of red-caped, Latin-spouting, incense-burning cardinals to cast the devil out of me. These fears are not entirely without foundation in my past, as you will recall from our experience with the fundamentalist Christians at Barclay, which I have rendered as another chapter in the long neglected *Story of an Epic Friendship*—one that rivals Gilgamesh and Enkidu's encounter with the beast Humbaba for bravado and danger.

❦

Chapter ???? (I've lost track!)

Fag Writers Save Val and Ashmont from Rabid Fundamentalists

Fall semester junior year, I dated Sally Rivens, whose initial attraction for me was that she was a cousin of Lettie Gorman. Like Lettie, she aspired to become a veterinarian. She looked like a shorter, rounder version of Lettie. She wore flannel shirts and overalls, and thick-soled leather workboots. At first, I thought she was bold like Lettie, too, because Sally was the one who asked *me* out.

Sally talked tough. She wanted to go to the Panther on our first date, but I talked her into pizza at Mario's instead. She told me she had been brought up in a fundamentalist Christian church which taught her that homosexuality was an abomination. She said her parents might believe such hateful nonsense, but she didn't. She hated her parents and wanted to be as *unlike* them as possible. That included having *abominable* sex with anyone she wanted. She was so tired of her mother warning her against the signs of a "perverted lifestyle"—ranging from swinging her arms when she walked to having short hair—that she couldn't wait to slide her tongue into another woman's mouth the first chance she got.

"You mean you never have?" I asked.

"What?" Sally replied. She'd been so absorbed in defying her parents that she'd forgotten she had an audience.

"You've never kissed a woman?"

"No!" she seemed shocked, and turned red. "Where would I find a girl who'd let another girl kiss her in my hometown? Lettie was the only— *you know*—that I ever knew. And she's my cousin. Lettie was the one who told me about *you*."

I knew that Sally would be T-R-O-U-B-L-E. But I thought she would be a certain *kind* of trouble. I thought I would show her how to make out. I would help her overcome her fears, point her toward the right books and organizations, offer her a crash course in Coming Out 101. And then let her down gently when it came time for her to find a girlfriend— since, of course, my heart then and for all time belonged to you, Ashmont.

I had no idea of the real T-R-O-U-B-L-E that lay ahead. When Sally and I returned to my room from Mario's, she tackled me and wrestled me onto my bed, pleading with me to let her kiss me. So I did. But once Sally's tongue found the inside of my mouth, she retreated immediately. Then she burst out crying. Not just crying, *wailing.*

"Oh, Jesus!" she moaned. "What have I done? I'm a sinner. Oh, Lord, save me. I'm going to hell for sure. Oh, I'm sorry. I'm sorry. Oh, Lord, forgive me." She shook with fear, and her voice rose into ever higher registers of anguish. It was then I knew that Sally was no ordinary scared baby dyke seeking initiation into the mysteries of lesbian sex. Sally was a tormented individual, who needed more than my amateur mentoring. Sally needed a shrink. And she needed one right away.

I walked Sally over to Student Counseling Services, and left her there, moaning and shaking. I felt sorry for her. And I felt stupid for not having seen through her facade of independence. I thought I'd never see her again. I was wrong.

Two days later, at 6:00 a.m., the real kind of T-R-O-U-B-L-E Sally brought into my life appeared outside my dorm room window. I heard droning voices break the early calm. Looking outside, I saw three figures holding Bibles, reading aloud. One was a middle-aged, balding man in a gray suit and tie who looked like my parents' insurance agent. One was a small, brittle-looking woman with a Pat Nixon suit and Annette Funicello hair. Between these two stood Sally, but not a Sally I'd ever seen. This Sally wore flat black loafers, white anklets, and a flowered shirtwaist dress. She looked acutely uncomfortable in these clothes, and kept her eyes on the pages in front of her, refusing to look up, even after I turned my light on and pulled back the curtain to lean out the window.

"Hey, Sally!" I shouted. But Sally simply raised her voice as she read.

Her father looked up. "She won't answer you. The Lord won't let her. We're here to save you from your perverted ways. To pray the devil out of your soul, and this dormitory, and this campus. To end the abomination of homosexuality at Barclay College."

"Praise Jesus," his wife answered.

"Okay, have it your way," I said. "I'm getting some sleep." But I couldn't, of course. I called campus security to have them removed. But the Rivens stepped back far enough from the dorm lawn and lowered their voices sufficiently so that they were considered to be exercising their freedom of speech. After the first morning, they weren't considered a nuisance by anyone but me—who endured snickering, stares, and graffiti on my dorm room door because of the Rivens' hectoring presence. Every morning I'd wake to scripture, come rain, snow, or sleet. They'd read until 7:30, when I assumed Mr. Rivens had to go to work. Thank God he was employed.

Some mornings, I'd stand near them, staring at Sally, trying to get her to meet my gaze, but she never would. She'd dropped out of Barclay, and enrolled in some Bible college in the South for next semester. Most of the passages they read were about sodomy. Very violent and vengeful. What sodomy had to do with Sally's and my little kiss, I didn't know. For some reason, all my irritation and anger with the Rivens focused on this one point. If God were going to bother condemning female homosexuality, he damn well ought to get the anatomy and the vocabulary right! I was sick and tired of lesbianism being the invisible perversion!

I stood in front of Mr. Rivens one morning, since he was the only one who ever talked, and asked, "Don't you have any passages about two women having sex? Nothing about clitorises? Vaginas? Does God only care about assholes and penises? Maybe God doesn't think it's wrong to be a lesbian. I mean, if it isn't explicitly condemned in the Bible, and you have only the Bible to go by, then God must think it's okay, or he would have made sure to say otherwise."

Mr. Rivens drew himself up to his full, not very substantial height, and puffed out his full, quite substantial chest, looked me straight in the eye, and pronounced in a loud, certain voice, "It's all sodomy in the eyes of the Lord. And you're all sodomites!"

Clearly, questioning the authority of scripture was not going to drive the Rivens out of their ministry. But then the campus newspaper began to run a daily feature: "The Rivens Family Scripture of the Day." Other students adopted the Rivens as pets, bringing them bagels and orange juice from the cafeteria and asking for autographs. At that point, *you* decided it had gone far enough.

You stopped by my room and asked if I had your permission to do whatever it took to get them to stop. I knew you hated sanctimoniousness, and I knew you were capable of imaginative, even dangerous capers when an important issue was at stake. So I merely asked if violence was involved, and when you said no, I gave you the green light, confident that the Rivens would soon be history. You lifted some books from my shelves before leaving, and then I didn't see you until the following day.

At 5:55 a.m., just before the Rivens usually made their appearance, I heard a different drone arising from their usual spot. I looked outside my window, and saw *you* reading aloud from my American Lit book. You were reciting Walt Whitman's "I Sing the Body Electric."

As the Rivens arrived, you were reading,

> . . . the expression of a well-made man appears not only
>   in his face
> It is in his limbs and joints also, it is curiously in the joints
>   of his hips and wrists,
> It is in his walk, the carriage of his neck, the flex of his
>   waist and knees, dress does not hide him,
> The strong, sweet quality he has strikes through the
>   cotton and broadcloth,
> To see him pass conveys as much as the best poem,
>   perhaps more,
> You linger to see his back, and the back of his neck and
>   shoulder-side.

Mr. Rivens lost his usual composure. "Ruth and Sally," he shouted, "Do not listen to these perversions. Do not listen." They walked down the street away from you, but you picked up your stack of books and followed. Finally, Mr. Rivens shouted at you, "Stop reading that fag writer!"

You looked up, stared him straight in the eye, and said, "No. Not only will I continue reading this fag writer, I have a whole stack of fag writers here, enough to last all year! Look—" You held up each book as you exuberantly called out each author.

"D.H. Lawrence! James Joyce! Oscar Wilde! Virginia Woolf! Plato! William Shakespeare! The thing about fags is, they're not only great writers, they're also prolific!"

And you resumed reading Walt Whitman. Mr. Rivens looked red and inflated, as though he might burst.

"Why are you doing this?" he shouted at you. "You look like a normal girl. Are you one of them? Are you a sodomite, too?"

You paused. And I waited breathlessly. I'd never heard you tell a lie before. Not ever.

You looked up at my window and locked your eyes onto mine. It was *me* you were looking at as you answered Mr. Rivens.

"Yes, Mr. Rivens. I am a sodomite in spirit. And I'm proud of it." And I felt a burst of love and admiration for you that swelled my heart to twice its normal size. You were, I decided, the most valiant and heroic person ever born.

"Ugh!" he said. "This whole campus is damned. You're way beyond saving. Come, Ruthie and Sally. God will smite this place."

And they left. Poof! They were gone and they never came back.

I flew down the stairs to meet you, nearly knocking you over, grabbed you and hugged you.

"Ashmont, thank you, thank you, thank you. You're my hero. How did you know it would work?"

You smiled slyly and said, "You have to fight sodomy with sodomy."

"Yes, I suppose you do," I laughed. But Ashmont, you do know those were not all fag writers you mentioned. I mean, some of them weren't really gay."

"Oh, yes, Val, I know." You smiled slyly. "But they are all sodomites in the eyes of the Lord, don't you think? Just like me."

"Yes," I laughed. "Just like you."

Anyway, Ashmont, sodomite in the eyes of the Lord though I may be, my relationship with Mary Patrick makes me realize that although I gave up relying on God for anything long ago, I have never been able to stop thinking about him—or her—or the molecule.

Wondering what she's up to. Whether she's changed since I last knew her. Whether she misses me.

I remember a story I read in a philosophy book about a group of Jews in Auschwitz who decided to put God on trial. God didn't have much of a chance in this horrible setting. They found no excuse for God's betrayal and found him guilty and worthy of death. Then, after announcing the verdict, the Rabbi pronounced the trial was over. It was time for evening prayer.

We can't live with God. And we can't live without her.

In these mortal meantimes, I thank whatever God there may be for you and for Mary Patrick. The closest I'll come to loving God—to knowing God—is in the love I feel for both of you.

Loving you eternally,

Val

November 1980
Dear Val,

I'm not shocked by your dalliance with a nun. I stopped believing long ago that just because someone assumes the responsibility of being a nun, priest, teacher, or parent, that they will act responsibly. At least Mary Patrick appreciates your "sweet soul." I give her credit for that. She will hurt you in the end, but it won't be calculated.

I'm not just being cynical. MP is caught in a triangle with God at one end and you at the other. Don't take it personally, Val, when God takes you down.

Your story about the uselessness of God reminded me of a similar childhood revelation of my own. Every child has such an epiphany, sooner or later.

I was about twelve, and it was a few months after the incident with my father. I think about this time in my life as little as possible. It's not important anymore. My mother took me to see our minister in his church office. Since no human had succeeded in diminishing my anger, she must have hoped God could. The minister, however, was less concerned with my feelings than he was with making sure that I wasn't blaming God. You're right, Val. Religious people are obsessed with God's innocence. On occasion, it renders them heartless.

"Do you believe that God is responsible for what happened?" the minister wanted to know.

"No, of course not," I said. "My father is." Considering what my father had done, this was an awful truth to hear from a child. But the minister smiled. He looked relieved.

"Of course," I added, "God did nothing to prevent it."

His smile faded. He furrowed his brow.

"While it's true," he sighed, "that bad things happen to people who don't appear to deserve them"—he peered at me over his half-frame glasses as if to imply that the jury was still out on *my* deservingness—"God never allows anyone to suffer more than they can bear. We all grow stronger through suffering." He sat back, satisfied with his brilliance.

His words disgusted me. My stomach curdled and my fists clenched. I would gain nothing from arguing with him.

I stood up, said "Good-bye," and opened the door to leave.

"Where are you going?" he asked.

"You've said enough," I answered.

"Oh, good," he said, and smiled. He thought he'd *reached* me. "Do you want to come back another time?"

"No, I don't," I said. "I will never enter a church again as long as I live."

"What a strange child," he muttered as I closed the door.

I kept my vow. I have never entered a church again in my life.

I work with people every day whom God has allowed to suffer more than they could bear. They are broken, battered, and hopeless. Huge chunks of their lives are wasted in pain. It's not redemptive. They're not improving because of it. They get worse.

I can hear you, Val. You are saying my outrage over suffering is by itself a sign of some transcendent impulse.

The problem and the wonder of you, Val, is that you are willing to find a saving grace in this sorry world at the merest flicker of compassion, the slightest ray of sun skimming off the murkiest of waters. You're not a libertine at all, but a saint or a terrible fool. I suppose you are both. Saint or fool, I'll be here to help you put the pieces of your heart back together after Mary Patrick breaks you. And she will.

I should go to bed now. My program budget is being audited tomorrow. How I hate bureaucratic hassles. Still, the program's success has given me more autonomy. No one thought I should focus on individual teenagers. Family systems is all the rage. We no longer have patients, but "identified patients"—meaning the whole family is emotionally troubled, but that symptoms often show up in one member, usually a child.

When this ideology takes children off the hook, I approve. When it takes parents off the hook, I despise it. Dammit, they chose to be parents. Who cares if their parents and grandparents screwed them up? They should have thought of that before they reproduced. The absence of accountability drives me mad. Like a mirror held up to a mirror, it reveals the generations in infinite regress—the pain in one generation's hearts hardening into the cruelty they extrude into their children's. Everybody is somebody's victim.

Where does the buck stop? Logically, it can't stop until we reach back to God—that feckless Olympian. Such thinking gets so morally murky, I can't abide it. It may provide an accurate map of the psyche, but like the schematic of a car, it tells us nothing about how to drive responsibly.

Besides, overhauling an entire family doesn't work. Families drop in and out of treatment. They change in cosmetic ways, but as soon as they're on their own, they break down in the same old ways. My colleagues hate me for pointing this out. It makes them feel futile. But hate me or not, it's the truth. They put Band-Aids on gushing arteries.

I take individual teenagers at risk for pregnancy and delinquency and shower them with encouragement and education. I keep them as far away from their families as I can. Through "One for One's" volunteer mentoring, each young person learns to do one important thing really well. Then, they heal themselves.

One girl showed a knack for calculus. I harassed the best math teacher in the city until she agreed to tutor her. For another kid it was gourmet cooking; I arranged for him to apprentice with lessons from the city's top chef. Once they start to feel successful at doing one thing well, they dress better, talk better, are friendlier, more hopeful, and begin to set goals for themselves. The farther they stay from the gravitational drain of their families, the better off they remain.

It's a ton of work discerning their gifts, but one of my own is sniffing out talent in kids from impoverished, culturally derelict backgrounds. Some have never been to a park, read an entire book, or seen *West Side Story,* much less *La Bohème.* But if I probe and push, I discover the nugget of absolute brilliance in each of them. The discovery of their gifts is thrilling for the kids. And it has the strangest, most profound effect on me.

I feel at peace with myself—a calm not of my body, but of my soul. It's as if I have fulfilled a mission destined for me before birth. At these moments I close my eyes and a voice in my head says—"Yes"— as if I were receiving the blessing of an angel. And for a fleeting moment that I can only describe as ecstasy, the demons that drive me are lulled to sleep. If the angel of death pays me a call when I abandon this mortal coil, I imagine her whispering in my ear, "You found Nikki's love of geometry, Malcolm's perfect pitch, Jordan's command of languages. You did what you were supposed to." Then I will die as I have not lived: in peace.

After I discover the children's talents, it's even more work convincing "volunteers" to mentor them. Next I track down donors to fund scholarships so the kids can go to college. I've given my evenings, my weekends—and when it meant the difference between keeping kids in the program or losing them to the streets—my money and my guest room. No one at the agency knows this last part. What I view as an alignment between my personal resources and my professional priorities, my colleagues would see as a violation of boundaries. For some psychologists, it would be. Not for me. It isn't so much that I hold myself above the ethical norms of my profession, but that my profession's norms have never come close to being high enough for me.

I've run myself ragged, but there are thirty kids whose lives have been permanently improved because of my program. Trouble is brewing, though. The agency views my program as a luxury, even though in the long run it's cheaper than therapy, welfare, or incarceration. After three years, the program will survive only if the agency is willing to continue funding.

They won't. Not because my program doesn't work, but because it works too well. These kids are going to succeed beautifully in life. And that's the problem. No matter how horrible their backgrounds, no matter what kind of abuse they've suffered, once they start doing well, they attract envy and resentment. People say they've gotten "special" treatment. There's a perverse need for children from poor families to fail. The world's dirty little secret is that people not only don't mind if these kids' lives are wasted in poverty, in jail, in violent and vagrant lives—they want and need them to fail. That's why you'll never see top-notch public education in inner cities. That's why you'll never find sex education and birth control made freely available to teenagers. Every social pyramid needs a bottom layer living in squalor so those on the top can savor their privileges.

While "One for One" has been my greatest success, it has also been the occasion for my most regrettable failure. Two teenaged boys were "fired" from the program—one for taking drugs, another because he got his girlfriend pregnant and I insisted that he find a job. Their departures didn't disturb me personally, except to revise the screening procedures that let them into the program.

But when Doreen dropped out, I grieved for weeks.

She reminded me of you, Val. Smart and filled with yearning to do something great in life. Both her parents are irredeemable alcoholics. Her absentee father lives in Florida. Her mother lives in squalor and stupor in Tonawanda, while Doreen takes care of her three younger siblings.

Doreen was referred to my program by the director of the family planning clinic. Doreen banged at the clinic door at 5 a.m. one Sunday morning looking for a "morning-after" pill because she'd gotten drunk and had sex on Saturday night. She hounded the security guard until he agreed to page the doctor on call. When the doctor asked her what the emergency was, she announced that she couldn't possibly get pregnant until after she won her first Oscar.

Doreen wants to become a costume designer in Hollywood, and while I ordinarily encourage more accessible goals, I indulged Doreen in hers because she has the talent to succeed. She arrived at her interview for "One for One" wearing an outlandish outfit—a white blouse, a huge bow in her hair, and a floor-length skirt. It turned out to be a replica of a costume worn by Katharine Hepburn in *The Philadelphia Story*. Doreen had sewn it to impress me with her skill and sincerity. It worked. I got her an internship with the university's theater department, and persuaded a film director on the faculty to look at some of her sketches. I'm confident I could have gotten her a full scholarship to film school if her goddamned "family system" hadn't gotten in the way.

Doreen's mother, Shammie (short for Shamrock, can you believe it?) has two modes. She's either a pitiful and helpless drunk, or a foul-mouthed, aggressive drunk. When she's hostile, she accuses Doreen of being a lazy, lying slut who'll end up in the street some day. And then, as if to prove herself right, she throws Doreen out of the house.

In spite of Shammie's tirades, Doreen felt deeply loyal to her family. She worked hard to keep her mother out of jail, and her siblings from dying of neglect. Small wonder that she loved lavish Hollywood movies and dreamed of escaping to California. I wanted to help her get free. Many a frigid Saturday night Doreen would wind up at my house sobbing, afraid she deserved her mother's wrath. I would reassure her that she didn't. And I would point out that her mother's behavior toward her dissolved any claim she might have to Doreen's loyalty. I was sure I was getting through to Doreen, that she would stay clear of her mother's deadly headlock. She was feeling good about herself. She was excited about her internship. Her grades were improving.

I expected Shammie to do something to sabotage Doreen's escape. I thought she would escalate her verbal and physical attacks. And I predicted this for Doreen, who said she was ready to ignore the worst insults her mother might hurl her way.

Shammie caught us both off guard. Instead of hurting Doreen, she hurt herself. The day before Doreen was scheduled to travel to New York to interview for a scholarship at NYU, Shammie got roaring drunk, "fell" on a patch of ice, and broke her ankle.

The night of Shammie's fall, Doreen stopped by my apartment to tell me that she had to stay home to take care of her younger siblings. She had already called NYU to cancel the interview. Since that meant missing the admissions deadline, she'd have to postpone college for at least a year. Doreen would be nineteen then, too old to meet the criteria for my program.

"Don't be angry, Doc, please. I'm sorry to disappoint you," Doreen pleaded.

"I'm not angry with you, Doreen." Indeed, I wasn't. I was furious, however, with Shammie. I felt as if she and I were pugilists sparring over her daughter's destiny. I was determined to win.

"Don't let Shammie do this to you, Doreen. She'll never let you go. After her ankle is healed, it will be something else. There will always be a reason to keep you at home. I thought you understood that."

"Oh, I do," she said, sobbing, letting her tears fall freely.

"I'm never going to Hollywood," she moaned. "You always tell us to face the truth. The truth is, I'll live and die in Tonawanda. I'll be taking care of Shammie until she dies of liver failure. By then, it'll be too late for me." She looked at me, her eyes lakes of pain, challenging me to tell her she wasn't speaking the truth.

"All right," I said, "that could happen. But it doesn't have to. The choice is yours." I wanted my words to challenge her, to provoke her into fighting back against Shammie. But instead, Doreen winced. Her eyes grew glassy and vacant, her voice hopeless and flat.

"Doctor Ashmont," she said, "you've helped me a lot. You're a wonderful psychologist. But you don't understand the first thing about weakness."

"But you aren't weak," I protested. "You're strong."

"I know," she said patiently, "but Shammie is weak. I'm not stupid. I know my mother is an alcoholic. I know she's irresponsible. I know almost everything she does is wrong. You're the one who has helped me understand that—"

"Yes," I interrupted, "if you understand that, then why—"

"Because," Doreen said forcefully, "the fact that it's wrong and it's not fair doesn't change anything. She won't change. And she *won't* take care of my sisters."

"But that's exactly why we have to get you away—"

Doreen put her hand across my mouth.

"Shush! Face the truth!" Doreen was speaking firmly and slowly, as if to a dull-witted child.

"You want everybody to be like you! You want Shammie to just grow up. You want me to forget about her. But look . . . look . . ." And she looked frantically around as if seeking something in my apartment that would communicate for her.

"Look at your apartment," she said finally. "You let me and the other kids in the program stay here. We're not supposed to. But you break the rules because you can't help it. You don't care how it's supposed to be. The reality is that sometimes we either stay here or we're on the street. Right?"

"Right," I said soberly. I hadn't considered what the kids thought about staying in my apartment. I mostly thought of what my colleagues would say. But of course they knew I was breaking the rules.

"You couldn't *not* break the rules and still be you. Well, it's like that with me and Shammie. It doesn't matter that what she does is unfair. I can't turn my back on her and my sisters and still be me, even if it's the dumbest thing on earth. I can't run off and do what I want to. Maybe that means I'm sick or weak like Shammie, too. But if so, that's who I am."

She sobbed heavily, and this time, she bent her head and buried her face in her hands. "I'm sorry, Doc. I don't want to disappoint you. I'm sorry to be such a fuck-up."

Instinctively, I began to think that Doreen had never been a good candidate for the program. I should never have admitted a girl so enmeshed with her mother. I should have foreseen her inability to individuate. But somewhere in the hardpack of these ideas, a glimmer of what Doreen was trying to tell me was breaking through—that the truth was more complex and demanding. I felt almost resentful of Doreen for pointing this out. To my surprise, it hurt me. I wanted to evaluate Doreen's "fitness"—not to miss her. Not to feel sad. Not to shed tears, as I had begun to.

Finally, when I could speak without my voice breaking, I said, "Doreen, you have never been and you will never be a disappointment to me. I am proud of you now. I will always be proud of you, whether you live in Tonawanda or Hollywood."

I had begun simply mouthing the right words, but as I spoke, I meant them, and something cracked open in my heart. I didn't understand it. Doreen's choice went against everything my program stands for—indeed, against everything that I myself stand for—but at that moment I accepted her decision. I embraced her, and she relaxed in my arms.

Later, as she was leaving, I called after her, "You will be careful, won't you?" I meant careful not to let Shammie walk all over her, but she thought I was talking about birth control.

"Don't worry," she grinned ruefully, "the only unborn spirit that would want me for a mother would be an even harder luck kid than I am. There can't be many of those."

"They'll have to wait until after your first Oscar. Don't give up."

"Right, Doc," she said with indulgent cheerfulness, pretending there was some merit in my fantasy.

I gave her money. Because it wouldn't have been me not to. Even if it was dumbest thing on earth. As I watched Doreen leave, a disturbing image popped into mind. I saw Doreen's face superimposed on Shammie's body. I saw Doreen slip on the ice. I saw Doreen's heart breaking into thousands of threadlike filaments that reached out to and wrapped around her children, and kept her from dying of pain. If I had known Shammie when she was Doreen's age, how would I feel about her now? If I met Doreen in ten years—and her life were just like Shammie's—how would I feel about her? I felt like I was slipping down a long, steep slope toward a lightless pit. I began to feel nauseous. I had to break my fall. I had to take a stand. I am right to draw lines. Lines give shape to chaos.

After Doreen was out of sight, I felt furious with Shammie. I did something I have never done before. I referred Shammie to the Family Therapy Program. Let the social workers tinker with Shammie's "system." If Shammie can leech off a caseworker instead of her daughter, Doreen will get some breathing room. At least, she can finish high school. I'd vastly prefer to kidnap Doreen and spirit her off to New York. But I know when I've been licked.

Shammie won.

Damn the phone! I ordinarily don't answer after 9 p.m. But when it rang ten times, I fantasized it might be Doreen needing refuge for the night. My fear for her mingled with a sudden uplift in my heart.

Of course, it wasn't Doreen. It was the agency administrator pestering me about some mindless bureaucratic report that she needs by 8 a.m. These petty details will be the death of me.

"One for One" takes so much of my time, I've given up trying to have a social life. I thought my relationship with Damon might work because his hours are as long as mine. He's a detective, not a "cop." I met him while he was investigating charges of incest against the father of one of my clients. I thought Damon was handsome, although most women wouldn't. He's tall and lean as a greyhound, with thinning black hair, and intense black—some would say beady—eyes. He talked about "putting perps away," and while my colleagues would quote Damon with sarcastic distaste, as though he were beneath their enlightened compassion, I agree with him. I want the perps put away.

I thought Damon was like me, that he was through with illusions about romance. I told him early on I never had sex with more than one man at a time because I don't have the time or energy. I didn't care if he had sex with other women, but I didn't want him to pretend he wasn't if he was.

I can't tolerate being treated as though I need to be lied to. It isn't through infidelity, it's through deceit that men control women. If men were honest about affairs, women would know where they stood. Knowledge would give women power. That's what lying prevents. Power is a far more important motive for infidelity than lust. I'm not saying women don't lie to men about affairs for manipulative reasons, too. They do. But I don't.

Damon agreed it took too much time and energy to have more than one sexual partner, and said that I needn't worry about his loyalty, because I was the most attractive woman he'd ever known. I emphasized that it wasn't his loyalty, but his honesty I was concerned about. He claimed he understood. But I was wary. I've been through this before.

So in a few months, I wasn't surprised when Damon began lowering his voice when answering the phone. When we were staying at my apartment, I'd receive frequent calls from someone who would immediately hang up. If Damon answered, he would whisper intensely, "I told you not to call me here." He would pretend the precinct was calling. I didn't have to wait for lipstick stains on his collar to know what he was up to.

I didn't ask Damon for the truth. I told him that he was having sex with another woman and pretending he had to hide it from me.

"I thought you said you wouldn't mind," he whined.

"I don't. It's not the sex. It's the lying. It's not even the lying. It's acting as if I need you to lie. I don't. You do. I can't stand that kind of weakness."

"Baby," he said, out of some script he's been through a hundred times, so often he doesn't hear what I've said. He hears someone who cares what he does. "I'm so sorry. I'll make it up to you. I'll never cheat again."

"You don't get it, do you? You could have sex with every hooker in New York and I wouldn't give a damn. What I won't tolerate is your pretending that I do care. That I need you to lie to me. If that's the only way you can feel powerful, forget it. You're weak and pathetic. And you're history. Good-bye."

As I turned to leave, I heard him move threateningly toward me as he muttered—so pathetically predictably—"Fucking crazy bitch. Fucking ball breaker. What are you? A dyke? I can't believe they let you anywhere near children at that agency."

I turned and looked at him with a gaze that said he could hit me if he wanted, but he'd only prove my point. He stopped. Then he snapped at me to get the fuck out of his apartment. Fucking right now. Fucking now. Get fucking gone. I left, looking backward to communicate how small and pitiful he was making himself with every "fucking" noise.

I paused long enough to say, "Good. . . . *fucking* . . . bye." As I closed the door, I heard something *thud* against it. Something hard that was aimed at my head.

I'm not sure what to do, Val. Nice guys like Cody want more from me than I can give. But I can't abide liars and jerks. That doesn't leave much in between. It's a good thing I'm not trying to have children.

You may find this impossible to believe, but I do get lonely. I long to be held. Not for sex. Just for closeness and comfort. Like what puppies in a heap derive from furry contact. Some visceral sharing of breath and pulse. I imagine being held by you in this way, Val. I envy your MP. And I get angry at you that I could never ask you for this, because you would turn it into something sexual.

Or would you? The truth is, I've never given you the chance. I'm afraid, Val. Not that you would kiss me. But that if I ever did let you hold me, I would fall and fade. My hide would melt and there would be nothing left but raw, frayed nerves. I'd never get my toughness back. I'd have to live not by principles, but through emotions. I couldn't stand it. I admire you for being able to. Doreen was wrong about one thing. I understand weakness. I am the weakest person I know. It makes me ever vigilant.

But now, to sleep. Perchance to dream. If I'm lucky, about our times at Barclay. About a child I long some day to have and to hold— but never shall.

Love and dreams,

Ashmont

December 1980

Dearest Ashmont,

She cheated on me, but not with God. It was Sister Mary Francis. You were right. I should have seen it coming.

One afternoon a few weeks ago, MP and I had been making out, and it finally dawned on me that her skills in this arena predated her relationship with me. I felt jealous wondering if the sexual preserves MP reserved for God had been *poached upon* by someone else. Being me, I had to ask. She admitted that she had kissed Sister Mary Francis. But she had reserved for God exactly the same intimacies that she had with me.

I felt a hot stab of jealousy in my chest. As casually as I could, I asked, "So where is this Mary Francis now?"

"Oh, MF is in El Salvador building a health center." I relaxed. Out of Massachusetts was good. Out of North America was better.

I felt confident enough to inquire about MF. "Is she a nurse?"

"Hah!" MP brayed. "I pity her patients if she were. She'd have a miserable bedside manner."

Her critical words should have reassured me, but the affection in her tone alarmed me.

"What's wrong with her? Is she rude? Obnoxious?" I hoped.

"Oh no, gruff and bossy is more like it. She has no medical training. But she's a wonderful organizer. She's a real bulldog, my MF—tenacious and strong-willed. When Jesus said 'blessed are the meek,' he didn't have Mary Francis in mind. Although when the meek inherit the earth and find it clean and well organized, they'll have the likes of MF to thank for it."

"Well, uh," I muttered, feeling sour at hearing Mary Francis—whom I now considered my archrival—praised, "so why are you here and she's in Central America?"

"Oh Val, you understand that I *must* go where my order assigns me?" She looked in my eyes with tender concern. I knew she was asking me if I understood that she would leave St. Mary's some day. Frolicking with me was all well and good, but secondary to her vocation. I knew that; I just didn't like to think about it.

"Sure. But can't you make *requests* or something?"

"Yes, but MF and I decided we needed time apart."

"You did?" My heart leaped.

MP sighed. "We did. You see, Mary Francis believes social action is the primary path to Christ. I believe in prayer and meditation. MF aspires to make the world a place worthy for Christ to walk. I aspire to prepare myself through prayer to become a worthy vessel for Christ to inhabit."

"*That* must have led to many a lover's quarrel." I couldn't help letting a gram of sarcasm ooze into my tone, although it escaped Mary Patrick's notice. To my amazement, she blushed.

"That's very perceptive of you, Val. Mary Francis says my reserving *some* intimacies for God is mystical mumbo jumbo. She believes doing good is more sacred than having 'esoteric thoughts'—which is how she refers to contemplative prayer. She claimed I was being stingy and cowardly by refusing to celebrate God's earthly gifts *fully*."

I paused, puzzled, then had to ask, "You mean by not 'going all the way'?"

"Precisely," she blushed again. "I told Mary Francis she was not respecting the mystical tradition of Hildegard of Bingen, Julian of Norwich, and of course, Teresa of Avila, whose sacred encounters with God had inspired me to become a nun in the first place. I reminded her that it was while St. Catherine was praying for a clean heart that God appeared and took her heart out—"

"My god," I interrupted, "how horrible—"

"No, no, Val. He put it back. Rather, he replaced it with his own, which beat more strongly than hers. After that, she was able to love others not just with her small human heart, but with the heart of Christ himself. So you see the power and importance of prayer."

"Of course," I said, trying to sound supportive. "And what did Mary Francis say?" I asked.

"She reminded me that it was also during prayer that Jesus told St. Teresa to abandon contemplation. She must learn how to see her Beloved—meaning himself, of course—in everyone. It is only through our neighbors, he said, that our true virtues are born. More important, Mary Francis said, this was the twentieth century, not the eleventh, twelfth, or sixteenth, and that I was nothing but a . . . a . . ."

"A what?" I was exploding with curiosity.

"Scaredy cat!" She laughed. Which gave me permission to laugh, too.

"Well," I said, "she needn't have used *invective*. Besides, you know what she is?"

"What?"

"She's a great big *meanie!*"

But instead of snickering with me, as I'd hoped, MP looked reflective. For the moment, she wasn't with me. She was with Mary Francis.

"Not really," she said dreamily. "She's really kind and sweet. She forces me to reflect upon my actions, which makes her dear to me." At that point, I changed the subject. I'd learned more than enough about the saintly, libidinous MF. For days after that, I pictured MF's face on guest room floors before I attacked them with my mop, and on the doormat as I scraped my boots. She sprouted deformities and grew more hideous every day. But she wouldn't go away.

Then one afternoon, we were lying naked in my bed, hugging and kissing—rather, I was lying naked and MP still wore her underwear. MP was braced on her palms over me. Somehow, I turned and knocked MP off balance so that she fell and rubbed her crotch along my thigh. She caught her breath and looked at me with astonishment—and either pleasure or horror. She slid slowly down my leg and closed her eyes tightly. "Oh, Val," she sighed, but whether it was a sigh of remorse or revelation, I couldn't tell.

"My God, Mary Patrick, I'm sorry. It was an accident!" I'd never before apologized to a woman for eliciting an orgasm. But as I've said, there is no one else like Mary Patrick.

"No, shush. I'm fine. It had to happen sooner or later," she said with such pathos I felt like crying, as if I'd shot a deer. She added sweetly, "I'm glad it happened with you."

"You are?"

"I am. But I'm going home now."

She left, and I didn't see her for a week. I was filled with dread. I expected to be struck dead by lightning or a sudden plague. Finally, MP called to say she was going to Boston for a few days and would call when she returned. Five days later she called again and invited me to visit her at St. Mary's. "There's someone I want you to meet," she said cheerily. I was sure I knew *who.*

As I drove up to St. Mary's and saw two women waving at me, I thought I had been wrong, that it wasn't Mary Francis. The woman standing next to Mary Patrick was about thirty, not 105. She was clear-skinned and rosy-cheeked, not pockmarked and dour. She was about 5'5" tall, not 6' or 7'. She had brown Prince Valiant hair, and cheerful, intelligent eyes. In spite of her sensible shoes, denim skirt, and crewneck sweater with the obligatory footlong crucifix dangling from her neck, Sister Mary Francis radiated authority, good cheer, and common sense. She looked like someone who could build a health center with one hand while she subdued a class of unruly children with the other. Although she didn't wear a habit, her manner reminded me so powerfully of the nuns at Sacred Heart that I was immediately intimidated. I cowered inwardly as I left the van and walked up to them, my hand extended.

"Sister Mary Francis, I presume," I said.

"Precisely," she said, and smiled at me so warmly, I couldn't hate her. I looked at Mary Patrick, and saw how happy she was.

I knew that we were over.

MF had succeeded where I had failed: she had vanquished God. And while I wanted to yell and scream and protest, I also knew that I loved Mary Patrick, *no matter what.* I would do nothing—*nothing*—to make this difficult.

So although it crushed my lungs and heart to do so, I asked breezily, "So when are you leaving? Where are you going? What great works will you perform?"

"Oh, Val, the order is sending us to Africa. We're going to build a school. It's so exciting."

I didn't actually hear most of what they said. I was too busy trying to keep breathing. I looked interested and cheerful. I nodded appropriately. I let Mary Patrick kiss me good-bye on the lips while MF looked on with a smile. She thanked me and said how much she'd miss me while I stared at my sneakers. I couldn't look at her without breaking down.

"Val," she said intensely, pulling my chin up so I had to look her in the eyes. A sob escaped me as I did so.

"You must remember how well loved you are, not only by me, but by God. No matter where I am, I will think of you. You will be with me, and I with you. Do you remember what St. Teresa replied when her Beloved appeared in prayer one day and asked her who she was?"

I remembered, and nodded.

"She said, 'I am Teresa of Jesus,' and when she asked him who he was, he replied, 'I am Jesus—of Teresa.'"

She paused a moment, then said directly to my soul, "I am Mary Patrick—of Val. Who are you?"

"I am Val—of Mary Patrick," I said, although my throat was so constricted it hurt to talk.

She grabbed my head between both hands and pressed it firmly, drawing it down to kiss the top of my forehead. It was a ritual gesture, and if I knew Mary Patrick, she was probably blowing the breath of Jesus into my sorry, sorrowful skull. I felt oddly light where her lips touched, and heavy and despondent everywhere else. She walked away, and didn't look back.

I stood for a few minutes after she and Mary Francis disappeared, not wanting to leave the spot where I had my last sight of her. Then I drove away. Feeling that although I was growing larger and stronger through the discipline of loving someone *no matter what,* that my *life* had been diminished by what Mary Patrick was taking away.

She was taking away a depth of faith and hope I'm not capable of generating from within. Before I met MP, I didn't care whether God loved me. But while I was with her, I felt as though Mary Patrick's light and warmth connected me with something transcendent— something larger and deeper than ordinary human love. Something healing and mysterious. Something enchanting and divine.

One morning a few weeks ago, Mary Patrick invited me to a sunrise prayer service. I expected it to be at St. Mary's, with other nuns and a priest and scripture and incense. But MP showed up on her bicycle and we rode to the outer Cape to watch the sunrise from the beach.

MP led us close to the water, where we sat back on our heels. The first hint of orange was brightening the otherwise gray-blue sky. As the orange smudge brightened, becoming streaks of yellow light, MP sighed, closed her eyes, and murmured, "The Holy Spirit welcomes us to another day. Can you feel it, Val?"

"No," I answered truthfully.

"Oh," she scoffed affectionately, "you're not accustomed to *letting* yourself. But it's so palpable. I can sense it. Like a stream." And she spread her arms wide, as if embracing the sunrays.

She lifted herself on her knees. "Ah, there now, I can feel it even more. Can you feel it yet, Val?"

"Yes," I said.

She squinted in my direction before closing her eyes again. "No lies, now. You're just saying that to please me. You don't have to *try* to feel God, Val. It's your natural state to be at one with God. Just allow the holy spirit to enter."

Then she proclaimed in an exultant voice:

> Open your mind to the light of eternity!
> Open your soul to the glory of nature!
> Open your heart to the love of the divine!
> Transform yourself body and soul into the pulse
>   of God!

"Don't try, Val. Remember, just allow!" She proclaimed exultantly.

I spread my arms wide like Mary Patrick. I closed my eyes and felt the warmth of the glowing sun. I wanted to allow God to enter my heart, because I wanted to be in the same place, the same mind as Mary Patrick. Okay, I addressed God, "Enter." I inhaled deeply, listening to my own breath, and to the waves.

And then I felt something. I swear I truly did. I felt something descend like a bird. Not a real bird, of course, but a brush of warm air that seemed to *enter* my head. I felt immensely pleased with myself. I didn't care if it was suggestibility or reality. In the happy plane I was inhabiting with Mary Patrick, there was no distinction.

"Mary Patrick," I announced proudly, "I feel it. I really do. Something came into my head."

"Then relax and let it spread, Val. Let's sit quietly now and pray."

So we did. I settled back on my heels, and the holy spirit traced her diaphanous tributaries down my spine, leaving lightness and peace in her wake. Blessing me and fortifying me for the day. When we left, I hugged Mary Patrick and thanked her. In her presence I felt something sacred. But she was my conduit to divinity. I could never conjure the holy spirit up on my own.

Now that she is gone, I am left with the *desire* to feel God's love— for that is what Mary Patrick calls it—but absolutely clueless as to how to feel, find, fire, or free it. The world is just the world. I am just me.

My loneliness is staggering.

I know it's stupid, but I feel resentful. Just as I was starting to feel that God and I were mending fences—that she or the molecule or what have you—was making up for past shoddy work with my parents by giving me Mary Patrick, then—wham!—God took her away. And gave her to someone more organized, more virtuous, more saintly, an all around better human being than *I*. It's as if God set the whole encounter up just to remind me how inadequate and undeserving I am.

I know this is nonsense. But it is a lingering and painful nonsense.

The only thing that has cheered me up in the last few weeks has been the unexpected, long-awaited sighting of the *head of a great mind*. No one could be more surprised than me to encounter the head in Provincetown rather than Nepal or Santa Fe. I call her the Boat Builder—BB for short. That's what she does for a living. She has a big warehouse in the East End where she builds sailboats. She rents out workshop space and tools, and that is how I met her.

I decided that *craft,* not art, is my true calling, so I'm going to paint furniture. You remember this fate was prophesied for me once. With MP gone, I need something to fill my time. So I rented workshop space and tools at BB's hangar.

I recognized BB as a *head* the first time I saw her. It's an ordinary head in most ways. BB's about my size, with brown, shaggy hair. Her eyes are gray, like mine, but lighter, with a clear gaze. They don't carry doubt or pain. But they don't carry judgment of those who do. She isn't overly this or overly that. She seems balanced, and at ease. Her attention is always focused on what she's doing, and nothing else.

She has a warmth that's different from Mary Patrick's. MP's warmth radiates indiscriminately outward from her heart, like sunlight. It relaxes you and makes you cheerful. BB's warmth is more like two focused beacons shining outward from her eyes. She has to be looking right at you before you can feel it. And then it's as if she is looking *through* you, from some place much farther back inside her head than her eyes, to some level of your being that is four or five feet behind you. It's tantalizing but disorienting—like being struck by a current of silent motionless wind.

Do you remember the Tibetan monks that came to Barclay to chant mantras and play their eight-foot trumpets? Their dignified, cheerful serenity reminds me of BB. Her movements are spare and graceful. She doesn't talk much, and I've learned not to pepper her with questions. She lets me watch her work, which I find deeply soothing. While MP used to *talk* to God, BB *operates* God—bringing spirit and matter together as hand and eye transform planks, nails, and glue into the beautifully curving surface of a sailboat. I tried to tell her this one day. I burbled and blathered. BB nodded silently while she continued working. But I was sure she understood.

Sometimes, I hear her proclaim brief, koanlike nuggets of wisdom. One day, she said, "When you row, you can't see what's in front of you. You just keep moving your arms." *That's right,* I thought. *That's what I need to do. Remain steady. Keep pushing forward without having to define where my life is taking me.*

But when I asked BB to repeat herself, she said, "When you're through with that, throw a tarp over it. It's going to rain."

I frequently hear her say profound things that she claims she never said. Am I making them up? Does she pretend she said something else? Is something else—the molecule, perhaps—speaking through her? Or do I have brain fever? Oh, all right, Ashmont, I know *you'll* say that I hear what I want to hear. Regardless of the source, what she says, whether about rowing or tarps, is helpful. I intend to continue making pilgrimages to her hangar. It's as close to church or temple as I'll ever come.

I know very little about BB. Don't know her name. Where she comes from. How she became a boatbuilder. How long she's been here. How long she plans to stay. She is a mystery to me. And I plan to keep her that way. The more you learn about a person, the more you distort them. I plan to keep BB *pure.*

Ashmont, won't you *please* reconsider coming to Provincetown for Christmas? You never come here to visit. And I've never complained. I always visit you in the Wasteland. It's been so long since you've come East. Please consider it, Ashmont. It would quicken my heart to see you.

In infinite love and deep loneliness,

Your friend Val

1983

December 1983

Precious Ashmont,

The bus from Boston rolled into Provincetown at 1 a.m. It is now 1:57 a.m. on December 26th, and I can't rest until I have done something to heal the rift that threatens our friendship. It is the first time in history that I have been afraid we will lose one another. For Val and Ashmont to split is inconceivable—like the oceans drying up, the sun reversing its tracks, or snow forgetting to fall in winter in New England. Today, for a brief time, the inconceivable appeared inevitable.

I will fill in my half of our conflict by writing another chapter of *The Story of an Epic Friendship*—because it suggests the events of yesterday were merely *another chapter,* not an *ending.*

∽

Chapter X?

Val and Ashmont Wrestle, After All

You might think this story begins with you driving through Coolidge Corner yesterday from the Howard Johnson Motor Inn to your mother's house in Chestnut Hill for Christmas dinner. By virtue of one of the world's great coincidences, you were snagged by the red light at Harvard Street. If you hadn't been, you would have driven right past me as I stood waiting for the next trolley car to Boston. Lucky for me, I was hard to miss.

I wore a sleeveless low-cut black sheath with black high heels and stockings. I was dragging a fur coat on the ground behind me as though it were fresh road kill. Oh, yes, and I was shivering and slowly turning blue in the 20-degree chill. You rolled your window down, shouted, "Hey you, get into this car *now!*" and saved me from hypothermia.

If you believed this story began there, you might think that if you'd driven faster to beat the light, or if I'd been dressed like an ordinary Bostonian in an identity-obscuring parka and boots, then our fight wouldn't have happened. It isn't true. It would only have been postponed.

The whole story begins a year ago. My half, anyway. I still don't know *all* of yours.

My half begins with a year of profound unhappiness. That's not an excuse, just a relevant fact. After Mary Patrick left three years ago, I lived on the fumes of her legacy of faith and hope for a couple of years. I tried to be good, optimistic, and cheerful. When I became discouraged about my life, I reminded myself that Mary Patrick believed that *God loved me*—whether I was an artist or a glorified maid.

But during the past year, the memory of Mary Patrick faded. *Trying* to be good didn't *make* me good. Believing that God loved me didn't help if God's opinion didn't count—and without Mary Patrick to champion her cause, God's clout diminished dramatically. I had no true profession. I had no one who loved me the way I wanted to be loved. I still believed that Love Rules, but I have proven unworthy of love. I felt useless and weary of myself.

The trompe l'oeil furniture I was painting sold well to tourists. Tables that looked like toaster ovens. Bookcases that looked like refrigerators. I knew it was kitsch. But it still killed me to hear the contempt in the Boat Builder's voice when she described my work as devolved. A pathetic excuse for real craftsmanship. Not only had I failed as an artist, I had failed at craft, as well. Oh, she never said those things in words. It's not as if I was worth talking to. But I could see it in her gaze. Besides, even if she didn't think it, I did.

Droplet by heavy droplet, despair seeped through every vein. The immense disappointment I felt with myself became a vast, voiceless fury. It polluted even previously sacred, safe havens. Desmond and Raymond, for example. These wonderful, generous men—who have given me all the home and family I have in the world—began to look like enemies. I blamed Desmond for my failure. If he had never invited me to spend the summer after college working at the inn, I might have remained in the city and gone to graduate school as planned. If he hadn't taught me how to run an inn and promoted me to manager, I would have been forced to find a *real* profession. I've been spiteful to both of them for a year, snarling at their goodwill, spurning their compassion. I don't know why they didn't fire me—*I* would have.

Worst, I watched in helplessness while anger began to infect my feelings toward you, Ashmont. I never before allowed myself to mind that I call you twice as often as you call me. That you *never* write. You continue to be secretive about your past and your family—even though you've known me for fifteen years. You have never visited me on the Cape, even when I've begged you. I have always told myself this unevenness was the price I paid for having you as a friend. You were worth it.

You *are* worth it. If it weren't for the other thing that gnawed at me, I would have swallowed my pride and concentrated on loving you more than my own ego. But I couldn't stand knowing that for fifteen years, I have been spilling out my guts to you in person, on the phone, and in writing. I have confided every stupid affair, every doubt and insecurity, every crisis of faith. And you have been there for me every time. You have offered love when I didn't deserve it, advice I would never have thought of, and faith and respect that I didn't earn. I ought to thank you for such devotion. And I do.

So what's the problem? The problem is that you *never, never, never* ask for anything in return. How can I continue this way? When I feel I have given the world nothing, have, in fact, nothing to give, how can I live knowing that even the best friend I have ever had, the one person I adore who knows me better than anyone, has so little regard for me that she has never asked for and has never taken one single itty-bitty solitary, miserable thing from me. I must be utterly useless. It makes me hate myself. And it has made me furious with you.

I felt so bad about being angry with you, so fearful of confessing my feelings to you, that I brooded and seethed in silence. I stopped writing. Stopped calling and waited until you called me. And when you said two months ago that you were coming to Boston to see your mother and brother for Christmas—for the first time since you moved away after college—and asked if we could see each other, I said I had plans.

I had a date.

You were supposed to feel punished. You were supposed to feel jealous. You were supposed to beg. You were supposed to ask me to break my date.

But you didn't. You said, and I quote: "Okay."

To whine and plead is not your way, and I know this. But it infuriated me, anyway. So, of course, I found a date. It wasn't hard, given that I'd been filling my empty hours dating women as eager for physical comfort and emotional detachment as I was. Disposable dates. Useful for a weekend. It worked not too badly, and kept me sane. The only problem was that I'll only date women who don't drink, and I usually found—or was found by—women at bars. I didn't say it was a smart or a healthy way to find dates, just the one I chose.

That's how I found Madeline, the woman whose apartment I was fleeing when you picked me up yesterday afternoon. It was Madeline's fur coat I was dragging. I'd filled several lost weekends with Madeline. I knew Madeline might be a problem. She claimed to be a "recovered alcoholic." She's been in AA for six years. But her last slip was only three months ago, just a week before I met her. I almost broke our first date when I found out, but she promised me she would never drink while we were dating. I wanted to believe her, and I didn't think I'd see her more than once or twice.

Madeline, however, was enormously fun. She is sweet, sexy, and impulsive—and only twenty-six. Her grandmother owns a fancy condominium in Brookline, which Madeline stays in off and on throughout the winter when her grandmother retreats to Florida. Madeline and I got in the habit of taking the bus up to Boston on weekends. She likes to dress up, go to fancy straight clubs, and hold hands and kiss while people stare. She craves the attention. I'm so tired of dating women who are paranoid about any public display of affection, that being with Madeline made me giddy. I knew our behavior was dangerous—it would have been more so in less expensive places—but danger was the lure.

We were supposed to go to L'Estate for dinner on Christmas day. We bought matching sheaths, hers in red, mine in black. She was going to wear the sable coat her grandmother had left behind. We were going to turn the restaurant on its ear with an extravagant display of Sapphic affection.

But then, while we were preening in front of the mirror, I asked Madeline if I could try on the coat. She seemed reluctant. I sniffed mischief. So I persisted. "What's the matter?" I goaded her, "Something hidden in the pockets you don't want me to see?"

"No," she said, laughing, emptying the pockets inside out. "Just some harmless breath mints, see?"

Madeline miscalculated. I am the daughter of rabid alcoholics. Breath mints are not harmless. They are not evidence of benign intent, but its opposite.

I was determined to unearth the cause of Madeline's nervous laughter. "Come on, let me try it. I'll look ravishing."

I aggressively grabbed for the coat, but Madeline held on tenaciously.

"Clink." We both heard. Faint but undeniable, coming from the coat's hem. "Clink. Clink."

"How many of them are there?" I asked. I tore the coat from her hands and pulled up the lining along the coat's back.

Five miniature bottles of Chivas fell to the floor.

"Well, you don't slip cheaply; I've got to give you that," I said, as I picked them up and put them in the coat's pocket.

"But," I added, "I'm not about to spend Christmas with you. You're a drunk, Madeline. I've had too many Christmases spoiled by drunks. I won't submit myself to another. Good-bye."

"No!" Madeline pleaded, "Please." And she flung her body across mine, trying to kiss me. But my mouth was stone.

"For God's sake, give me another chance!" she begged. "I haven't had a drink yet. I won't! Why do you have to be so . . . so fucking rigid?"

"Because I am," I said, moving toward my coat.

"Dammit," she exploded, angry now rather than contrite, "you can't go. I only stayed in Boston for Christmas so I could be with *you*. You can't leave me alone now or I really will have a drink."

"You should have thought of that sooner," I said, picking up my coat.

Then Madeline yanked my coat away, ran to the bathroom and stuffed it down the laundry chute.

"Now you have to stay!" she yelled triumphantly.

"Good-bye, Madeline," I said, opening the door. I didn't care how cold it was, I had to leave.

"Stop," she said. "Take this." I turned, and saw Madeline crying as she held out the fur coat for me to take.

"I'll be okay."

"No, please," she said plaintively. "Take it and the liquor, or I'll drink them all. You know I will."

The coat smelled vaguely of Scotch. It nauseated me. But I took it and closed the door. I couldn't bear to put it on. So I dragged it on the ground behind me as I marched to the subway stop, still so angry I was barely aware of the cold. I planned to take the bus home, and to carry Madeline's coat with me. I may be rigid. I may be cruel enough to leave Madeline alone on Christmas day. But I am not vindictive. I would not leave that coat and its contraband within twenty-five miles of Madeline's apartment. She would be scouring the trash barrels in her neighborhood for those liquor bottles later today, but she won't find anything. Madeline will be sober for one more day. She has me to thank and curse for that.

I waited for the trolley, sure that I would freeze to death, when I heard a car frenziedly honking. I looked up, and there you were, yelling, like a noisy guardian angel. Before I remembered how angry I was, I was overjoyed. As I stumbled toward your car in my unfamiliar high heels, I succumbed to a punishingly wistful thought. I imagined not Madeline but you sitting across from me at a candlelit table in L'Estate—wearing a red sheath dress, lightly running your nylon clad calf against mine. The pain of this fantasy nearly imploded my lungs—or was it the icy air? By the time I reached your car, I could barely breathe.

Wordlessly and efficiently, you shrugged off your camel hair overcoat and draped it over my shoulders. You drove me the few blocks back to your motel, guided me to your room, and covered me with blankets. While I thawed, I heard you mumbling on the phone.

"Mother, *caritas*," you said, "It's Christmas." And I knew you were persuading her to invite me to Christmas dinner.

Your face appeared over the horizon of the blanket. You smiled when you saw my eyes open, and asked me tenderly, "Are you all right?"

I was so happy to be the object of your solicitous attention that I couldn't bear to be angry. "I'm fine," I mumbled, my mouth still thawing.

"You're a little overdressed for Christmas dinner at the Ashmonts," you said, "But if you don't mind a more modest and boring gathering than whatever you originally intended—" you glanced at my high heels on the floor by the bed—"you're invited to dinner at my mother's house."

"But I've nothing to wear," I protested.

"Oh, you do now," you said, tossing me a red wool blazer with a blue and gold crest on the breast pocket to put on over my dress.

"It's an unusual look, isn't it," I said, looking in the mirror, the bottom hem of the jacket stopping just an inch or two above the hem of my dress.

"I look like a cross between a schoolgirl and a hooker, kind of a preppy slut." We both laughed. And I decided to be good for Christmas. To have a truce with myself about my anger at you. To simply enjoy what in the past would have been a dream come true—Christmas with my Ashmont.

As we drove to your mother's house, you didn't ask me any questions about the bizarre circumstances of our chance encounter. I knew you were being discreet, allowing me to tell you as much or as little as I wanted. I was dying to ask you why you were staying at a motel instead of at your mother's house, but I was preoccupied with annoyance at your merciless discretion. I wanted you to ask me questions. I wanted you to be nosy, intrusive. I wanted you to *need* to know, to *demand* to know, to be *dying* to find out what on earth I'd been up to.

So by the time we pulled up the circular drive to the front door of your mother's house—where I had never been invited before—I was thoroughly incensed. When I saw the large, immaculately kept colonial house where you grew up, I became even angrier as I realized that you, my friend Ashmont, grew up on Jefferson Avenue. You never told me. Perhaps you thought it irrelevant. Perhaps you thought I'd mind. You were right. I did.

The perfect fir wreath with a large red bow on the white wooden door with a brass knocker. The tasteful strings of small white lights glittering on the boxwood. The glow of amber light shining through the frosted glass of the living room bay window. The image had been stripped from my fantasy life and pasted onto *your* history. Your reality. *Ashmont is rich,* I thought. And I never knew. The rich part made me envious. But the never knew part made me resentful.

Your mother was gracious, in a detached, distracted way. I had only seen her once before, at graduation, but she looked the same frosted blonde picture of manicured, suburban perfection. She was impeccably polite to both of us. That's what was strange. You were both so terribly polite to each other, like an innkeeper and her guests—friendly, good-humored, and careful. I'm an expert on this style. And it isn't the way families usually behave—not after the first half hour.

Your brother, freshly divorced after three years of marriage, was rambling, self-pitying, and to my surprise in this home of fastidious women, disheveled and unshaven. He stared at my ass as I came in the door. I avoided his feeble efforts to converse. I recognized the symptoms of desperate loneliness and a crushing need to bend someone's ear. If I weren't careful, I realized, your brother would ask me for a date before the evening was over. But the angrier I got at you, the more I found myself stupidly laughing at his jokes. I touched his arm when I spoke to him. Just before dinner, I yawned and said, "My goodness, it's so warm in here, I'm getting sleepy," and I removed your blazer. After that, Dennis stared at my breasts, which, I'm ashamed to admit, gave me a truly, deeply stupid sense of power.

I was trapped. I knew I was being a moron. I kept telling myself, "This is idiotic. Not only is it rude, but you're a lesbian, for God's sake." But I couldn't stop flirting with your pitiful brother. And I couldn't meet your gaze, although I knew you wanted me to. I could sense your growing anger. And it pleased me. It energized me to further boldness, further idiocy.

"You know, Mrs. Ashmont," I said at one point, "I know so little about Emily's childhood. What kind of little girl *was* she? What kind of mischief did she get into?"

Dennis giggled nervously. Your mother looked profoundly uncomfortable, and paused just long enough for you to interrupt, "I'm sure there is nothing Mother could say about my childhood that would satisfy your hunger for scandal, Val." And you guided the conversation onto safer, duller ground.

I could tell that you were furious with me. In part I felt satisfied at provoking you. In part, I felt shocked at myself. I lost interest in Dennis, and made several pointed references to girlfriends and my favorite women's bars in Boston. Mercifully, he took the hint, and the evening ended with polite thanks and relief that it was over.

We drove in hostile silence back to your motel. I refused to start what I knew would be a painful conversation, and you were clearly waiting until we were safely ensconced in your room. Once we were, the battle began.

"What on earth," you said as you slammed the door, "were you doing flirting with my poor, pathetic brother? Whatever you were trying to say to me, just say it. You know I cannot abide indirection and lies!"

I stared defiantly back at you. Truth be told, I enjoyed the power of angering you. But like a child who's provoked her parents' wrath to get attention, I was afraid of the consequences.

"For the hundred millionth time," you exploded, "I can't help it that I'm not a lesbian! I love you in every other way, but I can't love you that way! It hurts me that you cannot or choose not to accept that!"

"Is *that* what you think this is about?" I mustered as much indignation as I could.

You stared at me. "Can you honestly say it wasn't?"

I remembered my wistful fantasy of you rubbing your calf across mine under the table at L'Estate. And I felt an ache radiate throughout my body. Here it was again, fresh as ever, that old yearning to touch you—that eternally deferred desire—that I remembered so strongly from our days at Barclay. The desire, and the pain of its hopelessness, were like a smashed and amputated limb, whose phantom pain exactly duplicates the past trauma. My thwarted desire for you was pain enough by itself, but it had become emblematic of the larger thwarted desire that I felt my whole life had become.

I looked at you, in love and misery, and I understood suddenly that I had been waiting—was still waiting—for you to change so that I could, too. I held my love for you as the greatest achievement of my life, my only claim to true distinction. And at some level, I still believed that sex with you would be my equivalent to the Coming of Christ—an event that would alter history, redeem my fate, clear away self-doubt and sin, and pave the way for grace and joy. The brush with transcendence that Mary Patrick had teased me with and taken away, *you* had the power to restore. And in my child's mind—for it is very childlike of me, isn't it Ashmont—I couldn't fathom how, with so much at stake, you could withhold yourself from me. I seethed in anger at you. But I wasn't ready to admit that. Not yet. So, I lied.

"Well, maybe it's a little bit about that, but that's not the major part," I insisted.

"Then what's the major part?" you demanded.

I told you how useless I felt. How hurt and angry I was that you never *asked* for anything. How tired I was of taking and never feeling like I had anything to give back. How *endangered* our friendship was because of what you refused to give. My words hurt you. Like a punching bag reeling back and forth under heavy blows, you flinched, cleared your face of hurt, and flinched again. I liked it that I could hurt you. I kept up my verbal onslaught until I noticed you were breathing heavy, deep sighs. You sank down on the side of the bed. I feared your hurt would soon turn to anger, so I shut up. But instead of looking angry, you looked exhausted.

"Oh, for God's sake, Val," you finally burst out, "of course I need you. For someone with an active imagination, I'm astonished that you never use it with me. It's true that I'm not good at asking for things, but that doesn't mean I don't want them. The truth is, I need you far more than you need me."

I loved hearing you say that. But I didn't believe you.

"But you never *show* me!" I protested. "You never say you need anything. You never ask for anything. You never say how I'm helping you. I can't guess. That's not fair. That's not like you, Ashmont, to be unfair."

"You're right," you said tiredly, "It's not fair, but it may be very like me, Val. Perhaps you don't know me as well as you think you do."

"And whose fault is that!" I shouted. This was my point. This was the hurt still stinging from today. "You never tell me anything! And you wouldn't let me find out anything from your mother, either."

This reignited your anger.

"Don't you ever do that again." You stood up and put your face very close to mine. "If you have something you want to know, ask me."

"All right," I said, standing up across from you with my hands on my hips. We must have looked like two gunslingers, ready to draw.

"Why do you hate your mother?"

"I don't hate my mother."

"You do, too. No one who loves their parents is as polite as you and your mother."

"I don't—"

"Ashmont, the truth," I prodded. "You have to try."

"Oh, I can't say," you said, looking as close to flustered as I've ever seen you. "Ask me something else."

"All right, there's Dennis. Why do I never hear anything about him. Why aren't you close?"

"Val, this isn't working." You pulled back.

But I wouldn't stop. "Then, there's your father. I always thought he was *dead.* For God's sake, you knew I thought he was dead, and in the fifteen years we've known each other, you've never corrected that impression. Then today, your mother casually remarks, thinking it would interest me, a fellow innkeeper, that your father, her ex-husband, runs an inn in Carmel. He's not a *ghost,* is he?"

By now, I was yelling. I'd pictured myself yelling at you for months. But it didn't feel good. It felt horrible. Especially as I saw you cover your ears with your hands.

"Stop!" You pleaded. "If you want to give me something, give me patience. I'm asking you, Val. Wait for me. I'll get there. I'll tell you everything you want to know some day. Not now. I can't." And you burst into tears.

I hated to see you sobbing. I was appalled at myself. And a little appalled at you. My bitter complaints about your self-sufficiency aside, it scared me to have smashed open a crack in your foundation. I relied upon your strength and calm. The enormity of the change I was initiating in our friendship frightened me. But it felt necessary.

It felt like progress.

Suddenly, I was exhausted. My anger drained away. I needed its brutal resolve to build up the courage to confront you, and its heat to melt through the fortress of your distance. Mission accomplished, I needed it no more, and it drifted off to infect some other friendship in need of its blunt force. In anger's departing wake, tenderness returned.

"I love you," I said, with all the passion I could bear to express without triggering tears of my own. "I'll never abandon you."

I sat down tentatively beside you, unsure if my touch would be welcome. I reached out my hand and—to my astonishment—you clutched it. Then you reached out for me, and you *hugged* me. I grew very still. As still as I could be. So I could feel every place where your skin touched mine. So I could breathe in and record this moment for eternity.

"All right," I said softly. "It will be all right." Because I could feel you needing me. I could feel *you* drawing strength from me, which I had never felt before. Maybe because, as you had suggested, I'd been blind. Maybe because, as I had argued, you had never done so before. But you were now. And it made me so *happy.* Happier than I have ever been. I knew then I could wait. You were trying. Hard.

I felt so close to you. I wanted to take care of you. I feared you might never allow me to get this close again. I couldn't bear the thought of pulling away from you. So I whispered, "Ashmont, let me stay with you tonight. Let me sleep next to you and hold you. No, no, no, shush—" I said as you started to murmur and squirm; I held you tight and talked over you—"no sex. Don't worry. Just let me hold you. Please. Let me do that for you. Just once."

I knew you were tempted when you didn't immediately pull away, but remained with your head nested on my shoulder, your breath tickling my neck. Hope expanded my heart. And then it contracted, as I heard you clear your throat. I sensed you reining your soul back before I felt you physically pull back and sit upright.

It hurt to have you do so, like adhesive tape torn abruptly from a wound. I had waited so many years for you to touch me, I couldn't bear it to be over so soon. I reached out to touch your face, but you caught my hand midair and returned it gently to my lap. You had retracted into your shell.

You wanted me to go, and I could see from the distress on your face that you were having trouble asking me. The only thing I could imagine that would be harder than going would have been to stay and know that you didn't want me there.

"Do you want me to leave?" I asked as calmly as I could.

You met my gaze, your eyes troubled and watery with tears. "Val, I'm so sorry. I can't lie. Yes, I want you to go. But if there's no bus, you can stay."

This was my out. I could have said there was no bus. You would never have thrown me out. You'd never suspect me of lying. I'd have gotten my way, sleeping in the bed next to you. I'd have bought one night of being close to you for the price of a lifetime knowing I had betrayed us both. Even at that steep price, I'd be lying if I didn't say I was tempted. The truth was, I didn't know if there was a bus. I'd been expecting to stay with Madeline.

"There's always a bus," I said, sounding existential and feeling deeply grown-up and weary.

I stood up, put on my shoes, and gathered Madeline's fur coat. You insisted I wear your blazer, and tried to convince me to take a sweater and your camel hair overcoat, as well, both of which I refused. I stepped over the threshold of your room, looking back once at the mussed up covers where we had been sitting in each other's arms just a moment ago, and feeling an odd little burst of envy for the sheets that would caress you overnight.

Leaving your room was the hardest thing I've ever done, Ashmont. All my heart, all my body, my very soul told me I belonged beside you. But you disagreed, and that was all that mattered. My child's mind resisted, but my grown-up will forced my legs to step outside your door.

We drove in silence to the bus station. You said good-bye politely, but you were eager, I could tell, in your sometimes vampiric solitude, to be alone. I decided not to take offense. Before I left your car, I kissed my hand and pressed it to your lips.

I said, "I love you, Ashmont, no matter what."

These were and always will be the *truest* words I ever speak.

There *was* a bus. I returned to the inn, where I have been writing for two hours.

I poured Madeline's liquor bottles out in a trash can at the bus station, and left the fur coat on a bench. My high heels are broken from such unskilled wearing. I'll mail the blazer back to you—it's not my style.

Forgive me for my impatience. I promise to wait. For as long as it takes. You opened your heart tonight. I'll cherish the memory and be grateful for your trust. I shall keep trying to grow up, and to become worthy of even more trust. Meanwhile . . .

All my love,

Val

1985

July 1985

Dear Ashmont,

You will be more astonished at this announcement than any I've made before: I'm involved with a *normal* person. She's not a nun, a drug addict, or a wealthy sexual adventuress. She's a social worker.

Even her name is normal: Nancy.

Nancy. Nancy. Nancy. Such a reassuring name. I'm hard-pressed to call my feelings being in love, since there's no melodrama or angst in our relationship. But I definitely love her. It's just that instead of wanting to get lost inside her, I like being outside her so I can appreciate her for who she is. Did you ever think I would grow so, Ashmont? I didn't.

She's very different from me. She's from San Francisco. She has a useful profession. Her parents are reliable and sober. She likes my furniture—she finds it whimsical rather than devolved. And she's *black*. Well, she's three-quarters black, although Nancy says that in America, if your skin isn't pink, you're black. She says there was so much rape of black slave women by white men in the South, and there has been so much interracial mingling since, that most "black" Americans are as much or more Scottish, English, French, German, or Irish as anything else. But in America, dark skin cancels out ethnicity. Her grandfather created a family scandal when he married her grandmother—a Swede from Minnesota. Nancy's cousins refer to them disparagingly as "the Swedish side of the family."

So Nancy is black, regardless of being Swedish, too. I'd never thought about how few blacks lived or vacationed in Provincetown until two months ago when I looked up from the reception desk, startled to see a black woman. She introduced herself as Nancy, and said she worked for an agency called New Starts for Cape Kids. She was selling raffle tickets to buy toys and books for the abused children she counsels. Aside from her dark brown skin and her head-hugging Afro, Nancy reminded me of Mary Patrick. She exuded warmth and goodwill. She was sensibly dressed in a plaid camp shirt, olive colored dungarees, and brown Oxford shoes. I checked for a telltale crucifix but found none dangling from her neck.

Nancy's much taller than MP, though. At five-feet-ten and one-half, she towers over me. And there's nothing cherubic about her body's construction. She's not thin, but she's not overweight either, although at first I thought she was. But it was only because she looks strong and she lets her body take up as much space as it wants to. Most women try to starve and shrink themselves to be as small as possible. Nancy enjoys feeling big.

Nancy ruthlessly negotiated the sale of raffle tickets. I bought $100 worth when I intended to spend $1.00! I was so impressed by her benevolent manipulation that I invited her to sip lemonade with me on the deck. Then I interrogated her about her work. Later, I realized I'd been asking her things I've always wanted to ask you. Nancy was surprised I cared. She said people usually cringe when they hear the word "abuse." Then they change the subject or walk away.

"Doesn't it make you angry all the time?" I asked. "Knowing these innocent children have been abused?"

"Oh *right*," Nancy said—she can be bristly. "And who am I going to be angry at? The abusers? Getting angry at them is like getting angry at a virus or an earthquake. They're dangerous and do horrible things, but they'll always be with us. Anger is a waste of time."

"Well, do you get angry at God?" I prompted, noting that Nancy did in fact sound angry. Or rather like she was trying very hard *not* to be.

Nancy hooted. "Sweetheart,"—I was flattered by the endearment until I observed that she used it with everyone from Desmond to her landlady—"don't bark up that tree. God is just another name for reality. I'd rather spend my time fixing things than pissing and moaning over how they got broken in the first place.

"That's the great thing about what I do, Val. Most people think social workers are bleeding heart 'do gooders.' But we aren't. We're a tribe of goddamned warriors. We don't just sit around and watch the carnage; we fight back. We're the bravest people I know. Second, of course, to the kids we work for."

Her eyes glistened with passion while she spoke, as if rebutting someone who had been devaluing her battlefield exploits. But when she stopped, she laughed self-consciously and looked away, as if she'd revealed more than she'd planned.

I admired Nancy's pragmatism, and I was eager to quiz her, but I suppressed myself out of fear of appearing nosy. *I know*—ordinarily that wouldn't stop me. But Nancy's opinion had grown important to me already. Her zeal and the way she described herself as working for kids, not for her agency, reminded me of you.

Ashmont, no one has *ever* reminded me of you!

In one of her trademark shifts from bristly to friendly, Nancy began asking about my life. I confided the steep decline in my aspirations over the past decade—from becoming my generation's Georgia O'Keefe to painter of the kitchiest furniture on the Cape.

Nancy refused to let me say anything negative about myself. As you have been opining every time we talk on the phone for the past year, Nancy views innkeeping as a valid contribution to society. She grilled me about what I had learned from each of my so called "failures," and insisted that if I had learned anything, I couldn't call them failures. Nancy's gaze is like truth serum—so attentive it melts resistance. I had to admit that I had learned at least *one* valuable lesson from each of my "failures," and I felt ever so grudgingly better about myself.

At one point, Nancy looked out at the view from the deck, the dazzling blue and sand curves of the inner Cape.

"Anyway, Val," she announced, "you live in paradise. That's better than having a high-powered, ulcer-inducing career."

I tracked her gaze around a view I ignored every day. And I flinched. The beauty and immensity of paradise made me aware of my own smallness. As always, I felt rebuked by nature's grandeur, not expanded.

Nancy studied my face. "But then," she said, "paradise is a state of mind, isn't it? It's getting late. Thanks for your hospitality, Val. I should go." She put her glass down and rose.

I felt ruffled by dismay. I didn't want her to go. Nancy had many of the virtues I'd admired in Mary Patrick. She helped people. She was kind and compassionate. Mary Patrick, however, declared that good works emerged not from her own virtue, but from the breath of God moving through her. Nancy appeared to brave the hazards of earth without divine inspiration. She generated her own goodness and strength, and I wanted to know how she did it.

"Invite her to dinner, you fool," I commanded myself, but the words would not emerge. I was sure Nancy was straight, and I was afraid she'd think I was coming on to her and take offense. I know volumes about coming on to women but little about how to proffer friendship. I felt clumsy, and stupendously shy.

Fortunately, while I was struggling to untie my tongue, Nancy invited *me* out to dinner the following night. I readily accepted. Well, it's easier for a straight woman, I thought. She doesn't have to worry about freaking another woman out with a simple invitation.

We had a wonderful time. Nancy was witty and charming. I remember thinking during dinner that she was the only other straight woman I'd met besides you who was well versed in "fag writers." She walked me home, and as we paused to say good-bye at the foot of the stairway that leads up to the inn, I reached out to shake her hand, thanking her for a terrific evening.

"Actually," she raised her eyebrows and glanced suggestively up toward the inn, "I was hoping you'd invite me up to your room for a while."

"You *were?*" I asked gracelessly, feeling confused.

She looked embarrassed. And I finally understood.

"Was this a *date?*" I asked, sounding astonished, feeling befuddled.

Nancy's eyes looked wounded. But her jaw jut out angrily as she began, "Look, Val. I'm not very subtle. I brought up every gay writer from Audre Lorde to Oscar Wilde over dinner—and you'd read them all. But maybe I misunderstood. Maybe you're just terribly literate. Maybe you aren't even *gay*—" she finished sarcastically. Nancy is usually so empathetic that her sarcasm cuts more deeply for the element of surprise.

She looked away and added, more levelly, "Or perhaps you don't find me attractive. I guess that's a possibility, too."

"Of course I'm gay," I protested. "How could anyone think otherwise? And of course I think you're attractive. It's just that you're . . . you're . . ."

She looked at me icily. "I'm what, Val? Aren't you going to finish your sentence? I hate it when people don't finish their sentences."

I felt like a complete idiot. "Nancy, I'm sorry. I just didn't think. I mean, ordinarily I always know when someone is gay. Ask my cousin Desmond. He'll tell you my radar is 100 percent accurate. But you . . . you're . . . I mean my radar wasn't even turned on. You see, I don't even know any black people, much less a black lesbian. You're the first I've ever known."

"Well, I'm glad to expand your horizons, but you need to get out more."

"Oh, look," I said, "do you think this makes me a racist?" I was afraid I was. I was afraid she thought I was. I was angry at myself for both thoughts. But, oddly and unfairly, I was also angry because if it weren't for *Nancy,* I wouldn't be in this humiliating situation.

I waited tensely for her to pass judgment, but all she said was, "I don't know, Val. I'm not your conscience. What do *you* think?"

"I think that I'm ignorant and idiotic. But I don't think that makes me a racist. And I'm sorry I hurt your feelings."

"Well, then," she said, gazing up the hill toward the inn, "how about it? Now that you *know* this is a date."

"You mean," I said, feeling confused again, "that you're still interested in me? But why? After I've been so . . . so . . ."

"So white?" Nancy grinned wickedly.

"Well, yes." I nodded. "And stupid. Although maybe they're the same."

"Sweetheart," she said laughing, "let me break this to you gently. You're available. Look around you. If I only dated black women, how many dates do you think I'd have this year?"

"Oh," I said, feeling thoroughly put in my place. "I guess I deserved that."

I must have looked as dejected as I felt, because Nancy again shifted seamlessly from bristly to tender. Her soft hand covered mine, and she spoke gently, "Val, lighten up. I'm teasing. I wouldn't really date you just because you're available. . . . You have to be available and *attractive!* Now how about it? Are you going to show me your room?"

She smiled warmly, and I was disarmed by the focused interest of her eyes. Nancy always knows what she wants, and right then, she wanted *me,* even if I couldn't fathom why. I decided that if she could put my ignorance behind us, so could I. Even so, I'm ashamed to admit I paused before inviting her up. I felt vulnerable. How much more racial blindness might I discover? How many other ways might I find to humiliate myself? Probably lots. It would be easy to say no. But Nancy would know why, and then I really would seem like a racist. And a coward.

I couldn't decide which would take more courage—saying yes or no. Finally, I impulsively clutched her hand and dragged her up the stairs. And when she gleefully yelled, "Atta girl," I was buoyed on the wave of her enthusiasm, and decided I had made the right choice. But we never made it to my room. Desmond had set his telescope up on the deck, and he and Nancy—an astronomy buff—talked quasars and supernovas for hours while I feigned wakefulness.

Finally, Nancy woke me up to say good-bye. As she bent over to kiss me, I leaned my head back, closed my eyes and for a microsecond—as her lips moved toward mine—I thought, "I'm about to kiss a black woman." The thought was exciting and strangely scary at the same time, as if kissing a black person connected me intimately with shadowy places in history that I felt curious about but afraid of. I've never thought of myself as a chicken, and I didn't want to start now, so I leaned forward and met her kiss. Which was soft, sweet, and not the least bit scary.

I wondered why I never think, "I'm about to be kissed by an Italian . . . a Jew . . . a Canadian." In fact, the last time I can remember having a similar thought was in eighth grade when I closed my eyes just before Betty Brandon puckered up to kiss me for the first time and I thought, "I'm going to kiss a *girl!*" In subsequent years, as you well know, I've learned to take the gender for granted and focus on the kiss. Perhaps you have to violate a taboo before you can shed it. The thing is, I didn't even know I harbored this taboo until Nancy showed up. It makes me wonder how many other taboos are lurking inside—unexplored and unexpressed.

When Nancy and I made love for the first time—well Ashmont, you knew this was coming, I don't know how to be just friends with a woman—I found myself gripping her hands and pressing our arms together so I could see her brown skin next to my pale skin. Pushing my breasts tightly against hers so I could feel the familiar soft tissue against my own while absorbing the contrasting colors of our flesh. Pressing my fingertips against the soft mat of her densely woven hair, then stroking my own thin, straight strands.

These differences amidst the familiar, expected shapes, textures, and sights of another woman's body aroused me sexually but also distracted me from the trancelike rituals of sex. Gradually, my languid hyper-awareness of every sensual detail faded as we shifted from foreplay to what Nancy calls sexual frenzy.

I shifted from perceiving Nancy as the black woman I was making love to, to perceiving her as simply the living, pulsing being at the other end of my own sensations. Afterward, as we lay together talking, I perceived her clearly as Nancy, this intricate individual I didn't yet know very well.

"Nancy," I whispered, "I need to confess something that may have been racist of me."

"Val, why do you whisper when you talk about race? And why oh why do you have to confess? God save me from Catholic girls . . . please just confide or inform or proclaim. I know I'm black, but that doesn't make me your confessor! I'm not interested! I'm not qualified! I'm Baptist, for God's sake. Or I used to be."

I sulked, feeling chastised.

"Come on. Talk to me, Val!" she commanded.

I turned away.

"You want me to say please, don't you?"

I nodded. Nancy understands what I want before I do.

"Please," she said once, matter-of-factly, without any blandishments. But she'd said it.

"Okay," I turned back to face her, and then said hurriedly so I wouldn't back out, "I thought about race the whole time we were making love. I couldn't stop, and I was turned on by it. There, I'm sorry. If you're disgusted with me and you want to go, I'll understand, but I had to tell you."

I braced myself, expecting a firestorm.

Nancy laughed heartily. "Sweetheart, did you think I wasn't aware of *your* race? Did you think I wasn't aware that you were aware of *mine?* Val, Val, Val . . ." She shook her head, as if to say my naiveté was so vast, words could not contain it.

"You really do need to get out more, Val. But you are the most earnest person I've ever met. I like that. Tell me—do not confess—what did you think about race?"

"Uh . . ." I floundered, not knowing how to put my perceptions into words. "Well, I liked the way we looked together, me so pale and you so dark. And I kept noticing how your body was different from mine. Like how the skin on the back of your hands is dark brown but your palms are pink, you know . . ." I trailed off, feeling idiotic.

"Oh, yeah," Nancy said dryly, "my palms are Swedish."

It took me a minute to fathom that she was teasing me. Then I laughed and began to relax. I told Nancy everything. I even confessed that at one point, I'd been curled like a ball inside her lanky frame and thought for a moment that from the ceiling, we must look like a Hostess cupcake. Fortunately, Nancy laughed. She confessed—I mean, she informed me—that she's always amazed at how incredibly pale naked white women are—she said she's afraid we'll fade into the sheets overnight and she won't be able to find us in the morning.

The second time we made love, I noticed other details about her body—the small mole she has below her left ear, the scar along her hip where she had surgery, and a tiny little cleft in the middle of her chin. But I didn't need to confess each and every one of these observations to Nancy. Or even to inform her.

As we spend more time together, I become more aware of how different we are in other ways. Nancy, for example, adores the ocean. We were hanging sheets outside on the clothesline behind the inn one day when Nancy said her favorite thing about Provincetown was that you could see sunrise from the eastern beaches, and sunset from the western ones. Then she asked if I wanted to accompany her on a whale watch the next morning.

"Ugh," I shivered, "no way. The ocean gives me the creeps."

"You're kidding," Nancy said, shocked. "Why live next to the ocean if you hate it? Why not Ohio or Iowa?"

"I live here," I said emphatically, feeling criticized, "because it's home!"

A breeze ruffled the sheet I was hanging, and I reached over to smooth it down. "I'll help you," Nancy said, and pressed the wrinkles out on her side.

"I didn't mean to offend you, Val. It's just that I love the ocean. I get the same thing from it that I do from the stars. There's no pettiness there. No race. No Swedes, Danes, or Guatemalans. No Catholics, Baptists, or Hindus. Just open space. I need that."

"Oh," I replied, feeling mollified. I threw the next sheet over the line, smiling to note that Nancy moved her nose close to the sheet exactly as I did to sniff the fresh smell. "I never thought of it that way. But why not the mountains? Or Big Sur? Why Cape Cod?"

"I chose Cape Cod because Karen was moving here," she said, giving far more concentration than was due to the precise placement of a clothespin in the middle of the sheet she was hanging.

I paused briefly, not knowing whether to feel threatened or relieved that Karen's name—and her presence or absence on the Cape—had never been mentioned before.

Staring straight ahead, I continued beating the wrinkles out of a striped sheet. I could feel Nancy watching me. Out of the corner of my eye, I saw her shrug slightly, as if to say, "What the hell . . ."

"Karen was a ranger with the Park Service. Is a park ranger. She *was* also my girlfriend. Not *is*."

"Oh," I said, relaxing and throwing a wadded up sheet at Nancy's stomach. "Hey, watch it," she said, batting the bundle away with both hands so it fell on the ground. She picked it up and shook it.

"She got a job up here at the national seashore, so I found this job at Cape Kids as a way for us to stay together. But before we'd finished packing, Karen got a better offer in Montana. She wasn't about to turn that job down, but I wasn't about to live through those godforsaken winters out west. At that point, we found out how much our relationship was worth to each other—less than our jobs or the weather," Nancy laughed ruefully.

"Anyway, I was already packed, and I'd been looking forward to living by the ocean, so here I am. I'd rather have found out here and now that Karen and I were doomed than later on in Montana! Brgh!" Nancy shivered.

"I suppose so," I said thoughtfully, trying to balance my pleasure at Karen's distance with sympathy for Nancy's loss. "Still, it's too bad."

"Too bad?" Nancy looked shocked.

"Oh, don't get me wrong. I'm delighted Karen didn't move here, or I'd never have had a chance with you."

"Don't underestimate your charms, Val," Nancy said quietly.

"But it's too bad for you. I mean, with Karen around you wouldn't have been the only black woman within a twenty-mile radius of Provincetown."

"Why do you assume Karen was black?" Nancy's voice was tense. I paused, biting into the wooden clothespin I held between my teeth. Responding defensively to Nancy over anything related to race makes her withdraw. She hates it when I ask her to judge, absolve, teach, or punish me.

"So, what was she," I asked casually, spitting the clothespin playfully at Nancy, "Swedish or something?"

"Norwegian," Nancy smiled. I sensed her relaxing. "And French. And Irish. A sweet little Euro-mutt like you." She threw the clothespin at me, but I caught it deftly with my hand and stuck it on the line.

Nancy lifted the next sheet out of the basket and waved it high in the breeze. It billowed up like a sail from the mast of her arms. She threw her head back and laughed and ran up and down the lawn with it whipping above her. I watched her, becoming somber as I was overtaken by a terrible premonition.

"Nancy," I said as she gathered the sheet around her like a shroud, with only her beautiful brown oval face showing through the white fabric, "you're not going to stay here, are you? I mean you won't stay on the Cape forever, will you? Maybe not even for very long."

"I don't have any plans to leave," she said, unbundling herself. "I like it here. I like you, Val."

"Thank you," I said, feeling suddenly weary while I thought to myself, *"That doesn't change a thing."*

Aloud, I said, "What's the longest you've ever lived anywhere?"

"Atlanta," she said. "That was for five years, ten years ago. After that I lived in Chapel Hill for three years and DC for two. Before that I lived in San Diego for a couple of years—now that was heaven. And before that I was in graduate school in Chicago for two years. Ugh! I was cold every day for two solid years."

A map of the United States lit up in my mind's eye, with a red light on every city Nancy had lived in. I knew that she would move on. She liked me. She might grow to love me. But she did not now and never would *need* me. She would never dig roots in some patch of earth just because *I* lived there. The rhythms of her life would propel her to other open spaces. It was only a matter of time.

At that moment, I knew that I would not, could not allow myself to need Nancy, either. I suppose this is healthy. It's just different from what I expected. For an instant, I felt like running away from Nancy—like tossing a sheet up into the wind and scaling its pluming heights into the big, scary, insentient sky.

But I decided not to. I will stay in place and love Nancy as long as she holds still and allows me to. This conscious choice makes me feel extravagantly mature. But wistful, too.

Ashmont, you know that my whole life long, I have yearned for exotic travel and romantic adventure. Slow boats down the Nile and Sherpa-led treks among the Himalayas would season me and make me wise. Why is it instead that movement toward wisdom transpires while I am standing still in the same place year after year? I feel like I've turned into a tree! What a perverse fate.

Nancy feels no sympathy at my plight. She reminds me that God placed knowledge in the fruit of a tree in Eden, not in the slithering of snakes or in the feathered flight of angels.

Anyway, standing still with Nancy is stretching me in ways I didn't know I had in me. For example, I used to think it was hard to be gay because you have to keep coming out all the time, no matter how old you get, no matter how often you've done it before. But for Nancy, secrecy about her skin color is not an option. She never knows when the viper of racism is going to strike.

A few Saturdays ago, we went to dinner at Crispi's, an expensive restaurant where Desmond, Raymond, and I have in the past enjoyed excellent service. Our waiter—the ironically named Christian—dawdled by the coffee station for twenty minutes before bringing us menus. Then he snarled when Nancy asked him to explain the dinner specials. Without speaking, Nancy and I studied the other tables. No one else was being treated rudely. No one else was black.

Christian continued his slow, abrasive service. Finally, when Nancy asked him politely to replace the diet soda he had brought her with the regular soda she had ordered, he muttered something inaudible under his breath and jerked his hand forward quickly. Nancy and I both thought he was going to strike her. She pulled back and I began to rise from my chair. At the last second, he moved his hand toward her glass, jerking it off the table, spilling it on the tablecloth without pausing to apologize or clean it up. He smirked, clearly enjoying having intimidated us, and disappeared into the kitchen.

"That cuts it," I said. "I'm going to go tell that asshole where he can put it."

"No, Val, sit down," Nancy said in a voice that brooked no dissent.

"But why? We can't let him get away with this behavior."

"No, Val. But this boy is *mine*. As the official black person here, I have dibs. That boy crossed my official dividing line between rudeness and harassment. Leave him to me."

Nancy's tone was calmly fierce. I'd been with her before when she let scrutiny from shopkeepers or surly stares at our linked hands from onlookers go by without comment. I'd assumed she valued inner harmony over confrontation with bigots. But apparently she was just picking her battles. I'm sure she has to, or she could spend every waking hour combating assholes.

So I sat back, curious to see what she would do. Nancy rose slowly from her chair and walked with poise and dignity toward the hostess. In a minute, the manager appeared, and listened to Nancy, looking worried at first, but then smiling and laughing as Nancy returned to our table. She was followed by a different waiter, who politely packed our food up in cartons and escorted us to the door.

I begged, but Nancy refused to tell me what she'd said to the manager. She insisted that I meet her at Crispi's the following night. I figured she'd arranged to have Christian fired, and she wanted to make sure he was gone.

But when we arrived at Crispi's the following night, who should arrive at our table to hand us menus with a forced, cold smile? *Christian.* I gasped and stared at Nancy while he recited the dinner specials in enormous detail and asked coldly but politely if we had any questions.

"You look like you've seen the devil," Nancy grinned after he'd disappeared to fetch our salads.

"Worse," I muttered. "Tell me why that man is still working here. And then tell me why we are enduring his insufferable presence as our waiter."

"Oh, the manager would have fired him. But I suggested that Christian be trained to wait politely on *every* customer, starting with you and me."

"He's not going to stop being a racist jerk because of *this.*"

"Well, of course not," Nancy said impatiently. "Nothing can stop Christian from being a racist jerk, but he can sure as hell can learn not to *act* like one in public. I don't think you can change people's opinions, Val. But people can change their behavior. If they're properly motivated. And I," she said leaning forward with a look of malevolent glee, "intend to be Christian's motivation all summer."

She sat back and scanned the menu. "So, order veal. Order pheasant. Order duck. This meal is on the house. And if Christian so much as puts a glass down on this table so you can hear it, dinner's on him," she said cheerfully.

After dinner, we walked out along the wharf to look at the tall schooners and the sleek double-decker yachts. I kept thinking about Nancy's toughness—her ability to gaze clear-eyed at prejudice without becoming cynical or bitter. If I were black, Ashmont, I'd hate all white people all the time.

The wind off the water was picking up, and I crossed my arms for warmth. "How do you stay sane and strong," I asked her, "in a world where there's so much hatred targeted at you because of your skin?" I brushed the hair out of my eyes to watch Nancy's face.

"What choice do I have?" Nancy shrugged.

"Lots," I said. "You could become bitter. You could turn to drugs and alcohol. You could become violent. Or at the very least, you could lead a selfish, unproductive life. That's what *I'd* do."

"Umm . . . and what kind of life would that be?"

"Not much of one," I admitted.

"Still . . ." I paused. There was something I was trying to figure out. Something I thought Nancy knew that I didn't. But I wasn't asking the right question to get at it.

"I knew a nun once," I said, "and faith kept her going. She believed in Jesus so vividly, it was as if he was walking beside her, whispering in her ear. And by being in love with him she could love the world.

"Jesus doesn't whisper in your ear. Yet you behave like Mary Patrick. How do you do it?"

"Do what?" We stood facing each other, the wind whipping our jackets and pants legs flat against our bodies.

"Not hate life," I said.

Concern mingled with annoyance on Nancy's face. "Val, what are you talking about? Is this about your neglected childhood? About not becoming Georgia O'Keefe? What are you really asking me?"

"Just answer the question!" I demanded.

"All right," Nancy sighed, looking tired. "I'll tell you what you *don't* do. What you don't do is give up. You keep looking for something beautiful that you can believe in. And then you get close to it and stay there." She sounded defiant, but whether of me or the forces of un-beauty in the world, I couldn't tell. She looked away from me over the naked masts of the schooners, her jaw set. She would say no more tonight.

Nor could I think of anything else to say, so we parted.

The next afternoon, Nancy arrived at the inn with a troupe of five-, six-, and seven-year-olds. Three little girls and two boys. They were one of her play groups. I showed them around the inn. They liked the little wooden footbridge over the fish pond, the Buddha-shaped cookie jar in the pantry, and the blue porcelain vases shaped like human hands on the breakfast tables on the sun porch. Then I sat them all down on the deck to draw with crayons and coloring books while they ate cookies.

Instead of drawing with the rest of the gang, one little girl followed me around like a duckling. She never said a word. When I sat on the swing, she clambered up next to me and grabbed my hand—pretty forcefully for someone who hasn't broken the four-foot mark yet—then sat holding it between her hands. She didn't move. She clearly didn't want me to move. Nor, indeed, did I. Her little hands were so sweet and soft, like a puppy's paws. Later Nancy told me this girl was physically capable of talking, she just chose not to. I kept wondering what horrible thing had been done to her to take away her voice— feeling hatred and fury for the adults who had damaged her.

Nancy's eyes followed her charges constantly, radiating patience and love. She was completely absorbed in watching them, in talking to them, in answering their questions. She treated them with extraordinary courtesy, more than most adults show to one another, much less children. "Randy," she said to one boy, "how many cookies would you like?"

"Twenty!" Randy exclaimed.

"Okay," Nancy said, "here's the first two." And of course, by the time Randy had eaten the first two cookies, plus one more, he was busy drawing and wasn't interested in more. Most adults, including me, would have gotten trapped in a nasty brawl with this six-year-old boy over whether or not he would be allowed to consume twenty cookies.

Later, when Nancy announced it was time to leave and asked the children to please start putting their crayons away, tiny but diva-voiced Coral howled in protest. I felt annoyed and critical, thinking, "What an obnoxious child." But Nancy stayed calm. Bending on one knee so she was at eye level with the girl, Nancy held Coral's hands gently, and said in a friendly but imperative tone, "Coral, look at me! Listen to me!"

Coral and I both looked into Nancy's warm, attentive eyes. Borrowing their calm, Coral became quiet. Nancy wiped a tear from Coral's chin, then placed her hands lightly on each of the girl's shoulders.

"We can either leave now and walk back by the beach path, or we can leave in ten minutes and walk back through town. Which would you rather do?"

Coral was magically transformed from a wailing banshee into a thoughtful decision maker. After a few seconds, she chirped, "The beach path!"

"Is that okay with everyone?" Nancy asked the other children. But they were already cleaned up and ready to go.

"Wait a minute," I called out impulsively as they lined up on either side of Nancy.

I raced onto the sun porch and grabbed five hand-shaped vases, returned and gave one to each child. I knew Desmond would kill me— or, worse, would make me accompany him on his next antiquing raid on the hill towns of northern Vermont in order to find replacements, but I didn't care. Seeing the children's faces light up as they cradled their vases filled me with joy. Making those children happy, however briefly, made me feel I have not lived in vain. Not that afternoon, anyway. I understood the allure of Nancy's work, and of yours, for the first time.

Nancy lifted a skeptical eyebrow at me as if to say, "Have you lost your mind?" But all she said was, "Children . . ." To which they instantly responded in a touching munchkin chorus, "Thank you, Val."

When Nancy returned that evening, we sat across from each other on the deck. I asked her if she had brought the children over to show me how selfish and self-pitying I was. That if I thought my life was hard, I should think about those kids and be grateful for what I had.

Nancy looked shocked, "For heaven's sake, no," she said. "I just wanted to show you *my* beautiful thing. You asked me, and I showed you."

"Oh," I said. "It's funny. You look at those kids and see beauty. When I look at them, all I can think about are the terrible things that somebody did to them. All I can feel is hatred for their parents."

"Look, Val. You can either choose to fill yourself with hatred or with other things. I don't know any other way to explain it."

She sounded frustrated. But I was actually starting to get it. I found myself remembering our old, epic friend.

"'*When the gods gave life, they also gave death,*'" I quoted.

Nancy groaned, "Oh no, not *God* again, Val. Give it *up*."

"No, no. I'm quoting *Gilgamesh*. After his friend, Enkidu, dies, Gilgamesh is torn with grief. He can't accept death, so he sets off on a journey to the end of the world, looking for the secret of eternal life. When he finds the guy he's looking for, this guy tells him that his whole trip has been in vain. He's been barking up the wrong tree. There's no way for Gilgamesh to become immortal.

"This guy is the only mortal ever made immortal by the gods—so he knows what he's talking about. Basically, he tells Gilgamesh to give up and go home.

"But he also tells him to enjoy his life *now*—good food, wine, clean clothes, dancing, and other good stuff. You know"—I waved my hand around the view of sunset from the deck—"just because you're going to die doesn't mean you can't enjoy paradise while you're still alive.

"In other words," I said, "what Gilgamesh had to do, and what I have to do, is grow up."

"Those are your words, not mine," Nancy said firmly.

"Okay, but it's the truth."

Nancy sat quietly studying my face.

"So what did he do?" she asked.

"Who?"

"Gilgamesh."

"Oh. He went back to work. Being king, I mean. I have the whole damn poem memorized. Do you want to hear the ending?"

Nancy nodded.

And I recited:

> He entered the city and asked a blind man
> If he had ever heard the name Enkidu,
> And the old man shrugged and shook his head,
> Then turned away,
> As if to say it is impossible
> To keep the names of friends
> Whom we have lost.

Gilgamesh said nothing more
to force his sorrow on another.

He looked at the walls,
Awed at the heights
His people had achieved
And for a moment—just a moment—
All that lay behind him
Passed from view.

"I think it means that after enough time has passed, Gilgamesh is involved with stuff in the present so much that he doesn't even think about the past."

"I see," said Nancy, who had been sitting across from me in a deck chair.

She moved to sit beside me on the swing. She put her arm across my leg, and we sat quietly, swinging our legs while watching the spectrum of light in the sky over paradise shift gradually from orange and red to indigo.

Ashmont, I can't remember when I've been so happy. Sometimes I'm afraid Nancy is too good to be true. I know she won't be around forever, but like Gilgamesh, I'm working on enjoying what I can while it lasts. She's the first person I've been involved with—nuns aside—that I'd actually be proud for you to meet.

I also want to say again how much I appreciate your calling me more often. It doesn't matter that you don't write as long as you call. I hope you realize that you have always been my source of beauty in the world—the *someone* I can believe in—that has kept me from completely hating life. I don't know how to thank you for this without sounding trite, but you have saved my life a million times.

Your ever-loving, happy-at-last-in-love friend,

Val

August 1985
Dearest Val,

Your letter about Nancy gave me such excruciating pain I could hardly breathe. I felt like my lungs were collapsing, and I had to deliberately draw long, steady breaths. It took me several minutes to figure out that I wasn't, in fact, dying, but was simply undergoing exquisite emotional pain.

Throughout your intrepid romantic career, I have felt amazement, pity, and fear on your behalf. But I have never, ever felt envy until now. But your love for Nancy sounds so positive, warm, and intimate. It is exactly the kind of love I wish for myself. It is exactly the kind of love I shall never have. And it was being reminded of that gap in my own life that hurt so much. That, and the fear that I will lose you. With Nancy in your life, you'll grow beyond me. I won't seem admirable and mysterious any more, just opaque and strange.

When I can stretch beyond grief and fear, I'm happy for you. Nancy can give you everything you need—which I never could. It makes me sad to say that. It feels like the end of an era. A Val who is happy and fulfilled in love—who is she?

I wish I could have told you more on the phone about the trouble I'm in—more than "I'm dealing with it." It was progress that I mentioned my troubles at all. Still, you have every right to be annoyed at my secrecy. Someday, I promise, I will tell you everything. Would you be surprised to find out that your righteous Ashmont spent a week in jail? Or would you grunt and say, "I always knew you'd end up in the slammer."

Jail was bad, but in different ways from what I expected. The noise was the worst part, the incessant yelling and whining throughout the cell block, all night long. But the isolation, the cold and impersonal treatment, felt strangely familiar and fated. Perhaps I myself always expected to wind up in prison. My therapist would say these thoughts prove I still feel guilty. I'm compelled to disagree with her. She would say that agreeing with her would mean I'm allowing myself to receive something from her, which is poison for me. Of course, I have to disagree with her about that, too. I disagreed with her so much over the past five months, that I finally fired her.

She said it would help to write about the past. I disagree, but I'm doing it anyway. This memoir will not help. It will reveal nothing about why I wound up in jail. All it will do is prove my ex-therapist wrong.

I'll start with the events leading up to my incarceration. Oh, of course, and to quitting my career as a therapist. It's hard to know where to break into the chain of events, but my involvement in the rescue network is as good a place as any.

It began as an underground network of people who helped runaway teenagers get away from families that damaged them. They were throwaways. Too old for the system, too young to fend for themselves. They were kids whose parents abused or neglected them, but judges kept returning them to their parents' custody, either because the parents could afford to hire unscrupulous lawyers who would label their children liars, or because the judges were too lazy, jaded, or corrupt to care.

These kids didn't have any good choices. They could stay home and be emotionally and physically destroyed. They could hit the streets and sell their bodies. Or they could take some cash and a bus ticket from the network and travel to a town where another network member would find them a place to stay and help them to get a job and a fresh start. I was the only therapist in the network. Most psychologists are terrified of breaking the law. Their primary loyalty is to their own careers—not to the people they work for. When these loyalties conflict, you can bet it will be their own privileged asses they'll cover.

You'd be surprised who else was involved. A Unitarian minister from Pittsburgh. Lots of so-called "housewives" from Buffalo and Rochester. A physician from Syracuse. A hospital chaplain from Cleveland. And two nuns from Erie. Everyone in the network shared a sense of urgency. An understanding that these teenagers were in danger. And an absolute inability to live with ourselves if we saw the danger and sat on our hands. The truth is, nobody really cares about troubled teenagers. Once the network whisks them away, the police don't waste time hunting for them. And after a certain amount of time and expense, the parents "wash their hands" of their unruly children. The network, therefore, operated without much risk of detection when we helped mainly teenagers.

The work became riskier when it expanded to helping mothers save children at risk of abuse from fathers whose custodial or visitation rights had been upheld by the courts. We know we are rescuing these children from further trauma. The district attorney and the newspapers call it kidnapping. The DA's office protects the sanctity of paternal rights, not children's health and safety. The newspapers simply generate scandal.

We began to ferry mothers and children from a safe house in Buffalo to safe houses in Rochester, Albany, or Utica, and to arrange plausible new identities in towns even further afield. We had to be very secretive. We couldn't afford for anyone—cop, social worker, or lawyer—to suspect a linkage between the sudden disappearances of mothers and their children and the members of our "organization." I have driven mothers and children from Buffalo to Syracuse or Utica and returned home the same night so I could be at work the next morning—just so no one could connect my absence from work with the timing of a child's disappearance. Such caution was particularly important for me, since I referred children to the network from my own caseload.

I always knew there might come a time when I'd be caught. If I hadn't been prepared for the consequences, I wouldn't have gotten involved in the first place. I always imagined it would happen because a mother would lose her nerve. Or a child would impulsively disclose her real name to a teacher. Instead, I was done in by a simple act of carelessness. Martha Gravitas—whose wealthy husband's lawyer managed to get the judge to order unsupervised visitation of their daughter even though the child had medically irrefutable evidence of molestation—dropped a small notebook from her handbag before being driven off at midnight in Sister Pauline's Duster. Clipped inside, the police found my business card with my home phone number penciled on the back. They called and asked me if I knew anything about the disappearance of Martha and her daughter Becky.

I could have lied, and my involvement with the case would have ended. Instead, I answered "Yes." I won't give anyone the power to turn me into a liar. When they asked me where Martha and Becky had gone, I said I would not tell them. I claimed therapist/client privilege as justification. I knew this argument would hold up like wet Kleenex in the face of an irate judge bent upon vindicating the rule of patrimony. But I held my ground. And for several days before the court hearing to which I had been subpoenaed to testify, I became center ring in a media circus.

While I was walking up the courthouse steps—my lawyer clearing a path for me among the throngs of reporters, while microphones were thrust in my face and flashbulbs popped like shooting stars—I had the experience that finally, after a lifetime dedicated to its avoidance, led me to enter therapy.

In the midst of anonymous faces and blaring voices, I recognized the angry, snarling countenance of someone I knew. And for a moment, time stopped. His face was the only one I saw. His voice was the only one I heard. Everyone else had frozen in place, and only George Gravitas and I stood alone in nearly identical tan trench coats on the granite courthouse steps.

"Are you happy now?" he snarled, glaring at me contemptuously. "You destroyed my family. Are you satisfied?"

I looked at him. This man knew that I knew for a fact that he had molested his daughter. I had read the medical reports. Becky Gravitas, who was *ten* years old, had symptoms of venereal disease and a torn hymen.

But George Gravitas had a ton of money and no shame. He had power, and he was used to getting his way. He confronted me now looking feral with indignation. He was speaking, I realized, without irony or deception, as well as without shame. From his perspective, I—not he—had ruined his family, because I blocked him from getting his way. In George Gravitas's mind, his family and all other human beings existed solely to gratify his needs.

I looked at that man's face—at the selfishness, the self-pity, the entitlement, the greed, and the arrogance. I knew the look. I knew the type. This man's narcissism was unassailable. You couldn't pierce it with a pitchfork. Not with reason. Not with guilt. Not with punishment. Not even violence. Suddenly, I felt overwhelmed not so much by hatred as by exhaustion. I couldn't bear to look at George Gravitas's face for another second. I had to get rid of it, and the only way to do that, I reasoned, since we were locked in a time warp on the courthouse steps, was to destroy it.

I reached inside my handbag for my gun. I'd bought and learned to shoot it when I began making house visits in Buffalo's worst neighborhoods. I prepared to discharge a bullet directly into his ugly, entitled face, looking forward with glee to his stunned expression —the last he would ever make.

My fingers flailed inside my pocketbook. The gun was missing. I'd removed it from my purse that morning. I assumed—correctly—that I'd be searched as I was taken prisoner for contempt of court. I assumed—also correctly—that it would look bad for me to be found *packing heat.* That fortuitous decision was all that prevented me from spending the rest of my life in jail for murder, instead of a week for contempt of court.

My fumbling search exploded the time warp. George Gravitas and I were released from stasis. The flow of time resumed and I was rushed up the courthouse steps, leaving him declaiming his victim's plea for justice to the TV cameras: "Men are discriminated against by the courts! Fathers have no rights!" He was pathetic and nauseating. But the spell was broken. Let George Gravitas lower himself to the bottom rung of hell.

My moment in court was undramatic. It was over in twenty minutes. I could have avoided jail time if I hadn't gotten ticked off by the judge's patronizing tone. My lawyer argued that Martha and Becky were by now long gone from their original destination—the only one I had any knowledge of. She pointed out that I had no knowledge of the identities or addresses of others who helped her flee. I was, in short, a useless witness harassed by the police because of their own ineffectiveness in turning up leads on the fugitives' whereabouts. The judge grudgingly agreed, and was ready to release me.

"Young lady," the judged lectured me in a booming, sonorous voice, "I hope you understand the gravity of what you've done. Your defiance of the law could well have landed you in jail."

My lawyer heard my subvocal growl and stepped on my foot—not lightly—under the table. I couldn't suppress myself.

"Your Honor," I said, "I fully understand the seriousness of my actions. But with all due respect, the court itself instigated this flight by ordering unsupervised visitation rights for a father who gave his ten-year-old daughter venereal disease."

The court erupted in startled gasps. This fact had not made the nightly news. While the judge pounded his gavel and tried to subdue the spectators into a respectful silence, I spoke up again.

"Also with all due respect, Your Honor, I am not a young lady. I am a thirty-three-year-old psychologist. How would Your Honor like it if he were addressed as 'old man'?"

That last comment got me a week, my lawyer said, rather than the mere fine or single night in a lockup that my first comment alone would have provoked. The week proved useful, however. After a day, I learned to tune out the cacophony around me, and I was forced to think carefully about the murder I'd been tempted to commit.

I had almost become one of "them." One of the purveyors of brute, impulsive violence who have mired the earth in trauma and suffering for millennia, and whom I have spent my whole life trying to vanquish. I have always prided myself on being different—on fighting back with cunning rather than simpleminded raw force.

Had I found the gun in my handbag, I would have killed George Gravitas as surely as my name is *Ashmont, Emily K*. And a far worse rung of hell than jail for me to burn in would have been the knowledge that I was no different from the enemies I bitterly oppose. The thought drove me wild, and directly into therapy as soon as I was released from the *slammer*.

Among the first questions my therapist asked was whether I had mistaken George Gravitas for my father. No. I knew exactly who he was. But I recognized the look of indignant narcissism because I'd seen it on my father's face. He'd worn it that night when everything changed, after I snapped on the light and stood with my mouth poised to shout for my mother, while I hid my father's pajama bottoms behind my back. We had been trapped in the same kind of time warp I'd been caught in with George Gravitas. My father whispered loudly, his face contorted with rage and fear, "Emily, for God's sake, don't. You'll destroy us all! Shut up! I'll give you anything you want, but be quiet!"

Time stopped as I absorbed his plea and his attempted bribe. And then, pitilessly, it began again as I opened my mouth and yelled.

"Mother!"

If the cost of saving us all from destruction was lying about what he'd done, I would destroy us all.

"Oh my God!" he whined, "Now you've really done it. What are we going to do?!"

We, mind you, he said, "we." What a piece of work is this man, my father.

But I'm skipping ahead. I must keep things in order. I was twelve years old. Before that night, I was a girl. I was in seventh grade. I was nearly normal, although dangerously precocious, forthright, and articulate for my age. I was building a scale model of the Acropolis with modeling clay. I was sneaking Lucky Strikes from my mother's purse and smoking them with Jemima Parsons behind her father's toolshed. I was scrubbing my face with lemon juice twice a day because Siobhan O'Brien's cousin—who was seventeen and had flawless rosy cheeks—had assured us this would keep our complexions clear.

I loved school. I belonged to the Debating Club and the Latin League, because I loved the beauty and power of language and because these activities kept me away from home. I had my own world, separate from my parents. Largely, I ignored them. And largely, they ignored me. My world was independent and adventurous. And I was the center of it. Only me.

After that night, I was . . . I don't know what I was . . . but I was not a girl any longer. And I was not the center of my own life. The *thing that happened*—that is how my parents' always referred to it—appropriated center stage. And retained it for a long time. I hated my father for usurping time and space in my life when I longed to be rid of him for good. It's a resentment shared by anyone who has been abused, attacked, raped, or robbed—the sheer volume of time and energy expended on the *parasitic slimeball perp* who has forced himself into the middle of your life and psyche without your consent.

The reason I knew what my father was up to that night was that he had tried it once before. A month earlier, I had woken up from a sound sleep to hear him moaning softly in the dark at the foot of my bed. There was enough light cast on the room through the cracked door so I could see him sitting on the edge of the bed, arching his back, rubbing his crotch while he whispered, "God, oh God . . ."

I knew he was masturbating. Jemima's sixteen-year-old brother Eddie had asked me to "help him" jerk off in their garage one day, and when I told him I couldn't think of anything more repulsive, he got angry and pulled his pants down and did it anyway, making similar, louder groans and grunts. I'd learned enough to know that sex was vaguely dirty, obscurely shameful, often dangerous for women, and compulsively fascinating to males. But that applied to *boys and men.*

This was my *father.*

I was terribly confused. So I didn't say a word while I tried to reason it out. First of all, think. This has been my response to danger for as long as I can remember. Why would my father come to my room? Didn't my mother let him "do it" in their room? Would he touch me? Would he hurt me? Should I be afraid? Should I hit him with the lamp and run? Would my mother come if I yelled? Would she be angry at me? What would he say he'd been doing? What would she do to me?

While I was still furiously thinking, trying to decide what to do, my father got up and left. He picked his pajama bottoms up off the floor, wiped his penis with them, and walked out of my room—without looking back to see if I was awake, to see if I was okay. He didn't care, I realized. This shocked me more than his masturbation had. He'd gotten what he wanted, and he was gone. In this moment, I understood everything I needed to know about sex. Everything I needed to know about my father.

All my confusion disappeared. *"You bastard,"* I thought, *"you won't get away with this."* I knew right then what I would do if he came back. And somehow I was sure he would return. I felt disgusted. I felt furious. I felt ashamed of him but also of *me*—I was humiliated that he would dare to treat me this way, but would not have done this to my younger brother.

My father was weak but charismatic. He was charming when he needed you, and cutting and sarcastic when he didn't. He lived in fear of my mother's wrath. I'd seen him lie outright to avoid her anger. It wasn't that she would yell if you did something wrong. Instead she would make you feel that you had become yet another disappointment in an infinite string of deep disappointments.

"Daniel," she would ask my father, "did you leave the milk on the counter? It's gone sour." "No, dear," he would lie, "it must have been one of the children." She would look at my brother or me and sigh a martyr's sigh, and we would feel guilty, even though we knew our father was the culprit. Then she would get a headache and go lie down. As far back as I can remember, my mother has had a headache. She has spent an astonishing number of days lying in dark, overheated rooms.

My brother and I were infuriated by our father's deceptions—his willingness to sell us out to save his own hide. It could have turned us into liars like him. But his behavior was so repellent that it turned me into a demon for truth.

I understood my father's shamelessness. It prepared me, unlike girls less bred to cunning, to predict that my father, if caught transgressing, would lie. He would betray me again, as he had already betrayed me by coming to my room to jerk off in the first place. I prepared to trap him in such a way that he absolutely could not lie his way out of it.

For nights, I slept lightly, anticipating his return. One night, I heard him pausing by my door, touching the doorknob, then moving on. Maybe I'd been wrong about him, I thought. Maybe he was too chicken to take the risk again. Maybe he was sorry for what he'd done. But then two nights later, just as I was drifting off to sleep, I saw a wedge of light spread across the carpet. I remember thinking, *"I knew you'd come."* But my certainty had been mingled with the hope that I was wrong—that he would never come back again—that I had dreamed the whole thing. As angry and determined to catch him as I was, my eyes, for an instant, filled with hot, burning tears.

I breathed deeply to feign sleep. I heard him whisper ever so lightly, "Playing possum, possum?"

This was a game from ancient childhood. As long as I was awake enough to answer, "yes," I was eligible for another story. I couldn't believe he thought this ploy would work with a twelve-year-old. I couldn't believe he would superimpose our childhood ritual onto this sordid pursuit. When I failed to answer, he tiptoed into the room. I heard the elastic band of his pajama bottoms expanding, I heard the cloth slipping down his legs. I felt the bed dip toward the end.

I heard him start to moan, and I knew it was time to act. I jumped out of bed, grabbed his pajama bottoms, hid them behind my back and fled across the room, turning the overhead light on. I opened my mouth to scream, "Mother," while he ineffectually tried to cover his penis with his hands. He lurched and grabbed for his pajamas. It was during these moments he pleaded with me not to "destroy us all." I ignored him, and shouted "Mother!"

Mother appeared, looking astonished. As soon as I saw her, I held my father's pajamas high over my head, pointing at him and stuttering, "H-h-h-h-he . . . he did it. Right there on the end of the bed. And it wasn't the first time!"

My father dropped not only his jaw, but his hands to his side. My mother's eyes widened as she stared at his still erect penis. I saw my father's jaws working. He was saying, "I didn't touch her. Honest. I just came in to check on—"

"Don't even try!" Mother hissed, grabbing the pajamas and handing them roughly to him. "For God's sake, cover yourself! And get out of here!" She turned quickly, confronting my brother, who appeared sleepily behind her, "Back to bed with you, now!"

My heart leapt when she snapped at my father. He would be punished. But as she turned around, my mother sighed deeply and put her hand to her temple. The headache was coming. Her instinctive response—before concern for me, before anger at my father—was pity for herself.

I knew I was in trouble when I heard that sigh. My heart sank.

Mother touched my cheek with her hand, looking at me with a mixture of worry and irritation—at the *problem* I had now become.

"Emily," she said, trying to sound gentle but unable to mask her annoyance, "Did he touch you? Did he hurt you?"

They were such different questions. My mother asked them as though they could be answered together, as though a *no* to one was a *no* to the other. I was confused, and hesitated.

"He—he—" I sputtered.

"Did he touch you?" she repeated sternly.

"No, but he—"

She held her hand up to shush me.

"Emily, go back to bed. I can't deal with this right now. We'll talk in the morning."

I was horrified. "Are you going with *him?*" My father had left my room. "Don't you even want to find out what happened? He'll lie. You know he's a big, fat liar!"

She looked at me forbearingly. She was starting to lose patience with me. With *me!* I couldn't believe it.

"Did he touch you?" she repeated, as if that were all that mattered.

"No, but he—"

"In the morning, Emily." She cut me off. "We'll talk in the morning, I promise. Now go back to sleep. Good night." And she left, closing the door behind her.

Go back to sleep? I couldn't believe she would even say it. I was so furious—now with them both—that I got dressed and went outside. I didn't want to be under the same roof with them. I sat on the curb across from the house for an hour. The light in their bedroom went off after fifteen minutes. Apparently, my parents were going to talk about it in the morning, too.

At 6:30, the lights went on in the kitchen. That would be my mother, slave to routine, making coffee. I rang the doorbell.

Mother answered the door, shocked to see me. Clearly, she hadn't bothered to check my room once during the night.

"Emily! What are you doing outside?"

"Since it isn't my house anymore—with *him* here—I thought I should ring the bell."

"Oh, Emily," she said, sighing. She gave me a look that said, "You're not going to make this easy for me, are you?"

And I gave her a look that said, "No, I'm not."

"Go upstairs and get ready for school, then come down to the kitchen and we'll talk." I complied because I wanted to hear what she'd say.

When I appeared in the kitchen a few minutes later, she gave me a cup of coffee with lots of milk and sugar, a favorite of mine.

She sat across from me, her face lined with worry, twisting her hands.

"Well," I said, realizing I would have to start. "What are you going to do, Mom? Is Dad going to jail? Or am I?" I was acting as tough and adult as I could. I had learned long ago that to act like a child and long for care and comfort like a child was to open myself to profound disappointment.

"What? Oh, Emily, don't talk that way. Nobody's going to jail. I was wondering if you'd like to see a psychologist—so you could talk about—" She stumbled, and I waited, curious to see how she would refer to my father's jerking off on my bed.

"—about the thing that happened last night."

"It wasn't just last night."

Her eyes widened. "What do you mean?"

"It happened once before. I was awake, but he didn't know it."

"Oh," she sighed, looking disappointed. "He told me about it. He thought you were asleep." Then something clicked inside her mind. Her eyes narrowed. Her tone was pleading, "For heaven's sake Emily, you know your father. If you'd so much as blinked or yawned, he'd have gotten up and left, and nothing would have happened."

So my mother thought I was the "destroyer," too. I was truly on my own. I couldn't look at her. I stared vacantly out the window and said, "No."

"No, what? Don't be cryptic, Emily."

"No, I won't go see a psychologist. In my opinion, *he* should go. Daniel. Don't expect me to ever to call him father again. Why don't you go, too? Maybe they can tell you why your head aches all the time," I said sarcastically.

"Emily," she hissed, and she leaned across the table and slapped me. Then she stared at her hand, as if it, not she, had hit me. She sighed and touched her forehead.

"I'm sorry," she said, and she buried her face in her hands, spilling her cup of coffee across the table and the floor. Neither of us moved to clean up the mess. It just kept spreading. We both watched it, as if in trance.

"I won't go," I repeated, standing up. "And if he stays here, I'll go to boarding school. And if you won't let me go to boarding school I'll run away. I mean it, Mother."

"I know you do, dear," she said tiredly. And as I turned to leave, I felt the strangest sense that she envied me. That if she could have run off to boarding school at that moment and left the spilled coffee and my father far behind, she would have jumped at the chance.

As it turned out, I didn't go to boarding school immediately, but I did go to see a psychologist. Several of them. My mother called her minister while I was at school, and he persuaded her that everyone in the family should go for counseling. Since my parents were going, I reluctantly agreed.

The sessions were worse than useless. I refused to talk. I insisted my parents were the ones who needed help. I could sense the therapist becoming frustrated with me and beginning to sympathize with my parents for having such a "strong-willed" child. My mother would say things like, "I understand what Daniel did was terrible, but it could have been worse. After all, he didn't even touch her . . ."

"Didn't even *touch her* . . ."

I waited for at least one therapist to take her on, to say, "Mrs. Ashmont, you're full of shit." Or "Mrs. Ashmont, how much worse would it have to be before you'd give a damn?" But no one ever did. None of them seemed to think it had been "so bad" either.

Every now and then, I would meet alone with a couple of different therapists. They would give me dolls or drawing paper, which I would throw on the floor. I was nearly thirteen years old, for God's sake. They would begin by saying things like, "You're pretty upset about what happened with your father, aren't you?" I would roll my eyes and retort sarcastically, "If your father was jerking off on your bed in the middle of the night while you were sleeping, wouldn't you be upset?"

I could feel their niceness retract as my hostility expanded. They all wanted to make things better. None of them understood that I wanted to make things worse. This had been entirely too easy on my parents. Nobody was getting it, which enraged me. How could they be so stupid! I couldn't understand why my father hadn't been forced from the house! Why hadn't my mother divorced him? I'd have been driven to delinquent acts if it hadn't been for Dr. Delong.

We were meeting in family counseling one day, in the room with the one-way mirror, where we'd been told consultants would sometimes watch in order to offer advice. As usual, we were sitting in sullen silence, when the red phone rang. This rarely happened, but it meant one of the consultants had an idea. The therapist picked up the phone and listened, then invited everyone but me to leave the room.

After a minute, Dr. Delong entered. She was a short, barrel-shaped woman, with steel-gray hair pulled into a bun. She wore gold wire-rimmed glasses, and had on a tailored beige suit with a row of tiny coffee stains descending the lapels of her jacket. She reeked of cigarette smoke and intelligence.

"May I come in?" She asked from the door. I was astonished that she asked, and I was immediately curious about her.

"You can come in," I said, eager to have her do so.

"Thank you," she said. "Do you mind if I sit?"

"No," I said, starting to like her.

"Is there somewhere you would prefer that I sit?"

I thought about it, and decided I wanted her to sit across from me, where my mother had been sitting a moment ago. I gestured, and she nodded and sat down.

"May I show you something?" she asked.

I nodded. She got up, flicked a switch, and lit up the mysterious mirror room next door. No one was in it.

"No one can hear us," she said "No one can see us. I just wanted you to know. Do you mind if we just sit for a minute?" she asked. "I'd like a smoke. If you don't mind smoking, that is?" She paused before lighting up.

I wanted her to stay. She could smoke all she wanted. She had brought an aura of hope into the room. Maybe she was someone who would finally get it, after all.

She smoked quietly, and I began to relax while I watched her. She smiled, noticing me watching her, and looked at me quizzically without saying anything.

I smiled, and spoke first, which I never did with the other therapists. "I know smoking's bad for you, but I kind of understand the appeal," I said.

"Uh oh," she laughed, a throaty smoker's laugh. "do you mean you understand the weakness of an adult who's become addicted to a behavior she can't stop? Or something else?"

"Something else," I said. I'd never thought of smoking as an addiction before, something you got hooked on, like alcohol. Years later, I realized Dr. Delong was also talking about my mother. Everything Dr. Delong said was deliberate and therapeutic. She was a true artist.

"It's like carrying a wand of fire around in your fingertips. You know, like you've tamed fire into this tiny stick you can carry around."

"Yes," she nodded heartily, "I like that. A wand of fire. Taking on the prerogative of the God's. You know the story of Prometheus?"

I nodded. Of course I knew Prometheus. I knew all the Greek myths.

"Then you must know Prometheus was punished severely for his boldness. He made the powers that be so upset."

I nodded. She gave me a serious, sad, knowing look, and I wondered if she was talking about me.

"Which doesn't mean in the slightest that Prometheus was wrong," she added. "He did what he had to do. In fact, he was very brave, don't you think?" She smiled, and I knew she was, in fact, talking about *me.*

"Yes," I said firmly, happy to have this understood about my actions for the very first time. "Yes, I do!"

"I do, too," she said. And I smiled at her. I hadn't smiled for weeks. I felt like the mask I had been holding in place to protect myself was breaking into pieces. I could feel tears falling down my cheeks. She smiled back, and held my gaze. And I felt like I was being hugged and soothed.

"Emily, there's something I want to ask you, if you don't mind, about what happened the night your father came to your room to masturbate. May I?"

I was shocked to hear her use the word "masturbate." None of the other therapists did. I was a little worried about what she was going to ask, but I nodded.

She took a long drag on her cigarette, blew it out in a huge puff, and said, "The way I see it, you wanted to nail him, right?" She was very serious.

"It didn't matter whether it was one night or two nights, or whether he thought you were asleep or not. Or whether he touched you or not. Because the crime had been committed, the damage had already been done when he allowed himself to think of you that way, and when he first set his foot on the floor to walk toward your room."

She understood perfectly.

"You hated him for that, didn't you?" she asked.

I nodded, lowering my gaze. I knew it must be wrong to hate your own father. I must be a monstrous child. I expected her to tell me I had to forgive him.

"Well, I'm here to tell you," she stubbed her cigarette out in the ashtray and I watched the embers die, "that you have every right to hate what he did. Every right." She spoke emphatically. I was amazed. If she understood this much, maybe I could confide my worst fear.

"Dr. Delong," I said hesitantly, "may I ask you something?"

"Anything," she said. She opened up a new package of cigarettes and as she pulled one out, I quickly grabbed her matches off the table and held it out to light her cigarette. We both smiled at this small civility.

"Thank you, my dear," she said.

I looked down, fearful to find disapproval in her gaze. "Maybe it was wrong of me to nail him. Maybe I should have done what my mother thinks I should have. Maybe I should have coughed the first night he came to my room, so he'd have run away and never come back. And then we could have avoided all this . . . mess."

"Never think that," she admonished me, lifting my chin up to meet my gaze. "Your father's behavior is not your responsibility."

"My mother thinks it is," I said.

"Your mother is dead wrong," she spoke crisply, and we both let her words hang in the air.

Dr. Delong was completely unlike the other therapists. She took definite stands. She wasn't afraid to criticize my parents. I'd never met anyone as honest. I probably never will.

"The important thing—and the only important thing—is that you stopped him! And you stopped him in a way that meant he couldn't lie his way out of it—couldn't come back later and try again!" We both sat silently, letting that settle in.

Dr. Delong sat back and chuckled, "Frankly, I'd have paid a pretty penny to see you holding those pajama bottoms up in the air. How high did you hold them? Show me, dear."

I grinned and held my fist way up high. "This high!"

"Stand up, dear, and show me how high!"

I stood up on my tiptoes, waving my fist in the air, "This high!"

Dr. Delong began to applaud. "Wonderful!" she said, and we giggled uproariously. I could never have imagined laughing again a few days ago, and now we were laughing about the *thing that happened*. Dr. Delong was proud of me and impressed with me—exactly what I wanted my mother to feel. Exactly what my mother was incapable of feeling.

When we stopped laughing, she became serious again. She pulled a drawing out of her briefcase. I recognized it as one I had reluctantly drawn for another therapist.

"Would you mind telling me about this drawing?"

"Oh, I hate drawing," I said. "I just did it to keep the other therapist happy."

"I know," she said, "but I wanted to ask you anyway. Who is this?"

"It's my father," I said.

"I thought so," she nodded. "It looks like a man shaped like a potato or a loaf of dough, with a very large erect penis sticking out. Am I right?"

I blinked. That was exactly right. That was how I saw my father. That was how I had drawn him.

"The only part of his body that has any feeling is the penis," she said. "The rest of him is numb like a potato. Am I right?"

I nodded. Dr. Delong had put into words what I felt, but hadn't known how to name. She rubbed her chin. "Well, you are a very clever girl, Emily. You understand your father perfectly. I just wanted you to know that I agree with you. Your diagnosis is perfect." And she put the drawing away.

"Emily, do you have any questions?"

"Why is my father still at home? Why hasn't he been arrested or sent away somewhere? Wasn't what he did bad enough?"

"Oh, it was very bad. Terrible. But the truth is, your parents and protective services—those are the people that would have sent him away—made a deal. He can stay as long as he comes for therapy with your mother. As long as the therapist thinks he's in no danger of repeating his abuse, they won't force him out."

My face fell.

"Emily, look at me."

I did.

"It's a flawed system," she said. "You need to know that. Sometimes it's worse than flawed. The deal your parents and the system has made may be lousy. It can be lousy and still be the best they could come up with. Don't let your anger about that get in your way. Don't let it eat you up inside. You'll find your own justice in here," she pointed at her heart, "by getting a good education, by making friends, by finding work you love.

"Your heart is bigger than this lousy situation. You're bigger than your parents. I know they look big to you now, but trust me, they're smaller than you think. You're tough. You're strong. You're smart and you're gifted. You're going to grow up and make your own life. Whatever bad or unfair decisions are being made right now *will not* get in your way."

I believed her. I believed she had seen my future. Dr. Delong convinced me I would be okay.

"Emily," she said, "you know that your parents and the therapists are talking about your request to go to boarding school. Is that what you really want?"

"Yes, Dr. Delong. I don't think I can live with either one of them any more."

I thought she would argue with me, but instead she didn't seem surprised. "Well, all right then. I'll support you."

"But Doctor," I said, "if I stayed here, could I see you? I mean would you be my therapist?"

"Alas, no," she said, "I'm here today as a consultant. I couldn't be your therapist. But I tell you what—you can write me. I'll give you the address of my clinic in Cleveland. Okay?"

"Okay," I said. "May I ask you one more thing?"

"What's that?"

"How come you're so different from the other therapists?"

She guffawed. "Because I'm three times their age, and I don't have to worry about getting fired. You know, they want to help, Emily. Their intentions are good."

"Yeah, but . . ."

"Yeah," she repeated, "I know. Good intentions don't cut it with Emily Ashmont!" She was teasing me! But fondly. Where had this woman come from?

I jumped out of my chair, my arms outstretched, feeling a burst of warmth and gratitude. But I stopped myself. No one in my family ever hugged.

Dr. Delong opened her arms out wide, "It's okay, dear." That was all the encouragement I needed. I hugged her solid, strength-and-sanity-inducing body, and she hugged me back. I whispered shyly in her ear.

"Dr. Delong, I don't believe in God, but if I did, I would think you were my guardian angel!"

"Thank you, dear. What a sweet compliment. Good luck to you. You've a long road ahead. But you'll be fine."

I let her go reluctantly. It was the warmest hug I'd ever received. I understood why Dr. Delong couldn't be my therapist, but couldn't she adopt me? Failing that, I decided that very day, I would *become* Dr.

Delong. She's the reason I'm sane today. She's the reason I became a psychologist. Sometimes I think she's the reason I'm still alive.

I went to boarding school. The distance between my father and me was sealed. He never apologized. All he ever said to acknowledge what he had done was that he knew he had "problems" to work on, and he hoped I wouldn't hold our "misunderstanding" against him forever. In his heart, he thought I'd let *him* down—by making a such a terrible "fuss" when he hadn't even touched me. After my mother divorced him three years later, I never saw him again. I asked my mother never to mention his name.

The distance with my mother was harder. Like my father, she never really "got" what was so terrible about what he'd done. She knew it was wrong, but since he hadn't actually *touched* me, how much harm could there be? She thought I was self-pitying and self-indulgent. She could never forgive me for "nailing" him and thereby confronting her with an infinite series of headaches. I didn't hate my mother. I just found it hard to love her anymore. Especially after she said to me—when I was seventeen and she was infected by a wave of sentimental-ity—"You know, dear, in spite of everything, your father really did love you." This comment destroyed any remaining respect I might have had for her.

I knew my father loved no one. Not me. Not my brother. Not my mother. No one but himself—and even that is true only if colossal self-absorption can be equated with love. My mother was too weak-minded, too faint of heart, to accept this truth. I despised this in her. From that moment on, I wanted nothing from her. I saw clearly that just because you have two parents alive and breathing on the planet does not mean that you are not completely on your own.

This aloneness in spite of our families—this is our bond, Val. This makes us blood sisters.

My therapist asked me once if I thought there was anything in my mother's own past that excused her for minimizing my father's behav-ior. Actually, what she *said* was, "How do you understand your mother's response to your father's sexual abuse?" But I knew what she was implying. That my mother was abused herself, and her history excused her pitiful maternal lapse.

Forget it. It's all very sad—pathetic, even—if she was abused. And it may indeed explain her peculiar "lapses." But if it's true, then for pity's sake, don't give birth! Unless you can keep your daughter safe from harm, don't even *think* about reproducing. Don't you dare. Goddamn you, Mother, don't you dare!

My therapist remarked one day that the dominant emotion in all my memories was anger. Surely, she said, I must have felt something else—sadness, fear, abandonment, frenzy, or despair? Actually, what she said was, "Do you remember feeling anything other than anger?" But I knew what she meant. I know the tricks of her trade.

And the answer is: No. I do not.

Even if it would make for an alternate history that my therapist would find more palatable. Easier to understand. To identify with. To like. The feeling I remember is anger.

But what I do remember other than anger is this:

For a while, I refused to sit at the same table with my family. I ate meals alone in my room.

If my father was in the car, I wouldn't get in. I took the bus.

I threw out half my stuff, everything my father had ever given me—a Bavarian cuckoo clock; a gold Cross pen and mechanical pencil set; the deluxe edition of *Great Works of Western Literature from Plato to William Shakespeare*. My other stuff I moved to the recreation room on the first floor, which I declared was now my "wing" of the house and off limits to everyone else.

I never obeyed another command my mother gave me in my life. If she said, "Emily, you may not buy the Beatles' *Abbey Road*," I bought it and left it out where she could see.

If she said, "Turn off the TV and go to bed," I increased the volume and shut my door.

No matter what she said, I ignored her. She would sigh, and move along. I always won. And after a while, she stopped telling, and started asking.

"Emily, who are you going out with?"

"Emily, what time will you be home?"

"Emily, did you get your driver's license yet?"

And not long after that, she stopped asking altogether. She would act surprised when I opened my mouth.

"Emily, what was that? Did you speak?"

The first time she sighed and walked away, I felt relieved.

The second time, I felt disappointed. I remember thinking, "Are you giving up so soon?"

The third time, I was contemptuous. My mother was overmatched. A featherweight against Mohammed Ali.

By the fourth time, I no longer cared what she said or didn't say.

Just before I fired her, my therapist asked me how I would know I was free, truly free, of the effects of my father's abuse and everything else "that happened" because of it. That's what she actually said.

I blurted out, "I'd have a child."

And then I felt sad. But irritated, too. I'd always viewed my decision not to have a child as my own impeccably reasoned choice. But what's disturbing about therapy—now that I am in the client's chair—is the way it takes things you have diligently organized into separate compartments and shakes them up wildly, so they come clanging together in irksome, disorderly ways. I resent that terribly. Not five minutes in therapy would go by without my therapist asking me, "Now what might *that* have to do with your abuse?" Abuse acts like a black hole whose fierce gravity draws everything into its swirling vortex. I hate this so much, I can hardly stand it. It shouldn't have so much power.

"But it does," is all my therapist said when I protested.

"I shouldn't let it," I'd retort.

"You don't have a choice," she replied.

This shut me up. Then I sulked.

Shortly after I began seeing this therapist I remembered something about that night—something I didn't tell anyone when I was twelve or since. I'm not sure it really happened.

I remember hearing a loud boom as the door opened and the wedge of light entered from the crack in the door, widening gradually to reveal my father. It was a visceral, deep, air-splitting boom like thunder after lightning—a sound that you feel in your viscera, not with your ears. I know my father didn't hear it—he didn't start or pause. There was no rain that night. No clouds obscured the sky.

I conclude there is only one thing that sound could have been.

It was the sound of my heart—breaking.

The sound of memories, hopes, and dreams bursting through the torn seams of my heart and crashing to earth. To death.

I would never stand at the podium on high school graduation day delivering my valedictorian speech—my voice catching with emotion as I cast around the audience and found my parents' faces glowing with pride.

I would never call my parents—homesick from my first year at college—and be invited to bring my dirty laundry and a friend home for pasta and wine.

I would never send a bound, autographed copy of my dissertation—by *Dr.* Emily K. Ashmont—to parents astonished and pleased by their daughter's scholarly pursuits.

I would never arrive at their door with a nervous young man in tow, announcing, "Mom and Dad, here he is—he's the one!"

I would never rent a cottage on the Cape and sunbathe on the shore while two proud grandparents scooped their wading grandchild out of the path of hazardous waves.

So be it. Let the dead bury the dead.

I quit my job at the clinic. They were going to fire me anyway. Jailbirds can't be therapists. I don't mind leaving the job. But I do mind leaving my clients behind. I still want to help children, I just can't do it within the rules. The director of the clinic asked me point blank if I could promise never to refer another child to the rescue network.

I said no, I could not.

Doing what's right is more important to me than obeying the law or the rules of my profession. I am either going to have to find a new profession, or some way to create my own rules. Regardless, I couldn't have stayed at the clinic. I felt like a leper at a cocktail party. Some of my colleagues were openly contemptuous. Most avoided me. A few were supportive in private, but too cowardly to say anything in public. While I was in jail, I kept asking myself, "Why do I want to work with these people?" The answer was, "I don't."

I won't. I can earn money by writing grants and doing the mano-a-mano fundraising I'm known for. I'm tough. I'm resilient. I'll get by.

I'm lonely. I'm poor. I'm a disgrace to my profession. And I'm an ex-con. But in some terribly strange way, I feel free. I imagine it's the freedom you feel once your house has burned down, you've been robbed of all possessions, and everyone you've ever loved has died or disappeared. There is precious little left for life to do to you.

My therapist would say that I feel free because I've finally received the punishment I was waiting for—and always felt that I deserved.

But she would be wrong.

Dead wrong.

Love,

Ashmont

October 1985
Darling, loyal Ashmont,

My stars are crossed. *Fate* intends me to live alone. My premonition that Nancy would leave was correct. Precious, *normal Nancy* is moving from Provincetown for good. Again, I am losing someone I love. Only this time—an improvement, I admit—there is no betrayal, no cheating, no lies. Only *loss*.

She is moving back to San Francisco to take care of her aging parents. Her mother fell and broke her hip, and her father has worsening Alzheimer's. Nancy feels duty bound to go help out. Actually, it isn't just duty. Nancy truly wants to help them. She loves her parents very much. She says they taught her everything of value about life. Can you imagine feeling that way about your parents? I feel a peculiar mix of emotions: I am acutely jealous of Nancy's parents because she's returning to them; I also wish they would adopt me.

I have to let her go!

It doesn't seem fair. Nancy says fairness is irrelevant. She says nothing in life—including her—comes with a guarantee. I know she's right, but my heart roils in protest.

Not only do I have to let her go, I have to do it graciously. Because Nancy deserves it. Because loving her as truly and deeply as I do commands it.

Admittedly, our relationship, sunny as it has been, has seen its share of conflicts recently. Last week, for example, Nancy announced that I sometimes repel her.

I had been feeling discouraged about my life. You know, poor me, destined for greatness, but wasting my days changing sheets and flushing toilets for spoiled travelers. I was sanding my frustration away on the chipped maple surface of an old coffee table on the inn's back lawn. That's where Nancy found me after work.

"Come on, Val," she said, throwing an arm over my shoulders, "let's go for a quick swim and out to dinner." I jerked abruptly out from under her arm. I found her high spirits abrasive. I was tired of being cheered up by Nancy, who never allowed me to cheer *her* up. But I felt guilty, too, so instead of speaking up, I shrugged her off.

"Don't do that," she said angrily, "if you want me to remove my arm, say so. Don't shrug it off."

I didn't answer. I felt too angry and self-pitying.

"Val, did you hear me?"

I nodded.

"Then answer me." She was very stern. I can never defy Nancy when she's stern.

"I heard you," I snapped. "Please leave me alone. I'm in a foul mood. Come back tomorrow."

I kept sanding. For several minutes all I heard was the scraping of sandpaper. I thought Nancy had left. I paused, feeling disappointed that she hadn't tried harder, and a little miffed that she hadn't said good-bye. Then I heard someone breathing behind me.

I craned my neck around, and saw Nancy standing stark naked, except for her socks and her sun visor, hands on her hips, looking like a female version of Donatello's *David,* smiling seductively, "Are you *sure* you don't want to go swimming?"

"Jeez, Nancy," I couldn't help but grin at her audacity. Ordinarily, she relied on gifts of chocolate and poetry to cajole me out of my bad moods.

She walked over and pressed her breasts against my back, reaching under my arms to pull me up. "How about it, Val?"

I was tempted. But something in me resisted. I wasn't through with my own bad mood, and didn't want to be cajoled on Nancy's schedule. Her seductiveness stirred up a resentment that had been simmering inside me for weeks—stemming from my observation that we only had good sex when Nancy initiated.

In the beginning of our relationship, sex was passionate and intimate. No one has ever made me feel as desirable as Nancy. It's the way she breathes—a deep, audible breath—as though she were inhaling my soul. When we made love, I felt as though we shared a rib. A giant bone that curved round and contained us both but had been badly fractured. While we touched, molecules on her side of the fissure leaped tenderly over to embrace molecules on my side, rendering them once again healed, whole, and bone-strong.

Lately, however, our sex life detoured onto more "adventurous" paths. Nancy calls it "erotic yoga," or "physical meditations"—whatever—sometimes they scare me, usually they excite me, and every now and then they make me terribly sad. Like the night we took our clothes off and sat in candlelight across from each other on the floor. Nancy set the alarm clock to go off in fifteen minutes and said our goal was to stare each other in the eyes until the bell went off, no matter what.

That sounded pleasurable and easy. But the longer I stared into Nancy's eyes, the sadder I became. I felt exposed, vulnerable, bare to an ocean of emotions that welled up in my soul and threatened to pour out of me so completely there would be nothing left. I felt my personality dropping away—until all that held me in place were the minuscule stars of reflected candlelight I saw in Nancy's eyes. Two focal points of consciousness I clung to until the alarm went off. Then I hurled myself on the floor, sobbing.

"God, that was awful," I exclaimed.

"God, that was great," Nancy said. As they had in mine, tears welled up in her eyes, but something else did, too—a feverish excitement that made her seem, for all our closeness of seconds ago, far away.

Nancy's favorite "meditation" is a game she refers to as "it." As in, one of us is *it*. Both of us start out buck naked. If you're "it," you have to keep absolutely still while the other one does whatever she wants to arouse you. She can stroke, lick, kiss, or whatever, but if you are "it" you have to hold still and keep silent. If you move, moan, grunt, or thrash (sighing is allowed, but that's all), you have to put a piece of clothing back on. You could call it strip poker in reverse.

The idea is to stay so still and silent during sex that your arousal has to find alternate pathways to orgasm than such trusty standbys as shrieking "oh my god," digging your heels into the bed, thrusting your pelvis up and down, or clawing the sheets. Nancy says that we all have an "energy body" superimposed on our physical bodies, but the only way you can kick-start these rarefied circuits is to remain absolutely still.

At first, this game felt weird—like an exercise in repression. It didn't help that whenever I was "it" I wound up fully clothed while Nancy remained nude. But Nancy encouraged me to keep trying, and at times I did feel as though some new "chutes and ladders" were opening inside my body—as if my torso were a chimney and orgasms wafted up my spinal column and exploded through a hole in the top of my head. Usually, sex leaves me feeling sweaty and worn—a sated, sensual beast. But this *wafting* and *dispersing* type of orgasm left me feeling disembodied.

Nancy is adept at having orgasms in this airy, celestial way. At first, her body tenses up and she looks as miserable as I do when I can't thrash and moan—but then her face clears. She looks blissful and quiescent, her closed eyes serene as Buddha's, her lips pressed together in a Mona Lisa smile. I know I should be happy that Nancy has attained the Nirvana she seeks, but I'm not. I miss her. I wonder where she's gone. And I miss the more companionable, unevolved thrash and grunt kind of sex we had in the beginning.

Whenever I asked Nancy for the old-fashioned, sweaty and sticky sex that I prefer, she would refuse. Or if she said yes, once we began to make love, she would withdraw to some faraway shore. Then, ironically, *I* would stop, feeling as though I must have done something wrong. I was afraid Nancy didn't like me touching her. I was afraid I repelled her.

Of course, I couldn't explain all this to Nancy as she hugged me from behind on the inn's back lawn. Emotions are fast, but thought is slow. Especially mine. And at the time, I didn't myself understand why a burst of annoyance at Nancy exploded inside me. So when she slipped her hands in my armpits and tried to pull me up, I went limp. I mean, a girl has to take a stand sometimes—even if she does so in stupid, self-defeating ways.

Nancy let go and stepped away from me. I could feel her angry gaze searing my back. "All right, I give up. Be that way. Hug your bad mood instead of me. Honestly, Val, sometimes you repel me."

"What?" I gasped in shock. There it was, my worst fear. Baldly, bluntly come true. Even though I feared Nancy felt that way, I never imagined she'd actually *say* it.

"You heard me," she said. "You could choose to be happy. You could choose to have a good time. But you prefer your own misery to my company." She gathered up her clothes.

"Well, the truth is out now, isn't it?" I snarled. "You're always trying to cheer me up. You treat me like one of your little clients. Well, just who is it who really needs cheering up? Huh? When you can't cheer me up, you get mad. But you'd eat me alive before you'd let me cheer you up. You never even let me decide when to have sex. It's all up to *you, you, you, you, you.*" I was ranting, but I couldn't stop.

I fell mute as I watched Nancy clutch her clothes against her stomach and stalk off. Somehow, my bad mood was no longer good company. I had been sorry for myself before, but now I felt pathetic. I looked down. The grass—lush and green—beckoned. I hurled myself on the lawn, rolled over to face the sky, and said aloud the first words that came to mind, "Oh, goddamn. Goddamn. Harumph. Harumph."

I heard a voice beside me and gazed up. Nancy had returned, now clothed in shirt and shorts. She lay down beside me. Then she turned and said one word.

"Harumph?" she said quizzically.

I laughed, having lost the will to be angry, "It was the best I could do. Being upset with you depletes my vocabulary."

We were quiet for awhile, staring at the sky. Then I said, "Nancy, do I really repel you?"

"Honestly, Val?"

"Honestly."

"Yes, you do sometimes. When you're sullen and moody. When you seem to detest life."

I sighed. And she hurriedly added, "I'm sure it isn't fair. I'm probably repelled by something in myself that I see in you. I'm sure my need to cheer up every wounded child—"

"Oh, Nancy, I'm sorry—" I started to interrupt, but she shushed me.

"No, Val, *do not* apologize for speaking your mind. Anyway, I'm sorry. I mean, I'm not sorry that I told the truth, but I'm sorry I said it in anger."

And the funny thing was, Ashmont, that after she said that, I felt okay. It was all right for Nancy to feel repelled by me at times, because she obviously felt many other things, too, including the respect to be completely honest. It made me trust her. I've always wanted someone who could fight well with me, and then make up equally well. And now I have her. Or, had her.

"Nancy, I've been thinking," I said as the air between us calmed and cleared. I stroked her bare rib cage between her breasts where her shirt fell open.

"About the sex thing?" she asked. "I wasn't aware you thought it was one-sided. I'm sorry. I'll try to be more responsive to you." She pulled my hand to her mouth and kissed my palm, then placed it across her breast.

"That's not exactly it," I said, returning my hand to her ribs. I wanted to tell her that I'd figured out that sex for her was what prayer had been for Mary Patrick. A way to transcend the ordinary. To love life by raising it to another level. But *I* was searching for a way to love the ordinary. To experience it in such a way that it didn't *need* transcending.

But as Nancy looked at me, curious, expectant, I couldn't find the words. Strong as Nancy always seems, I sensed that these words would ruffle the still surface of an underground pool—and I held back, uncertain whether speaking them would be courageous or cruel.

Instead, I decided it was my turn to cheer us up. So I stood up, took my shirt off, and turned it inside out before I put it back on. Then I extended a hand to Nancy to help her up. "I think it's time to go swimming, after all," I said.

"What did you do that for?" she asked, pointing to my exposed seams.

"I figured it must be a new fad," I said, pointing to Nancy, whose shirt was on inside out.

"Oh well, if you really want to be in vogue, you have to go all the way," she said, removing her shorts and putting them back on inside out. I took my jeans off and did the same, and we walked, pockets flying, to the beach, finding rapport in silliness.

I knew we hadn't resolved our problems. But I trusted that with time, we would. Learning to love with trust and respect has been Nancy's great gift to me. It is the lesson I needed to learn in the classroom of life.

Nancy has an alternate myth to the *round* people. She believes that lovers attract each other not to complete but to teach one another. Earth is a cosmic classroom where we perfect our souls. We choose our partners from some prenatal higher plane, because we recognize in them the teachers our souls require. It doesn't matter if the person you're attracted to irritates or enrages you—because you're not with them to have fun, but to educate your soul.

Nancy has taught me that you can love somebody and find joy and warmth in her presence—but even *that* kind of love doesn't take away a deeper loneliness and yearning for something you can only find inside yourself. Sometimes, I can't believe that I'm thirty-three years old and learning this for the first time. At other times, I feel precocious.

Anyway, I was afraid to ask Nancy what she has learned from me, because I was sure the answer was "nothing." But she pestered me for days, saying, "Don't you want to know, Val? I won't tell you unless you ask." Finally I burst out, "Yes, all right, I want to know."

Smiling triumphantly, Nancy said, "You're innocent, Val. And you're good."

"Am not," I muttered, looking down, feeling annoyed and embarrassed. "What gibberish. I'm a sinner. I'm selfish. I'm ignorant. I'm a big mess."

"Yes," Nancy said, bemused and undeterred. "Yes, you are. And yet you are innocent and good nonetheless. That's what I've learned from you."

Ashmont, I could not meet her eyes, although I felt them probing me. My heart filled with joy, as did my lungs with air, as if a rubber mold surrounding them had been dissolved. It is what I have always secretly hoped, but didn't dare believe. To hear Nancy say so was overpowering. I closed my eyes to steady myself. *I can die now,* I thought. For a moment, I felt at peace.

A few days later Nancy asked me if I wanted to move to San Francisco. Can you imagine, Ashmont? Me—Provincetown-bound, adventure-starved me—in *San Francisco?*

The odd thing was, I wasn't tempted. I expected to be, but I wasn't. Not because I don't love Nancy. And not because I'm not saddened at the thought of her leaving. But I didn't think seriously about actually packing up and moving to San Francisco for a second. Mind you, I was *thrilled* to be asked—even though Nancy warned me that her invitation came with no "guarantees."

"What would your family say about your bringing home a white girl?" I asked.

"They'd say I was no better than my grandfather," Nancy replied. "Listen, I could bring home a white *bear* without an eyebrow being raised as long as it was male. It's that damn gender thing they're still getting used to. But they'll just have to keep at it, because I'm not about to change."

But even while I compiled list after list of all the reasons why I ought to want to go, I knew I wouldn't. It puzzled me. So I sought out Desmond and Raymond one night to talk it over. As soon as I walked into their living room, Desmond looked at me wistfully, shaking his head, "California is so *far* . . ." he trailed off as he left the room to answer the telephone.

"What's Desmond been drinking?" I asked.

"He assumes you're going," Raymond said, kicking a magazine off the sofa so I could sit down, and handing me his just-emptied beer bottle. "Here, want to scrape the label?" (Some habits never die.)

"Why?" I asked, "I haven't said either way."

"Dez can't imagine you not going. He likes Nancy. She's the—"

"—most normal human being I've ever been attracted to," I finished with Ray. "I know you approve desperately. You both beam at me whenever she's around—as if I were pregnant or something."

"Perish the thought," Raymond said, feigning horror, "What a wretched mother you'd make!"

I finished peeling the label off one bottle and looked around for another. Raymond clutched a fresh bottle of beer to his chest, protesting, "You can't have it. Chew your nails or something. For God's sake, Val, learn to knit."

But I spotted Dez's empty bottle nearby, fetched it, and resumed peeling. We were quiet for a moment, then Raymond announced, "You aren't going." It wasn't a question, and I looked up in surprise.

"How did you know?"

"Because if you were going, you wouldn't have taken time to think about it. You'd have been in San Francisco as soon as Nancy told you she was leaving, before she even asked you. You'd have shot out of Provincetown like a rocket."

"Do you think it means I don't love Nancy?"

"No," Ray said slowly. "I do think it means there is something—or someone—you love more."

"But what? Who?" Raymond always sounds so sure of himself that I assume he has all the answers. He has admonished me more than once not to mistake confidence for knowledge.

"Oh, for heaven's sake, Val, I don't know," he said impatiently. "Maybe it isn't that you love someone else more than Nancy, but that you know in your heart that you *could*—that wonderful as she is, she's not your destiny. That whoever—or whatever—is, hasn't found you yet. Now leave me alone. I'm going to bed."

"Can I have your bottle?" I asked.

"No, I'm taking it with me," he said irritably as he left the room. But I knew he wasn't seriously mad because he didn't slam the door. When Raymond is truly angry, he always slams the door.

So I'm not going anywhere, Ashmont. Provincetown has a grip on me. And whatever it's doing to me, it isn't through yet. As scary as it is to think so, Provincetown must be my cosmic classroom. Every instinct I have says that whatever I'm on the planet to learn, I have to learn here. Whoever I am going to meet, I have to meet her here. Whether I like it or not.

To tell you the truth, when Raymond said that perhaps I knew there was someone I could love more than Nancy, my mind immediately turned to you. As much as I love Nancy, my love for you is deeper, stronger, stranger. I'm not saying that's a good or a healthy thing—it's simply the truth. As hard as I try not to, I sometimes feel that I am still waiting for you. That I have not aged a day in my emotions toward you since Barclay College. In the deepest strata of my mind—layers impervious to time and truth—I have a fixed belief that some day you will arrive, bag and baggage, at my side. My dream will come true, and you will recognize at last that your true home on earth is with *me*.

In the meantime, Nancy left.

And I stayed behind.

It wasn't a wrenching farewell, just a solemn and sad one. I knew Nancy had to go. I knew that she would be fine, that she would meet someone else, that she would work at being happy. And I know she assumed the same—with less reason—about me.

Truthfully, I've often thought that Nancy and I might not have stayed together even if she'd stayed. One evening a few weeks back I overheard her having a conversation with Desmond and Raymond about whether or not extraterrestrials had ever visited Earth.

Raymond said confidently that it was ridiculous to think alien life forms had visited the planet. It was too big a secret for blabbermouth governments to keep. But he looked forward to the day when they did arrive, because they would make differences between nations, religions, and races look minuscule in comparison to differences in planet of origin, not to mention in the number of heads, brains, or feet.

Desmond said with equal confidence that he was sure extraterrestrials *had* been here, that their superior intelligence and technology explained the Egyptian pyramids, Mayan temples, the inventions of the wheel and of democracy, and the Emancipation Proclamation. Desmond views all benign advances in human history as proof of alien intervention. He opined that the "military industrial complex" has conspired to keep evidence of alien visitations secret.

Raymond turned to Nancy and asked, "What do you think?"

"Sweethearts," Nancy said, her eyes liquid and dreamy as she stared up at the indigo sky, "they're here all the time. But they don't travel in ships. They live in another dimension. You can hunt your butts off in the material world and you won't turn up a single flying saucer or laser gun. They don't need them. They link up with your mind." She tapped her forehead, closed her eyes, and sat back, nodding.

Desmond and Raymond were speechless, and took advantage of Nancy's closed eyes to raise skeptical eyebrows at each other. Nancy had lifted the conversation from tabloid controversy to metaphysical speculation.

"Where's Val?" Desmond asked abruptly. "She said she'd bring me a beer ten minutes ago." He excused himself to fetch drinks, and Raymond stood up, stretched, and invited Nancy to walk down to the beach.

I took advantage of their absence to sit down in Nancy's still warm chair, and to look up at the sky as she had just a minute ago. Like strong perfume that lingers after the wearer has departed, I could almost smell the wistful yearning she left behind.

That's where she really wants to be, I thought. Not with me. Not with other people. Not on the planet. Her soul hungers for *elsewhere*. The depths of the ocean. The outer reaches of space. Other dimensions of space and time. She believes she will feel more at home there than she ever has here on earth. That's what sex was for Nancy, a way to leave earth behind. The problem was, she left me too.

And that made her just like my parents. Nancy has her own "amber sphere." The difference is that Nancy remains conscious while she travels. Over time, staying with Nancy might have left me even lonelier than I am without her.

The only person I've ever loved who shares my goal of surviving and enjoying life on Earth rather than fleeing or transcending it is YOU. It makes you more precious to me than ever—if that is possible.

Nonetheless, Ashmont, ultimate mismatch that Nancy and I may have been, I do miss her. I miss her when I see children. I miss her when I see Desmond's telescope. I miss her when I see black faces on television (there are so few in Provincetown—or on TV, for that matter). I miss her when I am sanding furniture. I miss her when I put my clothes on right side out. And I especially miss her when I have only my pillow to kiss as I go to sleep.

I pace the deck a lot, trying to appreciate paradise. And I spend a lot of time at The Boat Builder's. BB is an artist at being alone. I've never seen her voluntarily seek out the company of another person. Hanging around her is almost like being alone, so it's good practice.

Darcy likes her, too. That's the little girl that Nancy brought to the inn with her play group—the one who doesn't talk. I've become her volunteer "older sister" while she's in foster care. I've offered to take her to the circus and the beach, but what Darcy likes best is to follow me around and watch me work. Her favorite thing, however, is sitting near BB while she builds boats. They must recognize each other as kindred spirits, because BB actually says, "Hello, Darcy" and smiles at her when we arrive. Often, we'll eat lunch together. Darcy, me, and BB. We spread our sandwiches out on a tarp and eat without talking. The only sounds are crunching and slurping and crinkling paper.

The odd thing is, these meals have become my favorite time, too. Their silence acts like gravity on my spirit, rooting me to earth. I feel strangely peaceful and refreshed after these wordless picnics—as though I've been on a long retreat.

The less I talk, the more BB seems to like me. If speaking correlates to liking, that is, which, with BB, it may or may not. But lately she smiles at me when I arrive and says, "Hello, Val," even when Darcy isn't with me.

BB's pleased that I stopped making all that kitsch furniture. After Nancy left, my whimsy failed. I didn't have the heart for bright colors and fantastic shapes. What I do now is restore and repair. I sand for hours, rubbing off old layers of paint and varnish. And when I get down to the bare wood, I can no longer bring myself to paint the beautiful texture and grain. I see them with new eyes. Maybe they're simply BB's eyes, but wherever they came from, I see beauty now that I was too clouded or fearful or angry to see before. I actually take pride in my work.

BB must have sensed my moroseness one day. She invited me to sail out in one of her boats! I was infinitely flattered. But I declined. I'm still afraid of the sea's ominous belly. Somewhere out there, there's a blowhole waiting to suck me in.

So, Ashmont, your Val continues very slowly to grow up. Not to fear, though, I'll never grow out of adoring you. Now that you've quit your job (does this have anything to do with the mysterious "legal entanglement" to which you alluded on the phone? Surely you would tell me if you needed money for bail—I'm kidding, of course . . . I'm sure it's nothing so dire or you would tell me: *wouldn't you?*) why stay in dour Buffalo when Paradise is near?

Loving you, missing you, and
needing you,

Val

1988

June 1988
Dear Ashmont,

The tiger lilies are blooming in dense orange rows beside the fish pond. The hummingbirds perform their gravity-defying stunts at the bright red feeder near the rose garden. The sun rises early and sets late. The glory of summer surrounds me.

But so does death. Raymond died.

As you know, he's been ill for six months. After surviving pneumonia, several bouts of thrush, and starting to lose his sight to retinitis, a bout of meningitis pushed him past the hard edges of life and into the fine mist of death. That is how I think of the passage from Earth, Ashmont, as migrating gradually from the solid clarity of an ice cube into the formless vagueness of water, then the wandering diaspora of fog—and finally, the clear light of day. You remember the Sandburg poem about the fog coming on *little cat's feet*—that sweet, sentimental poem petrifies me, because I know the fog is death, which on some unannounced day will surround and trap me and disperse my molecules.

Anyway, Raymond is no longer here—but perhaps he is everywhere, restored to the intricate, eternal molecule I used to think was God.

Tending Raymond here at the inn was unbearable at times. He would lie propped up in his hospital bed, breathing shallowly. Gauntness gave every gesture a ghostly elegance. The light in his eyes dimmed with pain and confusion. It reminded me of the look I'd seen in the eyes of a beached young beluga whale in a documentary I saw on TV. It had swum onto a rocky beach to scratch its molting skin. The tide receded, leaving the whale to flounder helplessly on shore, its tender white skin bleeding from the rough rocks. It's eyes looked out from its massive, trapped body in mute protest and puzzlement: *What is happening to me? How can this be? Can no one help?*

The whale's fate unfolded with staggering indifference to his pain. I prayed desperately for the tide to return and free him. In Raymond's case, the tide I prayed for was death. And just as the waves mercifully returned and restored the whale to the comfort of his underwater home, the tug of death finally rose high against the shore of Raymond's life, and washed him free.

I miss him terribly. Each morning I wake up as if life were the familiar robust routine of last year or the year before, and then I remember: Raymond's dead. And the ache descends anew. It takes enormous effort to sit up, put my bare feet on the stiff rag rug, and plod my heavy way to the bathroom. Brushing my teeth can take ten minutes, and I sob spontaneously over small, ridiculous things—a dropped toothpaste cap, the sight of my own tired face in the mirror, a button whose last threads give way as it falls with a click on the floor.

Every day, I descend more deeply into the hole in my life that Raymond has left behind. He was more family to me—excepting Desmond—than my own kin. Kinder, truer, wiser. My mind struggles to grasp his permanent absence from my life. I keep thinking I see him in the inn, not his physical presence, but a rift in the air that holds his essence. And when I walk down the street, I keep thinking I see Raymond's crisp white trousers, Raymond's corduroy blazer, Raymond's scalp-hugging, salt-and-pepper hair. My heart lifts—then plummets when the resurrected Raymond turns out to be some stranger after all.

Raymond's dying wish was to be cremated and have his ashes strewn about Provincetown harbor. He asked *me* to sail out and sprinkle the sea with his remains. He chose sea-phobic, monster-fearing me. My fear was precisely why he asked.

A week before he died, Raymond commanded me to his bedside. Always prone to bossiness, he became a tyrant in his dying days. If Dez or I showed the least reluctance to fulfill one of his commands, Raymond would protest, *"How dare you disobey a dying man?"* I asked Desmond once if Raymond constantly referred to his impending death because he wanted to be sure we weren't denying his mortality.

"That's a sweet thought, Val," Desmond said, looking at me as though I had just suggested Santa Claus was real. "But Raymond is dying exactly the way he lived: bossy, bitchy, and opinionated. Frankly, I think he's practicing so he'll be ready when he gets to heaven and starts telling God how to run the universe."

Then Desmond grinned wickedly and added, "Of course, that's assuming heaven is Raymond's destination."

When I arrived at Raymond's bedside, he waved Desmond off and gestured with a single skinny finger for me to sit on the chair beside his bed.

He gripped my hand and I was surprised, as I was every time he touched me, at how light and bony his hands had become, how papery and soft. Where had he gone, I wondered. Where had Raymond's strength and substance gone? It was a mystery to me: how much smaller could he get and still be Raymond?

"I have a mission for you, Valerie Marie," he said enigmatically.

"Don't call me that. Only the nuns called me that. No, NO!" I said as I saw him opening his mouth to protest, "Not even dying men get to call me that!" He looked sulky for a moment.

"Say *please*," he commanded.

"Oh, okay," I said, losing heart to defy him, "Please don't call me that."

"Good," he said. "Now, Val, I've decided that cremation is the proper way to dispose of me, and I want my ashes tossed at sea. My sister Grace was right, water came before dust. I want to return to the source. And you will be the one to deliver my earthly remains to Neptune's depths."

"No," I said instinctively, scraping my chair back a few inches as panic swept through me. "Don't ask me. I can't. You know I'm terrified of the ocean. I can't go out in a boat. Besides," I whined, "it's Desmond's place to do something like that."

Raymond gripped my hand tightly so I couldn't get away from him. He was skinny, but powerful. *"Desmond,"* he said in an indignant whisper, "gets seasick. *Desmond* wants me buried in a big metal box he can visit in some cemetery. I will not rot in a can below the earth like some pickled earthworm! Not for Desmond; not for anyone!" Then in a louder, imperious voice he added, "Besides, this chore is yours. I've anointed you, and you must perform it."

"But I'm afraid," I said.

"Big fucking deal," Raymond retorted, unmoved. "I'm afraid of dying. So what?"

"But Raymond—" I started to protest, but he cut me off.

"I'm sick of it!" he nearly shouted, and I shut up. A hush fell over the room. I felt stunned by the impatience in his voice.

"I've been listening to you whine about the great sea monster waiting to eat you up for sixteen years!" His tone was cutting.

"Sixteen years! For God's sake, Val, you've been living on the Cape for sixteen years and you've never gone sailing, never swam more than ten feet from shore, never taken the goddamned *ferry!* And I'm just plain sick of it. Don't ask me why, but it irritates the hell out of me. I love you like a sister or a daughter or some strange hybrid in between, but if you'd been *my* cousin instead of Desmond's, I'd have tied you up, dragged you out to sea in a rowboat, tossed you overboard, and left you there to swim ashore. Goddamn fucking sea monster, indeed," he muttered.

I sat in shock. I'd no idea Raymond felt this way. I didn't know whether to be angry at his lack of compassion for my fears, or to be touched by how much he cared.

I also felt deeply humiliated. I looked down. I could feel Raymond searching my face. He was looking for resistance, defense, or protest. Not finding it seemed to soften him. He released my hand, and I used it to clutch my other, grasped them both in front of my stomach. I felt nauseous.

I could feel him waiting for a response. But I couldn't speak without crying, and I didn't want to give him that satisfaction. I knew I could outlast him in silence. It would be a small victory, but important for me at the moment.

"Oh for God's sake, Val, speak!" he finally burst out.

"Why? Why!" I said, my anger spilling out. "So you can squash me like a bug? Does it make you feel better about dying to see that you can squash somebody? Well, I'm an easy target. You ought to pick someone tougher . . ." My voice trailed off, already appalled at what I'd said.

"Is that what you think?" Raymond said levelly. I looked up and met his gaze, my eyes brimming with tears.

"No," I answered honestly. "But you made me feel very, very bad."

"Val," he said slowly, taking my hand back inside his, but gently this time. "Do this for me—"

"Oh, Raymond," I pulled back. "Give it up. I can't. I don't want to. Ask someone else."

"Listen to me," he commanded. "I want to tell you a story. Will you listen?"

"No," I muttered unhappily.

"Well, I'm going to tell you anyway. There was this Buddhist teacher, one of those very crazy wise men. He lived in a cave and one day while he was out gathering firewood, a bunch of demons moved in. He got home and they'd taken over like squatters. Now, being a great guru and all, he knew these goddamned demons had to be coming from his own mind. So at first he asked them politely to move out, but they wouldn't budge.

"Then he charged them like a bull, but they laughed. So the next thing he did was, he just sat down and started living his life in the middle of them, not paying any attention. And the next thing he knew, they had all disappeared. Except for one—the ugliest, most vicious one."

He paused and looked at me.

"What?" I said, interested. "What?"

"Just wanted to make sure you're listening. You see, Val, the way I figure it, that's exactly where you've gotten to in your life, exactly where this guy is when he's still got one big demon in the middle of his cave. And you've gotten *used* to it living there. You're not even trying to get rid of it any more."

"So what?" I said, feeling defensive. "Is that so bad?"

Raymond ignored me and went on with his story. "So the next thing this guy does is, he goes and stands in front of this vicious demon. He sticks his head inside its mouth, and says, 'Okay, demon, eat me if you want to.' And as soon as he does that, the last demon disappears."

Raymond shrugged, and fell silent, as if the story's ending proved that I must accept his challenge.

"But," I said, shaking my head, feeling inexplicably anxious, "what if the demon *didn't* disappear? What if it bit off his head?"

Raymond exploded in laughter.

"What's so funny?" I asked, feeling wounded.

"Nothing," Raymond said, wiping his eyes, "it's just that that's exactly what I thought you'd say. And it's a good question. It truly is. Heads do get bitten off. But you see, we have two choices when the demons surround us, but only one that we can live with."

I felt pleased that he had said *"We."* I started to relax for the first time since Raymond began this conversation.

"We can learn to live with a demon in the house. And we get so used to it that we don't even notice that we're walking around it, that we have to dust it, that we can't leave it alone in the house or invite guests over anymore. Or we can jump into its mouth and either get our heads bitten off or get rid of it for good.

"You're talking to a man who is sitting smack dab in the middle of the demon's mouth right now, Val. All I can tell you is I'd rather be here on the inside getting to know my demon rather than standing on the outside feeling afraid to jump in. Now, bottom line, will you do what I ask?"

"Okay," I said. I can't tell you why. Nothing had changed. I was still afraid. But once I'd said it, I couldn't weasel out of a deal with a dying man.

After Raymond's memorial service, BB volunteered to take Desmond and me—Dez insisted on coming, he said an afternoon of nausea would be his final gift to Raymond—out in one of her boats, so at least I knew the hull would be strong and secure, and the sailor guiding my way competent and skillful. To make it easier on me, BB chose a hot, clear day with soft breezes to nudge us gently forward.

Before we launched the boat, I made one last attempt to back out of my deal. Desmond carried the urn with Raymond's ashes with one hand, a packet of Dramamine in the other. As he stepped into the middle of the boat, he reached a hand out to help me in and I paused.

"You don't need me. You're the appropriate person to do this, Dez. I'd just be horning in."

"You will get in the boat this instant, Val, or you will leave my inn and never return." I had never seen Desmond so fierce.

"You're the one Ray wanted to do this. You promised a dying man you would honor his last wish. And if you break your word now, you're no cousin of mine."

Chastened, I stepped into the boat. As I reached out to accept the urn from Desmond's hands, I met his gaze. In them, I saw pure misery. I reached out to touch his shoulder, but he jerked it back.

"Don't touch me, Val." He said it calmly but definitively. Then he sat in the middle of the boat and turned his back toward me. And then I understood that the only way Desmond could get through this was silently. Stoically. Separately. And I would have to do the same.

I huddled near the back of the boat for the voyage out, staring at the broad blue belly of the beast, feeling absolutely petrified.

"So what if the beast takes me?" I thought as I stared at the opaque rippling surface of the sea. "What would be so awful about dying? The struggle is over then. You can rest."

I gripped the sides of the boat as we lurched along, balancing Raymond's urn between my knees.

"But I'm too young to die!" I protested. "I'm not ready yet! I haven't done anything I really wanted! I haven't achieved anything I'm proud of!"

Then I looked at Raymond's urn. I opened it up and stared at the ashes.

"Dez?" I asked. "Now?"

"Just do it," he said, staring straight ahead.

I started pouring the ashes over the side of the boat into the sea, trying to imagine how they could once have been Raymond. Suddenly, my fears seemed ludicrous.

"Oh, who the hell cares," I thought. *"I'm going to wind up just like Raymond some day. Fragments of carbon being sucked by seals. If the beast wants me, let her hunt me down! Let her suck me in and chew me up! I've done the best I can."*

I laughed aloud, a slightly demented laugh. Desmond glanced back quickly, looking glazed and seasick. And BB, who had been busy adjusting the sails, cast me a quick, approving look that said, "Yes, Val. Living and dying are perfectly absurd."

Then I remembered that Raymond always said I talked about BB as if she were a cocker spaniel—always supplying words for gestures and movements that don't require them. So I laughed even harder, doubling over and rocking the boat. A wave lapped roughly over the side, and I punched it right in its cold, moist, shape-shifting face!

I stood up, spread my arms out straight to the side, dropped Raymond's urn overboard, and dove into the demon's gaping jaws.

For an eternal moment that must have lasted less than a second, I felt certain I was about to die. The sky turned upside down and the water below waited to swallow me.

My head broke the surface, and the icy wet chill slapped my skin and spread through my hair, my clothes, and shoes. My eyes saw glassy green, and my nostrils filled with water as I sputtered and gasped for air. I sank down several feet into darker water, curled my knees against my chest, and turned my body upward. I kicked frantically. And I rose above the water's surface, spitting out salty water, and squinting into the reassuring sun. I was sure something would bite my foot and drag me underwater again. But I was still very much alive. I felt frozen and foolish but pleased. I hoped that Raymond had seen me. I believed he had died wondering if I would keep my promise.

BB tossed me a life preserver, and I grabbed it with one hand and paddled my way toward the boat with the other. She reeled me in. Desmond yelled, "Are you fucking nuts? It's not enough that Ray dies. Now you go berserk on me! Get your goddamn ass back on this boat. I'm not ready for you to die. I'm gonna goddamn kill you, Val!"

When I reached the boat, Desmond grabbed my wrists and pulled me roughly on board, shouting, "What the fuck's the matter with you?" He threw a towel at me, then crossed his arms and set his jaw and turned away.

BB remained calm. She placed the towel gently around my shoulders.

"Are you all right?" she asked.

"Yeah, I'm okay," I said nodding, pulling the towel tighter around my shoulders. "Just cold."

She looked at me severely and said, "Don't ever do that again." And she returned to adjusting the sails and steering the boat.

"I'm sorry," I said humbly. But I wasn't, really. I didn't, however, plan to repeat my death-defying leap ever again.

I don't know if I've conquered my fear of the monster sea for good, but I was calm, even cocky, the rest of Raymond's voyage. Watching his ashes disperse in the immense, impersonal ocean clarified the absurdity of all my previous ambitions and fears.

There is nothing to prove. Nothing at all of any consequence. Nothing that will stave off death. Nothing that will alter fate. If it is my fate to be swallowed by the beast, so be it. There is nothing I can do to stop it. As Raymond would say, "So what?"

Desmond wouldn't talk to me for the rest of the day. But I knew he wasn't so much angry at me as he was sad for both of us and for Raymond. That night, after I'd gone to bed, he rapped on my door, stuck his head in, and said solemnly, "Thank you, Val."

Then, in an uncharacteristic display of sentiment, he walked over to my bed and awkwardly kissed my forehead and tucked the sheets under my chin and my arms, as if I were a child. "He would be so proud," Desmond said, his voice catching, his eyes filling with tears.

"She did well," he said, patting my hand before he walked away. He was no longer speaking to me.

The only greater influence on me than Raymond's death has been Desmond's life during Ray's final days. I expected Desmond to react to Raymond's dying as Gilgamesh did Enkidu's. To rage and lament and thunder. But that wouldn't have helped Raymond. And helping Raymond was Desmond's sole priority. Every day, I watched Desmond winnow out the inessential emotions—his own rage and fear, his desire to flee, worries about his own death—which since he has the virus, too, will come all too soon, and will be endured without Raymond to keep him company.

Ashmont, I have always seen love as a psychic contraction that happens *to* you, not something you *decide to build*. When it is reciprocated, love comforts and consoles. When it is not, it torments and punishes. Desmond has shown me that love can be something else entirely—a discipline. A force that plunges you into a remote, rugged wilderness of pain and loss. If you make it through the trials of a lover's death, you emerge as Desmond has: an entirely rare and refined spirit, purified of human dross.

Desmond hates it when I speak of my admiration for him.

"What a load of crap," he snorts, turns his back, and leaves.

He thinks I've idealized him. But I haven't. Desmond can still be the world's greatest prick—irritable, sarcastic, and gruff. But I see now in Desmond that prickhood and nobility can co-exist.

Desmond and I are quieter than we have ever been, and we spend more time together. Raymond's absence speaks more eloquently of our loss than words. But every now and then, I will catch Desmond staring at me sadly. He'll shake his head and ask, his voice hoarse with suppressed emotion, "Are you ready, Val?"

And I know that those few words sum up Desmond's regrets, his pity, and his fear: *I'm sorry, Val, but I'm next. Can you take it?*

The truth is that I'm not ready. The truth is that I will never be. The truth is that I'll be here anyway, scrounging up the courage to do the right things.

"Of course, I'm ready," I say. And we fall back into silence.

The atmosphere here reminds me of lines from *Gilgamesh,* after the king's great grief has settled into a way of life.

> All that is left to one who grieves
> Is convalescence. No change of heart or spiritual
> Conversion, for the heart has changed
> And the soul has been converted
> To a thing that sees
> How much it costs to lose a friend it loved.

My heart is still changing, Ashmont. My soul is still learning to see. I need to slow and still my life while this rough education takes hold. This is the first summer in history I have dreaded the annual influx of tourists. I see a gaggle of guests climbing the inn steps and I groan, "Oh no, not humans. Stay away!" I have to be polite, especially with my expanded responsibilities for managing the inn, but I avoid unnecessary banter and keep to my room as much as I can.

The wonder is, silence no longer frightens me. I shall become as gorgeously stoic as my Ashmont! Will you miss my verbiage? Or be relieved?

But I am an ill-bred beast, for sure. So absorbed in my grief that I've forgotten life goes on. Pleasant, redeeming things happen even in the midst of tragedy, most significantly your promotion to Associate Professor! Congratulations!

I thought the university should have hired you as a *full* professor three years ago when you started teaching in the first place. So in my opinion, they're catching up. I'm glad you find teaching less stressful than counseling. The next time I visit you, I shall sit in on your class, *Professor Ashmont.* I promise to behave.

Oh, there is one more small thing. I didn't want to tell you until I got the test results back, so you wouldn't worry needlessly. Before Raymond died, I was helping him carry his "wheelie"—that's what we called his portable IV drip—up the stairs. I was behind him carrying the metal pole. He lost his footing, fell backward, and landed on top of me. The IV needle tore free from his arm and nicked me as we landed in a heap on the ground. At least I think it nicked me. There was blood on my hand, but I was also cut and scraped from falling. Anyway, to be on the safe side, and at Dez and Ray's insistence, I decided to get tested. The good news is that I'm negative. I found out this morning—and finally felt free to tell you.

It's funny, Ashmont, but while I waited for my test results, I thought a lot about the past. I assumed that confronting death would make me contemplate the future—all the things I'd never get to do. Instead, I thought about the lovers I've had, the books I've loved, the youth I misspent—and of you—of my love for you and how much I've learned from you. The journey I've been on hasn't taken me anywhere distinguished, but it's always been intense, frequently bizarre, sometimes messy, and of course, sinful. But in its own stumbling, inarticulate way, it has also been surprisingly beautiful—to me. In the end, that's all that matters.

The only wistful longing I felt toward the future I might never have was that I would leave you behind, that I would never have the chance to love you as long or as well as I wished. Nor to be as close to you emotionally and—shallow and single-minded as I am, apparently unto death—physically, too.

So Ashmont, fear not. I'll be around to pester you about moving to Provincetown for the rest of my life! I was convinced all along the results would be negative. When I found out I was right, my first thought was: I can't die of AIDS. I'm fated to drown at sea. The beast is biding her time.

Farewell for now. Stay as healthy as you can. I expect to live forever! And I want *you* with me!

Your adoring friend,

Val

June 1988

Dearest Val,

When I think about what happened in Provincetown last week, I feel as if I'm grasping at a fading dream. I fear the details—the sharp, savory specifics—will blur into the shapeless haze of ordinary time. Last night I did a Val-like thing. I immortalized these larger than life events in *The Story of an Epic Friendship*.

I have an envelope addressed and stamped, and I will mail this letter before my 2:30 seminar on post-traumatic stress disorder. Lest I chicken out, I plan to bundle this envelope with some other mail and drop them all into the mailbox at once. I have nothing to hide anymore. Secrecy—which I pretended was privacy—has become a bad habit, and I must break it. So here is my story. *Our* story. I hope you like it.

✎

Another Chapter

Our Heroes Discover the Secret of Eternal Life

I received your letter of early June, in which you informed me of your encounters with death—Raymond's actual death, Desmond's impending one, and briefly, the possibility of your own. Although your letter ended with the reassuring news of your negative test results, I panicked. I paced my living room all night. My thoughts raced, and I couldn't rein them in.

Grief and fear spread through me at the thought of your dying. I kept reminding myself that you weren't in danger. But news of your HIV test forced me for the very first time to imagine the world—*my* world—without you. I could not do it. Literally, I could not form any pictures of a world, a time, a life without Val Summer at the other end of my thoughts. If you stopped existing, I could no longer be me. I might still be alive, but I would not be the "me" I've always known, but some alien creature I'd have to invent.

Although I never admitted it to you, I've always assumed we would grow old together. I imagined hobbling down Commercial Street with you in our eighties—two cranky, arthritic, white-haired, lifelong friends. Or at worst, if one of us had to die first, I was sure it would be me. *I* would be the Enkidu, you the breast-beating Gilgamesh. But what if *you* were to be the dying Enkidu? *Me* the one to wander on alone?

I felt a sudden, overpowering need to see you. I had to appreciate you fully while you were still alive. I had to tell you in person how much I love you. I had to reveal my secrets now. I would no longer withhold myself from you in any way, and I regretted the years in which I had.

I couldn't *wait*. I felt impulsive and passionate and reckless. I felt exactly as I have always imagined you do, Val Summer, and I proceeded to act like you. I made airline reservations on the next flight to Provincetown. I packed only my toothbrush and my credit card.

I arrived at your inn the following evening. I paused on the deck to look out over the orange sky and your famous view of paradise—one I've pictured often from my remote porch in Buffalo. It was more beautiful than I imagined. And at that moment, I couldn't fathom why I had stayed away from paradise and you. Perhaps I was afraid I would never leave. That, like you, the light, the space, the sea would work their mysterious magic on me and I would remain, caught by their spell, forever. At the moment, I wished it had. I saw a different life, like a jet's tail streaming upward from the deck to the nearest cloud, that I might have led. I yearned for it, and for an instant, grieved it.

I knew exactly where your room would be. Your door, painted blue with a brass sign reading "Manager" on it, was open. I stepped inside. Your bed was a mess, the purple comforter trailing on the floor, lavender sheets heaped in a three-foot high mound around your feather pillows. Papers and a dozen pens were strewn across your writing desk. Your underwear was on the floor. It looked exactly like your dorm room. I heard the shower running in the bathroom. I heard you humming cheerfully, and I breathed my first easy breath since I read your letter. Val was here. Val was alive. You would emerge through that enameled white bathroom door any second—cheerful and clean and fragrant. I waited.

I heard the water shut off. I heard the doorknob squeak, I saw you shuffle into the room, your head bent down as you towel-dried your hair, a kimono draped over your shoulders, your breasts exposed.

You spied my black pumps, quickly lifted your head, gasped, and clutched the lapels of the kimono tightly closed.

"How unlike you to be modest," I said.

"How unlike you to show up unannounced!"

Your face lit up with delight. And then, perceiving my tears before I knew I had shed them, you said solicitously, "Emily! Are you crying?"

You christened me Emily. I don't know whether I had become Emily before you saw me, or whether the gentleness of your voice transformed me. But at that moment I was no longer Ashmont, but *Emily*— an emotional creature who bursts into tears at the touch of a soft-spoken voice.

This strange, sentimental Emily remembered the many times you had tried to seduce me in college by standing half-naked in my doorway, dripping wet from your shower, longing for a kiss. Beautiful as you were, back then I never wanted to kiss you. *Then* it seemed a terrible idea. Complicated and dangerous. But *now* it seemed simple to kiss you. Breathtakingly simple. Marvelous, apple-cheeked Val. How could I *not* kiss you?

Then Emily, this impulsive, emotional creature, walked toward you, untied your robe, pressed her body against yours, placed your head firmly between her two hands, and kissed you wetly and sweetly on the lips.

You were shocked. Val Summer, lover extraordinaire, shocked by a simple kiss.

"Emily," you gasped, "do you know what you're doing?"

"Yes," I said.

I knew. I removed the kimono from your shoulders, and you stood naked in front of me. You looked so beautiful. It was almost as if I'd never seen you before. But seeing you now, a beloved, mortal friend, you registered in a new part of my brain. Rather not just in my brain, but in the whole of my heart and soul.

You, Val, will remember the passage from *Phaedrus* in which Socrates describes our souls as having wings—in the nebular realm of pure light that is humanity's original home. When we're born and descend into mortal form, we lose our wings—and our vision of true beauty fades. The beauty we find in those we love is meant to remind us of our sublime source, and to revive our yearning for union with our luminous core. But instead, we fall farther from the light. Beauty commands not reverence but lust. Desire leads us into folly, not wisdom. Some souls, however, being possessed by the madness of the gods, are provoked by mortal beauty to remember *true* beauty. She who is so provoked is called a lover. As she remembers, her wings begin to grow.

Provoked by your mortal beauty, Valerie Marie Summer, I became your lover. I realized I had always been your lover in this important way—you are and always have embodied true beauty for me.

I removed my clothes, and touched you everywhere. It was simple to love you. It was simple to make love to you. Simple yet sublime.

Then you asked with your hands if you could touch me. You seemed to know this would be harder. I nodded. And you began to touch me lightly all over my body. You knew to move slowly, so I could grow to desire, not fear, your graceful touch. I felt oddly achy where your hands made contact, as though my body were bruised and tender. But in the wake of your hands, my skin felt soft and tingling, like new skin beneath a wound after the scab has fallen off. Vulnerable, but ready for new life.

Your hands kept asking, "Do you want this? May I?" And I kept saying yes.

You lifted your body above me, a solicitous king examining the body of his wild, wounded friend.

A lioness, you leaned in to lick me clean.

Your head was a golden orb, crowned by the glinting corona of the setting sun. Your eyes two tide pools, where dolphins leap and play.

Your hands were feathery fronds, brushing breezily over the desert of my body, drawing moisture upward from the earth, like dew.

Your belly, a hot ivory dome, descends and melts into my cool, bones, and I am warmed and rise through you, over and over and over again. A dove. I am free. My wings restored. I lift heavenward, and blue is all I see. And blue is all I taste and touch. Blue is everywhere.

Then white.

I am still. At last.

I have journeyed to a different galaxy, a different space and time. And in the distance traveled, I have shaken away the parochial fears and customs of my former self.

Moments later, restored to human form, we lift our heads and gaze into each other's eyes. And then I knew what that grief-stricken, fool Sumerian king had to travel to the ends of the earth to discover. Neither the king nor his wild consort were meant to live forever. Only the thing they had between them was immortal. The love of human friendship is the secret of eternal life—the only kind which the gods can neither steal nor hoard. I would never have imagined until this moment that you, Val, in the end would be proven right.

Love Rules.

Then, I confided my secrets to you. All of them. My whole sordid family history. I had waited so long to tell you that I no longer feared your response to the secrets themselves, but your anger at the amount of time it had taken me to confide them.

But you were neither angry nor hurt. Neither were you shocked or surprised. Instead, *I* was. Because you already knew my story. Not the details, but the shape of the sleazy truth.

Nancy told you. Hearing you describe me, she guessed the outlines of truth, guessed how I had responded, and guessed why I never told you. And she was right about damn near everything. She told you I would tell you when I was ready, and that you should neither rush me nor harass me when I finally did confide. She's a smart woman, your Nancy. I have to admit, I felt dismayed at being so transparent. And even more dismayed, having worked up the courage to tell you, to find my news was stale.

Still, it was my first time telling *you*. And my first time telling *anyone* other than my ex-therapist. I felt immensely relieved at your response. You were—aside from initially muttering that if you'd been in my bedroom at the time you'd have "whacked" my father's balls off—sweet and supportive and grateful for my confidence. And in the face of such unexpected comfort, I shook off more layers of pain. We held each other, and fell into a deep, exhausted sleep.

Hours later, I half awoke to the sound of your voice on the phone. I opened one eye, and saw a kimono-clad angel drenched in bright sun. *"I don't know where I am,"* I thought, *"but I know it isn't Buffalo."* Half convinced I was in heaven, I yawned and stretched, observing my naked condition with curiosity, and returned to sleep.

Then you pounced on the bed. I woke fully. The angel was you. A very exhilarated angel. You dragged me from the bed, draped me in your kimono, and escorted me to a small sunporch where you had laid out a breakfast of coffee and juice and wheat toast with honey—my usual morning meal. Reckless, possessed creature that I was, I stole instead the sugar doughnut from your plate and ate it in three bites.

You laughed, but then your eyes grew solemn and you brushed your hair back with your hand.

"Emily," you said softly, "why?"

"Didn't you enjoy it?" I avoided answering, feeling suddenly fearful that perhaps you hadn't.

"Enjoy it?" you screeched, wide eyed, "I'm not convinced yet that I'm not dreaming. It was the peak experience of my life."

Then your face grew pensive as you added, "But why now? After all these years?"

"The truth is I don't know," I said plainly, feeling embarrassed at my lack of insight and forethought.

"I didn't come here planning on making love to you last night. I came because your letter frightened me. I couldn't imagine my life without you. And I needed to see you right away. What happened last night just . . . happened."

"Really?" you asked, your eyebrows lifted in astonishment. "But that's so—"

"Unlike me? More like you?"

"Yes." You smiled. Then your face dimmed. "You aren't sorry, are you? I mean, that we had sex?"

"No, Val. I am happy about it."

And you sat and beamed at me. You reached out and placed your forearm against mine so that our soft pale skin touched from our wrists to our elbows. You grinned, and I relaxed into your impish, self-satisfied gaze, allowing our pulses to mesh.

"Emily, I love you," you said.

"I know. I love you, too," I said, and kissed you on the cheek. You turned your face to offer me your lips, with hope and sweetness in your eyes. And I cannot honestly say that I wasn't tempted. That I didn't feel desire. That I would not have enjoyed the softness of your lips.

But I couldn't. I retracted.

I could tolerate no more closeness. I had passed my limit. What was simple and sublime last night would be complicated and dangerous today. Timing is everything. And the time was wrong. I conveyed all this in a glance. You understood. You looked away to absorb your pain, while your hand gripped my elbow more tightly. Your eyes hugged your disappointment deep within your heart. And by the time your eyes met mine again, I could see that we were clear.

You are brave. Braver than me. I admire you.

I saw that you understood, as I did myself, that our touching—lifting our bodies into the harmony our souls have always felt for each other—profound as it had been, might never happen again.

The madness of the gods strikes once. But my pilgrimage served its purpose. Our souls now bear the imprint of mystery and death—a bond that can never be broken. Our mortal, human friendship—birthed at Barclay College and consummated on the lip of Provincetown Harbor—has yielded the secret of eternal life, without doing violence to woman, man, or beast.

We finished breakfast in silence—uncharacteristic for you but a necessity for me. We had exhausted what words could express. You showed me your cousin's bizarre, magnificent inn and we walked on the beach. I left on the five o'clock plane, feeling sad to depart but knowing I must. I have courses to teach, papers to grade. Duties to fulfill. For now, Val. I have much to finish before I'm fit for paradise.

Flying back to Buffalo, I wondered about the summer of 1973. What if I'd come to the Cape as you asked? Would I be an innkeeper now? A waitress? Or a carpenter? Would I have been happier? Stronger? Saner? Would I have become your lover years ago? Would you still love me now?

For a change, I had only questions, not a single answer.

The chapter closes. I have to finish now if I'm going to mail this before class. I miss you terribly. Think of me as I think of you. Thank you for everything, Val, especially for being your own exquisite self.

Your friend eternally,

Emily

July 1988

Dear, sweet Emily,

I received a large envelope today with many stamps but nothing inside! It's not like you to be forgetful. What could be *so* important? Please tell! If you can . . . I tried calling you today, but your answering machine said you were out of town until Friday. Emily, I demand an answer! What was in that envelope?

I think about your visit every day. Do you know how precious every moment was to me? Ironically enough, although you came because you were afraid of my death, I myself am less afraid of dying than ever. I now have *no* regrets. But not because we had sex. Because of what our having sex revealed that I was too ignorant before to fathom. Let me try to explain.

Years ago, when I was dating Mary Patrick, I confided to her my disappointment upon receiving First Communion. In Sister Matthew's zeal to ensure that the children in her catechism class would show proper respect for the host, she had told us a horrifying tale. A group of children preparing for first communion had been offered a bribe by some "heathen" children who wanted to "see" Jesus in the wafer. They persuaded three of the children to spit the host into their handkerchiefs after the priest had put it on their tongues. After mass, these foolhardy waifs took their handkerchiefs out of their pockets, but before they could unfold them and produce the sacred host, the sky broke loose with a terrible roar, and three bolts of lightning struck each of the young blasphemers stone cold dead! The hosts, of course, had disappeared.

"So don't imagine," Sister Matthew warned, "that you can play fast and loose with the body of Christ! That host is filled with lightning! If it sees the air after it enters your mouth, God will let the bolts fly! Pity your poor parents, and for the love of God, keep your mouths shut!"

No doubt you can now understand my fear of death by lightning, in spite of its statistical improbability. But you can also understand why I expected to feel electric currents coursing through my body when I received first communion.

Instead, I felt nothing. Just a thin patch of flour, melting in my mouth. I assumed God had turned the current off. That I must be defective. Unworthy. Too sinful for God to bother.

Mary Patrick was dismayed. "Oh no, Val," she reassured me. "The reason you didn't feel anything, you sweet soul, is that the current was already on. If all the lights in a house are already turned on, you hardly take note of one more bulb. You've never been without the light of God. Jesus was already there!"

I didn't believe her. But it was a lovely thought.

What I've understood, Emily, since we had sex, is how much your love has always been with me. I used to think that your having sex with me would prove that you really loved me. And that your not having sex with me proved that, in spite of my love for you, I was unworthy of you.

I expected having sex with you to lift me out of complete darkness. But what I discovered was that sex with you added one more bulb. A miraculously beautiful, incredibly important bulb, but only one more bulb. The current was already on. Your light and your love were already there. I have never been without them.

I just didn't know. I didn't know how to know. But I do now.

So, thank you. Not for one night of sex—although to be truthful, if anything would bring me to my knees in prayer, it would be to appeal for *more* nights of sex—but for the lifetime you have spent loving me.

Back to the mysterious envelope. You must call, and satisfy my curiosity. I shall not sleep until I know what was *supposed* to be in this envelope.

Love forever,

Val

1990

May 1990

Dear Emily,

So . . . now I am an innkeeper. It has been six months since Desmond died and left me the inn, but I still wake up every morning needing to remind myself that I own the bed I'm sleeping in . . . and the twenty-five other beds and rooms that surround it.

For months before he died Desmond fretted about what to do with the inn. As you know, our family tends toward sleaze, vice, and infamy. Precious few Summers could claim to deserve an inheritance so dear to Desmond's heart. And, let's face it, the clan is hardly close-knit. You know that I never see my mother—why should I go to Florida to watch her drink herself to death? In a few years she'll succeed in doing so just as my father did four years ago. As for Jamie and Ralph? Who knows where they are. It's been decades since I heard from either one of them. But if my family is distant and disinterested, Desmond's is worse.

For reasons that baffle me, Desmond *wants* to see his parents. Unlike mine, his parents are healthy as hippos, playing golf and tanning their hides to alligator toughness in Arizona. But they have steadfastly refused to see him since he told them he was gay when he was twenty four. They told him they couldn't have "that" in their house. Can you imagine . . . he no longer even merited a *personal goddamn pronoun*. A year ago, he wrote to tell them he was ill, but the only response he got was a mass card from his mother. As if he was already dead. Can you believe it? His brothers and sister have the same attitude. They disgust me.

A few years ago, after it become clear that Raymond would die before him, Desmond started discussing leaving the inn to me. He knows I love the inn, and that I would die *myself* before I would allow real estate developers to replace this regal estate with cheap condos. But Desmond wasn't sure I wanted the inn. He was afraid I would feel burdened and constricted by his legacy. The truth is, I was afraid of the same thing.

We procrastinated talking about Desmond's will, because it meant thinking about his death. Finally, a few weeks before he died, Desmond asked me to walk with him on the beach. He was due to see his lawyer the next day.

In the old days, Desmond would drag me off for brisk walks along the beach. I could never keep up with him, so he would strut ahead and jog back, circling around me. Now, Desmond hobbled along with a three-pronged cane on one side and me on the other for support. He was breathing heavily by the time we crossed the grassy dunes and reached the shoreline. I was afraid he was straining too hard, so I took several deep breaths, and said, "Desmond, slow down, for godsake, what are you hurrying for?"

He snorted. "Never kid a kidder, Val. If I walked any slower, they could bury me right here."

We stood still for a moment, gazing at the glassy gray sea. Desmond reached awkwardly down to pick up a stone in his bony right hand, and tossed it clumsily at the huge, wet target in front of us. But the stone fell short of the shoreline, landing on dry sand just a few feet in front of Desmond's sneakers.

"Story of my life," he snorted wryly. ". . . couldn't make it as far as I intended."

"Stop," I said, raising my hand like a traffic cop. "I can't stand it when you get mawkish."

Lately, I found myself responding as unsympathetically to Desmond's complaints as Raymond always had. I spoke with Raymond's crisp inflection and his extravagant hand gestures. I felt as though he had come back, through me, to take care of Desmond in his final days. He knew *exactly* what Desmond needed. The tough, unsentimental rejoinders Raymond channeled through me braced Desmond as sturdily as his cane.

"Suck it up, boyo, and let's sit down," I said.

"Oh, suck it up yourself," Desmond snapped with irritable cheerfulness.

"And don't call me 'boyo.' I'm five hundred times your age." He stood quiescent as a child while I spread the blanket out, and calmly accepted my hand as I helped him lower himself to the ground.

"I feel like I'm eighty-five and made of sticks," he groaned as he stuck his hands under his butt. He was so bony now that it hurt to sit.

I folded a towel and held it out to slip under him. Then I took his hands inside my own and rubbed them.

"More like twigs," I said, teasing him sadly. "We should have brought your gloves."

"Ugh," he grunted, yanking his hands back in disgust, "now *you* stop. I'm fine." And he folded his arms, warming his hands in his armpits.

"Okay," I said.

He pulled his knees up to his chest for more warmth, but I knew better than to offer to cover him with my jacket. He sat silently, gazing sidewise at me every now and then.

Finally, he sighed and burst out, "You know, Val, there are two things I regret."

"Don't tell me; I know. One, you make weak coffee. Two, you made me learn accounting, which left me only half of my brain."

"No-o-o," he said somberly. "And if you can't talk seriously, we won't discuss it." He stared straight ahead, sulking.

"Oh, all right. What?" I asked.

He continued staring.

"Please," I begged. "Please tell me. I promise to be serious."

"All right," he said, turning to face me, eager to unburden himself. "First, I'm sorry I never told you I was sorry that Mary Patrick left. So I'll tell you now. I'm sorry, Val, that she left. I know it was very painful for you."

"Mary Patrick!" I was stunned. She was the last person I expected to be preying on Desmond's mind in his final days.

"Yeah," he said, gently reminding me, "you know, the nun."

"Oh course I know. Do you think I could forget her? But that was years ago."

"I know, but it always bothered me. I know how much you loved her. But I was so caught up in my anger at the church, that I couldn't be there for you. I'm sorry, Val. Do you forgive me?"

"There's nothing—"

"Bullshit," Desmond interrupted. *"Do you forgive me?"*

"Yes," I said, chastened. Clearly, he'd been bothered for a long time. "One down, what's the other?"

He took a gold key from his pocket and held it flat in his palm. I recognized it. It was the master key to the inn.

"You know what this is?"

"Yes."

"You know I want the inn to be yours, Val. There's no one I'd rather leave it to. But I'm not sure you want it. Sometimes I worry that I did the wrong thing by inviting you to live here in the first place. Then maybe I did more wrong by promoting you and teaching you the business. But I wanted you here. Other than Raymond, you're my only family. But if wanting you here has hurt you, if it's been bad for you, then I'm sorry. I'm truly sorry."

"Oh, Dez," I said, looking deeply into his earnest eyes, feeling a whirlpool of sorrow in my throat. I thought I had long ago detoxed myself of all regrets. But Desmond stirred up old doubts, and I choked back tears.

"I've made my own choices," I managed to say, but not until I broke eye contact. I gazed down at my tightly woven fingers, twisting in my lap.

"Yeah, but I'm sorry anyway. Because if it weren't for me, you'd have been forced to make other ones. Maybe they'd have been better ones. Maybe you'd have been happier."

I could feel Desmond waiting for me to say I'd made the right choice. That I'd been happy. But I couldn't. I felt like I'd swallowed a rubber ball. I couldn't talk.

Desmond looked away, assuming he'd gotten an answer. "So," he said, his voice breaking slightly, then assuming a forced, unconvincing cheerfulness, "I guess you'll fly free once I'm gone, hey, Val? Well, I'm happy for you."

He held the key out, staring at it in his palm. I stared at it, too, mesmerized. And in a trance, I suddenly saw myself doing exactly what Desmond predicted—flying through the air, high over the ocean, away from the inn, away from Provincetown for good, following an overpowering urge for freedom, for movement, for a life, for a self—utterly different from the ones I'd had.

"Where will you go?" Desmond asked.

When I didn't answer, he balled the key in his fist and drew his arm back, preparing to toss it into the waves.

"Oh, hell," he muttered, "it'll be sold for condos, anyway. I'll just give the fucking inn to the ocean. Maybe Ray will find it," he chuckled bitterly. "No, he'd do worse than condos. He'd *redecorate*."

Desmond tossed the key into the sand in front of us, inches away from the incoming waves.

"Well, that's it," I thought, sighing deeply, looking away from Desmond's glum face to the dim gold shape scattered with sand. *"One life is over. A new life begins."* We watched as the waves lapped closer. Soon, it would grab the key and carry my fate out to sea.

And then, I felt the roots I had planted in this seaside carnival town reach up and grab me. I panicked. "Where will you go?" Desmond had asked. The problem was that I had nowhere to go. No place that lured me. I couldn't fly around forever. Some day I'd have to land. But the only home I knew, and, I abruptly realized, the only home I wanted, was *here*—and the key to it was burrowing deeper into a mucky sinkhole in the sand.

I ran forward and scattered the wet sand with my hands like a dog. I couldn't find it. So I dug wider, and deeper and faster. Then, discouraged, I sat back on my feet, flapped my muddy hands mournfully through the air, and said sadly to Desmond, "I can't find it. It's gone."

Desmond grinned wickedly, "I knew it. I knew it," he cackled. "It's the curse of the Summers. Don't know what we got till it's goddamn gone." He reached into his shirt pocket, withdrew another gold key, and waved it tauntingly back and forth.

I leapt up and ran toward him, grabbing for the key. "I want it," I said. "Can I have it? I'll take good care of it, Desmond. I promise."

Desmond held the key out, but when I grabbed it, he held on. I looked at him quizzically.

"Say you love the inn," he demanded.

"I love the inn," I shouted. "The inn's my home."

But he still wouldn't let go. "Say you love Provincetown," he insisted, with a malevolent glint in his eyes.

I paused. This was harder. I looked seriously at Desmond. I thought of Raymond. This patch of earth owned us all—had given us to each other.

"I love Provincetown," I said softly. "Can I have the inn?"

"Cousin," he said, "it's yours."

He put the key in my palm, curled my fingers firmly around it, put his arms around me, and held me tight. I felt his body shaking. And I realized Desmond was crying.

When we finally sat back, Desmond's face looked light and clear. "I'll sleep well tonight. Help me up, Val. Let's go home."

I pulled him gently up to his feet, and we shuffled slowly back to my *home,* Emily. My habitat. My sheltering cave between the great blue bowl of sky and the immense, hungry jaws of the sea.

After that day, ironically, while Desmond's emotional health improved, his body deteriorated. It was as if once he knew the inn would be taken care of, he didn't feel the need to stick around.

Most of the rest you already know from our phone conversation the day Desmond died. (Thank God you were home—I'd have lost my mind without you.) How he became too ill to stay at home, and had to be admitted to the hospital. God, was he pissed about that. But what you may not know, since I've been too busy managing Desmond's estate to call (I'm sorry . . .) is that I tried to get a special ordinance passed at Town Meeting that would have allowed Desmond to be buried in the rose garden behind the inn.

I did not succeed. Instead, we went with Desmond's second choice, which was, astonishingly enough, to be buried in the ancient, vine-covered cemetery at St. Mary's! His will included generous donations to a national gay and lesbian civil rights group, the local AIDS support committee, and the parish of St. Mary's Church. Who would have thought it possible, Emily? Desmond hated everything the Catholic Church stands for. But during his last months on earth, he asked me to drive him to St. Mary's several times a week. I have to assume that Catholicism bypasses the intellect and implants itself directly in sinew and soul.

Desmond found it soothing to sit among the brilliant crimson and violet stained glass windows, the golden-hued votives, and the still, white marble statuary. He said the dogma of the church be damned, its symbols evoked the Great Mystery. "I feel the promise here, Val," he said one day, his voice lowered an octave by pain, "that some day I will find the place of understanding.

"That's the Book of Job," he added thoughtfully. "Did you know that?"

"No," I said. I didn't know that Desmond read the Bible.

I hope he was right. I hope somewhere, in some form, Desmond is free of pain. And that he understands. But God, I do miss him. At least I had Dez when Raymond died. But now . . .

Well, now I've got the inn. And the funny thing is, that aside from being lonely, I am content.

I don't know how I got here, Emily. The two things I thought I needed most from life I never got: I am not an artist, and I never found a long-term lover to be the other half of my "round person."

Oddly, these gaps—which used to *flay* me with despair—no longer seem important. I have so many other things I never expected to have: a plot of land in paradise; financial security; a reputation as a *competent business woman* (!); and a single life which I enjoy more with every passing year. I have to say what I'm sure you thought you'd never hear me say: *I can't complain.*

Well . . . it isn't a complaint exactly, but I am perplexed by one frustration in my life. It will take you two seconds to guess that it is my long-standing demon: sex. Every now and then, I start to feel that I will explode if I don't have sex. But I cringe at the thought of dating. I don't want a "relationship"—I have neither the optimism nor the feverish industry that requires. It's hardly been my gift, anyway. But I feel too stodgy and reserved to have casual sex with someone I barely know.

Please believe that I am not saying this to make you feel guilty. My lust for you continues unabated, but that is my problem, not yours. I count myself lucky to have shared one night with you. And Emily, I knew before it happened that our first sex might be our last. That your mysterious libido, unleashed for one glorious flight, might retreat and fold its wings under the wrap of your privacy. Of course, I yearn for you. But I neither blame you, nor do I expect anything more from you. Hope is another thing.

A few weeks ago, I was feeling exactly as I used to on Saturday nights at college—itchy and cranky and pesty. I wandered around the inn dusting, rearranging furniture, and restocking salt and pepper shakers until I drove Dusty, the night clerk, crazy. She waved a ten dollar bill in my face and said she was paying me to disappear for a few hours so she could get her work done. She shoved me out the door and pointed me toward town, commanding me imperiously to "go find a twenty-year old at Aphrodite's Bar and work the excess estrogen out of my system." Dusty herself is twenty-five, which she considers to be ever so much older and wiser than twenty. She believes that hormones rule—especially estrogen.

I was too fitful and unfocused to argue, so I did as I'd been told. As I got closer to Aphrodite's, I began to feel bold and reckless. Why *not* find someone at the bar for one night of cathartic sex? I would do it.

I marched into the crowded, cacophonous bar, bought myself a beer, found an uninhabited corner, propped myself against the wall, and gazed around the room looking for a likely prospect. Someone young enough to want to experiment. Someone attractive enough to excite me in spite of her being a stranger. Someone without another woman hanging off her arm.

Someone lonely and desperate enough to be open to entreaties from: me.

It wasn't that I couldn't spot likely candidates. I did. But in addition to being young enough to be my love child, the women who looked available also looked even more lonely and desperate than I— their beer bottles clutched tightly in their fists, their hungry eyes scanning the dance floor, their hands self-consciously scratching their foreheads and touching their chins. I suppose this ought to have consoled me. Instead, it made me sad. I felt sorry for them. I felt like chucking them under the chin and telling them to cheer up, it's not so bad. They'll feel better in middle age. Needless to say, this solicitous frame of mind quelled my libido.

"I really am too old for this," I said aloud, but I understood now that it wasn't the effect of chronology alone, but of a burgeoning habit of empathy, which drove lasciviousness away. I shuffled from the bar, my beer bottle camouflaged in my jacket pocket, and decided to hike over to St. Mary's to visit Desmond's grave—a peculiarly soothing ritual I'd adopted.

It was about 10:00 p.m., and the streets were sparsely populated as I walked away from the town center, half a mile down the narrow, dimly lit blacktop that led past the last rows of houses, beside empty fields of dune grass, and ended at the small, white, narrow-spired church. Behind the church, I walked under the arched iron gateway into the cemetery. I passed the rows of small, toppled, slate-colored markers of the oldest graves, and walked down the stone path toward the larger, newer, granite markers at the rear. A single spotlight mounted on the rear of the church lit the ground a few yards behind Desmond's three-foot high tombstone.

"Hello, you old fart," I said, bending over and pressing my cheek against the smooth stone. "Didn't want you to be alone on a Saturday night, and Raymond's out cavorting with dolphins, so I came to party with you." I felt peaceful and strangely lighthearted amid the stillness of the graveyard.

"The nice thing about you dead people is you don't expect anything. You're content with things as they are. Here's a tribute," I proclaimed, lifting the beer bottle high and pouring a libation on the grass around Desmond's marker.

"Okay, now let's party," I said. I pulled my walkman from my pocket, put on my headphones, and began to play a tape of Village People songs, disco-ing in exuberant circles around Desmond's grave to the beat of "Macho Man."

"I know you hate this music," I called out as I danced, "but it's my duty to keep you as peeved in heaven as you were on earth." Finally, I collapsed, laughing, on the ground in front of the stone, and sat cross-legged, catching my breath.

"Ah, Dez," I sighed, "I miss you and Raymond." I began to feel heavyhearted, and traced my fingers around the sculpted letters of Desmond's name.

"Did you find the place of understanding? Why don't you come back and explain it to me? Ah, you're probably too busy. You probably opened an inn for the unbaptized babies in limbo—no doubt decorated with vases in the shape of ethereal hands." I chuckled, amused by myself, and sat back.

"Are you an angel yet, Dez? Or do they drum cranky old goats like you out of the seraphic corps?"

"As a matter of record," a voice said from the graveyard behind me, "the seraphim are noted cranks."

I jumped to my feet, my heartbeat racing, and whirled to see what ghost had spoken. I saw not a ghost but an angel standing on the path, lit by a round of bright light from the church's spotlight.

"Mary Patrick," I gasped, placing my hand over my pounding heart, "Is it really—"

"Valerie Marie," she said smiling, "I'm sorry I startled you. It's me, in the flesh."

"Oh my god," I breathed, "it's good to see you." As my heartbeat steadied, I studied her. Her flyaway Hayley Mills hair was still luminous gold, but was tamed and cut short in a Joan of Arc bob. She wore a tan trench coat open over a black knit sweater and pleated black slacks—in cuts more formal and sophisticated than the jeans and loose sweaters she used to wear.

My eyes honed in on a modest silver crucifix that hung around her neck.

"So you're still . . ."

"I'm still . . ." she smiled, lightly stroking the cross with one finger. Then she added, "For now," and her eyes clouded over with something somberly reflective—an introspective dimming I had never before seen obscure the purity of Mary Patrick's radiance.

She held her hands out, an invitation, and I walked over and received her embrace. She pressed me close and as she said, "Oh, Val, it's good to see you," I felt a bubble of joy transit up my spine. I laughed in sheer, undiluted happiness, and so did she. We rocked side to side in an extended hug. Finally, feeling self-conscious, I pulled back, but Mary Patrick held me in place a few seconds longer. There was something wistful and longing in the way she restrained me, and I remained in place as our moods softened and quieted.

Finally, I pulled back at arm's length. "How did you find me? What are you doing here?"

"A lovely young woman at your inn named Dusty told me she'd sent you to Aphrodite's, but that you'd probably be here desecrating your cousin's grave. I'm so sorry about Desmond, Val. He was a good man." She squeezed my hand and looked into my eyes with such extravagant sympathy, that it burned through months of healing, and I began to feel the raw grief of Desmond's loss. I looked away.

"I miss him so much," I sobbed briefly, and inelegantly wiped my eyes and nose with my sleeve. Then I forced a smile as I added, "I'm sure Desmond would be disappointed if *someone* didn't desecrate his grave."

"Anyway," I said, turning back to Mary Patrick. "You. Are you . . ."

"I'm here just tonight," she said quickly, "I'm sorry I don't have more time. I was supposed to fly to Miami today, but I wanted so badly to see you, I put it off until tomorrow night. I'm going to work with Hispanic immigrants—teaching them English and helping them find jobs. *Hablo español,*" she grinned, "I'm prepared."

"Oh," was all I could think to say. I felt blank and stupid. Without a scrap of evidence to support my assumption, I had begun to hope that Mary Patrick was back at St. Mary's for good. Finding out she was here for a single night cut my emotions off at the roots. There was no point in feeling anything—not even disappointment.

"Oh dear," she said worriedly, "perhaps I shouldn't have come at all. Have I hurt you all over again, Val?"

I couldn't bear to see remorse in MP's eyes. "Nonsense," I said emphatically, "I'm delighted you came, no matter how briefly. Now, please, come with me. You will have the best room at my inn."

I reached out to grab her hand and pull her along, but she resisted. "First, a prayer. Would you mind, Val?"

I'd forgotten what it was like to be with someone who prayed at moments when others would sulk, whine, or fidget. I remembered fondly what I liked about hanging around Mary Patrick—gaining a tourist's view of the terrain of mystics and saints.

"Sure," I shrugged, "but it's kind of late for the beach, isn't it?"

"I meant here, by your cousin's grave." And she knelt down by the marker.

"Oh, Desmond's okay," I said. "I'm sure he's not in purgatory or anything—"

"No, Val," MP gently interrupted me, "not a prayer *for* him, but to connect with his spirit—to invite his spirit's beauty and goodness to join with us and guide us." She said it sweetly, not the tiniest bit condescending, but I still felt like an idiot. So I shut up.

Mary Patrick spread her arms in front of her and looked up at the sky, and I sat down beside her and waited, expecting her to chant and conjure some grand spiritual presence from the stars.

But all she did was close her eyes and kneel silently. Apparently, prayer was a more mundane affair for MP today than it had been ten years ago. I felt nostalgic for the spectacle.

MP peeked sidewise at me through one eye. "Are you praying, Val?"

"What? Oh, yes."

Mary Patrick drew her eyebrows upward skeptically.

"In my fashion," I said. "I really am."

This satisfied her, because she closed her eyes again and prayed silently for several minutes. I was telling the truth. I felt a *presence*—but it didn't come from earth or sky. It came directly from my heart and spread like a comforter around Mary Patrick.

Eventually, MP stood up, smiled, and took my hand, and we began walking toward the inn.

I felt ridiculously happy ambling along, swinging our arms, silently grinning at each other. MP's effervescent aura made me feel content as a child. I pretended we were in the past, that I had just picked Mary Patrick up at St. Mary's in Desmond's van. We were about to drive past the beach, and MP would soon shock and delight me by suggesting an impetuous dip in the ocean.

The past ten years never happened. The dread Mary Francis never existed.

But they had. She did. And she was the love—the mortal one—of Mary Patrick's life. I felt guilty and churlish for not asking about her.

"So, how's Mary Francis? Is she meeting you in Miami?"

"No, Val," she said. It was as if I had taken a pin and exploded each tiny bubble in Mary Patrick's aura. She looked down as she spoke. A normal enough expression of sadness for most people, but not for Mary Patrick. She never looked anywhere but deeply into your eyes when she talked.

"MP," I said, lifting her chin, "what happened?" But she jerked her head away and rubbed the back of her hand across her forehead and then erratically in front of her as if making a tired, truncated sign of the cross.

I stood still and waited. Finally, MP looked me in the eyes, her own distilling quiet tears.

"Mary Francis is now Mrs. Lars Petersen. She fell in love with a Danish physician who worked at the mission hospital. If it's possible, he believes even more deeply in good works than Mary Francis. She left the order to marry him and moved to Denmark a year ago. It's taken me this long to get my transfer."

"Oh," I said, shocked. "I'm sorry."

"Don't be," MP said. "I understand now the purpose of vows of celibacy. Oh, it isn't that Jesus objects to sex—in fact, Val, you were the one who showed me it's possible to become closer to God through sexual intimacy."

"I was?" I gulped. Such a flattering recollection, but so different from my own. For a decade, I had felt depraved and selfish for destroying Mary Patrick's innocence.

"But," she sighed, "that only works if you're spiritually mature, which I was not. The darkness that descended when Mary Francis left was horrible. I lost the light of Jesus for a while. Do you understand?"

I paused and drew a deep breath, remembering my plunge into darkness when MP left ten years ago. *"Good God, yes,"* I thought. But all I said aloud was, "Yes."

"Of course you do," she replied thoughtfully. She stared at me meaningfully, and I felt as if she could see inside my past—that she saw my descent as clearly as if I were leaping off a diving platform in front of her, poised high over an oblivion about to embrace me. And for an instant, I sensed Mary Patrick leaning toward me in psychic space like a circus acrobat to catch and break my fall. I felt dizzy, and squeezed my eyes briefly shut to wake myself from trance. As I did, Mary Patrick continued.

"I became possessive of Mary Francis, Val. When she left to marry Dr. Petersen, I fantasized revenge on them both." MP paused, her voice a mixture of horror and sorrow. One hand flew up to cover her heart, as if to shield it from the enormity of her crime.

Shallow and craven beast that I am, I wondered what kind of revenge Mary Patrick could have fantasized—had she toyed with excluding MF and the lustful doctor from her prayers? Now, however, was not the time to ask. I felt dismayed by MP's discovery of the cannibal side of love, but I also felt heartened by her jealousy. Being joined by her in base emotions I was so familiar with somehow elevated them, and me.

I cleared my throat. "You did?"

"But what had she done?" MP cried out—as if the question gave new pain each time it was asked. "All she had done was follow her heart where Jesus led her. Instead of accusing her of running away from her vocation, I should have focused on following Jesus where he was leading me."

"And where was that?"

"Into solitude. Into examining my conscience. Into the life Jesus calls me to, not the one I wish for myself." She said it resolutely, but her voice leaked pain.

I understood finally that Mary Patrick was not a saint. Not someone whose faith was implanted in her genes like the gold in her hair or the green in her eyes. She was a human being who worked hard every day to have faith.

Mary Patrick looked down again, her face troubled.

"Mary Patrick," I said, "what?"

"I understand now what I put you through when I left with Mary Francis," she said, looking up and into my soul. "I thought only of myself, not of how hard it was for you. I'm sorry."

Now it was my turn to look down. I didn't want this. Didn't deserve it. MP had been my ideal of goodness for a decade. She was turning everything upside down.

"No, don't," I put my hand up like a traffic cop. "I'm no one to apologize to. I'm just a great big old—"

"Vessel of love, light of the true Christ," MP intercepted me, smiling. Meeting her gaze, I caught the glow of her sincerity. And smiled in return. Things weren't upside down, they were merely leveling out.

"Yes," I said, "exactly."

We resumed our walk to the inn, where I offered MP her own suite. But she asked if she could sleep with me. Chastely, she added. Of course, I agreed. MP surprised me by removing all her clothes as she climbed into bed. I followed her lead, and circled my body around hers.

"I see you still make your own rules," I said, cupping my hand around the crown of her head as if making a cap for a child. Her shorn hair made her head look small, her neck and shoulders bare and vulnerable. I felt large, protective, and sheltering beside her.

She laughed. "I suppose I do. You must think me a willful creature. But I never feel like I'm making them up. I feel like I'm discovering the rules as Jesus reveals them to me. It feels right to me to sleep in your bed, to touch you, to draw as close as we can. I know many people would think it was wrong—but to me it feels terribly, beautifully right."

I was silent for a moment, thinking over what she had said. Mary Patrick waited patiently, a questioning look on her face.

"What?" she finally demanded.

"Oh, I was just thinking."

"Praise Jesus," she said sarcastically—another new trait—"I feared you had been struck mute. Will you favor us with a sermon on your musings?"

"Mary Patrick," I pronounced, "you are the only person I have ever known whom faith has made good—has led you to love more fully rather than pinched and constricted you."

I expected her to argue with me. Instead she sighed wistfully, "That is a beautiful compliment, Val. I hope it remains true." With that, she closed her eyes. I turned out the light. And we slept.

The next morning, I drove her to the airport. After we hugged good-bye, I watched her walk across the concrete runway, her shoulder bag banging awkwardly against her hip, toward the small propeller plane that would transport her once again into a distant world. The past ten years had rendered her fully human. Saner and less demented. But also less magical. She glowed, but with wattage more human than divine.

I knew that Mary Patrick would have said her wattage had remained the same. My own had increased. Whatever, I admired her even more.

And when her plane lifted off, gradually diminishing into a tiny speck in the vast sky, she took only herself, not the best of me, along with her.

So now I follow Mary Patrick's example. I follow my solitude and my conscience into the life I am called to—by whomever—rather than the one I wish for. And I do so especially when I begin to yearn for you.

Fortunately, I don't have a lot of spare time for yearning. My life is busier than ever now that I'm running the inn. But at the same time, it is also quieter and calmer. Sometimes, I barely recognize myself. In a strange way, I feel I have returned to my true nature, to the shy, contemplative girl I used to be. I spent most of my childhood alone, with only my thoughts, my worries, and the stories I read and made up for companionship. At some deeper level, silence and aloneness are what I am accustomed to. I have come full circle, from desperately fleeing that child's solitude, to embracing it. It brings me peace to do so. The first I've had in decades.

The person I talk to most these days is BB, so I'm not exactly awash in chatter. Ironically, though, as I've grown quieter, BB has become more talkative. And I mean real talk, coming from her own lips, not imaginary commentary made up by me.

She takes me out in her boat regularly now. We stay out longer and sail farther each time. Sometimes, we sail all the way around the tip of the Cape and out to the open Atlantic, the land of whales and monsters. I am no longer afraid of the open sea and the great blue bowl of sky. They used to make me feel dwarfed and insignificant. BB has taught me to see them as mirrors of the vast unknowable self that lurks inside us all.

Oh all right, what she *really* said was, "Don't be afraid of the sky, Val. It's just water vapor." She tapped her head and said, "Your fear is all in your mind." Same thing.

BB has a name! It's Marie Rodrigues. She's one of five children of a Portuguese family from Fall River. Two of her brothers build boats as well. She lives in a small cottage in the far east end of town. She owns a cat named Ollie, likes anchovies on her pizza, and drinks a glass of red wine every night with dinner.

My fantasies about her to the contrary, she does not speak in koans. She has never traveled to Tibet. Does not think she was a lama in a past life. She does not even meditate, although she thinks that building a beautiful boat is a kind of prayer. And I agree.

She doesn't even believe in God. Well, not the way people usually mean it, not as a being. Not even an intricate molecule. She believes that life is all there is, but that life itself is sacred and eternal. It expands, explodes, colonizes, improvises, evolves, mutates, feeds on itself, migrates, and reproduces. But it never disappears. It adapts and keeps going. Not as individuals, but as a whole.

Okay, what she said was, "Life goes on." Same thing.

She believes that the idea of God expresses the best and the worst within our human selves. But there are no separate "beings," no angels, demigods, spirits, demons, or dominions of flying saints. We are all we have.

Those were her *real* words: "We are all we have."

The world, the future, are entirely in our own hands. They will only be as good or bad as our own most recent actions. The power of redemption or damnation rest entirely upon human shoulders.

What she said was, "It's up to us."

I said her philosophy implied that humanity must learn to live with an inescapable spiritual loneliness.

She said, "Yep. That's the way it is. You do your best. And you build good boats."

"And if you're lucky, you make good friends," I added, thinking of you.

BB's precise response was: "Yep."

In addition to BB's laconic wisdom, I have learned another profound lesson from her. Not from her words, but from the way she lives her life.

BB has shown me that there is another kind of love besides the kind people feel for each other. A love expressed by being kind and respectful, maintaining standards, doing good work. Holding a pattern of decency and hoping the world will catch up.

You create the rule of love through the way you live your life.

BB didn't say that. I did.

Last but not least, some news: I'm contracting for new construction on the inn this summer. It's something I've wanted to do for months. Desmond would approve, I think, since it will add more glory to this already glorious inn. I am building a new tower, higher and wider than the old one, with great round portholes on every side. It'll have the best damn view of paradise on the Cape! And it's not for rent. It will be my new living quarters. They'll be extremely spacious, with room enough for two very private people to lead two very private lives.

Not very subtle, am I? It's yours whenever you want it. Whenever you're ready. If you ever want to . . .

It's up to you.

All I ask is that you think about it. You know I'll always love you. No matter what.

All my love,

Val

July 1990
Dearest Val,

I felt a stab of jealousy at the brief return of the vagabond nun. Mark my words: she'll be back some day, unfrocked, seeking nights that won't be the least bit "chaste."

You would be surprised to find out how much your new tower tempts me. After reading your description, I was ready to quit teaching and come to work as your Assistant Manager in Charge of Domestic Maintenance. But fate delays the life I wish for, as you would say, and calls me temporarily to another. I have a mission to perform. If you had told me a few years ago that I would undertake this task, I'd have said you were insane.

It wasn't my idea. It was Doreen's. Rather, it was Doreen who showed me the way.

I was grading final exams in my office at the university in early May when I heard a knock at the door. I said, "Come in, but make it quick," and a pale, thin, distraught young woman entered. She had stringy blonde hair she kept brushing back over her ear. She looked nervous, expectant. She seemed vaguely familiar, and I assumed she must be a former student.

"Do I know you?" I asked.

"You don't remember me, Doc, do you?" Her face fell. "I was sure you would." She looked down, and her hands flew together in front of her like two small birds seeking reassurance. I recognized the gesture before I remembered the face.

"Doreen," I said.

It had been nearly ten years since Doreen left my apartment sobbing after she quit "One for One." I'd never felt good about the way we ended. Perhaps that is why I never tried to find her. I was afraid I'd hear what I expected to now—a sad tale of wasted potential and stupid choices. I felt a burst of pure hatred for Shammie—*male madre*—as I remembered the exuberant teenager dressed in an absurd costume from *The Philadelphia Story,* and superimposed this image on the drawn young woman standing in front of me today. I felt a wave of guarded affection for the girl Doreen had been. I smiled and asked her to sit down.

"I haven't won my first Oscar yet," she said shyly, looking as if she were going to cry. Watching her, I sensed the depth of her disappointment, and I suddenly felt heavy and sad myself.

"So what? Neither have I," I said. "They don't give Oscars for the truly important achievements in life, anyway. How have you been, Doreen?"

This triggered a violent burst of tears. "Oh, Dr. Ashmont, I need your help. I'm sorry, but I didn't know who else to turn to. I'm sorry to keep bawling. I never meant to turn out so weak." Her hand fluttered in front of her, and I met it with a wad of tissues, holding her fist within mine for a moment, till it grew steady and calm.

"You're not weak. What kind of help do you need?"

"It all started because of the baby," Doreen wailed. "Now there's this big investigation, and they might take them all away." Her voice grew more frantic with every word. I feared that one of my innocents had joined the enemy, that Doreen had become an abuser. The cynic in me said it was inevitable. My fondness for her insisted that I not assume. I made her slow down and tell me the facts. It took a long time, but the full story finally emerged.

Doreen had three children, all girls, aged seven, four, and nine months, from two fathers, neither of whom she had married. She lived on welfare. She wanted to work, but couldn't find a job with health benefits, so she couldn't afford to. Instead, she did some under-the-table work sewing costumes for theater groups.

Ordinarily she never allowed Shammie to babysit. One night a couple of weeks ago, however, Doreen had to turn some costumes in by an 11 p.m. deadline. Shammie had promised Doreen she was sober, and when Doreen left her house, Shammie seemed fine. But when Doreen arrived home, she found an ambulance at her front door. Shammie, it turns out, had drunk a bottle of wine before she arrived at Doreen's. She nodded off on the bed while holding the baby, who had fallen to the floor and started to cry.

The oldest girl had awakened to the baby's cries, found her on the floor and, unable to rouse her grandmother, had done what Doreen had trained her to do in an emergency—called 911. When the siren roused Shammie from her stupor, she had slapped the girl for this breach of secrecy.

The ambulance had arrived to find a seven-year-old being smacked by a drunken grandmother, and a four-year-old and an infant left without any responsible adult in charge. Although the baby wasn't injured, the EMT's filed a report with child protective services, which had launched an investigation and triggered Doreen's panic. She was convinced that she might lose all three children. She turned to me, since I was the only person she knew that might have some influence with the agency. And because, as she put it, I knew her from a time in her life when she'd "shown some promise."

"Dr. Ashmont, you've got to tell them. Tell them I can take care of my children. I do the best job I know how. You've got to tell them. I couldn't bear to live without them." Doreen's face crumpled in pain. Tears streamed down her raw, red cheeks.

I felt like I owed Doreen. I couldn't help but wonder how differently her life might have turned out if I'd allowed her to postpone her college interview for a year instead of kicking her out of my program. At the time, it never occurred to me to relax the rules. Why not, I wondered now. *Why not?* I'd been contemptuous of everyone else's rules, but rigid about my own. If I'd been more flexible, Doreen might not have an Oscar today, but perhaps she'd have a career, self-respect, and the dignity of supporting her own children. Maybe she *would* have an Oscar. Who knows?

These were the kind of sentimental, imprecise considerations that seemed more and more to be skewing my judgment. Like you, Val, I am starting to believe there are different, equally compelling truths, some of which contradict one another. Amazingly, this notion no longer seems stupid and reckless to me, but true.

While Doreen waited in my office, I called a former colleague at protective services. I lied and said Doreen was my private client, and the social worker looked up her file. After chatting for a few minutes, with mostly grunts and "okay's" on my end, I hung up the phone.

"Good news, kid, you're off the hook," I said.

Doreen sprang from her chair and flew across the room to hug me. Stiff and surprised as I was, I softened quickly, letting her lean forward and bury her face against my neck. I put my hand on her hair. "There, there," I whispered, feeling her immense relief radiate through me like a shock wave, "there, there." And as the wave passed through me, I could feel in its wake the agony Doreen had been in, not just today, but ten years ago, too—a vulnerable, goodhearted teenager torn between two fates: choosing her family, or choosing herself.

It was a dilemma I knew well. But I had chosen differently than Doreen. Life had punished us in different ways.

"Ah, Doreen," I sighed. I stroked her hair lightly, surprised and ridiculously touched by its childlike silkiness. I pressed my palm against the side of her skull and held it there firmly, as if to press a healing balm upon her. I knew in my heart that I would do everything in my power to help her. No matter what.

She knelt beside me, thanking me profusely. But I pulled her up to her feet and sat her down.

"Not so fast, Doreen," I said sternly. "We've got to get a few things straight. The case worker took your word that Shammie doesn't ordinarily babysit. But you've got to promise that you'll *never* leave Shammie alone with the kids again. The baby wasn't injured this time, but who knows what could happen in the future."

Doreen nodded gravely.

"And you've got to come see me once a week for a while. I told them you were my therapy client, and the social worker will be checking in with both of us for six months."

Doreen nodded vigorously. "Yes. Yes. I'll do anything. Whatever it takes. Thank you so much. How can I ever—"

I put my hand up to halt her, "Wait, Doreen, there's more. The case worker said you've been feeding the kids peanut butter and Jell-O four or five nights a week. That's not nutritious enough."

Doreen looked perplexed and embarrassed. "Well, all right," she said, "but that's what I was brought up on. That's pretty much all Shammie ever fed us. Well, Shammie didn't feed us, *I* did from about the age of seven on up. I don't know much about cooking. But I'll learn, I promise." And she looked up at me with open, deep, earnest eyes. She looked so young.

"Oh, Doreen, you're just a—" and I broke off, shocked at what I was going to say, which was, "You're just a child yourself."

But, it's the truth. Doreen spent most of her childhood acting as a "child mother" to her younger siblings, and now she was acting as a "child mother" to her own children.

Where or from whom would she have learned otherwise?

This question broke *all* my rules. I was turning into absolute mush the line that was supposed to separate the innocent from the guilty— the victims from the abusers. I knew Doreen had shown poor judgment. And as a result, her children had been endangered, however briefly. But I couldn't see Doreen as the enemy.

I *knew* Doreen. I knew her heart.

A peculiar brew of compassion, impatience, weariness, and practicality began to ferment in my mind. Dammit, there isn't enough time or money, there aren't enough case workers in the world to save all the lost and desperate children that need to be saved. Their goddamn parents are going to have to help. They are going to have to save their own children. And if that means saving the parents, too, so be it. I can't fight it anymore. It's too big.

If the truth was that Doreen was a child with children of her own, then I would help this poor, pathetic child to grow up. Even if I didn't like doing it. Even if it broke my rules. Because it was the only thing, at this late date, that could possibly help her. That could possibly help her children. And if I was willing to join this battle to help Doreen, then I might as well do it for others.

I must have been quiet for awhile, because I was startled when Doreen said, "What is too big, Dr. Ashmont?"

"What? Oh, call me Emily, please, Doreen. I'm sorry. I drifted off. I don't remember what I was saying. But there's one more thing you have to do."

"What's that?"

"You have to work for me."

Right then I offered Doreen a job helping me organize the program that was shaping itself as we talked. I call it "All for All." And it's growing slowly but steadily, without a dime of government money or an ounce of bureaucratic interference. I cut back my job to half time to build the program, and by the end of this year, I expect to quit the university and devote myself full time to All for All. And for once, since *all* the rules are mine, I don't have to break them. But I will bend them—when necessary.

We start by seeking referrals for "at risk" parents from obstetric wards at hospitals and from preschools. Of course, we don't label them "at risk" with our donors and sponsors. We don't call them "unwed parents." We don't even call them "single parents," even if they are—we call them "struggling young families" so they sound like human beings. Then through a network of churches and senior citizens groups, we track down grandparents and empty nesters—people with a reputation for integrity, warmth, and generosity—to match in partnerships with young parents. All the "senior parents" and all the "junior parents" (that's what they call themselves) meet together at a church once a month, and in their own homes as often as they want to. Voila, a *community* is born. Communities are made of equals. Clinics are not. Welfare programs are not. All for All *is,* because everyone gives and receives.

If we had asked these same individuals to donate money to help parents "at risk" of abusing their children, we wouldn't have gotten a penny. One of the great paradoxes of raising funds or finding volunteers is that the *more* you ask for, the more people are likely to give. But you don't start with money—you start with their souls. You ask them to donate specific talents for a tangible purpose. To give something they find valuable about themselves to something they recognize as valuable to others. And once they give time, money follows. Doreen had trouble with this notion at first. Once someone volunteered, she would back off. She felt shy about asking for more. Instead, I've taught her, go back and ask for more.

We harangue every corporation that makes money off kids. Toy manufacturers, clothing and diaper manufacturers, and drug companies. They sponsor classes and workshops on how to dress, bathe, and feed children. They get their name listed as donors, which gives them free advertising. But we also encourage them to attend the classes.

We introduce them to the parents and the kids. And then we develop ongoing newsletters and reports on the kids' progress which we send to the corporate contacts.

Corporations now seek us out to sponsor events. We have a free immunization campaign coming up in September funded by a pharmaceutical company. Of course, self-interest motivates most of this "generosity." As you know, I'm no Pollyanna about human nature. Still, whether you call it altruism or a more refined form of self-interest motivated by the desire to appear virtuous, it works. That's all I care about.

My next plan is to cajole the businesses we work with into creating jobs for these "junior parents." I'm very demanding. They have to be good jobs with generous health and educational benefits and day care. In some cases, I've gone back to sponsors from my old "One for One" program, and enlisted them in funding college scholarships—generous ones that include living expenses. I've never seen the point of doing anything halfway, or in offering people support that gives them *half* of what they need to thrive, which is what most programs do. That's like taking a man with only one healthy leg, surgically attaching a prosthetic to replace the missing limb, then hacking off the healthy leg he had in the first place—he's a lot worse off then he was before you messed him up.

In the course of my work, I've run into former colleagues from the agency where I used to work. A lot of them are supportive. But there have been a few who sniff and dismiss my work. "You're only changing things for a few families," they say. "You're singling some families out for special treatment. You're not changing the system."

"That's right," I say. "Instead of treating everybody equally, which means equally *ineffectually,* I actually help a small number of people become good parents and successful human beings. Instead of keeping clients dependent on my agency so I'll continue to have a job, I help people become independent. *Sorry.*"

Needless to say, I am no more popular now than I have ever been. I don't care. The program works. It's expensive. It's a huge amount of work. It helps a small number of families per year. And it suits me better than any of my previous jobs.

When I worked as a therapist, I would come home feeling used up, angry, and hopeless. I feared that I had not done enough to save endangered children who were slipping from my grip. And while I know I'm a superb college teacher—clear, concise, and fair—it disturbed me that many of the students I was helping to gain a credential to conduct therapy really ought to be in therapy for a dozen or so years themselves.

With All for All, I'm at my best. Fund-raising channels my aggressive instincts constructively. And my missionary zeal is fulfilled by watching the volunteers I've recruited do a far better job of providing contact, community, and warmth than I or any other professionals ever could.

I know that children continue to suffer beyond the reach of All for All. I know my program can't touch the parents who are way past "risk"—those who neglect and abuse their children every day.

I can't save all the children who need saving.

For the first time, I concede that limitation, if not without regret, at least without guilt and torment. (Well, without an unacceptable amount of guilt and torment.) I think of the abuse I'm preventing as a tribute to those valiant, suffering children whose lives I am unable to save.

I've even found my hatred of the evil Shammie abating. I found myself wondering what might have been different if she had had a competent "senior parent" to advise her when Doreen was growing up. Realistically, Shammie was far too selfish and corrupt to recognize that she needed help, much less to benefit from either kindness or wisdom. Still, I wondered, *"What if?"*

What if someone had reached out to her when she was fifteen? When she was twelve? When she was two? How young would she have to be to reverse the murky, undignified tide of her destiny? Pointless thoughts. But I kept having them.

Then, unexpectedly, I met the fiend herself.

I was helping Doreen move boxes into her new apartment. Her salary as Administrative Assistant for All for All enabled her to rent a small brick townhouse near the university. Doreen was inside washing windows and mopping floors while I carted tables and lamps down the moving van ramp to her front lawn. Her kids were with a babysitter—a former student from one of my seminars.

I heard a car with an unmuffled engine pull up across the street and sputter to a halt. The door creaked open and slammed shut. I felt a pair of eyes watching me. I turned. Next to the rusted green Impala stood a small, tense woman wearing black leggings and a long black tunic with silver sequins adorning the neckline. Her hair was dyed auburn and teased to frothy majesty, her eyes were shielded by enormous amber lenses in bright red plastic frames, her lips were a surprisingly muted shade of pink, and both wrists were adorned with bangles of silver and gold. Instead of the consumptive gargoyle I'd expected, she looked like a faded beautician. I knew it was Shammie from the expression on her face.

I had envisioned a meeting between Shammie and me as an epic encounter between archenemies. Clytemnestra berates Electra. Antigone skewers prissy Creon. Shammie and I would gaze at each other with a hatred befitting our rivalry for the soul of Doreen. We would wrestle and thrash—verbally, of course—until one of us cried "uncle" and forsaked her claim.

But Shammie was not gazing at me as would a warrior at a sworn enemy with whom she was about to cross swords. Instead, she looked at me as if I were the repo man about to pounce on her car. A nervous, fearful hostility puckered her brow as she raised a cigarette to her lips, lit it with a disposable lighter, and inhaled deeply, pausing before she blew the smoke my way.

She had been *my* enemy, I realized, but I had never been *hers*. I was an irritant, a danger, a threat. But not an enemy. Shammie was too small and helpless to merit them—too timid, too powerless, too afraid. In her eyes, we weren't Antigone and Creon: I was a rhinoceros; she was a squirrel. I'd seen that cowering, hostile look before. It is exactly the stance abused children take when they think they're about to get hit. I felt the tiniest ping of compassion for Shammie, and quickly doused it. Perhaps I didn't need to hate Shammie. But I wasn't about to feel sorry for her.

I put down the box I was carrying, and stared steadily back, curious to see how a squirrel would approach a rhino, wanting neither to help her, nor to scare her off. My lack of overt hostility must have given Shammie courage, because she suddenly threw her half-smoked cigarette to the ground, ground it out with her shoe, and sidled—I neglected to mention she was wearing three-inch black high heels, there was little she could do but sidle—toward me. She stopped about four feet away. Close enough to be heard. Too far for me to smack her.

She scrunched her mouth up a few times before she blurted out, "You're the shrink, right? Dorrie's doctor?" Her voice was high pitched, and she raised it even further at the end of each question. Its submissive qualities belied the anger that drew her lips into a frown.

"I'm the shrink," I said.

"Did you tell Dorrie I couldn't see the babies no more?" She spoke with wounded, muted venom, her outrage diluted by fear of angering me.

"I told her you couldn't be left alone with them, not that you couldn't see them," I said calmly.

"Oh . . ." she fumbled a moment. My calm and clarity had drained her anger. She'd worked herself up for a fight. She wasn't going to get one. What remained was hurt and confusion.

"Oh," she repeated, "well . . . why?"

I wanted to shout, "Because you're an irresponsible lush who has spent her useless life indulging in vice and endangering the health and safety of her own children. You're a parasite who feeds upon the strength, intelligence, and kindness of others to keep your pathetic soul alive."

But I didn't. It would have been like bludgeoning a flea. I searched for a weapon commensurate to the task.

"Because it's the law," I pronounced.

"It is?"

"Yes," I said definitively, "it is."

The law was large, hard-edged, and to be avoided at all costs. It brooked no debate. Wasn't something either Shammie or I could alter. If I were a rhino, The Law was a dinosaur. At least, I was betting that it was to Shammie.

"Well," she said softly, defeated, ". . . if that's the way it has to be."

"Yes," I said, almost sympathetically, "that's the way it has to be."

"Well, all right then," she said, sounding as resigned as a child who has finally accepted there really will be no ice cream after dinner, so that further beseeching is pointless.

She lit another cigarette, which seemed to give her strength. As she blew smoke in my direction, she called out "Bye." And she waved at me with a few quick stabs through the air of her cigarette.

As she wobbled away unsteadily in her high heels, she turned back quickly and added, "By the way, thanks for helping *my* girl." And then she nearly ran toward her car, like a child calling out a parting insult who feared retribution.

Did I imagine the emphasis on *my?* A territorial assertion?

My rhino's hide started to itch with irritation at this insult from a squirrel. But then I thought, what did it matter. Doreen wasn't Shammie's girl. She wasn't mine, either. She belonged to herself. She was beyond the reach of Shammie's maternal tentacles.

And so was I. I would make peace, I decided. And in a conciliatory gesture, I called out, "You're welcome," to Shammie's retreating back.

She looked back, surprised, and I waved and smiled, "Bye." My civility alarmed her, I observed, as Shammie leapt in her car, started the engine quickly, and sped away in a cloud of gray-blue smoke.

"You're burning oil, Shammie," I grinned to myself, pleased at her discomfort in spite of my conciliatory aims. "You're wasting gas."

As I turned around, I saw Doreen coming through the door.

"Dr. Ashmont," she said, "if that was my mother driving away—and I'd recognize the jet stream of her car's engine anywhere—I can't believe you're smiling. What did she say to you? If she insulted you, I'll wring her scrawny neck." Doreen looked worried.

"Never mind, Doreen. She stopped by to thank me for helping you. And please call me Emily. You keep forgetting."

Doreen looked skeptical. "I've never known you to lie, but that can't be the truth."

"It isn't a lie. It's just a partial truth. But it isn't anything you need to bother about. Come on, let's go out to lunch, my treat."

I felt suddenly, preposterously cheerful. I felt like Beowulf triumphant over Grendel's monstrous mother. As though all the *male madres* of the world had been vanquished and sent packing, following Shammie in her gray-blue wake, and even now dissipating into thin air.

I wanted to celebrate, and with Doreen's encouragement, although she, poor thing, had no idea what we were celebrating, I ordered a bottle of champagne—at midday! I felt the most unusual sensations. I felt silly, almost giddy. Oh, Val, I had fun.

After two glasses of champagne, I finally understood what I was celebrating. A voice, a memory had been trying to come into focus ever since I'd seen Shammie earlier that day. Finally, I heard the voice and I saw the face that was speaking to me.

It was Dr. Delong's raspy voice. It was her caring, sincere, and beautiful face. She was looking at me intently, as though our very lives depended on my understanding every word she said. She was telling me that *I was bigger than my parents. That they were much smaller than they seemed. That they would not get in my way. That some day I would understand just how small they really were.*

Today, I understood.

My parents are squirrels. But I am a rhino. They cannot hurt me. They cannot reach me. They cannot even scratch my hide.

Doreen and I stayed at lunch for three hours. And then, with apologies to Doreen, I went home and slept for the next sixteen. I have never slept that long before in my life.

I was way behind in my work the next day. Yet there is so much more to do. So you see, Val, I'm unable to retire yet, although I've never felt so tempted. The craziest thoughts pop into my mind. Living with you in paradise. Adopting a child. Yes, that's right, finally becoming a mother. I know it's crazy and impractical, but I keep picturing a small, dark-haired infant whom I gently cradle while I inhale the scent of her hair.

Sometimes, when I come home from work, I can almost hear a baby cry, can see her as a toddler, rushing from room to room. Then I see her as a young girl, scribbling homework at the kitchen table. Or scampering on the beach with the two of us—you and me—gazing on with pride. These images are so real that it startles me to remember they aren't. Then I feel wistful and sad.

I wonder if I'm losing my mind. Then I hear you say that I am simply being human. We are both probably right.

I will try to actually *mail* this letter this afternoon. I have addressed the envelope and only have to buy a stamp. Why is this still so hard? Perhaps because I write things down that I cannot yet speak about. Especially about the child. Why do I feel so shy about confiding in you, of all people? You know everything else about me. You would never make fun of me.

You would never tell me I'd be a terrible, cold, unloving parent. These are *my own* worst fears.

And here is another. I fear that you will fall in love. That you will follow the advice I dutifully gave you on the phone two weeks ago and remain open to dating, however awkward it may feel. You will find someone deserving who will scoop you up and absorb you into her orbit. Someone passionate and present. Someone who hungers for your body and thirsts for your soul. And by the time I—your monastic, missionary friend—get around to moving to Provincetown, there will be no extra room at your inn.

It's the risk I take. It's the risk I've always taken. There is nothing I can do but hope that some day in the future, the life I am called to and the life I wish for will miraculously merge into one.

Unfortunately, Val, the odds that this letter will ever reach you are diminishing by the second. But I will keep trying.

I always have.

I always will.

That is a promise I can keep.

In love and friendship,

Emily

1993

June 1993
Dearest Val,

I know you'll receive *this* letter, because I'll hand it to you as soon as I step off the plane, completing the last leg of my twenty-year journey to Provincetown.

I've written the introduction and compiled all the letters that tell the *story of our epic friendship.* This final letter is all that remains to bring this book of our lives to a close. Your first letter mourns the divergence of our paths; this letter celebrates their convergence, as my daughter and I arrive "bag and baggage" to live in your tower. It seems ironic yet fitting that I, the silent one, have claimed for myself the first and final words.

I do not want my daughter to grow up without you. And *I* do not want to grow older without you. I have heard the siren call of your inn for three years, but only recently have I removed the final barriers to its lure. Doreen can run the everyday operations of All for All. I made her Program Director, and put her in charge of a staff of ten and an annual budget of $3 million. I can now focus on founding chapters in other cities, work that I can do from anywhere, including Provincetown.

Doreen has become an expert advocate for children's rights, and is now as hard-nosed a fund-raiser as I have ever been. She brings a sweetness to her blackmail. She's more a cajoler than a harasser. All Doreen needed was the opportunity to bring out her best, and someone who believed in her as much as I do. I am so proud of her.

My success in helping Doreen "grow up" gave me greater confidence in my ability to nurture a child, and rekindled my interest in adoption. I've been on a waiting list for more than a year with an adoption agency that places South American babies. In its earliest stages, middle stages, and later stages, adopting a child means waiting and waiting for a phone call you fear will never come.

Doreen encouraged my maternal aspirations. Sometimes I feel she has "adopted" me. She's on a crusade to fill in the gaps in my life. For a while, she was on a not very subtle matchmaking campaign. She invited me out to dinner and then casually suggested that we stop for a drink at Buddies, a waterhole notorious for angling singles. We stayed for one drink, a total of half an hour. During that time, five young men with moussed hair, chest-baring, open-collared shirts, and thick gold chains asked Doreen to dance. None asked me. Doreen felt bad, thinking I minded, and began to apologize. I pointed out to her that I was ten—make that twenty—years older than the men in that bar. And I explained that being found uninteresting by boozy, horny guys in singles bars did nothing to mar my self-esteem.

I confided in Doreen that there had only been one man in my life I ever truly loved, and that was Cody. Doreen insisted that I should try to find him. She, like you, Val, cannot fathom anyone voluntarily giving me up, and seems to think that if Cody knew he might have a second chance, he'd snap me up.

Doreen's faith in my irresistibility aside, I assured her it was too late, that Cody wouldn't have a second chance. You told me in college that I was essentially a virgin, Val. At the time, you were trying to insult me. But you were right. Regardless of how much sex I have had or ever will have, my deepest desire is to belong to myself and myself alone.

What I didn't tell Doreen and what I've never admitted to you until now, is that I know exactly where Cody is. I've followed his career through professional journals and newsletters, and through a few strategic phone calls to our alma mater. As you know, I would have made a superb private eye.

Cody chairs the psychology department at a small liberal arts college in Kansas. He does research on thriving child syndrome—or the "mysterious" ability of some children who have suffered injury and abuse to adjust well emotionally and succeed intellectually in spite of their traumatic histories. Trust academics to take something magnificent and healthy and transform it into a "syndrome"; I blame psychology for that, not Cody.

He has been married for sixteen years, and has three children, a boy and two girls, ages fifteen, twelve, and eight. I can't fully explain why I have tracked Cody's life, except perhaps to continue confirming that I did the right thing when I broke up with him. I would not fit into

Cody's life, and he would not fit into mine. Every time I reconfirm this mismatch, I lay that particular road not taken to rest. Again.

Eventually, Doreen gave up on matchmaking, and decided to settle for inducing me to relax more. A year ago, she gave me a T-shirt and a pair of baggy blue jeans, and insisted that I practice wearing casual clothes. "Emily," she insisted, "if you're going to have a child, you've got to learn to dress for mess." So I practice wearing these loose, expandable clothes inside my house. I feel artificial and vulnerable in them, as though I can't be sure where my edges are. Finally, after much beseeching on Doreen's part, I agreed to wear them to her house three months ago to celebrate my birthday with a meal that she herself had cooked.

After I was seated at the dinner table, Doreen and her daughters—now aged ten, seven, and three—disappeared into the kitchen. The three girls reappeared in a solemn processional, the oldest carrying a covered tray, which she set down in front of me. "Mama says go ahead and start—she'll be right here," the girl said. I lifted the lid with a flourish, and saw a small plate with half a peanut butter sandwich and a cup of red jello. The girls burst out laughing, and so did I. On cue, Doreen appeared with another tray, whose lid lifted to reveal a plate of black beans and rice and some obscure dark greens Doreen insisted was kale.

"I've become a vegetarian," Doreen announced proudly. "This is one of the healthiest meals you'll find in Buffalo, Doc! Girls, you have Dr. Ashmont to thank for the change in your diet." For which I was roundly booed, as the girls teased, "Bring back Jell-O and peanut butter!" They laughed and the littlest one asked if she could sit in my lap instead of in her high chair, so I sat with my chin grazing her fine blonde hair, my body ridiculously comfortable in my soft, loose clothes. We held hands and said a brief blessing: "Oh how great and good it is, to sit and eat with friends."

This is what I want, I thought. This warmth and humor. This cozy informality. It is what I want my family to be. That night I decided that if I did adopt a child, I would move to Provincetown so I could share my family with you. After all, Val, you have been my real family all along. You have given me more care and affection than anyone. How could I raise a family without you?

Finally, two months ago, after almost giving up hope I would ever find a child, the adoption agency called. They had a six-month-old girl ready to be picked up the next week. I was thrilled and anxious. I had dreams about Alejandra Valerie Ashmont every night before I flew to South America. Most of them were variations on the same theme.

> I wake in bed to the sound of children wailing. I know it is the abused urchins who circle my bed every night, crying out for help. I hear them, but I can't see them. I run around my house flinging open doors, looking for them. Finally, I open the door to a single large room with rows of cribs. And I realize the crying has stopped.

> Alejandra stands, circled by light, among them. She has soothed them and appeased them, and put them to bed. And they sleep soundlessly, except for a chorus of soft infant sighs. Alejandra turns to me and smiles.

And then I wake up, feeling calm.

I flew to Alejandra's homeland, and took a bus to the mountain village where she was being cared for in an orphanage. Her parents had been killed on a narrow road like the one I arrived on. They had been riding on the back of a pickup truck when an oncoming bus lost its brakes, careened out of control, and smashed into the truck.

Alejandra had been strapped in a basket her mother carried in her lap. The sturdy wicker basket had been thrown clear of the accident, and landed in a river that flowed nearby. Alejandra was found unharmed, floating with the current like a latter day Moses. They called her the "miracle child." When I heard her story, I felt like her kin already. We have seen a lot of loss in our lives, Alejandra and me, regardless of the difference in our years.

When I arrived at the orphanage, I entered the nursery, a large room lined with rows of cribs. I walked straight to the first crib on the right. "It's her," I declared. And it was. I picked her up, a robust, sturdy child with a rug of black hair, brown eyes, and eyelashes thick as baby caterpillars. The smallness of her parts astonished me. Tiny ears and fingernails and toes—everything in scale.

Alejandra fussed, and I carried her outside, onto the terrace overlooking the lush, forested valley beneath us. Immediately, she stopped crying. When I moved to take her back inside, she began to fuss again, and when I turned back to the open air, she quieted down. I gazed out at the dark greens below, the open lands before us, and the immense blue sky above. My daughter was born in a land of great vistas. She should grow up in a place with big skies and vast spaces that soothe her and remind her of home. My decision to live in Provincetown was sealed.

The first few times I held Alejandra, and felt her impossibly small infant fist clutch itself around my massive finger, I felt joy, then a wave of fear. Would I grow to need this joy too much? Could Alejandra trust me—and could I trust myself—not to drain her joy to fill my own emptiness?

But each time I felt afraid, Alejandra fretted and cried. And when I forced myself to breath in joy once again, she beamed radiantly back at me. Joy, I learn, is a two-way street. Alejandra asks the best of me—the courage to bear this joy, so that every time my daughter looks upon me, she sees my face inscribed with joy, and learns through our exchange, the mysterious nature of her own true self, and the secret of eternal life.

This is my triumph—holding this joy and trusting that it is, and through it, I am, in at least one particular way—good.

I have had to slay so many Humbabas to get here, Val. Hell, I had to clear the whole damn sacred forest.

But here I am. In a place I never expected to be. I have sailed across the Sea of Death. And returned. More alive than when I departed.

It took a few weeks to settle my affairs in Buffalo. There was nothing, aside from Doreen and her kids, that I minded leaving behind. But give me a year to raise the funds, and I'll transfer the headquarters of All for All to Boston—then Doreen and her children can move here. But *not* Shammie. If the squirrel wants to visit, let her get a job, spend some bucks, and take the bus.

I have shipped my books, sold my furniture, and packed what Alejandra and I need in one trunk and three suitcases. When I boarded the plane an hour ago, I felt light and portable. I knew that my last flight out of Buffalo would be free of turbulence. And I was right. The tray table remains calm and steady as I write with my right hand, and my daughter slumbers soundly as I cradle her in my left arm. As I lean over Alejandra, eight months old today, to kiss her forehead and inhale her sweet fragrance, the love I feel for her stretches around her and expands my heart.

I hope I am worthy of her. I hope I am up to the task of raising her. I am proud that she chose me to be her mother, for I feel that in some mysterious way she did choose me, just as you did, Val, more than twenty years ago. And now I am hers, as I was yours, for life.

I am grateful to share Alejandra with you. Perhaps it was both of us she chose. I feel the strangest sense of completion, as though all my previous life were preparing me for this great task. And as though, with Alejandra and with you, I am now settling into my proper sphere. I can hear you, Val. You will say this sounds like those reprobate *round people*. I can only laugh and agree, but with the caveat that there may be forms of roundness that serve to make one, not less, but more oneself than before. If so, I shall settle into my side of this sphere with the loudest, most resounding sigh this earth has heard since Gilgamesh found his Enkidu.

But unlike that half-mad, half-god tyrant, I shall not be fool enough to lose my friend. You are right, Val. Love is a virtuous and necessary thing. And the fact that many things pass for love—and go by that name—when they are not, is not love's fault. Love calls us to find what she is, and what she is not. She calls us to find her highest self, and thereby develop our own. I have always called love by your name, Val. And now I call it by Alejandra's, too.

The flight attendant commands us to fasten our seat belts, put our seats and tray tables in their upright position, and to store our belongings under the seat in front of us.

We are about to land. As I gaze behind us, I see the great blue bowl of sky. As I gaze below, I see the airport tarmac, and the future it represents. By the tiny terminal, I see a woman standing that I know is you. And for a moment, Val, for one powerful moment of grace and eternity,

> All that lay behind us
> Passed from view.

With love, my Enkidu,
from your Gilgamesh,

Emily

Appendix

Val Summer
Humanities 210: The Epic
Paper #3: Critical Synopsis

September 29, 1970
Dr. Woolrich

What Gilgamesh Means to Me

Gilgamesh was a Sumerian king of truly epic proportions. His story is thousands of years old. He was half-man and half-god. But he was lonely, and pined for a special friend. One night, Gilgamesh dreamed of a shooting star. His mother said the dream meant that Gilgamesh would soon find his friend.

Meanwhile, deep in the forest lives Enkidu, half-human, half-animal. Rumors of the wild man reach Gilgamesh, who wonders if Enkidu might be his long-awaited friend. He sends a woman from the palace to find Enkidu, give him clothes, and teach him to talk.

Enkidu comes to the palace to meet Gilgamesh. As soon as their eyes meet, they recognize each other as soulmates. It's as if they were the two original halves of a single round being, like the ones in Plato's creation myth in the *Symposium*. At last, they are whole.

Next, Gilgamesh and Enkidu engage in a monumental wrestling match, from which they emerge exhausted and sweaty and loving each other. No doubt, this is where D. H. Lawrence got the idea for the homoerotic wrestling match between Birkin and Gerald in *Women in Love,* another example of epic friendship (before things went so wrong). If there is ever to be a story of epic female friendship—the need for which Virginia Woolf so keenly observes in her brilliant essay "A Sitting Room of One's Own"—it should begin with a wrestling match in front of a fireplace.

Briefly, our heroes are happy. They share dreams, take long baths, and hike around the kingdom. Then Gilgamesh gets the idea of setting off to kill the monster who haunts the sacred cedar forest. The problem is that the beast, Humbaba, is protected by the gods. As punishment for slaughtering Humbaba, the gods decree that one of the friends must die. They pick Enkidu.

The scene of Enkidu's death is one of utter desolation. Gilgamesh cannot bear the thought of living without his friend. And Enkidu cannot bear the thought of leaving Gilgamesh to grow old alone. It is one of the most moving and tragic death scenes in all literature, and vastly superior to the end of *Romeo and Juliet*. Gilgamesh and Enkidu really knew each other, whereas Romeo and Juliet were children caught up in romantic infatuation.

The story slides downhill from there. Gilgamesh is crazy with grief. He wanders off to seek the secret of eternal life, hoping to bring Enkidu back to life. Finally, he finds the only person ever granted immortality by the gods, Utnapishtim, who was given eternal life after he survived a flood as bad as Noah's. Sadly, the guy says "no way" to Gilgamesh's request for immortality. However, he does give Gilgamesh a plant that's supposed to restore youth. On the way back to Uruk, however, Gilgamesh puts the plant down, and a cunning snake eats it, leaving behind its sloughed off skin.

Our lonely hero returns to Uruk, where he dedicates the rest of his life to the memory of his friend. There is never anyone in Gilgamesh's life—not family, friend, wife, or child —whom he comes close to loving as much as dear, departed Enkidu.

Grade: **B**

Miss Summer: While you have captured the passionate friendship between our heroes, you omit much of the narrative and many important themes. Your fanciful efforts to link Gilgamesh to D. H. Lawrence and Virginia Woolf lack historical or literary context. I encourage you to season your impressionistic readings with some regard for the actual text. Do please check your Woolf reference—I don't believe Miss Woolf was as specific as you in her title.

Dr. Woolrich

Emily Ashmont
Humanities 210: Epic Heroes
Paper #3: Critical Synopsis

September 26, 1970
Dr. Woolrich

Gilgamesh: Heroic Fool or Foolish Hero?

Archeologists discovered clay tablets with fragments of the myth of Gilgamesh in the ruins of ancient Ninevah in the late nineteenth century. Oral traditions recounting the exploits of this Sumerian king are thought to date back to the third millennium BC. Babylonian scribes later recorded and elaborated his feats.

Gilgamesh was a despot, bored and corrupt. As an example of his tyranny—and the contempt for women which passes for heroic virility in epic literature—Gilgamesh insisted on having sexual intercourse with brides before their weddings. Today, some of us would call this rape. In those days, it was simply the king's prerogative.

Enkidu represents the king's unspoiled complement. While Gilgamesh is part human, part divine, Enkidu the forest creature is part human, part animal. Free of the corrupting effects of civilization, Enkidu lives purely and simply. He runs with the animals and frees them from the hunters' cruel traps. Frustrated with their loss of prey, the hunters persuade Gilgamesh to send a palace prostitute to seduce Enkidu and lead him to Uruk.

In a display of misogyny worthy of Christian interpretations of Eve's role in the Garden of Eden, the myth recounts that sex with the prostitute weakens the wild man. He begins to dress in human clothes and learns to speak. The animals—once his closest friends—shun their now civilized companion. Alone and homeless, Enkidu arrives in Uruk.

Gilgamesh responds to the sight of Enkidu as would an unneutered German shepherd to the sight of an alpha male. The two engage in a brutal wrestling match which, in the way of epic male friendships, cements their bond.

Soon, however, the dissolute Gilgamesh is bored again. He concocts a foolhardy and dangerous plan to slay Humbaba, the divinely appointed guardian of the cedar forest. Although Enkidu warns him against such bravado, Gilgamesh—who has never seen death—persists. He taunts Enkidu, saying he will go alone if his friend is too fearful. Enkidu gives in and joins Gilgamesh on his mission. Of course, it is Enkidu who is wounded in the ensuing struggle with Humbaba.

The two heroes must then face the wrath of the gods for slaying Humbaba. The goddess Ishtar is portrayed as responsible for the heroes' undoing. She offers a plea bargain to Gilgamesh for the murder of Humbaba, but he spurns it and her. She then sends the bull of heaven to assault Gilgamesh. It is Enkidu, however, who is killed while protecting his friend.

The attitude of the gods throughout the myth is one of capricious manipulation, mixed with fits of compassion. The bull of heaven is allowed, for example, to wreak havoc on innocent lives in retaliation for Gilgamesh's transgressions, but the gods agree that not *everyone* should starve to death. Their power is raw, and they enjoy using it; they are the most realistic and human of gods.

With Enkidu's death, Gilgamesh encounters mortality for the first time. He shows a regard for his friend in death which, had he shown it earlier, might have saved his friend's life. His grief leads him on yet another fool's errand. He decides to find Utnapishtim, the lone survivor of the legendary great flood, who was granted immortality by the gods. From him, Gilgamesh hopes to learn the secret of eternal life.

After a typical epic quest, including a sea voyage and encounters with supernatural beings, Gilgamesh finds Utnapishtim, who tells him that his voyage has been fruitless: immortality is reserved by gods for gods alone. In the most moving passage in the epic, Utnapishtim—touched by Gilgamesh's devotion to his departed friend—tells him that

> friendship is vowing toward immortality
> And does not know the passing away of beauty . . .
> Because it aims for the spirit.

I interpret these words as meaning that true immortality derives from loving someone so much they become a part of you, and the love you share becomes itself an eternal being, separate from and surviving the physical deaths of the lovers. I do not believe that human beings are capable of such love, but if we were, that would be a heroism worthy of the name. Finally, Utnapishtim tells Gilgamesh to return home, finish grieving, and move forward with his life. He also reveals the location of a secret plant that provides eternal youth.

Gilgamesh retrieves the plant from the bottom of a river, only foolishly to leave it unguarded while he rests. A snake eats the plant, leaving behind its shed skin as a reminder to Gilgamesh of his carelessness. The loss underlines the epic's harsh but realistic message, that death and loss are humanity's fate. Keep busy. Be realistic about what you expect. Don't assume the gods are on your side.

Grade: **A**

Miss Ashmont: Excellent synopsis. Your view of our hero is, however, a bit jaded and clinical. Your critical perceptions are so informed by feminism and modernism that you never allow yourself to meet the epic on its own terms. I am not suggesting complete cultural relativism, simply that you might at times give poor Gilgamesh a break.

Dr. Woolrich

ABOUT THE AUTHOR

Mary Jacobsen is a psychotherapist and career consultant in private practice in Arlington, Massachusetts, and the author of the nonfiction book *Hand-Me-Down Dreams: How Families Influence Our Career Paths*. Dr. Jacobsen has taught literature, writing, and family systems theory at various colleges, and has worked as a medical social worker at Massachusetts General Hospital, a public affairs writer at Brandeis University, and a counselor at Lesley College. *Blood Sisters* is her first novel.

ALICE STREET EDITIONS™
Harrington Park Press®
Judith P. Stelboum
Editor in Chief

Women of Mystery: An Anthology edited by Katherine V. Forrest

Glamour Girls: Femme/Femme Erotica by Rachel Kramer Bussel

The Meadowlark Sings by Helen R. Schwartz

Order a copy of this book with this form or online at:
http://www.haworthpress.com/store/product.asp?sku=5427

BLOOD SISTERS
A Novel of an Epic Friendship

_____in softbound at $19.95 (ISBN-13: 978-1-56023-322-0; ISBN-10: 1-56023-322-2)

Or order online and use special offer code HEC25 in the shopping cart.

COST OF BOOKS_____

☐ **BILL ME LATER:** (Bill-me option is good on US/Canada/Mexico orders only; not good to jobbers, wholesalers, or subscription agencies.)

☐ Check here if billing address is different from shipping address and attach purchase order and billing address information.

POSTAGE & HANDLING_____
(US: $4.00 for first book & $1.50 for each additional book)
(Outside US: $5.00 for first book & $2.00 for each additional book)

Signature_____

SUBTOTAL_____

☐ **PAYMENT ENCLOSED: $_____**

IN CANADA: ADD 7% GST_____

☐ **PLEASE CHARGE TO MY CREDIT CARD.**

STATE TAX_____
(NJ, NY, OH, MN, CA, IL, IN, PA, & SD residents, add appropriate local sales tax)

☐ Visa ☐ MasterCard ☐ AmEx ☐ Discover
☐ Diner's Club ☐ Eurocard ☐ JCB

Account # _____

FINAL TOTAL_____
(If paying in Canadian funds, convert using the current exchange rate, UNESCO coupons welcome)

Exp. Date_____

Signature_____

Prices in US dollars and subject to change without notice.

NAME_____

INSTITUTION_____

ADDRESS_____

CITY_____

STATE/ZIP_____

COUNTRY_____ COUNTY (NY residents only)_____

TEL_____ FAX_____

E-MAIL_____

May we use your e-mail address for confirmations and other types of information? ☐ Yes ☐ No
We appreciate receiving your e-mail address and fax number. Haworth would like to e-mail or fax special discount offers to you, as a preferred customer. **We will never share, rent, or exchange your e-mail address or fax number.** We regard such actions as an invasion of your privacy.

Order From Your Local Bookstore or Directly From
The Haworth Press, Inc.
10 Alice Street, Binghamton, New York 13904-1580 • USA
TELEPHONE: 1-800-HAWORTH (1-800-429-6784) / Outside US/Canada: (607) 722-5857
FAX: 1-800-895-0582 / Outside US/Canada: (607) 771-0012
E-mail to: orders@haworthpress.com

For orders outside US and Canada, you may wish to order through your local sales representative, distributor, or bookseller.
For information, see http://haworthpress.com/distributors

(Discounts are available for individual orders in US and Canada only, not booksellers/distributors.)

PLEASE PHOTOCOPY THIS FORM FOR YOUR PERSONAL USE.
http://www.HaworthPress.com   BOF04